FOSTER

FOSTER

A love story

ISBN-13: 978-1-7377043-4-8 (Paperback)
ISBN-13: 978-1-7377043-3-1 (Ebook)
ISBN-13: 978-1-7377043-5-5 (Hardcover)

Cover design by: Ryan McCrory

To my husband, Ryan McCrory,
the leading man in my own love story

And to our rescue pets, both past and present,
Tsunami, Brodi, and Jaxson

Dear Reader

(I)

I'm not sure how to start this little writing endeavor, so I guess I'm going to get right down to it. Why beat around the bush, right? I have a lot to say, and not a whole lot of time to say it. I want to get one thing straight right off the bat, though—I never expected for any of this to happen. I didn't *plan* for it. And I sure as hell didn't want it. All I was trying to do was help. That's all I ever wanted. But things got carried away—they spiraled out of control, you see? I know it was stupid not to go to the police when it happened the first time, but you have to understand—*I did it out of love*. Everything I did, it was out of love. I didn't expect it to lead me where it did, but what's done is done. I've had to come to terms with it, and now so will you. It was the only choice I had at the time. And you know what? I think if it happened to you, you would have done the exact same thing. When love is involved, you can wind up doing some pretty crazy shit.

That's how I ended up in that parking lot at 2:30 in the damn morning. It was cold that night. I know you don't expect Arizona to be cold, but let me tell you, in the winter months it can get pretty dang chilly. I was shivering in my hoodie on that early March morning, and it wasn't just because of what I was doing out there, it was also because of that frigid midnight breeze. Even my heavy-duty work gloves had trouble keeping out that cold.

Anyway, I parked my car as close to the dumpster as I could. The parking lot was deserted, thank God. Not that anyone expects a bustling scene in the loading area of a shopping center in the middle of the night. With what I was doing, though, you can understand why I was still worried.

I chose the dumpster behind the Outback Steakhouse because I figured it already smelled pretty rancid. And it did, let me tell you. There's nothing like the stench of decomposing shellfish and fatty chunks of rib eye drifting on the breeze to get your stomach rolling. So anyway, I chose right. Because that dumpster already reeked of rotting meat. Nobody was going to notice if I added a little bit of meat myself. Not rotting yet, but just give it time.

So I parked back there, right next to that Outback dumpster. I must have looked around at least a dozen times to make sure nobody was nearby. I can't even come close to articulating how scared I was at that moment—you see, I had never done anything like this before. I was damn near terrified. I made sure to turn off the headlights so I wouldn't catch anyone's attention, and I kept my hoodie pulled over my head the whole time just in case there were cameras back there. Turns out there weren't any—people or cameras, that is.

I got out of the car and ran around to the back. One more look around, just to make sure I was alone, and I opened the trunk. The trash bags filled most of the space inside. They were the big trash bags, too—those black ones at the grocery store with the pull ties on the top. I had filled five of them with the mess. I didn't think it would take that many, but it did. Just goes to show how naive I was back then. That's when I noticed there was a small red smear on my car's bumper. *Jesus!* I drove all the way to the damn shopping center and I had drops of blood on my car the whole time? Like I said—naive.

So I grabbed the first trash bag and was ready to lift it when I realized I hadn't opened the dumpster yet. And these bags were *heavy*, mind you, especially for a woman of my size. I will never win a weightlifting contest, and if the zombie apocalypse happened and the only way to escape was to pull myself up a high wall, I would probably end up getting eaten alive—my innards getting pulled out as I screamed and tried to shove them back inside. One more zombie for the army of the dead—sans intestines.

Anyway, I'm getting off track. I'm nervous, you see. Writing this down—confessing to it—it's pretty scary stuff. I was more scared out behind that shopping center, though—that's for damn sure. So I put the trash bag down and ran over to the dumpster to open the lid. The stink inside! Wow! I went back to my trunk and grabbed the first bag. Such a lumpy thing. It's not like grabbing a garbage bag full of regular trash. All the large, awkward shapes inside made that bag very difficult to move. And don't forget *heavy*.

So I lugged it over to the dumpster and tossed it in. It made a squishy sound as it plopped down on top of the other trash that was already inside. Then it was back to the trunk for round two . . . and three . . . and four . . . and five. Somehow, I managed to get all five trash bags into that dumpster. I was actually starting to work up a sweat by the time I was done. I thought I was shaking from the cold, but with how much I was sweating, I think it was more fear than cold that was causing my hands to shake like that. When I was finally done, there were a few more drops of red on my bumper. I found a napkin lying on the ground—damn litterbugs—and used that to wipe off the red as best I could. Blood smears *so much*—did you ever notice that? Perhaps not, if you never had to run such a disturbing errand as I had to do that night.

I tossed the napkin in the dumpster with the rest of it. Then I slowly shut the lid, taking extra care to not make any noise. Maybe a homeless person was sleeping back behind the shopping center that night—you never know. So I closed the lid as quiet as I could and then leaned real close to the side of the dumpster. "It wasn't supposed to be like this," I whispered to the contents inside. "I'm sorry."

I hurried around to the driver's side of the car and was about to jump back inside when I realized I hadn't closed the trunk. God, I was really frazzled that night! So I went over and closed the trunk, just as quiet as I closed the dumpster lid. I checked to make sure there were no more red smears, then got in my car.

I was crying by this point. I may sound pretty heartless with what I did, but I really was just a young, innocent girl that had a bad thing happen to her. Well, sorta young. Is thirty-two young? I choose to think it still is. And I was such a good, law-abiding girl before that particular evening.

Never even got a traffic ticket, if you can believe it. I cared about others, and I cared about doing the right thing. I still do, but I guess not as much as I used to. *Obviously.*

It's because of love. That's what did it. That's what *changed* me. I didn't experience a lot of that particular emotion growing up. My parents died when I was pretty young, and I was raised by an aunt that didn't care much for children. She ended up passing away when I was not much more than nineteen. I didn't cry for her nearly as much as I did my parents. Now *them* I loved. But you forget things quickly as a child. Those feelings of love fade away, and I never knew that feeling again. Not really. Not until just recently.

So you can understand why I did what I did. It was because of love, and because I never really felt it before. So I had to—*had to*—protect who I loved. Anyone would do whatever they possibly could to protect their loved ones. Mothers die to protect their babies. Men die to protect their women. And I drove to a deserted shopping center and got rid of what needed getting rid of. I did it out of love. I thought that would be it—I thought I would do that one fateful midnight errand and that would be the end of it. I could move on—*we* could move on—and forget about it. Remember when I said I was naive?

So things got worse after that, like they always seem to do. And I did more things I was not proud of. Things that were by far worse than a traffic ticket. It was all out of love, though. Stupid, *mindless* love. And I realized something along the way. I'm not sure if anything would have changed if I had realized it sooner—to be honest, probably not. But

I'll tell you what I realized all the same. Maybe it will help you to make better choices than I did.

So here it is: Love can be the death of you. If you aren't careful, and hell, maybe even if you are. Love can change everything. It can turn you into a person that you never thought you could be. It can kill the person that you were. And it can kill the people around you. That's what happened to me anyway. So if you take away anything from this rambling confession, take that. *Love can be the death of you.*

I have to go. I will write more later. I know there is still so much more to say. And so much more to confess. So until next time, just remember what I said about love. And about death. They are so closely linked. I'm sure most people don't really realize that until it is too late. I didn't.

Skyler Seabrooke

CHAPTER 1

October 8, 2017
3:05 p.m.

"What's the address, Trish?"

"Eight-six-one West Primrose Avenue. The caller said they could hear crying coming from underneath their porch. Older couple. They said they couldn't crawl down there on their own. The man has a bad back and his wife recently had knee surgery."

"Got it. And they thought it was a cat, right?"

"Multiple. Maybe a litter. The couple doesn't own a cat, but they said there are some strays in the neighborhood. They think the mother might have died or abandoned the litter."

"Okay, let them know I'll be there in fifteen. Who do we have working at the vet center today?"

"Doctor Fischer. He'll be in 'til five."

"Perfect. I'll call back after I take a look."

"Thanks, Skyler. I'll get a kennel ready just in case."

"You're the best." Skyler Seabrooke ended the call and tossed her phone onto the passenger seat of her Sentra. Two pet carriers took up the majority of the back seat, one large and one small. She glanced in her rearview mirror, hit the signal, and let the Nissan drift into the right lane. She got off at the next exit, grateful to leave the freeway before an approaching semi had the chance to barrel past her small car, then started making her way down Sagebrush Avenue.

Ten minutes later, the Primrose street sign came into view. Skyler slowed the Sentra and turned left onto a pleasant-looking street lined with cozy, cottage-style houses painted in various shades of pastel. 861 was the seventh house on the right-hand side.

Skyler pulled up to the curb and parked the car. She flipped her visor down and took a quick look at herself in the mirror. A sprinkling of freckles covered her cheeks, and her large, hazel eyes stood out even though she seldom wore makeup to accentuate them. She smoothed her auburn hair and brushed a few loose strands behind her shoulder so her name tag would be visible. Next to her name was a logo for the Agave Animal Care Center—a purple paw print with a red heart inside.

Skyler reached across the car and popped open the glove compartment. She grabbed a pair of work gloves and shoved them between her belt and her cargo pants. She debated bringing a carrier along, but decided against it until she knew what she was dealing with. She hopped out of the car and made her way up to the house.

An elderly gentleman opened the door before Skyler had a chance to mount the steps onto the porch. He had a thin frame, flexed posture, and a small tremor in his left hand. "Hello there," he said, and offered her a warm smile.

"Good afternoon, sir. My name is Skyler. I'm from the Agave Animal Care Center. I heard you might have a situation underneath your porch."

"Thank you so much for coming," the man said. "My name's Henry. And my wife is Abigail. She'll be out in a moment." Henry descended the porch steps one at a time, holding the handrail to steady himself. Once he reached the sidewalk, he extended his hand.

Skyler shook with him, taking care to not squeeze with too much force. The arthritis there was clearly visible, the skin inflamed and the knuckles bulging. "It's nice to meet you, Henry."

"Likewise," Henry said. "Say, you look awfully young to be an animal wrangler."

"Well, if it's kittens, I can usually handle 'em by myself. A little more iffy if it's a large dog." A frail woman opened the front door and stepped outside. Skyler waved and introduced herself.

"Yes, of course. I'm Abigail." The woman made her way across the porch, holding a cane in her right hand. A long incision ran down her left knee. It was bright pink with scabs woven in and out of the scar tissue. "Knee replacement," Abigail said. She grabbed the handrail and carefully descended the steps, one at a time, just like her husband.

"I'm terrified for the day I'm going to need one of those," Skyler said, and shook Abigail's hand.

"Oh dear, you don't look a day over twenty-five. You have a long, long time before you ever have to worry about your joints giving up on you."

Skyler laughed. "I think twenty-five is generous, but I thank you for it. So, tell me what's going on under your porch."

"Well, the other day we saw a dead cat in the road. Run over, I'm sure. Poor thing. Some people on this road just drive too darn fast. Our neighbors helped us bury it. As you can see, we are not at the peak of physical fitness."

"I've seen a lot worse," Skyler said with a smile.

"Well," Abigail continued, "last night we started hearing some noises coming from underneath the porch. Squeaking sounds. It kept going on, and getting louder. By today we realized it was actually crying. What we suspect is the cat in the road was the mother to a litter of babies under the porch. I can't bear the thought of them down there crying for their mama."

"I can't stand the thought of that either. It breaks my heart. So how about you show me where you're hearing the crying, and I'll take a look."

"Right around this way," Henry said. He ambled over to the side of the porch steps, and pointed to an opening at ground level.

Skyler knelt down and listened. She could hear whimpering coming from somewhere in the darkness below the house. "Yeah, it definitely sounds like you have some upset babies down there," she said, standing up. The opening looked big enough for her to fit through without too much difficulty. She was a petite woman, five foot three and 130 pounds. "Anything under there I need to be concerned about?"

"Nothing of the sort, dear," Abigail said. "At least I hope not!"

"Good to know. I'm gonna go grab a flashlight and a carrier from my car. Hang tight." She returned a minute later, carrying a heavy-duty flashlight and wearing her gloves. She held the smaller pet carrier in her other hand; the larger of the two wasn't going to fit underneath the porch. "Here goes nothing," she said, and dropped to her knees.

Skyler flicked on the flashlight and peered inside. Sunshine filtered in below the steps, but the light faded away as she looked deeper under the house. Heavy support beams stood in various locations, going from the ground up to the house's foundation. The floor was muddy and soft. She panned the flashlight back and forth, looking for movement. The whimpering ceased as she swept the light from side to side.

Skyler looked up at Henry and Abigail. "Looks like I'm gonna get a little muddy. You guys wait up here, okay? I'll see what I can find."

"Would you like a towel, dear? I don't want your pretty face getting covered in mud."

"A little mud is good for the pores," Skyler said. "Keeps the face looking young." She winked.

Abigail chuckled. "Well, alright then. Good luck."

Skyler crawled through the opening and underneath the porch. It was humid down below, and much cooler. She could feel her gloves sinking into the soft earth. Luckily, it wasn't as muddy as it appeared to be; most of the soil she could brush off her gloves as she went. She crawled further into the open space below the house, checking the base of each support post for signs of life.

She had made it almost twenty feet when she heard a tiny hiss off to her left. Skyler panned her flashlight in that direction and saw a set of tiny, golden eyes shining in the beam of light. The eyes disappeared and another hiss came, this time from behind a nearby post.

Skyler crawled over to the post and peered around the side. Five sets of eyes stared back at her, huddled together and not moving. She crawled toward them, lugging the carrier beside her. As she got closer, she could make out the faces of five very small kittens. The one in the center hissed at her again. It burrowed between two of the others, and then turned back to growl at her.

"Hello, little ones. My name is Skyler. I'm here to help." She crawled forward a few more feet. The gray kitten in the center grumbled in response. "My my, aren't you the vocal fella?"

Three of the kittens scurried around one of the posts and back into the shadows. The angry gray one stood its ground and continued to hiss. Skyler reached over and scooped up the docile white kitten that was beside the gray one. It squeaked in protest and began flailing its tiny back legs in the air. "It's okay, it's okay. I'm here to help, sweetie," Skyler said. Other than being dirty and frightened, the kitten looked fairly healthy. *Probably starving, though,* she thought. She pulled the carrier around, opened the front, and placed the white kitten inside.

When she looked back up, the gray one was gone, probably taking the opportunity to join its siblings in the shadows. Skyler pulled the carrier along until she was around the side of the support post. The three quieter kittens were there, staring at her with glimmering yellow eyes. She snatched them up as quickly as she could, not wanting them to run off in different directions. They squealed and hissed as she placed one, two, and—finally—three kittens into the carrier along with the white one. Space was running out, and there was a commotion of angry whimpers going on inside.

Skyler went back to the flashlight and panned it around the underside of the house. *Where the hell did the gray one go?* The smell of dank soil was getting overwhelming, and her knees were beginning to feel damp. Her arms prickled with gooseflesh in the cool air, and she wanted to get back out into the sunshine. But not without the gray one. "You can hide all you want, little guy, but I'm not leaving here without you," she called into the darkness.

Skyler pivoted on her hands and knees, turning her body in a circle. She had almost made it back to her starting position when the flashlight picked up on something huddled in the corner—a small ball of gray fur. She crawled toward it, slow and steady, keeping her flashlight pointed straight ahead. She was five feet away when the gray ball turned to look at her, its eyes lighting up in the warm glow of the flashlight.

The gray kitten attempted to dart away, back into the darkness and away from Skyler. She lunged at it, landing face down in the mud with her arms outstretched. She turned her head to the side and took in a breath of air. Grains of bitter soil fell into her mouth and she spit them out, trying not to gag. She struggled to her knees and elbows, keeping her hands together. Little needles poked at her fingers, one managing to make it through the leather of her glove and then sinking into her thumb.

"Ow, you little shit. Stop biting me!" Skyler looked at the gray ball of fury in her hands. "You, sir, are not very nice." The kitten growled and squirmed inside her gloves as it tried to free itself. "I do admire your spirit, though," she said. The kitten sank its tiny fangs into her thumb again. "Yowzers! Those things are sharp!"

Skyler crawled toward the pet carrier on her elbows, holding the enraged kitten in front of her. It continued to chew on her gloves, its teeny teeth poking at the flesh beneath. When she reached the carrier, she carefully transitioned the kitten to one hand so she could open the door and stick it inside. "You're a tough little guy, aren't you? I think I'm going to call you Thor."

Once Thor was secured, Skyler retrieved her flashlight and turned to leave. The carrier growled and hissed and squeaked as she crawled her way back to the front of the house. Daylight loomed ahead. She could see the silhouettes of two sets of feet, and one cane, standing by the porch. She pushed the carrier through the opening first and then followed it out.

"My goodness!" Abigail exclaimed. "You're positively filthy! I'm embarrassed to think the underside of my home could be so dirty!"

Skyler laughed and stood up. "I doubt it's very easy to sweep under there." She leaned over and brushed off her pants. Some chunks of dirt fell to the grass, but most of it just smeared. She shrugged and decided to leave it.

"So it sounds like you were successful," Henry said, looking down at the crate of angry squeaks.

"Yeah, five in total. Including a very feisty little gray one."

"Heavens," Abigail said. "Poor things. I'm so happy you were able to come out and save them."

"Absolutely. Saving animals is what I live for."

"God bless you for it." Abigail's lips curled into a mischievous smile. "Say, did any of them look like they might be a little *less* feisty? Perhaps one that a couple of old folks would be able to manage?"

Henry looked at his wife and raised one of his white, bushy eyebrows.

Abigail shrugged helplessly and gestured toward the pet carrier. "They were born right here. It seems like we should have one." She looked at Henry with hopeful eyes.

He sighed and shook his head. "Forty-two years, and she can still get me to say yes to damn near anything."

"Oh goody!" Abigail said, clasping her hands together. "What about you, dear? You think you might want to take home one of these cuties as well?"

Skyler shook her head. "No, I'm not looking to adopt. But I do a lot of fostering for the animals we rescue. Get them healed up, healthy, and ready for adoption. I imagine these little guys might stay with me for a while until they are old enough to be on their own." She looked down at the carrier.

One small gray paw was sticking through the metal gate, waving wildly in the air, tiny claws splayed and at the ready. "And to answer your earlier question, yes, there is a little sweetie in there that I think would be perfect for you. She's all white."

"She sounds beautiful. What do you think we should name her, Henry? Snowball or Snowflake?"

"I like Avalanche," Henry said.

Abigail scoffed. "I guess the name will be a work in progress." She turned to Skyler. "So when might our little one be ready for adoption?"

Skyler considered for a moment. "They look like they are around five weeks old. We usually keep them until they are a minimum of eight weeks. So I'm guessing, give or take a month from now, she can be all yours."

"Perfect. It will give us plenty of time to go get her a litter box, food, and plenty of toys."

"Oh boy, here we go," Henry said, and chuckled. He extended a hand to Skyler. She removed her gloves and shook hands with both of them.

"I'd hug you, dear," Abigail said, "but like I mentioned earlier, you are quite filthy."

Skyler smiled. "No worries. I get that a lot." She unzipped one of her cargo pockets and pulled out a business card with the AACC logo in the center. "Here's the name of the shelter and the address if you have any questions. We will give you a call when *Avalanche* is ready for adoption." She winked at Henry.

"Oh no! Not you, too." Abigail rolled her eyes. "I want something a little less ferocious."

"Luckily, you will have a few weeks to discuss it." Skyler grabbed the carrier and started walking toward her car.

"Thank you again, dear!" Abigail called after her.

"Of course! Anytime!" Skyler got to the Sentra and carefully placed the carrier in the back seat. Thor grumbled from inside. She glanced into the carrier and then down at her hand, where two bright red pinpricks were in the pad of her thumb. She looked back at Thor. "I think once you have a bath and a full belly you're going to feel awfully bad about this." She held up her hand in front of the carrier. Thor reached through the gate and swiped at it with his tiny claws. "Such a tough guy."

Skyler got into the driver's seat and turned the car around. Henry and Abigail waved from the porch. She returned their wave and started making her way back toward the shelter. In the back seat, Thor yowled the entire way.

CHAPTER 2

October 8, 2017
4:22 p.m.

It was a beautiful autumn day in Diamondback, Arizona. The early October sunshine filtered through the trees, and the summer heat was finally beginning to fade. Before long the evenings would become crisp and refreshing, and the residents of Diamondback would get to break out their light jackets and fall sweaters. Maybe even a scarf or two if the temperature dipped below average.

Diamondback was located on the eastern edge of central Arizona, with an elevation much higher than its neighbors to the west and to the south. While Phoenix and Tucson simmered in the summer heat, Diamondback's weather was much more akin to that of Flagstaff or Sedona in the northern part of the state. Each winter the town saw its fair share of snowfall, and late autumn often produced some beautiful fall colors to the delight of residents and visitors alike.

It was a smaller town, with a population just over sixty thousand. Locals found it was large enough that they were not able to recognize everyone, but small enough that they were likely to run into a friendly face at the supermarket every now and again. The town had a decent mix of age groups, ranging from small children to the elderly. The only demographic that was lacking were those of college age, since there were no colleges located within the town limits. Most college-bound students went off to Phoenix or Tucson to earn their degrees, although many ended up calling home to complain about the heat while they were attending the universities.

Diamondback's downtown area was the typical maze of one-way streets that were often seen in Arizona's city centers, although none of the buildings made it much past five stories in height. The street level was bustling with locally owned shops, mom and pop restaurants, craft breweries, and pubs.

Just north of downtown was the Agave Animal Care Center. It was a sprawling brick building with an adjoining fenced courtyard littered with pet toys. Potential adopters could often be seen in the courtyard, tossing a ball or playing tug-of-war with a lucky dog that was about to get brought to its forever home.

The building was painted a light, misty gray, and just above the glass double doors of the main entrance, *Agave Animal Care Center* was printed in large, purple letters. A purple paw print was beside the letters, with a red heart inside.

Skyler pulled into the main parking lot, then veered to the right to go around the side of the building opposite the courtyard. She parked in one of the staff spaces off of the main lot, next to the employee entrance. She hopped out of the car and stretched her arms over her head. Her crawl under the Primrose house had left her shoulders aching and her lower back feeling stiff. *Thirty-two going on sixty,* she thought, and opened the back door of the Sentra to grab the pet carrier.

She headed up to the employee entrance and punched the code into the keypad to open the door. She waited for the lock to disengage, then pulled the door open and went inside. Thor, who had taken a moment to rest his vocal cords, perked up and began to bellow his mighty squeaks again.

Inside, a long corridor ran the length of the building, with the doorway on the opposite end opening up to the courtyard. On the right side of the hallway were the staff lockers, administrative offices, and veterinary facility. On the left was the adoption center, with a large lobby and two kennel zones—one for cats and one for dogs. The hallway was painted the same misty gray as the outside of the building, with white tile that did little to conceal the dusty paw prints that often covered its surface. It smelled like a cross between a hospital and a daycare center, with a splash of wet dog mixed in.

Skyler's steps echoed down the hallway as she made her way to the vet center, which was located midway down the corridor. The veterinary facility took up the majority of the west-facing side of the building and housed Diamondback's only twenty-four hour veterinary hospital, equipped with a surgery suite, observation unit, and ICU. Beyond the hospital quarters was the Agave Pet Clinic, with a separate, public entrance for those bringing in their pets for checkups and vaccines.

As Skyler neared the double doors, a young volunteer came out with a black Labrador. The lab had a cone around its neck, and was turning its head rapidly from side to side to inspect the hallway. It noticed Skyler, looked at her with inquisitive eyes and its tongue hanging out, then peered down at the pet carrier she was holding. The lab lunged forward to sniff the carrier, its tail wagging energetically in the air. The volunteer stumbled, struggling to hold onto the leash.

"Sorry, bud," Skyler said, and raised the carrier above waist level. "I think if you stuck your nose in there you might end up with a kitten paw embedded in your snout."

"Sorry, Skyler," the volunteer said, holding onto the leash with both hands.

"No worries, Seth. Looks like you got your hands full with this one."

"Yeah! If he would just leave his incision alone he wouldn't have to go into The Center sporting the cone of shame." Seth gave Skyler a smile, then headed across the hallway and into the adoption center, which the staff had nicknamed "The Center" long before Skyler began working at the AACC, some sixteen years ago.

Skyler went into the vet hospital and smiled at the veterinary technician who was sitting at the nurses' station. "Hey, Kelsey. Is the doc available?"

Kelsey looked down at the hissing pet carrier, eyebrows raised. Her red hair was pulled back today, showing off the dark-rimmed glasses she was wearing with magenta rhinestones glinting in the corners. "Sure is. Whatcha got there?"

"Litter of kittens that lost their mom," Skyler said. "They look pretty healthy, though. I just need a wellness check."

"I'll let Doctor Fischer know you're here, Sky." Kelsey pointed at the carrier with one of her manicured nails. "That little gray one sure doesn't seem to like you very much."

Skyler lifted the carrier and peeked in at Thor. "Oh, him? We're just getting to know each other is all." Skyler blew Thor a kiss. He squeaked angrily in return. She looked back at Kelsey. "Exam room one open?"

"You bet."

"Thanks, Kels." Skyler went around the left side of the nurses' station and into the wing of treatment rooms. She could hear Kelsey on the phone, notifying Fischer of her arrival. She went into the first exam room, reserved for incoming animals, and placed the carrier on top of the metal table in the center. Skyler then went to the sink and washed her hands, scrubbing where Thor's tiny teeth had punctured her skin. She grabbed the antibiotic ointment from the top drawer. "Little turd," Skyler said to the carrier as she applied the ointment to the scarlet dots on her thumb.

Alan Fischer arrived a few minutes later. He was in his mid-forties, with an athletic build and wavy brown hair that he often had pulled back into a small ponytail. He was a handsome man, with a sharp jawline and eyes the color of rich chocolate. He was also an excellent veterinarian. Fischer started working at the AACC shortly after Skyler started volunteering there. As a teenager, she had a crush on him, even though he was over ten years her senior. Now, she respected him as a vet and valued him as a colleague, but nothing more.

"Hey, Sky," Fischer said. "Whatcha got for me?" He knelt down and peered into the carrier. He looked up at Skyler and raised his eyebrows. "Well, that little gray one certainly has a lot of attitude."

Skyler held up her thumb. "He's also a biter."

"Duly noted." Fischer grabbed a pair of gloves from a box mounted on the wall. "These guys look pretty young. How's your foster list going? Can you take on any more?"

"The three pups I was fostering just got adopted out last week. I can take 'em."

"They'll probably still need some bottle feeding," Fischer said. "You okay with that?"

"Sure thing. I've got all the time in the world."

"Someday you're going to have to find some time for yourself, you know? Perhaps meet a nice, dog-loving man that's worthy of your affection?"

"Eh, people are complicated. I much prefer the furry variety." Skyler pointed her finger at the carrier on the exam table. "Let me know when those little ones are ready for me. Oh, and the white female is already spoken for. The couple that called them in wants her."

"Lucky lady. I'll take a look and let you know when they're good to go."

"Thanks, Doc." Skyler went to the door and stepped out of the room. As the door swung shut behind her, she heard Fischer exclaim, "Ow! You little biting bastard! Stop that!" Skyler giggled to herself, and headed to the locker room to change.

CHAPTER 3

October 8, 2017
5:14 p.m.

Skyler stepped out of the locker room, wearing jeans and holding a gym bag containing her muddy clothes. Instead of going out to the parking lot, she headed back down the hallway toward the administrative offices at the opposite end. She stopped at the first admin office past the veterinary center, where a plaque on the door said "Trish Morgan, Director of Animal Services".

Skyler poked her head inside. "Trish? I'm heading out for the day."

A thin woman with blondish-gray, shoulder-length hair looked up from her desk. She was pretty in a simple sort of way, the wrinkles of age having taken mercy on her thus far. She wore a beige blazer with an AACC name tag pinned to the lapel. "How'd it go at the Primrose place?" she asked, setting down the pen she was holding.

Skyler stepped into the office, holding the door ajar with her boot. "It went well. Litter of five kittens under the house. All seem to be in good health. Looks like they will need a few weeks of foster care until they're old enough to go to The Center. The couple at the house would like to adopt one of them."

"That's great news," Trish said, repositioning the delicate, golden frame of her eyeglasses with one hand. "You want to foster them? Or would you like me to look up our foster list and see who is available?"

"I can do it," Skyler said. "I'm pretty sure one of them is already *quite* fond of me."

"Did you get bit again?" Trish asked, raising her eyebrow and looking over the frame of her glasses.

"Just a little." Skyler shrugged. "If a giant monster came at me in the dark I might just try to do some biting, too."

"You are far from giant," Trish said with a shake of her head.

"Tell that to the one-pound kitten that bit me."

"Touché." Trish stood up and came around the desk. "Let me see the bite."

Skyler rolled her eyes. "It's *nothing.* I swear. I already disinfected it."

Trish grabbed Skyler's hand, turning it over to inspect the puncture wounds. "Yeah, well you know how dangerous cat bites can be. I don't need any more of my employees going to the ER with cat scratch fever."

"That was a volunteer," Skyler said. She remembered the incident well. A new volunteer was bitten by a feral cat and failed to adequately disinfect the wound. She ended up with a nasty bacterial infection and an impromptu visit to the local urgent care. "They gave her some antibiotics and she was good as new."

"Even so, I want you to be careful." Trish released Skyler's hand. "Looks pretty superficial. I think it'll be okay as long as you washed it thoroughly."

"Thanks, Work Mom," Skyler said, and gave Trish a goofy grin.

Trish sighed and rolled her eyes. "Yeah, yeah." She went back to her desk and sat down. "You're off tomorrow, right? Do you have anything fun planned? Perhaps a date with a fine, upstanding gentleman?"

"Why does everyone keep saying that today? Do I have a 'Future Spinster' sign taped to my back?"

"You are such a smart, beautiful girl, Sky. I just want you to be happy."

"Yeah, well, animals make me happy."

Trish nodded thoughtfully. "Very true. But animals aren't going to get you laid."

Skyler burst out laughing. "That is not a very work mom thing to say."

"Just because I act mom-like sometimes doesn't mean I'm an old fogy. I'm fifty-four, not eighty." Trish flipped her hair back with a flick of her wrist and readjusted her glasses, looking at Skyler with mock disdain. She pulled a stack of papers into the center of the desk. "Now, I have payroll to do.

Why don't you stop by Sawyer's Pub on the way home and see if a nice gentleman would be willing to buy you a drink. I bet you ten dollars there will be more than one that would be happy to do that."

"Oh, geez. I was planning on just grabbing some takeout and binging *Game of Thrones* or something."

"Ten dollars would help take care of that takeout. Just saying."

"Yeah, yeah," Skyler said, and stepped into the hallway.

"Oh, and Skyler?"

"Yeah?"

"If you do go to Sawyer's, can you at least wipe some of that dirt off your face first? I don't want to just *throw* my ten dollars away." Trish winked.

Skyler reached up and rubbed her cheek. She could feel grains of soil rolling underneath her fingers and scratching at her skin. She swiped at her face, trying to brush the dirt away. "Huh. I thought I got it all."

"Oh, what am I going to do with you?"

Skyler laughed and ran her fingers through her hair, searching for more dirt. "I'm telling you, it's a lost cause." She pulled a few strands into view, saw mud crusted to their tips, and pinched it off with her fingers. "See ya Monday?"

"You got it." Trish grabbed a new pen from a mug with puppies painted on the side. "Now get out of here."

"Yes, ma'am." Skyler gave Trish a nod and let the office door fall closed behind her.

CHAPTER 4

November 6, 1993
1:52 p.m.

Skyler tugged at the black seat belt, which pressed firmly into the crease of her narrow hips. She wiggled her eight-year-old body back and forth, trying to slacken the taut belt, which begrudgingly resisted her efforts. *Why is the seat belt so tight?* she thought. She wrapped her small fingers around the shoulder strap and pulled forward, but the seat belt refused to budge. With a defeated sigh, she relinquished the belt and slouched back in her seat. In the front seat, her mommy and daddy were deep in conversation and hadn't noticed her struggles to free herself.

Instead of interrupting them, Skyler turned her attention to her car window and to the blurred landscape that was shooting past the glass. The road they were on was cut into the side of a mountain—or at least it looked like a mountain—and the rocks swept upward at a steep angle where the asphalt met the earth. On the opposite side, a guardrail ran along the asphalt's edge, turning inward and outward along with the winding road. From Skyler's vantage point, she could see nothing beyond the guardrail, just blue sky and a few fluffy wisps of clouds.

Skyler picked up her stuffed doggy that was on the seat beside her. His ear was slightly torn and one of his eyes askew, but he was still her favorite traveling doggy. Ruff Stuff was what her daddy and her had named him when she opened up the bright red box on Christmas morning last year. Eleven months had passed since then, and Ruff Stuff had seen his fair share of wear and tear. He was certainly living up to his name, though, because Ruff Stuff was, in fact, some *rough stuff*. With Christmas only a little over a month away, Skyler wondered if maybe Ruff Stuff would get a friend on Christmas morning. Perhaps a little stuffed kitty—or even better, a *real* Ruff Stuff that barks and wags his tail and follows Skyler all around the house. That would be the best Christmas *ever*.

Skyler tried to lean forward again, but the seat belt still held her firmly in place. She wanted to let her mommy and daddy know that if Santa was considering giving her a real Ruff Stuff this Christmas she wouldn't mind at all, not even when she had to pick up his stinky poop. That's how much she wanted a real Ruff Stuff.

Her parents still seemed to be pretty busy talking, though—they hadn't so much as *glanced* in her direction in longer than she could remember. They were even talking about her like she wasn't even there!

"I don't know, Sean," Teresa was saying. "Inviting Regina over for Thanksgiving might not be the best idea. You know how she is around kids. Maybe—"

"I know, hon. But she's my sister and we haven't had her over for the holidays since Sky was a baby."

Teresa sighed. "Yeah, and you remember how that went when Skyler spit up at the dinner table? I thought Regina was going to run out of the house right then and there!"

Sean laughed and reached over to pat his wife's leg. "I think Skyler is a little old for spitting up at the table now, don'tcha think?"

"Well, alright then. We can invite her, but don't get your hopes up too high about her actually accepting the invitation."

The car shifted gently to the side as Sean went around another embankment. In the back seat, Skyler asked why Aunt Regina wouldn't want to come to their house for Turkey Day, but her parents went on talking as if she hadn't even spoken. Outside the window, the blue sky hovered overhead. The clouds seemed to have melted away, and the blueness suddenly felt heavy and suffocating, much like Skyler's seat belt was becoming.

"I would love to show Regina what we've done with the place since she was here last," Sean went on. "Hell, the house wasn't even blue last time! And all the trees in the neighborhood were so small back then. Now they're getting as tall as some of the houses. And I really think the fall colors would take her breath away."

"It really has turned into a lovely neighborhood, hasn't it?" Teresa looked at her husband and smiled. "You certainly picked a good one, Mr. Seabrooke."

"Nothing but the best for my girls," Sean said. Skyler could see him wink at her mommy through the rearview mirror. Now why didn't she get a wink, too? Or at least a glance, for goodness sake.

"Daddy—" Skyler began, but then stopped. No sound had come out. Where had her voice gone? She was sure she had spoken, but why wasn't there any noise? "Daddy . . . Mommy?" Still nothing. Just the sound of the wind outside and the tires humming on the winding road. The silence felt strange . . . menacing even. Like the moment in a scary movie right before the monster popped out from behind the closet door.

Instead, the silence was broken by Skyler's mommy, who seemed unphased by her daughter's growing frustration in the back seat. "Can you imagine how big all those trees will be when Skyler is all grown up? *She'll* be the one coming over for the holidays, and maybe we'll get to watch *her* kids playing on those trees someday."

"Let's not get ahead of ourselves, hon," Sean said. "She's still got a lot of growing to do before she has any kids of her own. Hell, I'm not even gonna let her start dating until she's at least twenty-five." They both laughed.

Why are they talking about me like I'm not here? Skyler thought. "Mommy?" she called to the front seat. Silence. Where the heck had her voice gone? And why wouldn't they turn around? Something was wrong—it had to be. It *felt* wrong. *"Daddy!"* Skyler yelled as fear started to take hold of her. She struggled against the seat belt, but it felt tighter than ever. She reached forward, trying to grab her mommy's shoulder, but she was just out of reach.

The car drifted around another embankment. Outside her window, all Skyler could see was the side of the mountain, the rocks blurred and moving way too fast. Skyler tossed Ruff Stuff to the seat beside her and tried to crawl out of the seat belt. She needed to warn her parents. Something was wrong— something bad was going to happen.

As Skyler tried to slip out of the belt, it pulled back on her with sudden, nauseating force. It dug into her stomach, and the shoulder strap pressed the wind out of her lungs. She tried to scream, but now she had no voice and no breath. She reached for the front seat, but now her mommy was feet away instead of inches.

Skyler leaned forward with all her strength, but the belt pulled back harder. She looked down and was horrified to find there was now *another* seat belt wrapped around her. Skyler's eyes widened as a third belt slid out from between the seats and slinked around her shoulders, like a snake wrapping around its victim.

"No!" she tried to scream, but nothing came out. The snake belts constricted against her, squeezing tighter and tighter. A fourth belt emerged and wrapped itself around her neck, another around her mouth. She reached forward desperately, but now the front seat was five . . . six . . . eight feet away.

The belts started to pull her down, away from the front seat and away from her parents. Skyler became aware that the seat she was sitting on felt sticky—gelatinous even. And she was getting pulled down into it. Where the snake belts weren't coiled around her skin, the gooey, leather seat was now grabbing at her as well. Pulling her down, deeper into the seat. She was going to drown in it, wrapped in snakes and drowning in dark goo.

Skyler looked at the front seat, her eyes bulging as the snake belts squeezed against her. She still needed to warn her parents—warn them they were in danger before she was sucked down completely. But they were so far away now . . .

"Speaking of Skyler," Teresa said, "I know we were discussing the possibility of visiting the animal shelter before Christmas, but we still haven't decided what we would be adopting."

"Yeah," Sean sighed, "I know. I think I'm leaning toward a—"

Her mommy's gasp cut off whatever her daddy was going to say, or maybe he just simply stopped talking. And now the car was spinning, the back end whipping around so the vehicle was gliding sideways along the road. Skyler shot forward, the snake belts gone and the back seat returning to just a seat. She was in a normal car again, and her parents were only an arm's reach away. But now it was already too late.

Outside her window, Skyler could see a curved road that disappeared around the side of the mountain. Her head spun to look out the opposite window. The suffocating blue sky was gone. Now all that loomed outside the glass was the front grill of some gigantic truck, looking almost like an angry mouth that wanted to swallow their car whole. Without even chewing.

Skyler screamed. She wasn't sure if she made a sound, but even if she did, she wouldn't have heard it over her mommy's and daddy's screams from the front seat.

The car struck the angry-mouth truck, but instead of being swallowed, it was jolted to the side and slammed over the guardrail. And now the world was spinning instead of the car. The sky became the earth and the earth became the sky. The windows shattered inward and outward. Ruff Stuff somersaulted through the back seat and was gone. Luggage was flying by the windows, the trunk now hanging open. Skyler saw her daddy's toiletry kit smash into a giant rock jutting out of the side of the steep embankment. Her mommy's nightgown was fluttering through the air, a single white cloud in an expanse of blue sky. And then the sky was gone and the ground was back, harsh and biting and so, so hard. Skyler kept screaming her silent screams, but her mommy and daddy were no longer making any noise. Now the only sound was the earth grinding under metal, and rocks tumbling past the car as it came to a stop some eighty feet below . . .

Skyler jerked awake, a silent scream caught in her throat. She tried to cough it away, desperate for cool air to fill her lungs—air that wasn't choked with dust and bits of flying rock. She sat bolt upright in her bed, flinging the sheets from her body in fear that they were snakes in disguise that would grab her and pull her down at any moment. The darkness in her bedroom made her feel like she was buried under the mountain she went tumbling down, instead of shattered on top of it. And she was suffocating—suffocating from the blue sky, suffocating from the snake belts, suffocating from the gooey, black leather seat . . .

Finally, Skyler was able to suck in a great mouthful of air. The gasping sound that accompanied it made her jump. So she was able to make a sound, after all? She reached across the dark and grabbed at the glowing red dot that was on her bedside table. She pulled up her phone and jabbed at the screen until harsh blue light cut through the darkness. It was 2:47 a.m. on the morning of October twentieth. It was 2017— not 1993, which was the year her parents crashed into a tractor trailer on their way back from visiting relatives. She was not in a crumpled vehicle but in her own bed, inside the blue house with all the trees outside. There were no snakes. There was no black goo. Ruff Stuff was not lying on the side of an embankment next to her mother's nightgown—he was packed away in a box in her closet, tattered and worn but something that Skyler was never quite able to part with. He had never been inside her parents' car on that horrible day in 1993, and neither had Skyler. She had been at her friend's house having a sleepover, and Ruff Stuff had gone with her.

Skyler placed her phone back on the nightstand with a shaky hand, then allowed herself to lie back down. She pulled her knees up to her chest and wrapped her arms around her pillow, squeezing it tightly against her trembling body. *Just a dream, just a dream, just a dream,* she reassured herself. The same dream she had every fall as the anniversary of her parents' death crept near. A little girl in the back seat, getting dragged down by some unimaginable monster as she tried to warn her parents about the danger that lurked around the next corner—a warning she could never give and a danger that was inevitable.

CHAPTER 5

October 31, 2017
5:18 p.m.

Alpine Ridge Estates was located on the western side of town. The community was a quiet one, with mature trees that towered over the well-kept sidewalks that lined the streets. As dusk arrived each evening, lamp posts flickered into life, creating a warm, comforting glow for those going out on their nightly strolls.

Most of the residents of Alpine Ridge were of retirement age and beyond. Kids were rarely seen playing in the yards, and children's laughter could only be heard when one of the neighbors had their grandkids over for a visit. The afternoons were calm and peaceful, and the community safe and reliable.

Skyler wove her way through the neighborhood, her Sentra gliding through the long shadows cast by the trees up above, before finally turning left onto Oak Ridge Drive. As expected, no trick-or-treaters were out that evening. It had been many years—decades even—since the sidewalks of Alpine Ridge bustled with trick-or-treaters on Halloween night. Instead of witches and goblins prowling the streets, only fallen autumn leaves drifted along the paths, stirred up by a gentle, late-afternoon breeze.

9713 East Oak Ridge Drive was located on a cul-de-sac at the far end of the community. It was a large, two-story home, with a slanted gray roof that hung over a generously sized front porch. The porch and window frames were painted a brilliant white, in contrast to the stormy blue color of the house itself. It was also one of the largest houses in the neighborhood, with an expansive backyard and plenty of space between it and the adjacent homes.

Skyler pulled the Sentra into the driveway and hit the button on her visor to raise the garage door. She gave her rearview mirror one final glance for any sign of approaching costume-clad children, then pulled into the garage and shut the door with another press of the button.

Inside the house, the heater had already kicked on and was humming softly up above. The temperatures in Diamondback were starting to drop into the thirties at night, and Skyler had to keep the place warm for her foster kittens. She dropped her keys and purse onto the kitchen table and stripped off the jacket she was wearing, tossing it onto the living room couch as she headed toward the two spare bedrooms at the end of the downstairs hall. Her boots clomped on the hardwood floor as she passed the foyer, staircase, and guest bathroom. At the end of the hall were two shut doors, one on either side.

Both rooms had been converted into foster spaces, one of them catering to dogs, and the other to cats. When Skyler was at work, she kept her fosters in their rooms, where they would be safe and unable to get into mischief. In the evenings, depending on the foster's health and age, Skyler would let them out of their rooms to explore the lower level of the house. She placed a pet gate across the foot of the stairs to prevent any furry explorers from venturing too far, where there might be loose cords to chew on or clothing to tear up. Upstairs was for her and downstairs was for them, or so she liked to think.

Skyler opened the room on the left—the cat room—and left the door ajar. Thor was immediately at her feet, with two of his sisters fast on his heels. Avalanche—*sorry, Abigail*—strolled out a moment later, her pink nose looking like a piece of strawberry candy surrounded by white fur. Skyler leaned over and scooped Thor off the ground. He started purring and burrowed his face into her neck.

"Where's your brother?" Skyler asked, looking at the kittens surrounding her feet. Ser Alliser still hadn't come out of the room. Skyler pushed the door open a little further and peeked inside. Alliser scrambled out of the litter box, grains of sand flying off his back paws, and ran over to greet her. "Good evening, ser," she said, and set Thor down so she could scratch behind Alliser's ears. Thor grumbled and pawed at Skyler's arm, wanting to get back up. "Needy needy," she said with a shake of her head, and picked him up before heading back to the kitchen.

The rest of the kittens followed, squeaking and meowing and falling over one another. Tonight was their last night at Casa de Skyler before heading to The Center tomorrow to go up for adoption. Skyler was going to be sad to see them go, especially Thor. He was going to get snatched up quickly, with his fluffy, oversized ears and piercing green eyes.

Skyler grabbed cans of kitten food from the cupboard and pet dishes from the cabinet. She prepared five bowls of food, taking care to not step on the kittens that were running around her feet and meowing with excitement. Thor dug his claws into her jeans and attempted to climb her leg, a skill he had been trying to perfect for the last week and a half. Skyler plucked all two-and-a-half pounds of him off her shin and set him back on the ground. "You, my dear, have got to learn how to be patient." She lightly bopped the top of his head, and he immediately scrambled for her pant leg again.

Skyler set the bowls down, a couple feet apart, and the scurrying madness around her feet ceased as the feeding frenzy commenced. She left the kitchen, stepped over the pet gate at the foot of the stairs, and headed up to the second floor to shower and change.

A pair of double doors was at the top, closed and with a heavy layer of dust collecting on the doorknobs. The master bedroom. This had been her parents' room, and then her aunt Regina's. Out of love for her brother, Regina had begrudgingly moved to Diamondback to raise Skyler following the tragic accident. However, Regina's disdain for children was not lost on Skyler, and their relationship had never been a close one. They tolerated each other as two unhappy roommates will do until the lease runs up, but Skyler received little love from her aunt during her teenage years.

Regina suffered a fatal heart attack a few weeks after Skyler's nineteenth birthday. While Skyler felt sad about her aunt's death, she did not grieve for her as she had done with her parents. She had Regina buried at the Tranquil Springs Cemetery, in the plot next to Sean and Teresa. When Skyler visited her parents' grave on holidays and on the anniversary of their death, she always brought fresh flowers for them— lavender dahlias, her mother's favorite. She left the bouquet of dahlias near their adjoining gravestone, and would then lay one flower on Regina's grave, out of respect for the woman who had attempted to raise her.

Following Regina's death, Skyler restored the master bedroom to how it had looked when her parents were still alive, and then shut the doors and left it. She couldn't stand the thought of moving into her parents' old room, despite how many years it had been since they slept inside its walls. Skyler moved all of Regina's things to one of the spare rooms, and then did what she had done to the master bedroom to the remainder of the house. The furniture was now dated, and the offensive, mustard-colored area rug worn thin, but each time she returned home for the night the house looked like it did when she got home from school as a kid. She would imagine her mother was in the kitchen making supper, and her father in the living room watching the Red Sox try to win the series.

Skyler turned away from the double doors and went down the hallway to her bedroom—the same one she had since she was a child. The bedroom was the only room in the house that she had updated with new furnishings and decor. Pictures of animals hung on the walls—some paintings, some watercolors, some photographs. Her queen-sized bed sat atop a modern bed frame, free of dust ruffles and with an upholstered headboard attached. Across the room was a walk-in closet with a collection of work boots scattered across the floor.

Skyler stripped down and tossed her clothes into the closet. She then hurried across the bedroom, shivering despite the running heater, and went into the attached bathroom. She reached into the shower, turned on the nozzle, and the sound of running water filled the room.

Skyler looked at herself in the mirror as she waited for the shower to heat up. No dirt on her face this time, so that's good. She leaned forward, the lights of the vanity reflecting in her hazel eyes, and swept her hair back with one hand so she could study her forehead, where a couple of small lines were beginning to form. *Where the hell did these come from?* she thought. *I'm too young for wrinkles, right?* Skyler poked at her forehead, moving the skin up and down to see if the fine lines disappeared. They didn't. She stepped back from the mirror with a defeated sigh.

At least there aren't any wrinkles anywhere else, she thought, then added: *yet.* Skyler wasn't one for exercise, but she had a lean frame and toned arms from her work at the shelter. There was a lot of scrubbing and cleaning required when she had kennel duty, not to mention the amount of lifting she had to do on a regular basis—bags of dog food, containers of cat litter, eighty-plus-pound dogs that were too sick, injured, or uncooperative to lift themselves. Skyler had also taken on the role as an animal rescue officer four years ago, which was physically as well as emotionally demanding. Whenever the shelter received a call about strays in the community, or animals that were trapped or injured, one of the officers on staff would go out to contain the animal and bring it back to the shelter. Occasionally the work was dangerous, but more often than not, it was just labor-intensive. Like crawling around in the dirt underneath somebody's house.

The mirror began to cloud as steam clung to its surface, drifting out from behind the lavender-colored shower curtain and filling the confines of the bathroom. Skyler turned away from her foggy reflection and stepped into the inviting warmth of the shower, trying and failing to keep her thoughts on something other than giving up Thor tomorrow. She had grown rather fond of him, and he was going to be a hard one to say goodbye to. It was something that had to be done, though, before she found herself getting even more attached. Better to be sad now than devastated later. A few tears inevitably fell every time Skyler had to give up a foster pet for adoption, but they were tears of relief as well as sadness, because she knew she would never have to see those animals wither away and die.

Skyler leaned forward and let the hot water pelt her back. The chill of the day was finally draining from her skin, and she could feel the tension in her muscles beginning to subside. Instead of thinking about Thor's departure, she decided to consider her movie options for the night. It definitely had to be something scary—it was Halloween, after all.

♥   ♥   ♥

Three hours later, Skyler sat in the living room, Thor peacefully dozing on her lap. Michael Myers had just finished chasing Jamie Lee Curtis around with a ridiculously large kitchen knife, and now some naive teenagers were reading from something called The Book of the Dead—definitely not a good idea while staying in a cabin in the deep, dark woods. Her phone buzzed on the coffee table, the vibration eliciting an unhappy grunt from Thor. Skyler paused the movie and carefully leaned forward to retrieve the phone. She glanced at the clock mounted on the wall near the fireplace. It was a quarter to nine.

"I don't have any candy," Skyler said, after seeing Trish's name on the screen and answering the call.

"Hi, Sky. Sorry to call so late."

"It's okay. Except I'm worried about what you're gonna say. It *is* Halloween."

Trish sighed. "Yeah, a really shitty day for stray black cats. Luckily, that's not why I called."

"Thank God." When Skyler started working at the shelter, she thought the violence done to black cats on Halloween was nothing more than a myth. It didn't take her long to realize there was more fact to the myth than she had originally thought. Apparently, it was easy to underestimate the cruelty of humanity. It was a hard lesson for her to learn, and one that proved true time and time again.

Skyler scratched under Thor's chin, and he lifted his head up to allow her better access for more scratches. "So what's up?"

"Got a call from Aspen Park. Some teenagers said there's an animal stuck in a storm drain out there. They could hear it crying. I'd ask Arthur, but he's already on a call and it sounds like it might take a while."

"Any idea what kind of animal?"

"They didn't say. It sounded like they might have been drinking. Didn't give their names either. Probably because they didn't want to get caught after stealing Daddy's booze. Anyway, I know it's late. I can get Justin on this one if you want to pass. I know you hate Halloween."

"It's not that I hate Halloween itself. It's the assholes that think torturing an animal is an acceptable way to show their Halloween spirit that I hate."

"Yeah, I know," Trish said with a heavy sigh. "At least it doesn't happen every year."

"Thank God for that." Skyler listened to Thor's contented purr as he snuggled on her lap, his paws kneading the fuzzy blanket that was draped over her legs. "I think Justin was going to a Halloween party," she said. "I can take it. It's gonna get cold out tonight, and I don't want whatever it is stuck out there until morning."

"You sure?"

"Yeah, I got it. They say where in the park?"

"One of the runoff drains near the wooded area at the south end." Trish hesitated for a moment. "Ya know, on second thought, I don't really like the idea of you going out there alone at night. On Halloween, no less. How about I call Justin and see if he's able to go with?"

"You can if you want, but Aspen Park isn't exactly a dangerous area. I don't think Diamondback has a dangerous area."

"Even so, I'll at least shoot him a text."

"Okay. Thanks, Trish. I'll head right out."

"Thanks, Sky. And be careful out there."

"Yes, Work Mom," Skyler said, and ended the call.

CHAPTER 6

October 31, 2017
9:23 p.m.

Aspen Park was on the edge of town, right before the mountains swept upward and became rocky and uninhabitable. A few hiking trails wove their way through the surrounding forest, but their paths were steep and only suitable for experienced hikers. The park itself was on level ground and divided into three sections. A playground took up the northern end, equipped with a jungle gym, swing set, and matching slides that the kids loved to race down to see who was the fastest slider. In the middle of the park, picnic tables and charcoal grills were set up over lush grass that tickled your ankles and was sprinkled with dandelions in the summertime. To the south, there was a sandy area with a volleyball net stretched across the center, although it was used much more often as a children's sandbox than for a game of volleyball.

At the far end of Aspen Park, in the direction of the mountains, was a small pond—the result of a few runoff drains that kept the neighborhood to the north from getting flooded during the rainy season. Skyler walked past a group of picnic tables, heading toward the tree line and the inky, black pond that looked more like tar than water in the silvery moonlight. A few coals were still flickering bright orange in one of the grill stands and she could smell the faint aroma of smoke in the air. The park was deserted, the teenagers that made the call long gone. Skyler reached the pond, which was fairly shallow at the moment because Diamondback had not received any rain that October. She flicked on her flashlight and pointed it at the surrounding woods. Silence greeted her. A soft rustle went through the trees as a breeze trickled through, and then the forest fell silent again.

Skyler shivered. It was going to be a cold night. She couldn't see her breath just yet, but she suspected it wouldn't be much longer before soft white plumes, like ghosts, started to form each time the air escaped her lungs. She held her breath, listening for any cries or whimpering. Still nothing.

Skyler went around the side of the pond and past the first few pine trees that marked the forest's edge. She turned off her flashlight, closed her eyes, and listened. A minute passed. Then two. She was beginning to wonder if the teenagers had made a prank call, when she heard a soft mewling sound coming from somewhere off to her left. She turned as quietly as she could in the direction of the noise, keeping her flashlight off. More whimpers, coming from the runoff drain furthest from the tree line.

Skyler made her way through the trees and dropped to her knees in front of the drain. She placed her hand on the cement pipe and leaned down to peer inside. She was about to flip her flashlight back on when an owl hooted somewhere up above. She then heard pine needles crunching behind her, followed by the snap of a breaking branch.

Skyler felt her skin break out into a wave of gooseflesh that was almost painful in its intensity. *What the hell is that? Did I stumble into some animal's den? Oh God, did I just put myself between a bear cub and its mother?* Skyler knelt on the ground, frozen in place, gripping her flashlight tightly with one hand. The mewling in the drain had stopped, replaced by the sound of breathing coming from behind her. Another branch broke, closer this time. Skyler willed herself to turn around, but she felt like she was stuck—like her fear was holding her down. All she could do was stare into the dark mouth of the drain as whatever it was closed the distance between them.

Seconds later, something grabbed onto Skyler's shoulder. Her scream drifted across the empty park, although there was no one around to hear it.

CHAPTER 7

October 31, 2017
9:35 p.m.

"Jesus Christ, Justin!" Skyler cried. "Are you trying to give me a goddamn heart attack?"

Justin was doubled over, laughing hysterically. When he got control of himself, he offered a hand down to Skyler. She shoved it away and stood up, brushing pine needles off her knees to hide the fact that her hands were still shaking. Finally, she clicked on her flashlight and pointed it at him.

Justin, a fellow AACC employee and animal rescue officer, was just over six feet tall, with a winning smile and shaggy, blond hair. He was wearing a long overcoat and a top hat. Splashes of fake blood were splattered on his shirt, and he had a sharp, wooden stick poking out from one of his pockets. He put the hand Skyler had rejected up to his mouth, trying to ward off another bout of laughter.

"And what in the hell are you supposed to be?" Skyler asked. She could feel anger and relief inside her chest, competing to see which would come out as the dominant emotion.

"*Abraham Lincoln: Vampire Hunter*," Justin said, pulling out the wooden stick and holding it up like a stake.

"Oh God. You twentysomethings sure are creative, aren'tcha?" Relief came out victorious, and with it, Skyler could feel the tension in her shoulders beginning to ease off, along with the pounding in her chest.

"Come on, Sky," Justin said. "It's a decent costume, right?" He put the stake back into his pocket. "Look, I'm sorry I scared you. It's just . . . it's Halloween. And it seemed like too good of an opportunity to pass up. I really am sorry."

"Okay, fine," Skyler said. "But you probably scared off the animal that's in there." She threw a thumb at the storm drain.

"It was probably you that scared it off. You did scream pretty loud." Justin giggled.

"Oh, shut up." Skyler smacked him in the shoulder. "You can either help me or go back to your party."

"I'll help, I'll help. What do you want me to do?"

"Here," she said, handing him the flashlight. "Hold this." Skyler dropped back onto her knees and looked into the storm drain. "Shine it in here."

Justin knelt down beside her and pointed the flashlight into the drain. An inch of water was sitting at the bottom, with brown, crumpled leaves floating on top. Five yards from the entrance was a small heap of wet fur. Skyler tried to make out what it was, but it was too dark inside the pipe to discern any distinctive characteristics. The lump of fur let out a soft, frightened whimper.

"I'm going in," she said without hesitation. She had already crawled a foot forward when Justin grabbed her arm. Skyler stopped and looked up at him. "What?"

"We don't even know what it is yet. Should you really be just crawling in there in the dark without knowing what it is?"

"And how do you propose we find that out?" Skyler asked, annoyed.

"Well . . ." he trailed off. "Okay, fine. But take this." He pulled the wooden stake out and offered it to Skyler.

She looked down at the stake, then back up at Justin. "It's not a freaking vampire, Justin."

"Yeah, I know," he said, exasperated. He peered into the drain again, then back at Skyler. "Just in case it's rabid or something."

Skyler sighed. Justin was a nice guy and he meant well, but the idea that she would stake a rabid animal to death in a storm drain on Halloween was ridiculous. "I'd rather just stick to my gloves, thanks. Just keep the light steady for me."

"You think you can fit in there? It looks pretty tight."

"I can fit better than you can anyway," she said, and entered the pipe. "Try to keep the light pointed to the left side. Otherwise, all I see is my shadow." Justin redirected the flashlight, and the drain in front of her became vaguely illuminated by the light reflecting off the concrete wall of the pipe. She would have liked to bring the flashlight with her, but the drain was narrow and she wasn't sure if she was going to be able to maneuver down there with the animal *and* the flashlight.

Skyler crawled forward, moving slowly so as to not frighten the animal that was cowering up ahead. She didn't like it inside the confines of the drain; it smelled like mildew and she could feel the pipe closing in on her. She had crawled into a lot of weird places to save animals, but this one might take the cake. Especially since it was dark—and Halloween.

The closer she got to the heap of fur, the darker the pipe became, her body blocking out more and more of the reflected light from the flashlight. She was only a couple yards away now, and could feel the cement walls of the pipe pressing against her shoulders as it began to narrow. She wasn't going to be able to crawl any further on her hands and knees. Skyler considered for a moment, let out a reserved sigh, and lowered herself onto her belly. Frigid, dank water soaked into her clothing, reaching her skin in seconds. She felt the water saturate her bra and seep down into her pants. *Happy freaking Halloween,* she thought, and continued her forward crawl, using her elbows to pull herself along.

She heard the mewling again, coming from directly in front of her. The pipe was now bathed in shadows, and she couldn't make out anything except for a fuzzy black blob. She reached forward and wrapped her gloves around the dark shape. It went rigid, then cried out in fear. It attempted to wiggle out of her grasp, but it wasn't moving very well.

Skyler began inching backward through the cold muck, which, unfortunately, was vastly more difficult than going forward. On the upside, the further she went, the more light managed to filter through. The animal in her hands gave a final, weak whimper, and ceased struggling. After she made it back five feet, Skyler came up onto her knees and elbows, and started crawling backward, holding the animal above the dirty water.

"How's it coming, Sky?" Justin called from outside. "It's pretty creepy out here."

"How do you think it is in here?" she asked.

"Good point."

Justin held the flashlight steady as Skyler crawled the rest of the way out of the pipe. Once outside, she breathed a sigh of relief and sat down heavily on the forest floor. The front of her shirt and pants oozed with muddy water, and crumpled bits of leaves clung to the dripping fabric. Justin redirected the flashlight onto the small animal in her hands.

"Hey, Sky," Justin said nervously, "it's not moving. Is it—I mean, did it—do you think it died?"

"What? It was moving and making noise in the pipe." Skyler looked down at the crumpled ball of fur now laying limp in her gloved hands. *"Fuck!"* she exclaimed, transferring the animal to one hand and pulling the soggy glove off the other with her teeth. She spat out the bits of leaves and grime that came with it. "It's not breathing."

An image of Skyler's mother—cold and lifeless—flashed through her head. She was lying in her coffin, her skin waxy, her chest not moving. It was so strange to see her so still, to see her *not breathing.*

"Shit, Sky—"

"Just hold the flashlight steady, okay?"

Justin did as he was asked, centering the beam of light onto the unmoving form in Skyler's hand. She began vigorously rubbing the animal's back up and down, simultaneously trying to warm it up and restart its breathing. "It was alive a second ago," she said, more to herself than to Justin. "It's just cold . . . and scared . . ." She continued to rub the animal's back with her bare fingers, oblivious to the cold. "Shit shit shit. Come on. You can do this, sweetie. You got this. Just breathe. Just. Breathe. *Please.*"

The animal stirred, its small, fragile legs reaching up to Skyler's fingers. It mewled softly, then began to shiver. *"Oh, thank God,"* Skyler whispered. "Get me a blanket, Justin. Over in the carrier."

Without a word, Justin stood up and headed in the direction of the pond, moving quickly through the trees. The light from the flashlight dwindled as he left Skyler sitting in the dark with the shivering infant animal. She pressed it to her chest, trying to use her body heat to warm it up. "Hang in there, sweetie. Just a little longer, okay? I'm gonna get you warm and safe. I promise."

Justin returned with the carrier a moment later. He pulled out the blanket and handed it to Skyler. She quickly wrapped the baby inside, trying to rub off as much of the water from its fur as she could. It whimpered softly from inside its swaddled cocoon.

"What is it?" Justin asked, leaning closer.

"A kitten," Skyler said. She continued to rub the outside of the blanket, wanting to get the kitten as warm as possible. "Looks like a newborn."

"Kinda big for a newborn, right? I mean, size-wise it looks like it has to be at least a month or two old."

"Yeah, but its eyes aren't even open yet. And that happens in the first two weeks."

"Huh," Justin said. "Well, maybe it's underdeveloped for some reason? Disease or illness or something?"

"Could be." Skyler peered into the blanket at the shaking ball of damp fur. "We should get going. It needs to get to the vet center ASAP." She looked up at Justin. "You got the carrier?"

"Yeah, right here." He set it down in front of her and unhooked the latch.

Skyler reluctantly placed the bundled kitten inside, not wanting to let it go in fear that it would stop breathing again— in a box, not breathing, just like her mother. She tucked it in as best she could, then shut the carrier door.

Skyler let out a shaky breath and looked at Justin. He offered his hand down to her, and she allowed him to help her to her feet. He reached for the carrier, but Skyler stopped him. "I got it," she said, and lifted the carrier herself.

"You sure? A gentleman always offers to carry things for a lady."

"But you aren't a gentleman, Justin. You're a vampire hunter."

Justin laughed. "Only for tonight, though."

They headed across the park, walking side by side, and Skyler was grateful to not be alone in that empty, shadowy place—Halloween or not.

"You want me to come with you to the shelter?" Justin asked once they reached the parking lot.

"Naw, I got this. You go back to your party. I don't want you to waste a perfectly good Halloween costume." Skyler opened her car door and placed the carrier onto the passenger seat, taking a moment to peek inside to make sure the kitten was still breathing.

"Oh, so now you think it's a good costume?" Justin grinned.

"Decent costume. Shitty movie," Skyler said, and smiled. She wished Justin a good night and got into her car. In the seat beside her, the kitten whimpered once more, then fell asleep.

CHAPTER 8

October 31, 2017
10:42 p.m.

Doctor Alan Fischer placed the kitten onto the scale in Exam Room One. "Two-point-one pounds," he said. He removed the kitten and set it back on the examination table, taking a moment to enter the weight into the computer that was mounted on the wall. Skyler leaned against the counter on the opposite side of the room, watching with rapt interest. Fischer returned to the kitten and felt along its front and hind legs, then moved on to its neck and abdomen.

"Any injuries?" Skyler asked.

"Not that I can find," Fischer said. "She is missing a tail, though."

"She?"

"Yeah, she. And the lack of tail doesn't appear to be from trauma. It doesn't look like she was born with one. Not one of regular length anyway. It might be a bobbed tail."

"Like a bobcat?" Skyler asked.

Fischer laughed. "Yeah, but she isn't a bobcat. There are some domesticated cat breeds that have bobbed tails as well. Or it could potentially be a genetic deformity." Fischer placed his stethoscope on the kitten's small chest, falling silent as he listened. "Sounds good," he said after a moment. Then added, "Surprisingly."

"Surprisingly?" Skyler raised her eyebrows. When Fischer didn't respond, she went on. "How old do you think she is? Her eyes are still closed, so that would mean less than two weeks. But she's already over two pounds. Isn't that odd?" Skyler came over to the exam table. Now that the kitten was clean and dry, she could see it had tan fur with a sprinkling of brown spots.

"It's not common, but it could happen. If she is developmentally delayed, it might take longer for her eyes to open. Hell, this level of underdevelopment could be why the mother abandoned her in the first place. The rest of the litter was developing at a normal pace, except for this one, whatever the reason, so the mother decided it wasn't going to survive and abandoned it."

"Sad," Skyler said with a frown.

"Nature's rough, kid. You know that."

"Should I go back to the park and look for the rest of the litter? Or the mother?"

"I don't think it will do any good," Fischer said. "With how underdeveloped she is, I think it's safe to say she was abandoned. The mother and the rest of the litter are probably long gone. Safe and cozy under somebody's porch, perhaps."

Skyler gave Fischer a wan smile. "And *why* is she so underdeveloped? What aren't you telling me, Doc?"

Fischer sighed and lifted his hands, palms up. "Disease, genetic disability, illness—it could be any of those. Her body shape and proportions are abnormal, so there's some level of deformity going on here as well. Sorry to say it Skyler, but I wouldn't get your hopes too high about her making it through the night. With the level of deformity here, it might actually be a mercy if she passed sooner rather than later."

"But . . . *I saved her*. She stopped breathing and I got her to start again. I saved her life." Skyler stroked the kitten's head with her index finger. When Fischer didn't respond, she said, "It's *possible* she could make it, isn't it?"

"Anything is possible," Fischer said with a shrug. "She already had one miracle tonight when you brought her back. Who's to say she won't have another?"

Skyler sighed, nodding. "Okay then. Thanks for taking a look. How much longer do you think you're gonna stick around?"

"At least until midnight. If they don't get brought in by then, then they don't get brought in at all."

Skyler looked at Fischer. "It's really good of you to always volunteer to do the late shift on Halloween, just in case some abuse cases come in."

"Hey, I'm happy to help," Fischer said. "And every Halloween I just end up sitting around here on my ass doing nothing, I count it as a blessing."

"Amen, Doc. Anna okay with being left all by her lonesome on Halloween again?"

"Yeah. My lovely wife told me she had a date with Hannibal Lecter, and from what I hear, he is quite the entertainer."

"Maybe you should pick up a bottle of Chianti on your way home."

Fischer chuckled and removed his gloves. "Good call. Anything else for now?"

"Nope. I have a kennel set up with a thermal blanket. And the vet tech knows to feed her every two hours." Skyler looked down at the exhausted kitten. She couldn't have survived that storm drain just to die in a kennel—she had more fight in her than that. "If all goes well tonight, do you think I could take her home tomorrow?"

"I commend you, Skyler—doing all that fostering. These animals are lucky to have you." Fischer crossed the room, heading toward the door. "And yes, if the night of observation goes well, you are welcome to take her home tomorrow. But like I said, please don't get your hopes up too high with this one."

"Yeah, I understand." Skyler wrapped a blanket around the kitten and carefully placed it back inside the carrier.

Fischer paused, one hand resting on the door, and turned back to look at her. "Happy Halloween, Skyler," he said.

"I'm just happy it's almost over."

"Yes, at least the black cats can be safe again until next year."

"And people ask me why I like animals more than I like humans."

"With some of the stuff I see around here, I don't blame you," Fischer said, and went out into the hallway.

Skyler lifted the carrier and peered inside. The kitten had already fallen asleep, her belly steadily rising and falling from beneath the blanket. "Okay, little one," Skyler whispered, "you're gonna be *real* strong tonight. And if all goes well, you get to come home with me tomorrow. And I know you're gonna do just fine, because you're my little fighter. You've already proven that out in the woods."

Inside the hospital's observation unit, Skyler went to the kennel she had already prepared when she arrived that evening and placed the kitten inside. It collapsed on the thermal blanket, instantly asleep.

Skyler looked over at the neighboring kennel, where a gray pit bull with a swollen eye and lacerated forehead was peacefully dozing. "You'll look after her while I'm gone, won't you Cinder?" The pit bull looked at Skyler with tired eyes, then drifted back to sleep.

Skyler watched the kitten for some time, not wanting to leave her alone in case she stopped breathing again. "Remember, you're a fighter," she whispered. "That's what I'm gonna call you. *Athena.* She's the goddess of war, because she's tough. And so are you."

It took another twenty minutes for Skyler to finally leave the kennel and go home for the night. As she drove through town, all the trick-or-treaters gone from the streets and tucked snuggly into their beds, she said a silent prayer—to whoever may be listening—that Athena would make it safely through the night.

CHAPTER 9

November 1, 2017
9:22 a.m.

The morning of November first was a crisp one, with a gentle breeze that tugged at Skyler's hair as she headed back over to her car for the second pet carrier. The trees that lined the AACC parking lot were alight with the fiery colors of fall; oranges, reds, and yellows fluttered in their branches, looking like dancing flames. Skyler took in a deep breath, relishing the chilled air as it filled her lungs, and surveyed the visitors' lot. Quite a few spaces had already been filled, and it looked like it was going to be a busy day at The Center.

Skyler grabbed the carrier from the back seat and shut the door. She peered inside, and Thor immediately stuck out a paw when he saw her. "Alright, my dear," she said. "You're gonna be strong today, okay? You and me both. No crying."

Despite the words, Skyler could feel her eyes burning with the threat of oncoming tears. She blinked them away, sniffled, and let out a long breath. First saying goodbye to Thor, then finding out if Athena was still alive—this was going to be one rollercoaster of a day.

Skyler walked slowly toward the staff entrance. She had spent the majority of the night tossing and turning, wondering if Athena was still breathing inside her kennel. Now that she was about to find out, she almost wanted to delay the moment, in fear the answer would not be what she hoped for.

She entered the building and went down the hallway until she reached the adoption center on the left-hand side. She passed through the double doors and stepped into a large lobby that was already strewn with people. In the center of the room stood a circular service desk, with a reception counter on one side and multiple stations for people to sit and sign adoption paperwork on the other. Five people were manning the desk that morning—two staff members and three volunteers. A young couple was already seated at one of the stations, leaning over the desk and talking with one of the employees as they signed various adoption forms.

Skyler walked across the lobby with the pet carrier, weaving her way through the various stands of pet toys, treats, and accessories that were erected like pylons in the open space. The shelter was thriving with the donations and government funding it received, but every little bit helped, and all proceeds from the merchandise sales went straight into feeding and caring for the animals. Skyler swerved to miss a toddler that was sprinting across the room, beelining for a

Siberian husky mix that was walking with one of the volunteers. Two parents followed, trying to reach the toddler before the toddler reached the husky.

The glass doors that served as the main entrance were surrounded by a two-story window that took up the majority of the east-facing side of the lobby. Outside, Skyler saw an older couple making their way across the parking lot, walking hand in hand. She recognized them immediately—Abigail and Henry from the Primrose house. She had called them earlier in the week to let them know that Avalanche would be ready for adoption on Saturday. Avalanche was already in the Cat Cabana, where she was patiently waiting with a sign on her kennel that said "I already found my furever home". It didn't look like she was going to have to wait for long.

The Cat Cabana was located on the left side of the lobby, opposite the Dog House. It was a large, open space with kennels—eighty-four in all—lining the walls. Skyler went across the room to where the rest of her foster litter was located. She placed the remaining kittens inside the kennel with Avalanche, stopping to give Thor one last hug. Tears, feeling more like acid than saline, stung at her eyes, and Skyler had to rub the sleeve of her hoodie across her face to keep them from falling. She shut the kennel door, her breath hitching in her throat as she fastened the latch.

"You could keep him, you know," someone said from behind her. Skyler whirled around, startled. Trish was standing in the center of the Cat Cabana, her arms crossed and a motherly expression of concern on her face. "The one you call

Thor. You don't have to give him up for adoption. It's about time you adopt one for yourself."

Skyler stared at Trish, her vulnerability causing her to feel naked and exposed. She could feel her face growing warm. "Yeah, but then I wouldn't have room for the next ones. I can't keep all the animals I foster."

Trish walked over to where Skyler was standing and looked into the kennel. Thor was on his back and batting at his brother's tail. "I'm not talking about keeping them all. I'm talking about keeping one. *That one.*" She pointed at Thor, whose gray, fuzzy legs were splayed in the air as he wrestled with Ser Alliser.

"I can't, Trish. You know that."

"I know that you don't want to get too attached to *anything* that might one day get sick and die. But Skyler, I'm telling you, that's no way to live your—"

"Yeah, I know, I know," Skyler said, cutting her off. "I just . . . can't." She brought her sleeve up to her eyes again, catching a rogue tear before it had a chance to descend her cheek.

The Cat Cabana doors opened, and the cheerful chatter of the lobby filled the room, hovering in the air until the doors swept closed again. Skyler looked over eagerly, hoping there would be something—anything—that could get her out of this conversation. She sighed with relief. "Abigail, Henry, it's so good to see you again." She hurried over to them, leaving Trish standing by the kennels.

"Hello, dear!" Abigail called out. The cane she had when they met was gone, and she walked over to Skyler with only the faintest trace of a limp. "It's so good to see you," she said, taking Skyler's hand. "And I am so very excited to see our little bundle of joy as well! Where is she?"

Skyler pivoted on her heels and pointed to the kennel where Trish was still standing. "Right over there, next to the woman who is looking at me with disapproval."

"Disapproval?" Abigail scoffed. "I don't think there is anything you could do that would warrant disapproval."

"These kids," Trish said, stepping away from the kennel. "Sometimes it's like talking to a brick wall." She gave Skyler a sarcastic grin. Skyler smiled back at her and batted her eyes. Trish sighed and rolled her eyes in return. "Okay then, I'll let you guys get down to business." As she passed Skyler she leaned over and lowered her voice. "Just think about it, okay?"

"Yes, Work Mom," Skyler said with a nod. She waited for Trish to leave the room, then turned back to Abigail and Henry. "Are you excited, Henry?" she asked.

"Maybe not for the litter box, but I think it will be nice having a little fuzzball around."

"Well, come on over then." Skyler went to the kennel, then brought her hands up to one side as if she was showing off a prize on a game show.

Abigail hurried over and looked inside. "Oh Henry!" she exclaimed. "She's adorable! Look how fluffy she is!" Abigail stuck an arthritic finger through the bars of the kennel and wiggled it at the kittens. Henry joined her, and stuck a couple of his fingers in as well.

Skyler couldn't help but smile. She watched them for a moment, then asked, "Would you like to hold her?"

"Absolutely!" Abigail said. She took Henry's arm and they stepped back to allow Skyler access to the kennel.

Skyler opened the door and reached inside to grab Avalanche. She placed the white kitten into Abigail's arms, and the delight on the elderly woman's face caused ten years of age to instantly melt away. Abigail extended one finger to Avalanche, and went into a fit of giggles when Avalanche grabbed onto it with her tiny paws. Henry reached over and scratched the kitten behind the ears, a smile spreading across his face.

Skyler felt a bit of sadness over losing Thor drain out of her. This is what she lived for—to see the smiling faces of the people who adopted her foster pets. Soon, maybe today even, someone will be overtaken with that same joyful smile as they adopted Thor into their family.

"Did you settle on a name for this little one yet?" Skyler asked.

Abigail looked up, beaming. "Blizzard!" she said. "Much more manly than Snowball, but a little less fearsome than Avalanche." She gave Henry a sly smile.

Henry nodded, his eyes still on the kitten. "Yes, our little Blizzard." He looked up at Skyler. "I still might call her Avalanche when Abby's not around," he whispered, and then gave Skyler a wink.

"Oh, you," Abigail said, although her attention was focused only on Blizzard.

Skyler laughed. "Okay, you two. It was wonderful to see you again. I'll send in one of our volunteers to get Blizzard all ready to go. And then one of our staff members at the front desk will have some adoption papers for you to sign."

"God bless you, dear." Abigail gave Skyler a warm smile, then looked back down at Blizzard and ruffled the fur on her belly.

"Take care," Skyler said, and headed back out to the lobby. She went to the service desk and rested her forearms on the reception counter. "Hey, Samantha, I have a couple who are ready to adopt in the Cat Cabana. Can you head over with a carrier?"

"You got it, Sky," Samantha said.

As Skyler left The Center, the persistent fluttering in her stomach gave way to an even more unpleasant sensation—a gnawing worry that made her insides shrivel and fold in on themselves. The soft cries for help in the storm drain. The tiny ball of shivering fur—wet, cold, and terrified. And then little Athena fading away in her hands, only to be revived by Skyler's insistence that she must live. And did she? Did she live? Was the crawl through that pipe for nothing? Did Skyler revive a kitten that was so damaged it was doomed to die for a second time in one night? *Freaking Halloween.*

Skyler continued down the hallway until she reached the vet center on the opposite side. She went in, said hello to Kelsey, and then made her way past the nurses' station. One more deep breath and she stepped into the observation unit, where Athena may or may not be waiting for her.

CHAPTER 10

November 1, 2017
3:28 p.m.

Skyler sat in one of her downstairs bedrooms—the one she had converted into a cat-oriented foster room many years before. She was on the floor in the center of the room, sitting with her legs crossed and a blanket draped over her lap. An empty pet carrier was beside her, the door hanging open.

Nuzzled inside the blanket, eyes closed and ears folded, was Athena. Skyler gently stroked the tawny fuzz atop her head with one finger, and the kitten lifted her face and squeaked in response. "You may be underdeveloped, little lady, but you certainly have size on your side," she whispered. "I think you're gonna end up being a big, healthy kitty in no time. Especially with my help."

Skyler reached over and grabbed the bottle of kitten formula that was on the floor next to the carrier. She popped the cap off, being careful not to jostle Athena in the process, and lowered the bottle to the kitten's face. Athena stirred and started searching blindly for the formula bottle. Skyler placed the tiny nipple on her mouth, and Athena immediately latched on and started drinking. She kneaded the surrounding blanket rhythmically with her frail paws as she suckled the bottle, as if in a trance.

Skyler giggled. "You, my dear, have quite the appetite." She held the bottle in place and let Athena guzzle the rest down. There were only a few drops left when she finally unlatched and curled into a ball, falling asleep within seconds.

Skyler set the blanket down on the floor and bunched up the sides to turn it into a makeshift nest. She got to her feet and collected the carrier and formula. "I will be back in a couple hours, my dear." She was about to shut the door when she stopped and turned back to look at the snoozing kitten. "Thank you for living," she whispered, and then quietly closed the door behind her.

She placed the carrier in the foster room across the hall, then headed toward the kitchen. It was about time she had something to eat as well. She put the rest of the mixed formula into the fridge and set the timer on her watch for two hours. For the next few weeks, Athena was going to require feedings every couple of hours. It wreaked havoc on Skyler's own sleep schedule, but she was used to the midnight feedings by now. A lot of the foster kittens and puppies required it, and it felt good to be needed.

Skyler started rummaging through the kitchen cabinets, trying to figure out what sounded good for an early dinner.

Her eyes got caught on the wall calendar that was hanging over the breakfast bar, saying it was still October. She went over and flipped the calendar page up, grateful for the month of Halloween to be behind her. In October, Athena had almost died—well, did die, if only for a moment. In November, she was going to thrive. Skyler was sure of it, regardless of what Fischer had said.

The November calendar picture was of a wolf standing in a heavily wooded area, sprinkles of red-leaved trees standing out among the pines. *Hello, November,* she thought, and began humming a song to herself as she grabbed a pot from under the stove and started cooking dinner for one.

Seven nights later, as the clock drifted past midnight and one day gave birth to the next, Athena finished off a bottle of formula with a contented yawn and a stretch of her not-so-frail paws. Skyler rubbed the drops of leftover formula from Athena's whiskers, then ruffled the fuzz on her tiny chin. Athena's eyes fluttered once, twice, and then were still. Skyler let the empty bottle fall to the floor and placed her hand on Athena's full, rounded belly. The kitten breathed in and out, strong breaths that in no way resembled the labored breathing from the night out in the woods.

"How ya doing, sweetie?" Skyler asked, watching Athena's eyes flutter yet again. Then, in the warm glow of the table lamp, as 12:03 became 12:04, Athena's eyes opened for the first time. They went from side to side, unseeing, before finally settling on Skyler. Athena blinked slowly, her eyes clearing and their stormy blue color becoming more pronounced with each blink. The blue was almost startling, with streaks of indigo extending from rounded pupils. A small gasp escaped Skyler's lips as she stared into those eyes. She couldn't recall ever seeing such unique and captivating eyes on a kitten before.

"Hi, baby," she whispered. Athena's eyes remained locked on Skyler, and she let out a soft squeak at the sound of Skyler's voice. Skyler smiled. "That's right, sweetie. I'm here to take care of you." Athena squeaked again. "I'm gonna keep you safe, okay? That's my job. To keep you safe and warm and full and happy. I promise."

Athena's eyes, never leaving Skyler's, drifted slowly closed, and she soon fell asleep in Skyler's arms. Skyler sat there, watching Athena sleep, as a chilled breeze rustled the trees outside, sweeping away the fall colors that clung to their branches.

It was nearly 12:30 by the time Skyler finally forced herself to leave the foster room to go back upstairs, and even though she knew she would be back in less than two hours time, it was still extremely hard to leave Athena's side.

CHAPTER 11

November 10, 2017
11:19 a.m.

Athena took one wobbly step after another, her behind swaying from side to side as her hind legs struggled to support her own weight. Small, chocolate-colored brown spots covered her tan coat, and her bobbed tail stood out like a fuzzy baton. When she neared the edge of the exam table, Skyler scooped her up and placed her back in the center. Athena reached out a paw and grasped Skyler's finger, attempting to nurse from it.

"You just ate, goofball," Skyler said, and patted Athena's head. Athena let out a dejected squeak, then started wobbling across the table again.

The door to the treatment room opened, and Alan Fischer stepped inside. His hair was pulled back into a small bun, and his lab coat was open, revealing a festive fall shirt with orange and red stripes. "How's it going, Skyler?" he asked, stepping up to the exam table as he donned a pair of gloves.

"Great!" Skyler exclaimed. "She's doing so much better. Just look at her!" She gave Athena a scratch under her chin.

Fischer looked down at Athena, but the relieved smile Skyler expected didn't materialize. Instead, the furrow in his brow deepened and a crease appeared between his eyes. "Hmm," he said, then cleared his throat.

"What?" Skyler asked, alarmed. "What is it? Isn't she doing great?"

"How much weight has she gained?" Fischer asked as he leaned forward.

"Just over a pound," Skyler said. "I weighed her when I came in."

Fischer pulled his stethoscope from where it was hanging around his neck and placed it against Athena's small body, listening. "And how much has she been eating?"

"A ton. Twice as much as I would have expected for her age. I'm thinking she might be older than we originally thought. She just looks younger because of how developmentally delayed she is."

Fischer felt along Athena's limbs and then gently pressed his fingers to her abdomen. "When did her eyes open?" he asked.

"A couple days ago. And her ears started to unfold yesterday. Typical development, just very delayed."

Fischer grabbed a thermometer from one of the drawers. His lips were pursed and his expression unreadable. He took

Athena's temperature, checked the results, then tossed the probe cover into the trash.

Skyler watched him, unaware she was chewing on her lower lip until it began to ache. She looked down at Athena, who was wobbling toward the edge of the table again. She reached over and gently placed her back in the center. "What is it, Doc? What aren't you telling me?"

Fischer sighed, shook his head, and then leaned back against the countertop opposite the exam table. "She's growing quite quickly, Skyler," he said. "Too quickly."

"Too quickly? Growing is a good thing, though. It means she's healthy." Skyler shrugged helplessly.

Fischer removed his gloves. "It's too fast. It's not normal development. And her proportions are all off—pathological even." He tossed the gloves into the trash can, where they landed on top of the thermometer cover.

Skyler looked down at the discarded gloves, confused. She glanced at Athena, then back at Fischer. "What are you talking about? What do you mean *pathological*?"

"Her growth rate, her body proportions—they are not typical of a normal, healthy cat. Not even a developmentally delayed one. The size of her head, her forelimbs . . . she's *deformed*. And the only thing that could explain that is . . ." Fischer sighed again and squeezed his eyes shut.

"Is . . . ?" Skyler asked, her voice raising to an anxious whine. "Is what, Alan?"

"Cancer, Skyler. Tumors. In the bones, in the muscles. Who knows where else? This amount of deformity—"

"She's not deformed," Skyler snapped, startled by the anger in her voice. She wasn't one to snap at people, no matter how troubling the news might be. Once she regained her composure, she said, "She's growing. She's eating. She's recovering from almost dying. That's it."

"A kitten can't grow that fast, Skyler. *You know that.* But tumors can."

"But she's eating so well . . ." Skyler trailed off.

"Cancer eats calories. Everything she eats is going to the tumors."

Skyler shook her head. "But . . . it can't be. She's fine. Just look at her."

Fischer was quiet for a moment. "Then how do you explain her size? She's enormous for her stage of development. Skyler—"

"No, Doc. I think you're wrong about this one."

"Skyler."

Skyler's eyes, which had been frantically looking around the room, locked on Fischer's. The look she saw there made her jaw clamp shut, then tremble. The social worker who told her about her parents' accident had worn the same expression.

"She's not going to make it," Fischer said, his voice kind but stern. It was the voice he reserved for pet owners when it was time for them to make the tough choices. The "it's time to let go" voice.

"Keeping her alive would only be cruel," he went on. "We can euthanize her now so she can pass peacefully."

"I saved her, Alan. She stopped breathing and I saved her. I can't just stand back and watch you do that to her. I can't watch you kill her."

"It's so she won't suffer, Skyler."

Skyler looked down at Athena, who had flopped over on the table, exhausted. *How the hell am I going to survive losing her again?* Skyler scooped Athena up and gently tucked her into the crook of her arm. "I can't let you do that," she said. "She's not suffering. And until she is—*if* she ever is—we will deal with it then."

"Alright, Skyler," Fischer said, resolved. "Keep caring for her for now. When things start to decline—"

"*If* things start to decline."

"Right. If. Bring her back then and we can make her passing peaceful and humane."

"Uh huh. Yeah, sure," Skyler mumbled. She placed Athena into the pet carrier on the counter and latched the door. Fischer gave her a nod and stepped out of the room. Once alone, Skyler leaned forward and peered into the carrier. Athena watched her with brilliant, shimmering blue eyes.

"It's okay, sweetie. He's just jumping to conclusions. I won't let anything bad happen to you." Skyler picked up the carrier. "You're my big tough girl," she whispered. "I've known it since the night I found you. You're my little warrior. And you're going to be just fine. I promise."

Skyler's voice sounded steady enough, but inside she could feel fear growing and spreading throughout her body, like tumors.

CHAPTER 12

November 13, 2017
10:40 p.m.

Skyler stood on the darkened landing midway up the stairs. She tapped her foot anxiously on the hardwood, listening to the soft, pitiful cries coming from the foster room down the hall. She had just tucked Athena in for the night, and the heart-wrenching cries began as soon as she shut the door. Skyler made it midway up the stairs before her body refused to take another step. She stood there in the dark, listening to Athena's lonely pleas, as an internal battle waged inside her head. Should she keep Athena in her foster room, or take her upstairs and into the bedroom? It would mean breaking a rule she had not violated once in all her years of fostering.

Before Skyler realized what she was doing, she descended one step, then another, and another. She reached the first floor landing and looked down the hallway to the foster room at the far end, where the desperate squeaking continued with unwavering vigor. Skyler crept down the hall and stopped just short of the door, where a soft, amber glow was spilling out from underneath.

She watched as a small shadow passed by the door, then returned a few seconds later. *Just turn around and go back upstairs,* she thought. *Fosters stay in their rooms at night. Not to mention they aren't allowed upstairs anyway. And definitely not in your bed.*

Skyler watched the shadow totter by again. *You can't let them sleep upstairs with you. You'll get attached and then it will be too hard when they go up for adoption.*

But Athena might not get adopted, she thought. *If Fischer's right, she won't make it that long. So I should take her upstairs where she could get all the love she can while she's alive . . .* Skyler gnawed on her lower lip. *But he's probably wrong. Definitely wrong. She's way too healthy to be dying of cancer. There's no way. So then I should just leave her here—*

Athena stuck her paw under the door, sensing Skyler's presence on the opposite side. Her tiny arm stretched to its limit as she reached blindly into the hallway, swiping back and forth as she searched for purchase. When she made contact with Skyler's foot, she stopped. She curled her paw around Skyler's big toe, then stuck out her other arm in a desperate attempt to cling to her.

Skyler's breath hitched. "Fine," she said, "you win." She opened the door and looked down at Athena, who squeaked expectantly. "You win," Skyler said again. Athena stumbled over to her and pressed her small body against Skyler's ankle.

With a sigh, Skyler collected Athena and her nest of blankets and headed back down the hall. Athena sat silently in her arms, looking up at her with sparkling blue eyes. "This is against the rules, missy," Skyler said as she reached the top of the stairs. "I didn't even let Thor up here." She went into her bedroom and placed the bundled blankets on top of her bedspread, then set Athena inside.

Skyler hurried around to the other side of the bed and crawled underneath the covers, shivering as she pulled the duvet up to her chin. She reached out and fluffed the nest of blankets beside her. Athena squeaked softly from her cozy cocoon, then drifted off to sleep. Skyler watched her, feeling both unnerved and comforted by Athena's presence in her bed. Athena's small belly rose and fell in a steady rhythm, and before long, Skyler found herself growing tired as well. She drifted off into a peaceful sleep, one where she didn't find herself waking in the night and straining to hear if Athena was still crying somewhere down in the darkness below.

When Skyler awoke the following morning, Athena was curled into the hollow of her neck, feeling like a fuzzy, breathing scarf. Skyler reached up and scratched behind the kitten's ear. Athena stirred, and began kneading at Skyler's shoulder. *Don't get attached, don't get attached, don't get attached,* Skyler thought as she ruffled the kitten's downy fluff. However, deep down in the depths of her consciousness—a dangerous sea of thoughts and memories where Skyler rarely, if ever, allowed herself to go—she knew it was already too late for that.

Athena breathed in content little rumbles as she lay against Skyler's neck on that sunny November morning, but she didn't purr. A thought flickered through Skyler's mind, fleeting but undeniable—*I've never heard her purr, not once*—and then it dove down into the depths, where she chose to leave it lurking in the shadows.

❤ ❤ ❤

Nearly two weeks had passed since Athena joined Skyler in the upstairs bedroom. Now, on a not-so-sunny morning in late November, Skyler lay in bed and watched Athena sleeping beside her, once again transfixed by the rise and fall of her belly as she breathed in and out.

Athena's belly, along with the rest of her, was not nearly as small as it had been on her first night in Skyler's bed. There were, however, no bulges, no lumps, no growths—nothing that would allude to a rapidly growing tumor or malignancy. Athena was just . . . *growing*. Her energy was up, her demeanor playful, and her appetite insatiable. None of these things were indicative of cancer, and Skyler's insistence that Fischer was wrong was becoming more and more founded with each passing day. Athena was a healthy cat, after all. But there was *something* different about her.

Skyler reached over and began petting Athena, who was stretched out on the bed and making the gentle snuffling noises of deep slumber. She was more than seven pounds now, and approaching the size of a regular house cat. Her baby teeth had erupted, and looked like nubby, white daggers when she opened her mouth to suckle her bottle. Her ears had completely unfolded, and were rounded instead of triangular. The indecipherable mushy features of a newborn were transforming into the more pronounced features of the cat Athena would become, and she was not the typical house cat that Skyler was expecting. Not even close.

Skyler had stubbornly attempted to keep her thoughts about Athena's origins at bay, but her mind kept circulating back to the same realization: Athena doesn't purr. Not when she's feeding. Not when she's snuggling Skyler or getting pet. Not when she's kneading a blanket or falling asleep. Not once . . . *ever*. Skyler was aware that some cats purr more than others, but to never purr? That wasn't normal. Not for a house cat anyway. Big cats, on the other hand, are incapable of purring. Big cats are the ones with rounded ears, and the ones that put on so much weight so quickly. Not because their bodies are overcome with tumors, but because they are growing into *big* cats.

Skyler ran her hand down Athena's side, feeling the downy softness of her fur. She had already spent the better part of the week googling big cat species and what they looked like at various ages, and Athena did not resemble any of them. She was too stocky in her build, and her coat pattern unique. The spots on her flank alluded to the possibility of her being a young lion or a cougar, but after scrolling through hundreds of Google search images, Skyler was convinced Athena was not either of them. She was different. *She was special.*

One thing Skyler *was* certain of was that she could not keep a big cat in her home, nor take it to the AACC for adoption. Keeping big cats in houses was morally wrong, and she knew the day would come when she'd have to take Athena to an animal sanctuary, no matter how hard that might be. Skyler had always thought the big cat sanctuary in Camp Verde was a fantastic facility; they cared for their animals and didn't do any of the inhumane junk that a lot of "sanctuaries" took part in. No cub petting, no abuse, no *Tiger King* bullshit. However, even though Skyler knew keeping Athena was wrong, she was still struggling to accept the fact that she would have to give her up. Athena wasn't your average big cat—not an average cat at all. She was special, and she required special care. Care that Skyler thought she was fully capable of giving, perhaps even more so than a sanctuary.

"What are we gonna do?" she whispered to Athena, who continued to sleep the tranquil sleep that only a feline seems to be capable of.

What am I capable of? Skyler thought. *What lengths am I willing to go to to keep Athena safe with me? I know she belongs in a sanctuary, but . . . does she really? What could they give her that I can't?*

Skyler could feel her morals and rationality draining out of her, like blood seeping out of a deep wound. No matter how much she tried to close the hole, the blood continued to ooze and flow. At some point in the past month, without her even realizing it, she had suffered a fatal blow. Her sense of right and wrong had been cut out of her, and no matter how stringently she had previously followed her moral compass, it was beyond saving now. *Let them leak out,* she thought. *The morals and the blood and the rest of it. They've never gotten me anywhere before, and why hold onto something that has never helped me in any way? Something that will leave me all alone in this house again, just like I've always been.*

Skyler placed her palm on Athena's round belly, feeling her hand rise and fall with the cub's breathing. Someday Athena would have to go to the animal sanctuary—*obviously*—but it didn't have to be now. Not *right* now anyway. She was still too fragile, still too helpless. And what if the people at the sanctuary didn't know how to care for a cub of her size and at her level of dependence? What if she died because of it? Skyler shuddered at the thought. Athena wouldn't be going to any sanctuary—not until she was a little older, and a little stronger. Until then, she was going to stay right here with Skyler, where she was safe.

CHAPTER 13

November 25, 2017
3:42 p.m.

Skyler poured a generous serving of kibble into the steel bowl inside the kennel, where a terrier was eagerly devouring every kernel that made it to the floor instead of inside the bowl. She gave the dog an absentminded pat, then stepped out of the kennel and shut the gate, latching it into place. Athena was scheduled for a wellness exam with Doctor Fischer in a few days, and Skyler had spent her entire shift mulling over the options she had to keep Athena away from that appointment. There were only two ways that checkup would play out, and Skyler didn't care for either one of them.

The first involved Fischer continuing to say that Athena was deformed from terminal cancer—better to think that than to consider the possibility that a big cat was roaming the eastern Arizona countryside. And if Fischer did still think it was cancer, he might be much more insistent with his plan to euthanize her to ease her inevitable suffering.

The other, more likely, outcome was that Fischer would realize his error during the previous wellness exam and be on the phone within minutes to have Athena transferred over to an animal sanctuary. And who even knows which one it would be? San Diego? Florida? Instead of some place within driving distance, Athena might get shipped across the country. Somewhere Skyler would seldom get to visit to make sure Athena was being cared for properly. Athena couldn't go somewhere like that—not until she was ready for it, of course.

By the time Skyler crawled into bed that night, she had come to the conclusion that there was only one course of action that would lead to her getting to keep Athena. She didn't want to do it—knew how difficult it would be—but after spending the day brainstorming, she hadn't been able to come up with any other feasible options.

A late autumn breeze rustled the trees outside her window, creating warped shadows that danced across the ceiling and stretched down the darkened walls of her bedroom. Skyler felt her eyelids growing heavy as she watched the shadows merge into one large sea of darkness, and she fell into a fitful sleep. Dreams drifted in and out of the blackness, like the wind slithering through the trees outside.

Skyler dreamt of her parents, not in the unreachable front seat of their doomed car, but laughing in their bright, sunlit kitchen as they cooked breakfast together. The room was filled with the crackling sounds of frying bacon, and a vase of lilac dahlias sat atop the kitchen counter. Skyler went forward—

towards the warmth, the laughter, the love—but as soon as she stepped into the room, everything began to dim and fade away. Sunlight gave way to shadows, and grass began to grow from the hardwood floor. The sounds of cooking and laughter ceased, replaced by the rumbling thunder of an oncoming storm, and the vase of dahlias shattered, sending shards of glass shooting across the room like broken stars. The walls dropped away, and then it wasn't a kitchen at all. It was a grass-covered hill in Tranquility Cemetery, and her parents' gravestone stood where the kitchen stove once was. The dahlias from the shattered vase had fallen onto their graves, the flowers now dry and wilted, and bits of their petals broke off and blew away in the quickening wind. Another grave materialized, still open, with crumbling black earth falling down its sides. Skyler dropped to her knees in the thick grass and peered down into the grave. There was a huddled ball of fur at the bottom, cold and shivering in the surrounding wetness. Skyler looked up at the sky. She wasn't sure when, but a light rain had started to fall. "I can save you," she said, turning back to the terrified ball of fur. She grasped the edges of the grave and lowered herself inside. Cemetery dirt tumbled down on top of her, sticking to her bare shoulders and clinging to her hair. She brushed the dirt off her face and went toward the animal that was cowering in the corner. "I won't hurt you," she whispered. The rain pelted down harder, and up above, thunder boomed with increasing intensity. Clods of dirt started tumbling into the grave, brought down by the pounding rain. To Skyler's horror, she saw the grave was starting to fill with water. She grabbed the small animal before it could drown, and then tried to pull herself up and out of the grave . . . but more and more dirt kept pouring down its walls. Her fingers sunk into wet, sodden earth as she tried to claw her way out, searching for a root, a rock, *anything*, to help her escape. The baby animal against her chest cried out in fear, only no sound came from its mouth. Instead, Skyler heard a deafening roar from somewhere up above. She looked toward the sound, but all she could see from the bottom of the grave was gray, swirling clouds and water. Skyler tried desperately to crawl out of the pit she had willingly crawled into, but now there was so much water, and so much black earth. All around her. Covering her. Weighing her down. The baby against her chest opened its mouth to cry out again, and again the sound came from somewhere up above—a snarling growl that was as enraged as it was frightened. "What are you?" Skyler screamed, not sure if the question was directed at the ball of fur she had cradled in her arms, or to the unknown beast that was up above, or both. She looked at the infant, trying to identify what she was holding, but there was just too much soil and too much water, blurring her vision and scratching at her eyes. Skyler looked down and was horrified to see the water was up to her waist now. Dirt kept falling in from the sides and splashing around her, and the liquid surrounding her was changing—growing thicker and more viscous. It was holding her down . . . *pulling* her down. Like the seat belt snakes. Like the melting back seat. She was in a grave of black sludge and it was trying to drag her down. And the ball of fur clung to her chest, terrified and whimpering and digging its small claws into her skin. *"What are you!?"* she screamed.

Skyler jerked awake with a gasp, her body drenched in sweat. Rain was pounding against her bedroom window, and for a moment she wasn't sure if she was still dreaming. There was just too much of her dream in this reality. The rain . . . the crying . . .

Crying? Where was the crying coming from? Skyler felt a trickle of terror. There was something in her bedroom. The animal from the grave? Had it followed her out of the dream and into this new, disorienting reality? Was it creeping through the shadows, crouched low and inching toward her through the dark?

Realization dawned, and guilt immediately followed. There *was* something in the room with her, but it wasn't a monstrous dream creature. It was Athena. Athena who had been sleeping next to her for the past two weeks. Athena who was now crying beside her. How long had she been crying? Had Skyler screamed out loud and frightened her? Or was it Athena's cries that had caused such a vivid nightmare to occur in the first place?

Skyler reached across the bed with a shaky hand, found Athena's trembling body in the darkness beside her, and pulled her close. She cradled Athena with one arm and placed the other hand on her belly. Athena's crying tapered off, and she nuzzled into the crook of Skyler's shoulder. Skyler closed her eyes and took in a long, tremulous breath, forcing herself to let it out slowly and deliberately. *Just a dream, just a dream, just a dream,* she thought, letting the gentle rise and fall of Athena's breathing help her to relax. *Just a horrible, awful dream. Nothing more than that.*

"It's okay, Atty," she whispered. "Everything's okay. I won't let anything bad happen to you. I'm going to keep you safe. No matter what, I'm going to keep you safe. I promise."

CHAPTER 14

November 26, 2017
9:17 a.m.

Skyler sat in her car, staring at her reflection in the visor's mirror. She rubbed her palms up and down her face, smearing the little makeup she was wearing and making the skin around her eyes puffy and red. She blinked hard several times, happy to see blooms of pink and red blood vessels appear in the whites of her eyes. *Good,* she thought. *Looks pretty good.*

Skyler hadn't cried—*really* cried—in many years. Sure, a few tears would spill every now and then, usually when she gave up a foster pet she was particularly fond of, but as for sobbing—the kind that racked your body and left you breathless and numb—she had not experienced that level of weeping since she was a child. Not since her parents died. Now, sitting in her car outside the AACC and looking in the mirror at her inflamed, ruddy complexion, she thought she had gotten pretty close. Close enough to be believable anyway.

She got out of the car and hurried across the parking lot, quickly punched in the code for the employee entrance, and went inside. She walked straight to Trish's office, keeping her head down and her eyes on the floor. When she reached the door, she knocked twice and let herself in before she heard a reply.

"Skyler!" Trish gasped. "What's happened? Are you alright?" Trish was up and around her desk so quickly she was still speaking when she reached Skyler. She grasped Skyler's shoulders and looked at her with frank concern, lines of worry etched deeply into her brow.

"It's . . ." Skyler trailed off. "It's Athena. She . . . she . . ." Skyler sucked in a shaky breath. *"She died,"* she said finally, and then lowered her head and let her body shake in the same way she had practiced earlier at home. She kept her face to the floor, blinking hard, trying to force tears into her eyes. Once they felt wet, she looked up at Trish.

"Oh God, Sky . . . I'm so sorry." Trish led her over to one of the two chairs near the desk and sat her down. She then sat down in the opposite chair, leaned forward, and took Skyler's hand in both of her own.

"I was really hoping Fischer was wrong about her being sick," Skyler stammered. "I mean, she had been doing good. *So good.* And then a few days ago she stopped eating. I just thought—I thought maybe she was out of this growth spurt and just wasn't as hungry." She shrugged helplessly. "But then she kept getting weaker. Yesterday she could barely stand up . . . and now . . . now . . ." Skyler bent forward, squeezed her eyes shut, and did another performance of her rehearsed sobbing.

"Skyler, I am so very, very sorry. I know how attached you got to this one. More so than I've ever seen before." Trish rubbed Skyler's hand, a motherly gesture that Skyler vaguely remembered her own mother doing so many years ago. "I was hoping Fischer was wrong about this one, too."

Skyler sniffled, keeping her head down. "I was stupid not to believe him in the first place," she said, then paused. "I thought . . . I thought I could save her."

Trish squeezed her hand. "You can't save them all, Sky. You know that. You gave Athena the best shot she had at life. If it weren't for you, she never would have known what it was like to be loved and cared for. *You* gave her that."

Skyler looked at Trish and forced a weak smile. "Yeah, I guess," she said, then added another sniffle for good measure. "Do you mind telling Doctor Fischer what happened? I know he was supposed to do a wellness check on her the day after tomorrow. I just—I just want to go home for today. Would that be alright?"

"Absolutely," Trish said. "I'll take care of it. Do you need any help with, um, with her remains?"

"No, I already buried her in my backyard. I didn't want her body just *lying there* all night. I hope that's okay." Skyler rubbed at her eyes with her free hand. When she lowered it back into her lap, her fingers were smudged with dark mascara.

"Of course," Trish said. "I'm just so sorry this happened."

"Me, too," Skyler said softly.

"Why don't you come over to my place for Thanksgiving tomorrow? I hate the thought of you being all alone for the holiday, especially with what just happened."

Skyler looked at the mascara on her fingers, then rubbed it off on her jeans. "Thanks, Work Mom, but I heard your in-laws are in town this year. And from what I recall, your mother-in-law is not a very fun person to be around."

"That's why I need your help, Skyler!" Trish exclaimed.

Skyler smiled and shook her head. "Next time, okay? I'm no stranger to a solitary holiday, and I'd really just like some time alone for now. I—I got attached to this one."

"I know you did, my dear. And I am so sorry it turned out this way."

"Thanks for understanding, Trish," Skyler said, and then stood up.

Trish joined her. She smoothed out her skirt, then pulled Skyler in for a long hug. Skyler wrapped her arms around Trish's thin shoulders, feeling like she might actually cry for real this time—no rehearsal necessary. A sickening wave of guilt surged through her, wrapping itself sinuously through her intestines like a well-established tapeworm. *You're gonna burn in hell for this,* she thought.

"Let me know if you change your mind," Trish said, finally releasing Skyler from the tight embrace. "My mother-in-law isn't that bad after she's had a couple of drinks. Well, make that three or four."

Skyler forced a meager laugh. "Thanks, but I'd rather just stay home." She walked over to the office door, pausing before she opened it. She looked back at Trish, her hand resting on the doorknob, all the while feeling the guilt gnawing at her insides like a hungry parasite. "I hope it ends up being a nice holiday, regardless of how much she ends up drinking."

"Thank you. Call me if you change your mind."

"Of course," Skyler said. "And thank you again." She left Trish's office and went down the hallway, rushing past the entrance to the vet center on her way to the exit. She didn't want to bump into Fischer until Trish had a chance to talk to him. After her performance in Trish's office, Skyler didn't think she had it in her to spout off any more lies. Not just yet anyway.

Skyler half-walked, half-ran across the parking lot to her Sentra. She wanted away from the shelter, away from the lies, and away from the guilt parasite that was refusing to give up its hold on her gut. She had lied to her work mom, and she had done it well. The thought caused the guilt parasite to take another hearty bite out of her inner tissues and start chewing.

Skyler started the car and forced herself to drive out of the lot at a respectable speed. Her mind lingered on the guilt parasite; she could almost hear its teeth grinding from somewhere deep inside. However, if she had to choose between the guilt parasite and losing Athena, she chose the guilt parasite. Let it have a whole goddamn Thanksgiving dinner in there, for all she cared. As long as she got to keep

Athena, and as long as she never had to wake from another nightmare afraid and alone in the dark.

Skyler turned onto Sagebrush Avenue and headed toward the pet store. Leaves lazily drifted down from the sparsely covered trees to the damp pavement below, the final golden bits of fall landing in murky puddles along the sides of the road. Before long, winter would tighten its grip on Diamondback, and snow would fall from the gray mass of clouds above instead of rain. *No more rain,* Skyler thought with a sigh of relief. Between last night's deluge and her nightmare downpour, she had had just about all the rain she could stand.

Skyler pulled into the PetSmart parking lot, sending a spray of water and leaves flying as she went through a sprawling puddle. Luckily, it would be a quick stop; all she needed to pick up was some more kitten formula. It's not like she could be getting it from the shelter anymore, now that Athena was officially "dead". And with Athena going through the formula at such a rapid rate, Skyler expected by the time she got home her foster pet would already be growing hungry.

CHAPTER 15

December 18, 2017
6:42 p.m.

The first real snow of the season arrived during the third week
of December, the darkened sky bursting into life in a sea of
white confetti. The first snowflakes that managed to reach the
ground melted away, the earth still too warm to accept them.
However, as the flakes grew in size and number, a shimmering
white blanket began to appear, coating Diamondback in a
layer of fairy dust.

The trees, now stripped bare, were strewn with twinkling
lights of red, green, and silver. Warm golden globes adorned
the awnings of the downtown storefronts, and frosted
snowmen sitting atop cherry-colored sleds were displayed in
the windows, beckoning passersby to come inside. An
enormous, stand-alone Christmas ornament was in the town
square, illuminated with sparkling blue and white lights.

Children giggled as they ran underneath, and lovers stood inside the sphere, taking selfies and stealing kisses.

Inside the community of Alpine Ridge, houses glimmered with Christmas lights in every color imaginable. Plum purples, emerald greens, icy blues, and cheerful reds lined their roofs, wrapped around their porches, and dangled from the surrounding trees. Plump red Santas stood next to driveways, holding strands of lights that were attached to present-stuffed sleds and elegant reindeer. Inflated penguins stood beside polar bears that prowled the lawns, and candy canes lined the walkways. Elaborate wreaths of pine and poinsettias hung on the doors, welcoming families and visitors alike.

The Seabrooke house, as always, was less remarkable than its festive, jovial neighbors. Its decorations were modest, and its inhabitants much less interested in competing for the annual "Best-Dressed House" award. A single line of white icicle lights ran along its roof, and a humble wreath hung from the front door. Inside, the house was devoid of holiday decorations. The living space looked much the same as it did in July, save for the whispers of snowflakes falling lazily outside its windows.

There was something very unique about the blue house at the end of Oak Ridge Drive, however—something that all the other houses in Alpine Ridge were lacking. It bounded from room to room, pouncing on fuzzy mice and batting at the laces of discarded tennis shoes. Its paws padded along the hardwood floor as it ran through the hallways, often tumbling into walls or nearby furniture while in a clumsy pursuit of one toy or another.

Skyler was in the kitchen, cutting small pieces out of a raw chuck roast. She placed the bits of meat onto a food scale she purchased on Amazon, measuring the serving size exactly from what she had researched on the internet. Skyler introduced Athena to solid food a week ago, but it wasn't until the day before last that Athena finally took a few tentative nibbles, followed by a few hearty gulps. The process of transitioning her to solid food would be a slow one, and for now her diet still mainly consisted of formula. A lot of formula.

Athena's growth had been steady and unyielding as the weeks went by, and when Skyler weighed her last, she was nearly fifteen pounds and well on her way to exceeding the size of a large house cat. Her resemblance to a house cat, however, continued to diminish as she aged, and by that snowy evening in mid-December, had all but disappeared. Her paws were now large and heavy, and her structure stocky and solid. Her ears were rounded and covered in soft, downy fur. Her tawny coat had thickened, and brown spots covered her back and haunches. And her eyes, which were once a brilliant blue, were now starting to show hints of glimmering amber.

Athena tottered into the kitchen, carrying a half-destroyed stuffed clownfish toy in her mouth. She dropped it on the floor as soon as she smelled what Skyler had on the counter, her interest in pretend prey momentarily forgotten. She bounded over to Skyler, slowed too late, and bumped heavily into her legs, causing Skyler to drop the piece of meat she was holding. Athena looked up at her with her amber-streaked blue eyes, startled.

"Careful Atty!" Skyler exclaimed. "No bumping into people that are holding knives, okay?" She looked down at Athena, and the cub squeaked at her. Skyler felt the corners of her mouth curl into a smile in spite of herself.

Athena got up on her hind legs and pressed her front paws against the cabinet, struggling to reach what was on the countertop. "Down, Atty. Patience is a virtue here in the Seabrooke house." Skyler gently nudged Athena's paws off the cabinet and cut a few final bits of meat from the chuck roast. Finished, she placed the beef into a bowl and set it down on a mat she had removed from one of the foster rooms.

The doors to the foster rooms now stood open and the spaces unused; Skyler had not brought in another litter of foster pets since deciding to keep Athena. She told Trish it was because she was still heartbroken over Athena's death, which Trish accepted without complaint. She reassured Skyler they still had many other foster volunteers they could call on until Skyler was ready to resume her role as a foster parent.

The guilt parasite, which had come into being following Skyler's lies to Trish, continued to gnaw at her insides, but as the days turned into weeks and her bond with Athena continued to grow, the parasite started to lose its hold on her. By that December evening, as Christmas rounded the final bend and was about to come in for the home stretch, Skyler's guilt parasite was sluggish and unmotivated at best. If anything, she was more plagued by the disintegration of her morals, the shame of which seemed to be like a parasite in itself. Every now and then, like a sultry whisper in a lover's ear, the thought would recur to her that keeping a big cat in the house was wrong. Morally wrong, ethically wrong, undeniably *wrong*. She knew it deep down in her gut, but like the guilt parasite, it was getting easier and easier to ignore. Each time the thought surfaced—while she was cleaning a kennel in the Cat Cabana, or taking a shelter dog out for a much needed walk—she found a new justification for her actions. Something to silence those incessant whispers of wrongdoing; to sweep them away like the smoke of an extinguished match on a windy day.

Skyler still intended to take Athena to the animal sanctuary in Camp Verde, but only when Athena was ready. Once she was strong enough, and once she became too big to handle. Whenever the morality police whispered in Skyler's ear, she repeated the same mantra, over and over again, until the words started to lose their meaning. *Once Atty is grown, I will take her up there. I can visit every weekend. And she can live the life she is supposed to live, surrounded by other big cats.* However, as Skyler lay awake at night, waiting for sleep to take her and listening to Athena breathing beside her, she could feel the cogs in her brain turning, trying to configure a new justification to keep Athena a little bit longer, to wait until she was a little bit bigger.

The blanket of snow on the ground had thickened considerably by the time Skyler crawled into bed that evening. She rolled onto her side and wrapped her arms around Athena, feeling the comforting rise and fall of the cub's chest. "I'll bring you to the sanctuary one day," Skyler whispered. "But not until you're ready."

Skyler listened to the wind rattling the bare branches of the trees outside. She closed her eyes and tried to convince herself that she was doing nothing wrong, that keeping Athena a few more weeks was in her best interest. Until Athena was strong enough to handle the transition. And until Skyler was strong enough to let her go.

CHAPTER 16

January 30, 2018
1:55 p.m.

"Skyler, can I have a moment?"

Skyler jumped, dropping the lathered brush she had been holding. Soap splattered onto the concrete floor of the empty dog kennel. She came up to her knees, which were already wet with sudsy water, and wiped her hands off on her jeans. She looked over her shoulder and saw Trish standing behind her, arms crossed and an indecipherable expression on her face.

"Uh huh," Skyler said, and got to her feet. "What's up?"

"I just wanted to chat for a bit," Trish said, uncrossing her arms.

Skyler nervously rubbed her hands on her shirt, even though they were already dry. "Sure," she said. "I have kennel duty all day, but I can always find time for my work mom. What's up?"

Trish sighed and leaned against the cinder block wall that served as a partition between the kennel Skyler was standing in and the next one over. A shaggy, brown dog came up to the chain-link fence of the kennel and sniffed tentatively at Trish's skirt. She glanced down, offered her fingers through the fence for the mutt to lick, then turned back to Skyler. "I'm a little bit concerned," she said.

"Concerned? About what?" Skyler felt her stomach sink, and a tangled knot materialize in its place. *Oh God, does she know something? Fischer must have known I was lying and said something to her.* Skyler kept her outward appearance as neutral as she could manage, while inside her stomach did a relentless series of nauseating somersaults.

Trish looked down at the shaggy dog, which was eagerly wagging its tail for more attention, and then back up at Skyler. "You haven't taken on any new foster pets," she said finally.

The somersaults in Skyler's stomach ceased, and she felt the knot of dread begin to loosen. This she could handle. She had actually been waiting for this conversation to come up and already had an answer all picked out. She stepped out of the kennel so she could face Trish directly.

"I understand losing Athena was very hard on you," Trish went on, "especially after the losses you suffered when you were a child. And I already know there is *nothing* I can say or do to make up for any of that. But I feel like you are . . . *struggling* right now, and I want to help. If you'll let me."

"I'm not *struggling*," Skyler said. She watched the shaggy dog meander over to its dog bed and flop down inside its cushioned walls. "I'm just taking a break. I was taking on so many foster pets there for a while, and you know how much work they can be, especially if they're sick or newborns. And Athena was *both*. I was up all night, every night, trying to save her. And I just . . . couldn't." Skyler let out a shaky breath. She hoped she hadn't rambled through the explanation like a rehearsed speech, which was what it was. She looked down at the shaggy dog, partially because she didn't want to meet Trish's eyes, and partially because the guilt parasite had resurrected itself and was now squirming around her insides, tearing chunks out of her gut and chewing at them hungrily.

Trish's head dipped down into a sympathetic head tilt. She reached out and rubbed Skyler's arm, which caused the guilt parasite to tear off another piece of something deep inside. Skyler shifted uncomfortably and wrapped her arms around herself.

"I understand your aversion to resuming foster care," Trish said. "But I'm not going to lie,"—*guilt parasite: munch munch munch*—"it really does trouble me. You seemed to derive so much joy from helping those animals, and I worry about you all alone in that big house of yours. If you really don't want to foster anymore, then maybe adopting one of these guys would help ease the pain." Trish gestured down to the dog in the kennel, which jumped out of its bed and hurried back over to the fence to lick her fingers again. "One of these guys would be lucky to have you."

Skyler watched Mr. McShaggy Mutt as it sniffed at Trish's hand, its tail swishing from side to side. She smiled—a sad, helpless smile which she often found on her face when she looked at the shelter dogs that went day in and day out without getting adopted. The old, the sick, the unattractive. Try as they might, some of those dogs would never get to leave the shelter, always getting passed up for a dog that was younger, cuter, or both.

"If I adopted one of these guys," Skyler said, "eventually it would grow old, get sick, and die. And I'd have to watch it. I just *can't.* I'm sorry, Trish, but I don't have it in me. Not after what happened with Athena, and not after what happened to my parents."

Trish nodded, her expression sad but resolved. "Okay then," she said, "I will stop pestering. I just can't stand the thought of you being alone every night, though. Those foster pets kept you company."

"I hope to resume fostering eventually, once I'm ready." *Finally, not a lie.* Skyler did plan to return to her fostering duties as soon as she took Athena to the sanctuary, whenever that ended up being. And once Athena was safely relocated, she could tell Trish what happened. Maybe they could even go visit Athena there together, and Trish could see how well she was doing, all because of Skyler's help. And maybe when Trish saw that, she would be able to forgive Skyler for all the lying and sneaking around. In the end, it was all for a good cause, right? Trish will understand that. She *has* to. She loves animals just as much as Skyler does.

Yes, Skyler would definitely tell Trish everything as soon as Athena was settled at the sanctuary. So the only real question was *when* will Athena be going to the sanctuary? Skyler had already managed to justify her way into keeping the cub for another month and a half, but now that January was coming to a close, she was running out of justifications. Athena was now three months old, and in no way too small or fragile to go to the sanctuary. In fact, she was bigger than the shaggy dog wagging its tail inside the kennel, and that dog was at least fifty pounds, if not more.

"I just need a little more time, Trish. That's all."

"Well, I'm always here for you. You know that, right?"

"Of course I do. And thank you." *Guilt parasite: bite, tear, chew chew chew.*

"What about a nice strapping young lad to keep you company then?" Trish raised an eyebrow, the corner of her mouth curling into a mischievous smile.

Skyler laughed. "I haven't met any strapping young lads as of late, I'm afraid."

Trish let out an exaggerated sigh. "*None?* Not even over the holidays?"

"I already told you I went on a couple of dates around New Year's." Skyler took a step toward the empty kennel, where the soap was threatening to turn to scum. She needed to hose it off or she'd have to start all over again.

"Yes, you mentioned that. But only first dates, no second dates. And why was that?"

"The guy I went out with in December said he doesn't like dogs. Now what kind of a sick bastard doesn't like dogs?" Skyler reached down and grabbed the hose that was lying on the concrete floor near the entrance to the kennel.

"Okay," Trish said with a nod, "I will attribute that lack of romance to irreconcilable differences. What about the other one? From a few weeks ago?"

"He lives with his mother."

"Well, shit. There really aren't any good ones left, are there?"

Skyler's laugh echoed through the Dog House, causing a few of the resident dogs to bark in response. "Not that I can find, apparently." She grabbed the nozzle of the hose and stepped back from the kennel, ready to spray it down.

Trish stepped back to avoid getting splashed. "Alright Sky, I'm done work mom'ing for the day. You let me know if you need anything."

"Absolutely," Skyler said.

Trish turned to leave, then stopped herself and looked back at Skyler. "Have you taken a look at the Happily Ever After page on the website recently?"

"Yeah, it's always a mood booster to see our animals in their new homes. Lets me know what we do here is worth it."

"Did you see Thor's picture on there?"

Skyler nodded, a wistful smile spreading across her face. "Yeah, him and Alliser. I love that they got adopted together. Still not sure how their owner got those Santa hats to stay on their heads for the photo, though."

"Photoshop?" Trish asked.

"Perhaps. Or maybe Thor posed in that hat without complaint."

Trish snickered. "Doubtful," she said, then turned and started walking along the row of kennels toward the entrance to The Center. Skyler watched her go, Trish's sensible business heels clicking on the concrete floor as she went.

The guilt parasite inside Skyler's gut took one final bite, then settled. It would be back, though. It always came back eventually. Just like the killer in a slasher movie. No matter how many bullets she put into it or how certain she was that it was dead for good, it would rise again.

Skyler accepted that the parasite would be with her until Athena was safely at the sanctuary. Until then, it would always be lurking in the shadows and waiting for the next opportunity to resume its endless chewing. And since Skyler didn't plan on giving up Athena anytime soon, she was going to have to learn how to live with the guilt parasite. Or find a way to silence it.

CHAPTER 17

March 3, 2018
7:40 p.m.

Athena was asleep on the couch when Skyler got home, her legs splayed and her belly pointed up at the ceiling. Her body now spanned the length of two couch cushions, which dipped down beneath her eighty-plus pounds. She had become increasingly stocky in her build over the past couple of months, and the thickness of her muscles, especially in her forelimbs, was now much more pronounced.

Athena stirred when Skyler stepped out of the garage and into the kitchen. Skyler stomped the bits of remaining snow sludge from her boots, then removed them and discarded them by the door. Athena's paws were against her stomach before she got a chance to remove her coat, the cub's weight causing her to stumble backward.

"Whoa, Atty," Skyler said. "Let me get my jacket off first." She held her hand to her side, her palm flat and fingers splayed—a gesture she had been training Athena to understand as "stop". As Athena continued to grow, training was becoming more and more important to manage her behavior, which was that of a rambunctious teenager. Before long, she would become too big to control, and then it would be imperative for her to be properly trained. Luckily, Skyler was well versed in training unruly dogs at the shelter, and training Athena was not much different than training one of them.

Athena obediently lowered her front paws to the floor and sat down. She watched Skyler with large, amber eyes as Skyler removed her jacket and her scarf.

Once Skyler was through, she snapped her fingers— "go"—and then opened up her arms. "Okay, I'm ready!" Athena launched into the air and wrapped her front paws over Skyler's shoulders. Skyler staggered backward another foot and fell against the door, laughing. "I missed you, too, Atty."

She lowered the big cat back down to the floor, then went over to the fridge and pulled open the bottom drawer. Inside, it was filled with raw meat. She grabbed a turkey breast and the remains of a bottom round roast and brought them over to the kitchen counter.

As soon as she set them down, Athena's head popped up on the other side. She swiped at the poultry with one large, floppy paw. "Atty, stop that!" Skyler lowered her hand down to her side and splayed her fingers. Athena looked at Skyler's hand, seemed to debate her options for a moment, then lowered herself back down to the floor with a huff. Her kittenish squeaks had deepened in the past month, and sometimes Skyler could hear a guttural rumbling inside her throat at feeding time.

Skyler glanced at the kitchen window, making sure the curtains were still tightly drawn. She had started keeping the curtains closed in February, once Athena was large enough to be seen from the outside. It made the house eerily dark, but it kept any peeping neighbors from catching a glimpse of what she had inside. Due to her home's large lot size, Skyler doubted any neighbors were close enough to see through her windows—*thanks, Mom and Dad*—but she still didn't want to take any chances.

Skyler prepared Athena's dinner of turkey breast, then adorned the top of the pinkish-white flesh with the few remaining pieces of roast. Redness from the beef seeped down into the poultry below, turning the milky pink muscle into a darker, more pronounced shade of pink. She placed the bowl on the floor, then looked at Athena, whose eyes were ping-ponging from the food to Skyler's hand and then back to the food again. Skyler snapped her fingers, and Athena hurried over to the bowl and began to eat. Skyler sat down on the floor and watched her, listening to the deep vibrations in Athena's throat as she chewed.

Athena's molars gnawed through the raw meat easily. Bits of turkey bones crunched as they broke in her jaws, and white tubes of tendons lay across the flesh like dead worms as Athena tore chunk after chunk out of the piece of poultry.

"You're lucky I don't have a mortgage to pay," Skyler said to Athena, who ignored her as she ate. "Otherwise I wouldn't be able to afford your hearty appetite." In truth, Skyler's parents had left behind a comfortable nest egg, and money had never been a significant concern—not that she was going to run out and buy a Lamborghini anytime soon.

Skyler leaned down, closer to the floor, and tilted her head so she could see Athena's mouth better as she ate. All of Athena's baby teeth were in, glistening white and sharp as razors. To Skyler's surprise, her canine teeth still appeared to be growing, though. They had appeared fairly normal in size and shape a few weeks ago, but now they looked exceptionally long.

Skyler got onto her belly and pulled herself a little closer to Athena, watching closely as she finished off the remaining pieces of turkey. They were too long, alright. The canine teeth were just too long. *Why haven't they stopped growing?* Skyler thought. *All the others have stopped growing. Why haven't these?*

Athena's top canines now protruded from her mouth, and looked like sharp white spears as they rested against her chin. Skyler wondered why she hadn't noticed them before. *I guess I just never really looked at them that close.* Now, as she lay on her stomach and stared at Athena's teeth with frank fascination, something other than the guilt parasite stirred inside her stomach: unease. The shape of the teeth was familiar, but she couldn't put her finger on it. *Not a lion, not a tiger . . .*

Skyler pushed herself up from the floor, leaving Athena to finish off her dinner in peace. She grabbed her phone from the kitchen table and headed into the living room. She sat down heavily on the couch, letting out a soft *oomph* as she landed. On her phone, she tapped on the Google icon and started scrolling quickly through the various pictures of the big cat species, paying close attention to their canine teeth. She had searched through Google images countless times trying to figure out what species Athena was, but not once had she focused solely on the size and shape of the big cat's teeth.

Skyler stopped on one of the pictures, her eyes widening and her breath catching in her throat. She stared at the picture for a long time, wondering how she possibly could have missed it before. *Because it's insane,* she thought. *Because that would be absolutely batshit insane.* She clicked on the picture anyway, the unease in her stomach steadily growing.

Athena stalked into the living room, silent and low to the ground. The fur on her belly brushed against the hardwood as she inched closer and closer to the back of the couch, her bobbed tail twitching from side to side. Once she was directly behind Skyler, she sunk into a crouch and launched herself up and over the side of the couch.

Skyler screamed and dropped her phone on the floor. It landed next to her foot, faceup, with the picture still open on the screen. Athena settled on the cushion beside her, then flopped down onto her lap and playfully reached a paw up to Skyler's face, attempting to lick her forehead.

"Athena, ick! You have turkey breath," Skyler said, pushing Athena's head back down. The protruding canines caught her attention again, and she pressed a finger to Athena's whiskered cheek, lifting her lip up so she could see the full length of one of the teeth. She leaned over and looked down at the picture on her phone, and then back at Athena, looked at the phone, at Athena, the phone, Athena. *"Holy shit,"* Skyler murmured, and lowered Athena's lip back down. It covered part of the tooth, but not all of it.

Skyler absentmindedly stroked Athena's head, and soon the cub was asleep on her lap. Skyler stared at the closed curtain on the opposite side of the room, lost in thought, her phone's screen having faded to black long ago and the picture no longer visible. "What are we going to do?" she whispered. "What am *I* going to do?"

Skyler sat that way for a long time, her hand finally coming to a rest on Athena's side. Her unease gave way to fatigue, which in turn gave way to drowsiness. Skyler could feel the tentacles of sleep reaching out for her, and then enveloping her, like the arms of a kraken wrapping around a doomed ship and pulling it down to the depths below. She went down with it, letting herself get submerged into a dark and troubled sleep.

That night she dreamt of the cemetery. Only this time, as she stood in the open grave with water and soil pouring down from above and thick, viscous mud rapidly rising from below, she didn't have to ask the bundle of fur what it was. This time she already knew.

CHAPTER 18

March 4, 2018
7:29 a.m.

Skyler awoke on the couch, disoriented and afraid. Something heavy was on top of her. At first she was convinced it was dirt and mud—the soil from her dream finally covering her and burying her alive. Only it wasn't cold and wet like in her nightmare, it was warm and soft. She reached down to the weight on her legs and felt fur. Athena snorted, woken up by Skyler's frantic movements.

Skyler sat bolt upright and clutched the cub to her chest. She squeezed her eyes shut and waited, willing her heart rate to slow and her breathing to regulate. The panic from her dream seemed to have followed her into her waking state, a stowaway in the depths of her mind as she drifted into consciousness.

A minute passed. Then two. Skyler let out a slow breath, feeling the nightmare's overpowering hold over her finally releasing its grip. The thudding in her chest lessened, and she felt the panic leaving her body. Athena nuzzled against her neck, attempting to comfort her.

"I'm sorry, Atty," Skyler said. "I squeezed you too tight, didn't I?" She stroked Athena's head, then carefully moved her to the other side of the couch so she could stand up.

Skyler stumbled across the dark living room, avoiding the coffee table and adjacent chairs by memory. "God, what time is it?" She reached the curtain and pulled it back. Bright sunlight shot through the window, the room suddenly bathed in the brilliant light of morning. Skyler winced, her eyes sending a bolt of pain directly into her skull. "Shit," she muttered under her breath. She blinked repeatedly, trying to ease the strain in her eyes and adjust to the brightness. Once the pain subsided, she looked over at Athena, who was in the center of the living room with her back arched into an elegant feline stretch.

"Good morning," Skyler said. Athena chuffed in response—a pleasant, breathy snort of air through the nose that tigers often used to communicate. Only she was not a tiger.

With the morning light filtering in, the vividness of the nightmare began to fade. Skyler walked over to Athena, knelt down, and ruffled the fur behind one fuzzy ear. She saw her phone lying on the floor in the same spot where it had landed the night before. Skyler remembered her evening Google search and groaned. She looked at Athena and said, "Mama's gonna have to go on a little trip today, my dear."

Athena's golden eyes went from Skyler to a lone sock that was lying on the rug a few feet away. She burst into action, pouncing heavily on top of the sock and knocking the coffee table askew. Skyler watched her tear at the sock for a moment, holding it between her front paws and easily shredding it into pieces with her teeth, then trudged upstairs to shower and change. *I wonder what else she can tear apart,* she thought, and headed into her bedroom.

An hour later, Skyler arrived at the AACC, this time using the front entrance to go inside. The lobby was alight with spring sunshine, and the pleasant sound of happy chatter filled the open space. She walked through a beam of sunlight, feeling the momentary warmth on her back, and up to the service desk in the center of the room.

"Hey, Samantha," she said, leaning forward and resting her forearms on the counter. "Who's on kennel duty today?"

Samantha looked up from the colorful stack of adoption folders she was in the midst of organizing. She was a pretty blonde of seventeen, volunteering at the shelter in hopes it would look good on her college applications for veterinary school one day. "'Morning, Skyler," she said. She pushed the folders aside and looked at the printed schedule that was tacked above the desk. "Kennel duty today is you and Justin. Aren't you on kennel duty all week?"

Skyler tilted her head and eyed the man that was standing behind Samantha. He was inside the desk's service area and facing the opposite direction, talking to a woman who was holding a hefty bag of dog bone treats. The man had dark brown hair, and his muscular frame was only somewhat concealed by the purple volunteer shirt he was wearing. He said something, and Dog Bone Woman laughed in response. Skyler didn't recognize him.

"Yeah, I am," she said, distracted. "Who's that?" Skyler gestured toward the man with her chin.

Samantha glanced briefly over her shoulder. "Oh, that's Peter. He just started. New volunteer." Samantha leaned over the desk, her long, blonde hair brushing across the countertop. Quieter, she said, "He's *super* cute." Samantha blushed and a schoolgirl smile spread across her face.

Skyler grinned and leaned forward, their foreheads almost touching. "Don't you already have a boyfriend?" she whispered.

"Yeah," Samantha giggled. "I can still look, though. He's too old for me anyway." She pushed herself away from the counter and flipped her hair back with one hand. "What about you?" she asked, and winked. "I bet you guys are right around the same age."

Skyler sighed and shook her head. "I swear, this entire place is trying to play matchmaker with me."

Samantha shrugged. "Wait 'til you see him." She waggled her eyebrows up and down and giggled again.

Skyler took another look at Peter, who was still talking to Dog Bone Woman. The woman was blushing and looking at him with starry eyes. *Well, the posterior view is certainly promising,* she thought. No time for that now, though. She turned her attention back to Samantha. "I have something important I have to do today. Do you think there is any way I could bribe Justin to cover kennel duty for me? I can make it up to him next week."

Samantha sighed. "I dunno, Sky. It sounded like he had plans for later today. You can ask, though."

"I can cover for you," Peter said. He walked over to join them, having just finished his conversation with Dog Bone Woman. Samantha looked over her shoulder and her cheeks flushed again. She looked away, grinning sheepishly.

Skyler could see why Samantha was so flustered. Peter was even better looking from the front than he was from behind. He had a broad chest, and his shirt sleeves were taut over his defined, muscular arms. His eyes were a dazzling green, and his jawline pronounced and chiseled. His hair was combed back, but a few loose strands fell across his forehead, making him look endearing—the boy next door. No, the *man* next door.

Skyler felt her own cheeks growing warm as she stared at him. "I, uh—we haven't met yet. I'm Skyler." She extended her hand over the desk.

Peter shook with her, a grin spreading across his handsome face. "Nice to meet you. I'm Peter. I just started volunteering."

"Welcome to the team," Skyler said, trying to sound casual.

"Glad to be here." Peter's eyes lingered on Skyler's. "Sorry to interrupt, but I heard you needed help with . . . kennel duty? I'm assuming that's cleaning out the kennels."

Skyler nodded, her voice having evaded her. Inside, her heart fluttered around like a caged butterfly. "Yeah," she said finally. "Cleaning, scrubbing, and hosing them down. It's not exactly the funnest of ways to spend your day."

"I don't mind," Peter said, his grin widening, revealing white, radiant teeth.

"Are you sure? You just started and I don't want to scare you away just yet."

"I'm hoping to someday land a full-time gig here, so anything that makes that more likely, I am willing to do."

"Well, Trish does appreciate a go-getter." Skyler forced herself to look around the lobby, not wanting to openly gawk at him. When she looked back, he was watching her with a small smile touching his lips, as if he knew she was trying not to stare. "Are you sure?"

"Absolutely. I can have Justin show me the ropes."

"Well, that would be very much appreciated," Skyler said. She glanced at Samantha, who was looking at her with wide eyes and a large, animated grin spread across her face.

"I'll go find Justin now," Peter said. "Nice to meet you, Skyler."

"Nice to meet you, too," she said. Then added, "Thanks again."

Peter nodded and went over to the partition in the desk. He stepped through and started making his way toward the Dog

House. Samantha and Skyler watched him go in silence. He slipped through the double doors and was gone.

Samantha turned to Skyler, her grin larger than ever. "Told you," she said.

Skyler felt herself blushing again. "Yeah, girl, you sure did. See ya tomorrow?"

"You got it. I hope whatever you gotta do today goes well."

"Me, too." Skyler turned and headed toward the main entrance, glancing over at the Dog House once more before she left.

CHAPTER 19

March 4, 2018
11:58 a.m.

Three hours later, Skyler arrived at the Natural History Museum of Phoenix, Arizona. The lobby was a large expanse of white tile, its walls stretching up to three stories in height. Glass balconies hung over the lobby, each level containing different eras of history, like layers of sandstone along a cliff face. A *Tyrannosaurus rex* skeleton was in the center of the room, standing tall and ferocious on a platform of artificial rock. To the right was the admissions counter.

Skyler walked over to the counter and pulled out her credit card. Her boots were silent on the tile, and the girl on the opposite side of the desk didn't hear her approach. It wasn't until Skyler placed her card on the desk that the bespectacled girl with purple streaks in her hair looked up from her phone. "For one?" she asked.

"Yes, thank you." When the purple-haired girl was finished ringing her up, Skyler asked, "Where's your ice age exhibit?"

"Second floor," the girl said. "First floor is dinosaurs and stuff, second floor has the ice age and the dawn of man, third floor is present-day and the future." The girl handed Skyler a ticket with *Day Pass* stamped on the front. "You can come in and out all you want for the day. Just hold onto this."

"Thanks so much." Skyler took the ticket and stuck it in her back pocket along with her credit card. She left the admissions counter, walked past the towering *T. rex*, and headed for the elevators.

On the second floor, she went straight to the directory sign. To the left was the Cenozoic Era and the Pleistocene Epoch. To the right was The Last Ice Age and The Emergence of the *Homo sapiens*. Skyler turned right. She stopped at the entrance to a large room with high ceilings that had a partition going down the center. One side had models of early humans, with mountains of black, scraggly hair and heavy beards. Their hips were draped with furry pieces of spotted cloth. The women were topless, and one had an infant clutched to her breast.

On the opposite side, a woolly mammoth dominated the center of the room, its tusks stretching at least twelve feet in length and hovering ten feet above the ground. Skyler walked toward the woolly mammoth, passing beneath a large sign that said "The Last Ice Age: The Era of Giant Mammals". She strolled around the room, looking at illustrations of the American lion and a sculpture of a giant sloth. A group of Neanderthals huddled around an artificial fire, sharpening spears. At the far end of the room, she saw what she was looking for—what she had driven nearly three hours to see.

Skyler had been to this museum before, taken by her parents when she was six years old. Although the memory of their visit was fuzzy and incomplete, she still remembered seeing the animal sculptures that captured her attention all those years ago and caused her mouth to drop open with awe. The life-sized models were still there, set up with a savanna-type backdrop and artificial grassland underneath. Skyler's heartbeat quickened, and her throat suddenly felt scratchy and dry. She hurried across the room and came to a stop in front of the three sculptures, her mouth falling open like she was a girl of six again.

The three saber-toothed cats stood side by side, going from the biggest on the left to the smallest on the right. All three species were heavily muscled and robustly built, and their thick forelimbs were elongated and more pronounced than those of modern-day big cats. They had tan coats, the two smaller species also having spots running along their backs and hind legs. All had bobbed tails. And all had incredibly long canines, stretching well past their jawlines and at least half a foot in length, if not more.

Skyler went to the placard on the wall next to the models. The top said "*Smilodon*: The Most Well-Known Creature of the Ice Age". Below the title, in smaller letters, it said "The Story Behind the Saber-Toothed Cats".

Skyler read the paragraphs that followed, unaware she was holding her breath until she started to feel lightheaded. She could hear her pulse thudding in her ears, and a child off to her left yelling "woowy mamoof" over and over. The child's shrieks barely registered to her as her eyes went from one line of text to the next.

"Smilodon, more commonly known as the Saber-Toothed Tiger, was not actually a tiger at all. In the early Miocene Epoch, the Felidae family split into two subfamilies. Those that continued on the Felidae path of evolution eventually became the modern-day cats we all know and love today: the African lion, the tiger, the leopard. Those that went down the other branch of evolution became the Smilodon.

Smilodon was a formidable predator during the ice age. It was heavily built, its bones stronger and thicker than those of modern-day big cats. It was an ambush predator, using its mass and strength to pin down prey so it could use its elongated canines to slash and stab at its victim. The canines could grow as long as seven inches in length, and had a razored edge for shredding meat. Smilodon's jaw was capable of opening 120 degrees (that's twice as wide as the lions and tigers we see today!) to accommodate its canines.

The Smilodon genus consisted of three species: Smilodon populator, Smilodon fatalis, and Smilodon gracilis. Smilodon populator was the largest of the smilodons, and lived in the grasslands of South America. Smilodon fatalis was the next largest in size, and the most common of the species. It lived in North America and grew to the size of an African lion. The smallest, Smilodon gracilis . . ."

Skyler looked down at the illustration near the bottom of the sign. In the picture, a *Smilodon* with spots—probably the *Smilodon fatalis*—was standing near the entrance to a cave with two cubs sitting nearby. Skyler leaned in, carefully inspecting the cubs. They also had spots along their flanks, and somewhat resembled the cubs of a modern-day lion. Unlike a lion, they had elongated canines—although not nearly as long as mama's. *Those are the baby teeth,* Skyler thought. *And then their adult canines will grow in, and they will be seven inches long.*

The woowy mamoof kid was now smacking the giant sloth statue with gusto. The hollow sculpture made a *bonk!* noise each time the kid's hand wailed down on top of it. Skyler ignored the enthusiastic bonks, still lost in thought. She turned back to the three *Smilodon* sculptures.

A small plaque was in front of each statue. *S. populator*, the model on the left, was enormous. It came up to Skyler's shoulders, and the plaque said it could grow up to 960 pounds. The middle model was the *S. fatalis*, which weighed up to 620 pounds, and the smallest was the *S. gracilis* at 200 pounds.

Skyler walked from model to model, eventually ending up in front of the *S. fatalis* in the center. She read the plaque again. "*S. fatalis.* 350-620 pounds. Lived in shrubland and forest." Skyler looked up at the model, studying it closely. Its shoulders were level with her waist, and its head came up to the height of her chest. "Holy crap," she mumbled. She looked around, searching for a model of a *Smilodon* cub. She was peering around the side of the statues when she heard a voice come from directly behind her.

"Can I help you?"

Skyler jumped and spun around, feeling like she had just been caught doing some sort of illegal activity. The guilt parasite stirred, then settled.

A man of retirement age, wearing a khaki shirt and matching tan shorts, stood behind her. A name tag was pinned to his left breast pocket. "I'm Andrew," he said. "I'm a docent here. I'd love to answer any questions you might have about our beloved saber-toothed cats." He leaned in, as if to tell Skyler something in confidence. "They've always been my favorite," he said, smiling warmly from underneath a bushy, gray mustache. "I guess you could say that *Smilodon* makes me smile." He chuckled.

Skyler forced a smile of her own. "Yeah, I—uh . . . I was wondering how you could tell which one was which."

Andrew looked slightly confused, then covered it with a polite nod of his head. "The labels are right below the models." He lifted his palm, gesturing toward the small plaques erected in front of each statue. "We presume the *populator* had a solid, tan coat because it lived on the open plains. The *fatalis* and *gracilis* often lived in forested areas, so paleontologists theorized that they might have had spots on their coats, like a leopard or jaguar."

"Yeah, that makes sense," Skyler said, looking back at the *S. fatalis*. "I was actually wondering more about when they were younger. Like, how would you differentiate between the species when they were babies."

Andrew shook his head. "That is something we have yet to discover, I'm afraid. Although I sure would like to see what one of those little guys looked like." He smiled wistfully. "Probably like a lion cub, but with bigger teeth." He winked.

Just like Athena, Skyler thought. She forced another smile. "Yeah, I bet. So you think the cubs would have large canines, too?"

"I would imagine so," Andrew said, nodding. "Although not nearly as large as the adults, obviously. The adult canines took nearly two years to grow to their full size. It is theorized that in adolescence both sets of canines were present—both baby *and* adult teeth. That way the adult teeth had a support system as they grew. *Smilodon's* canines may be fearsome in length, but they are not as strong as one might suspect. That's why they have that razor edge." He pointed to one of the canines on the *S. fatalis.* "So they can shred and slice their prey."

"Shred and slice . . ." Skyler trailed off, staring at the curved, saber-shaped teeth.

"Could you imagine one of these incredible predators being alive today? What animal—or human—could ever stand a chance against *Smilodon*?"

"I couldn't even imagine," Skyler said. She turned away from the models and looked at Andrew. "I just have one more question, if you don't mind."

"Not one bit. Fire away!"

"At what age would a cub become dangerous?"

Andrew looked at Skyler with a puzzled expression. "You sure are curious about what these youngsters must have been like."

Skyler shrugged. "I just find them fascinating, that's all."

Andrew nodded, satisfied. "Well, there is no way to know exactly when these guys would have started hunting on their own. I have read that today's tiger cubs start hunting around eight to ten months old, although they can become dangerous to humans in as little as four months. Perhaps you should research the La Brea Tar Pits in Los Angeles. A few juvenile skeletons were recovered from—"

"The what?" Skyler asked, cutting Andrew off mid-sentence.

"The La Brea Tar Pits. A lot of animal remains from the last ice age were recovered from there. The herbivores would get stuck in the tar, and then the predators would get stuck themselves while trying to get at the herbivores. As a result, a lot of giant mammals ended up getting preserved there. Sad for them, but lucky for paleontologists today. Here, come take a look!"

Andrew led Skyler over to a large sign covered in heavy plastic. At the top it said "The La Brea Tar Pits" in bold, black letters.

"Now, to passersby, La Brea might look just like any other city park. Grassy areas to relax, plenty of walking paths, a lake. But there is so much more lurking just below the surface! See here," Andrew pointed to a picture of a lake, "this is the main tourist draw. The lake near the entrance. Part groundwater and part tar. Very memorable because of the mammoth sculptures."

Skyler looked at the picture on the display sign. In it, a medium-sized lake was surrounded by a heavy fence. The lake looked fairly normal, except for its darker color and the swirls of oil covering its surface. What captured her attention were the mammoth sculptures at the lake's edge. One of the mammoths was partially submerged in the tar lake, struggling to free itself, while a baby screamed in terror at the tar's edge. It was horrifying.

"Now, the lake is great for taking pictures, but here's where the real action is." Andrew moved his finger over to another picture which was some sort of dig site. "Less than a five minute walk from the lake is Pit 91. This is where the scientists make their discoveries. It even has an observation deck so visitors can watch them while they work."

Pit 91 was a large, square-shaped hole cut into the earth. The hole was at least twenty feet down and thirty feet across in either direction. A wooden railing wrapped around its edge, with a single opening where a ladder was propped up for researchers to go in and out. The walls of the pit were lined with wooden planks, probably to keep the earth from crumbling in and burying the paleontologists below.

"Kinda like a swimming pool, isn't it? Only below ground. And with wooden platforms around it instead of cement. I sure wouldn't want to go swimming in there, though." Another chuckle.

Skyler studied the picture of Pit 91. Just as Andrew described, there were wooden platforms situated over a tar pit. It did look something like a swimming pool, only with viscous black muck instead of water. There was a second, much smaller tar pit positioned next to the larger "pool". *A spa,* she thought. *A swimming pool and a spa set twenty feet below the earth's surface.* In the "pool", animal bones protruded from the dark, oily sludge, with eager scientists hunched over them. The "spa" pit was much deeper, with a ladder that descended down its side and disappeared into the darkness below. Skyler couldn't see the bottom.

Like an open grave, she thought. *A grave too deep to see the bottom.* A flash of last night's dream went through her head as she looked at the smaller, deeper pit. *Standing in an open grave. Waist deep . . . not in mud, but in tar.*

Skyler looked back at Andrew. His lips were moving, but she could no longer hear him. She was sweating, and her head was spinning at a nauseating rate. *Not mud, but tar. A tar pit grave. Standing inside a tar pit grave . . .*

"Ma'am? Ma'am, are you alright?" Andrew's voice, hovering somewhere off in the distance.

Skyler felt herself snap back to reality. She was suddenly aware of the woowy mamoof kid, running back and forth and shrieking with obnoxious delight. The *Smilodon* statues stood beside her, looking fearsomely large, but also pathetically plastic. And then there was Andrew, the eager-to-please docent, standing in front of her and looking concerned. "I'm sorry. I—I must have spaced out there for a bit."

"I'd say!" Andrew said, sounding relieved. "You went as white as a sheet there for a minute. Would you like to sit down? We have benches—"

"No," Skyler said, a little too quickly. "I mean, no thank you. I appreciate the information, but I have to get going now." Skyler didn't wait for Andrew to reply. Instead, she whirled around and hurried toward the exit to The Last Ice Age. She had seen enough.

CHAPTER 20

March 4, 2018
4:31 p.m.

Athena was waiting by the kitchen door when Skyler arrived back at home. As soon as Skyler stepped inside, the cub jumped up and pressed her front paws against Skyler's chest, nuzzling her with her head and chuffing softly.

"Hello, my dear. How's my Atty doing?" Skyler ruffled Athena's neck, which came up to her chest when the big cat was standing on her hind legs. Athena looked up at her, their faces only a foot apart. Skyler placed a thumb on each whiskered cheek, then lifted them up so she could see the full length of her canines. They were almost three inches long. *Too long,* Skyler thought. *Saber-tooth long.*

"You hungry?" Skyler asked. She gently lowered Athena's front paws to the floor and then went across the kitchen to retrieve a piece of beef from the fridge. Instead of cutting it into pieces, Skyler put the entire chunk of meat onto a plate and then set it down on the floor.

Athena looked at the large portion of meat. Confused, she tilted her head in a way that was very much human. She then smacked at the meat with her front paw—a gesture that was very much *not* human—and the plate skittered across the floor. Athena looked up at Skyler for permission, then hunkered down in front of the beef as soon as Skyler snapped her fingers.

Fascinated, Skyler sat down beside her to watch. Athena opened her mouth wide—too wide, saber-tooth wide—and sunk her teeth into the wet, reddish-purple flesh. She lifted the entire piece of beef, shook it a few times, then dropped it, discouraged. After a moment, she tilted her head and instead slashed at it with her canines. This maneuver cut a piece loose, and she then used her molars to tear it free.

Now having the technique down, Athena made quick work of slicing and tearing the beef apart, gulping each piece down until there was nothing left. When she was done, she flopped down next to Skyler and settled her head into Skyler's lap. She looked up at Skyler with her wide, amber eyes, where only a few flecks of blue remained.

"I love you, Atty," Skyler whispered. "I have no idea what I'm going to do with you, but I love you very much." Skyler lay down on the kitchen floor next to Athena, feeling the cub's beefy breath warm on her face.

The entire drive home, Skyler had weighed her options about what to do with Athena, determined to come up with a solution before she arrived back in Diamondback.

Unfortunately, as she turned into her driveway and waited for the garage door to rumble up on its track, she was still undecided. She had narrowed her choices down to two possibilities—one that was rational and safe and "right", and one that was not. Now, lying on the floor next to Athena and looking into her golden eyes, Skyler realized she really only had one choice—and it wasn't the rational one.

The original idea of bringing Athena to a sanctuary was no longer an option. If Atty was in fact a *Smilodon*—which Skyler was now fairly certain she was—then she wasn't going to get to live out her days running around in the sunshine inside the safe walls of a sanctuary. Instead, she was going to be collected and taken to a lab somewhere—to be studied, poked, and prodded. An extinct species that turns out to not be extinct? Athena would spend the rest of her life locked in a cage, only to be removed for countless experiments and tests. She would lie on cold examination tables with harsh lighting and loud machines as scientists collected samples and injected her with God knows what. Athena would have a miserable life, alone and unloved and scared. Just a specimen in a metaphorical petri dish. If people could treat today's big cats so badly—illegal breeding, exploiting cubs, killing them for fur and body parts—what would they possibly do to an extinct one?

Skyler ran her hand down Athena's side, feeling her belly as it rose and fell in steady intervals. The other option— correction: the only option—was to keep her. To keep Atty where she was safe, and to hide her as best she could. Skyler's house was large and fairly secluded; she could keep Athena concealed at least until she was nearly full grown. And then . . . Skyler closed her eyes and pressed her face into Athena's fur . . . and then they will have to go somewhere. Somewhere away. Somewhere where no one would ever find them. She could do it, if she had to. Mexico wasn't *that* far away.

The thought of leaving her parents' home was a distressing one, but then again, it hadn't been their home in many years. The decorations and furnishings—the ones her aunt Regina hadn't destroyed anyway—were theirs, but the house itself was just a house. Her parents were gone and her aunt was gone, too, not even their ghosts existing inside these walls. But Athena . . . Athena was *here*. She was *alive*. And she greeted Skyler at the door every day when she got home and slept next to her every night. Athena *loved* her. Right? Can saber-toothed cats love?

"Do you love me, Atty?" Skyler whispered into the scruff of Athena's neck. The cub chuffed in response. Skyler smiled, the fur tickling at her nose. "I'll take that as a yes. I love you, too. And I'm going to keep you safe. I promise."

CHAPTER 21

March 5, 2018
10:27 a.m.

"Ya know, when I volunteered to do kennel duty, I didn't realize what a pain in the ass it would be."

Skyler whirled around, dropping the bag of kitten food she was holding. Kernels of salmon-flavored kibble tumbled out, and the four kittens inside the kennel rushed over and started chewing at it noisily.

"Sorry," Peter said, "I didn't mean to startle you. Are you always this jumpy?"

Skyler blushed, her cheeks feeling like she was in front of a heated stove. Peter was standing in the center of the Cat Cabana, his thumbs hooked into the pockets of his jeans and a sly smile at the corner of his mouth. "I just didn't hear you, is all," Skyler said. "You always sneak up on people?"

Peter's grin widened and he took a step forward. His volunteer shirt was stretched across his broad chest, and Skyler could make out the definition of his muscles through the fabric. *God, he can even make a volunteer shirt look sexy.* She looked away, overly conscious that she was staring again.

"Sorry about that," he said, and walked over to where Skyler was standing. He stopped in front of the kennel, his body dangerously close to hers. When he reached inside to pet one of the kittens, his arm brushed against her, then came to rest with his shoulder lightly pressed against her own.

Skyler held her breath, savoring the touch. Seconds ticked by, Peter petting the kittens while Skyler stood in silence beside him, their arms touching. Finally, she took a step to the side, away from Peter and away from the kennel. "So," she said, trying to sound casual, "not a fan of kennel duty, huh?"

Peter turned his head and looked at Skyler, his green eyes sparkling. He continued to pet the kittens with one outstretched finger. "I don't know if it was the kennel cleaning itself, or having to spend the day with Justin. He sure can talk a lot about nothing." Peter collected the toppled bag of kitten food and gently closed the kennel door. He offered the bag to Skyler.

Skyler stepped forward and snatched the bag of food, pulling it to her chest. She felt like she was trying to use the bag to conceal her obvious attraction to him, but it wasn't working. He knew she was attracted to him, that's why he was smiling like that. Skyler felt her cheeks burning again. Since when did she become a fumbling schoolgirl drooling over a guy? *God, get your act together,* she thought. *He's not* that *attractive.* And then her mind corrected her: *Yes, he is.*

"I much rather have been doing kennel duty with you," Peter said, still smiling.

"Well, since you were covering for me, I don't think doing it together would have been possible."

Peter raised his eyebrows and stifled a laugh. "What was that? Doing it to . . . ?"

Skyler's cheeks burned, the stove now turned on to full blast. "I—I didn't mean . . ."

"I know," he said. "I'm just giving you a hard time. So what did you have to do yesterday that was so urgent?" Peter casually hooked his thumbs back into his pockets.

Skyler caught herself following his hands as they made their descent to his jeans, then snapped her eyes back up to his. "Nothing important, just some errands," she said too quickly.

"Nothing important? So I had to spend the entire day scrubbing the kennels with Justin for *nothing important*?" He took a step closer to Skyler.

"He's not all that bad," Skyler protested, still clutching the kitten kibble like a makeshift shield.

"No, he's not. He's just not you."

A nervous laugh escaped Skyler's lips. "You, sir, know nothing about me."

Peter took another step forward, leaving only a few feet between them. "I know that you are very well liked around here, and that if I want to get offered a full-time position at Agave, then you are the one to talk to. Am I right?"

"Well, Trish would be the one hiring you, not me."

"I'm sure you could put in a good word for me, if you feel so inclined."

"I could . . ." Skyler said, letting the words hang in the air, then added, "but I'm not sure about you yet. I mean, what if you're a horrible dog walker?"

"I didn't know my dog walking abilities were so important here at the Agave Animal Care Center."

"Dog walking is *very* important. It's often the only time the dogs get out of their kennels all day."

Peter nodded thoughtfully. "Okay, then I will make sure to hone my dog walking abilities."

"You do that," Skyler said, and then began walking toward the entrance to the Cat Cabana.

"You know," Peter called after her, "I could really use some more pointers on how to succeed around here. Perhaps I could take you out to dinner, and then you could share some of your secrets about top-notch animal care."

Skyler turned back and stared at him, mouth ajar. "Are you asking me out?" she said, then instantly regretted it. *Who says that? Fifteen-year-olds in rom-coms—that's who.*

"Yeah, I think I am. Although, after covering your kennel duty, I think it should be *you* who is the one to take *me* out."

"You want me to take you out because you had to clean some dog kennels?"

"I'll let that slide, *if* you agree to go to dinner with me."

Skyler looked down at the bag of kitten chow, feeling both anxious and excited at the same time. How long had it been since she was actually interested in going on a date with someone? She looked at Peter—his handsome face, his muscular build. "Alright," she said, willing herself not to blush again.

"Alright," Peter agreed, nodding. "Now the only question is, where do I take the best dog walker in all of Diamondback?"

"I'm sure you can figure that one out yourself," Skyler said, unable to keep a smile from creeping across her lips.

"Tomorrow night?"

"Yeah. Tomorrow night." Skyler turned and hurried out of the Cat Cabana, not wanting to say anything stupid that might cause him to change his mind. As she went through the double doors, she almost collided with Trish, who was standing just outside with her foot propping one of the doors open an inch.

Trish looked up, startled. "God, you walk fast," she said, a sheepish grin plastered to her face.

Skyler's jaw dropped open. "Eavesdropper!" she exclaimed. She furrowed her brow and contorted her expression into one of mock outrage.

Trish grabbed Skyler's arm, which was still holding onto the kitten food, and pulled her away from the door. "Sorry, couldn't help myself," she whispered. "You two will have such beautiful babies."

"Oh my God," Skyler groaned, keeping her voice low. "You are ridiculous." She rolled her eyes and glanced at the closed doors of the Cat Cabana. "And keep your voice down. I don't want him hearing your crazy talk."

"Want me to help you pick out something to wear?" Trish asked, grinning.

"I'm thirty-two. I am fully capable of dressing myself." Skyler gave the bag of food to Trish, then started walking across the lobby, away from the Cat Cabana.

"Just promise me you aren't going to wear your work boots!" Trish called after her.

Skyler threw a quick glance over her shoulder, her lips curling into a smile. "But that's all I own!"

CHAPTER 22

March 6, 2018
6:29 p.m.

Skyler stood in her bedroom, her body bare except for a towel that was clutched loosely to her chest. Her eyes darted between the various articles of clothing that were spread across her bed. Three pairs of jeans lay before her, two bootcut and one skinny. She leaned forward and pulled the black pair of skinny jeans into the center of the bed. She then reached up and pulled down a red T-shirt from the assortment of available tops. She wrinkled her brow and turned to Athena, who was lying next to her bare feet and looking up at her with bright, golden eyes.

"What do you think, Atty? Too Hot Topic?" Skyler glanced at the black pants and red shirt combo again. "Ugh, you're right. Way too Hot Topic." She snatched the red shirt off the bed and tossed it onto the floor.

Athena jumped up, ran over to the shirt, and flopped down on top of it. The shirt disappeared beneath her, concealed by her bulky frame. She was now over eighty pounds and a little past four months old. Her muscles had thickened considerably, and they stood out underneath her tan coat.

Athena rolled off the shirt, pinned it down with one large paw, and then bit into it with her three-inch canines. The red fabric split easily, making a sharp, tearing noise.

"Athena!" Skyler cried. "Bad girl!" Skyler stomped across the room and attempted to retrieve the ripped shirt. In response, Athena pressed down harder with her paw, pinning the shirt against the carpet. Skyler pulled at the material, which tore instead of budging from under Athena's paw. "Hey, Schwarzenegger. When did you get so strong? Gimme that!" Skyler yanked harder on the shirt. Athena batted lightly at her hand, hopped up, and crouched into a playful pose. A shredded piece of red fabric dangled from between her teeth.

Skyler sighed, defeated. "I don't have time to play, Atty. I'm supposed to be getting ready. He's gonna be here in half an hour."

Athena sat down heavily on her haunches, looked at Skyler with hopeful eyes, then turned her attention back to the tattered shirt. The tearing sounds resumed.

"Here, use this." Skyler grabbed a knotted rope toy she put together a few weeks ago using a heavy-duty rope she purchased from Home Depot. None of the dog toys she bought recently were a match for the growing cub, but this makeshift toy had managed to hang in there so far. She tossed it next to Athena, who immediately grabbed it and started shaking it from side to side. She pinned it to the ground and attempted to tear it in half, but the rope toy stubbornly held on.

Satisfied, Skyler went back to the bed. She grabbed a sky blue sweater with an enticing yet respectable V-neck and positioned it over the pants. "This works," she said, and tossed her towel through the open bathroom door behind her. She dressed quickly, throwing on the black pants and blue sweater. Finally, she sat down at the edge of the bed and pulled on her boots. *Sorry, Trish,* she thought. *Fresh out of high heels.*

Skyler glanced at her watch. Twenty minutes until seven. She went into the bathroom, stepped over the discarded towel, and looked at herself in the mirror. She had blow-dried her hair after showering and put in a moderate effort trying to style it—something she rarely did. It now rested on her shoulders, a few red highlights standing out among the loose waves. She leaned forward and examined her makeup application. *Not too bad,* she thought. Especially for someone who is used to only applying a dab of powder and a flick of mascara. All in all, she was fairly pleased with her attempt at being girly, even if she was still wearing work boots.

Skyler could hear enthusiastic chomping noises coming from the other room. She gave herself one last look in the mirror, then walked out of the bathroom. "What do you think, Atty? Am I presentable?" Skyler held her arms out to either side to give Athena a better view of her outfit.

Athena looked up, the saliva-covered rope toy dangling from her jaws. She dropped the toy and plodded over to Skyler, rubbing against her legs with the side of her neck.

Skyler squatted down and took Athena's large head into her hands. "You're gonna be a good girl tonight while I'm gone, right? No destroying the house. And no watching any R-rated movies. You know you're way too young for those." Skyler kissed the top of Athena's head. "Okay, let's feed you real quick before he gets here. I want you in the kitchen and occupied when I head out the door." Skyler stood. "C'mon, Atty. Dinner time."

Athena jumped up and bolted out of the bedroom as soon as Skyler snapped her fingers. Skyler could hear her eighty-plus pounds thudding on the floor as she ran through the hallway, bounded down the stairs, and headed into the kitchen.

Skyler went to her dresser, opened a small jewelry box, and pulled out a thin, golden chain with a small, aqua-colored diamond pendant attached. The necklace had been her mother's. Skyler wrapped the delicate chain around her neck, muttering under her breath as she fumbled with the tiny clasp. Finally, it clicked into place, and she let out a sigh of relief as the diamond settled in the center of her chest.

You got this, she thought. *Just don't act like a drooling idiot the whole night.* She jumped up and down a few times, shaking out her hands and trying to will the nervous energy from her body.

Athena let out a disgruntled moan down in the kitchen, where she was not-so-patiently waiting for her supper.

"I'm coming!" Skyler called down the hall. She turned off the bedroom light and left the room.

CHAPTER 23

March 6, 2018
7:10 p.m.

"So where exactly are you taking me?" Skyler asked as she watched the welcome sign for Alpine Ridge glide past her window. She looked over at Peter, who was casually slouched in the driver's seat with one hand draped over the steering wheel. Skyler could see the veins in his forearm standing out, and cords of muscle working their way toward his shoulder.

Don't stare! she thought. *For Christ's sake, it's only been five minutes and you're already staring.* She forced herself to look straight ahead. The traffic was light, rush hour having already passed. Peter was heading down Willow Street in the direction of downtown. Skyler's mind quickly sifted through the possible destinations in the downtown area. A few bars. Restaurants, both fancy and laid back. A pool hall. An old-school arcade.

"You'll find out soon enough," Peter said, and gave Skyler a flash of his dazzling smile.

Skyler smiled back, a little too long. *Don't stare!* She snapped her head forward again.

"So," Peter said, "are you gonna tell me a little bit more about yourself? Or do I have to wait until dinner?"

"Well, there's not too much to tell, I suppose. Born and raised here in Diamondback. Worked at Agave since I was in high school, first as a volunteer and then full time after I graduated."

"And you're damn good at it, from what everyone tells me at the shelter. You're very respected over there."

Skyler blushed. "I've just been there a long time, that's all."

"How long *exactly*?" Peter asked, turning the Toyota FJ Cruiser onto Sagebrush Avenue.

"If you, sir, are trying to sneakily ask me how old I am, your attempt has failed. A lady never tells. You must know that by now."

Peter laughed. "Touché. Though I doubt you'll be celebrating the big three-oh anytime soon."

"Blatant flattery will get you nowhere, Peter."

"Duly noted." Peter turned off Sagebrush Avenue and entered Diamondback's modest downtown area. "So what about family then? Do they live in Diamondback as well?"

Skyler shifted uncomfortably in her seat. "No, no family here." Her hand went up to her mother's necklace, her fingers tracing the edges of the gemstone as she stared out the window.

"Oh," Peter said, sounding surprised. "I thought you said you were born here. Did your parents move somewhere else?"

"Actually, they passed away when I was little."

"Oh God, I'm sorry." He paused. "That it happened, *and* that I brought it up." He shook his head. "Way to go, Pete," he mumbled under his breath.

"It's okay," Skyler said. "It was a long time ago. Car accident. My aunt ended up raising me. Well, sort of."

"I'm really sorry that happened, Skyler. I know losing a parent sucks . . . but losing both? *God.*"

"You lost a parent?" Skyler asked, taken aback.

"Yeah, my mom. A few years ago. Heart attack. And they say heart attacks are a guy's thing. Guess not."

"I'm so sorry, Peter. If you ever want to talk about it, I'm here." Skyler briefly rested her hand on Peter's arm. She felt a tinge of electricity as her fingers touched his skin.

"Thanks. I'll keep that in mind." Peter looked over at her and smiled. "She's actually the reason I came here. After she died, home didn't feel like home anymore, ya know? So I've been traveling around a lot, trying to find a new place that fits. I think Diamondback might be it."

"I hope it is," Skyler said.

Peter pulled the FJ Cruiser up to Minstrel's Steakhouse and parallel parked just past the storefront. Skyler looked at the red, illuminated sign reflected in the side-view mirror. "Minstrel's?" she asked, not quite believing that's where they were going.

"Yeah," Peter said, sounding nervous. He shifted the car into park and turned off the engine. "Is that okay? I went to the one in Tucson once and loved it. I guess I should have asked if you were a vegetarian first."

Skyler laughed. "Oh, I'm definitely a carnivore. I just didn't expect steak on a first date."

"Well, Skyler, I'm a fancy kinda guy." He gave her a ridiculous grin and waggled his eyebrows up and down.

Skyler giggled. "Well, okay then." She went to grab her door handle, but Peter bolted out of the car and jogged around the front before she had a chance. Skyler watched him, fascinated. He arrived at the passenger door, opened it, then held out his hand. Skyler felt the same electric tingle as their hands met.

Peter closed the door, then gestured toward the entrance to Minstrel's. "This way, my lady."

They headed into the restaurant, and as Skyler stepped into the subtle yet elegantly decorated lobby, she felt Peter's hand press softly against the small of her back as he walked beside her. *Oh dear lord,* she thought, *I'm in trouble.* Skyler bit down on her lower lip, trying to stop the grin that was spreading across her face.

CHAPTER 24

March 6, 2018
9:19 p.m.

"Dessert?" Peter asked. A busser had just swept up the empty entrée plates and disappeared around a nearby corner.

Skyler sighed. "Oh God, I don't think I can eat another bite." She placed a hand against her stomach and shook her head with regret.

"Well, you can't say I didn't try." Peter finished off his beer and raised his eyebrows at Skyler's near-empty glass. "Another glass of wine?"

"No, thank you. I think if I consume one more calorie I might burst."

Peter smirked. "Like the guy's stomach in *Alien*?"

"Hey!" Skyler exclaimed. "I told you the reason I liked that movie was because everyone died except for the lady and her cat."

"You *also* said that all movies should end that way."

Skyler laughed. "What's wrong with that? I think that would be a perfectly acceptable ending for most movies."

"Maybe you're right," Peter said. He brushed a few loose strands of hair from his forehead, and Skyler found herself staring again.

Peter pulled out his wallet and selected a few bills from inside. He tucked them into the checkbook that was resting on the edge of the table.

"You sure you don't want me to help out with that?" Skyler asked. "I did stick you with kennel duty, after all."

"You also gave me plenty of helpful advice tonight about how to perfect my dog walking skills. And how to get on Trish's good side so I can maybe get myself a permanent gig at the shelter. I think I owe you more than just one dinner."

Skyler smiled. "You think there might be another dinner, huh?"

"Absolutely. If you're interested."

"Absolutely," Skyler said, and blushed in spite of herself.

Peter pulled the FJ Cruiser up to the curb in front of Skyler's house. She looked up at the porch, and to the single porch light that cast a warm glow on the front door. All the curtains were drawn—for obvious reasons. The blue house looked dark and uninhabited, save for the porch light.

Skyler's eyes went to Peter. She didn't want the night to end. It had been a perfect evening, and she could already feel swirls of hope in her stomach that there might be more perfect evenings to come.

Peter hopped out of the car and walked around the front to open her door. Skyler watched him pass by through the windshield, her eyes lingering on his chest and the alluring curve of his biceps. Her mind shifted to whether or not he would kiss her goodnight. And, if he did, would she be any good at it? How long had it been since she kissed a guy? She hadn't even hugged the dog-hating idiot from December goodnight, let alone kissed the sicko.

Skyler jumped when the passenger door opened, snapping her out of the whirlwind of thoughts that were spinning around inside her head. She glanced up at Peter and forced an anxious smile. God, she must look like such a nerd to him. She took his hand and allowed him to help her out of the car.

They walked along the sidewalk on the way to the porch, Peter's hand resting softly on Skyler's lower back. She felt her stomach fluttering and her heart pounding away in her chest. Had she ever felt this way about a guy before? It was like she had been transformed into a giddy schoolgirl, no longer the independent, thirty-something-year-old woman that she was. They ascended the steps onto her porch, their skin now bathed in golden light.

"Hey, I really hate to intrude . . ." Peter said, his voice cutting into the serene quiet. A chirping cricket fell silent. "But could I by chance use your bathroom? I should have stopped on the way out of the restaurant. Damn beers." He shrugged and looked down, embarrassed.

Skyler felt a wave of relief. She had been agonizing over whether she should invite him inside for a hot chocolate or something—maybe say she wanted some dessert, after all, and she had ice cream in the fridge. But then she decided against it, thinking it made her sound too much like a little kid to offer ice cream to the handsome man with the bulging biceps. Or too much like a slut for inviting him in at all on the first date.

"Yeah, sure," she said. The thought of Athena asleep on the couch, big cat legs splayed and saber-teeth hanging out, slammed into her like a freight train. *Oh shit,* she thought. "But, um, first," she stammered, "let me go in real quick. The, uh, the bathroom is a little dirty. Out of soap. Just wait here for a second, okay?" She gave Peter an awkward grin, her eyebrows raised.

He laughed. "Yeah, that's fine. It's not like I'm the Pope or anything, though."

Skyler shrugged helplessly. "Even so, I'd like to get the clean laundry off the couch. I don't want you seeing my unmentionables." She didn't mean to bring up her underwear, but there it was. And she had called them unmentionables. Maybe he was going to decide he didn't have to pee that bad, after all.

Instead, Peter nodded, a serious expression fixed to his face. "I understand the concern. I will just be out here jumping up and down and clenching my bladder."

"I'll just be a second." Skyler unlocked the door and darted into the house, shutting it quickly behind her. She hurried over to the couch, where, sure enough, Athena was lying in an unabashedly shameless position with her legs in the air.

"Hey, you," Skyler whispered. "Wake up, Atty."

Athena stirred, and considered Skyler with one cranky eye.

"Atty, I need you to go into your old room. Remember? From when you were a baby. Let's go. Just for a little while."

Athena jumped off the couch and sunk down into a deep stretch, her front legs splayed out and her back arched. She then rubbed up against Skyler and chuffed.

"Shh, Atty," Skyler whispered. "C'mon." She tugged on Athena's shoulder and started guiding her down the hall toward the foster rooms. Athena walked into the dark room and turned to look at Skyler with a puzzled expression.

Skyler flicked on the light. "Just for a little while, okay? Just please be very quiet. I'll give you an extra dinner tonight if you just stay *quiet*."

Athena stared at Skyler, uncomprehending. She then noticed a rawhide chew toy in the corner and lay down next to it. She grabbed the toy and started licking at it lazily.

"Good girl," Skyler said, and slowly shut the door. She rushed back down the hall, quickly glanced into the living room to make sure there really were no unmentionables out and on display, then went back to the front door.

"Sorry," she said to Peter, stepping aside to allow him into the foyer. "Thanks for waiting."

Peter smiled and hurried past her. "Not a problem. Which way to the little boys' room?"

"Oh yeah, sorry! It's the first door on the right." Skyler pointed down the hallway she had just come out of. She watched Peter turn into the bathroom and shut the door. Light stretched across the hardwood from the crack beneath the door. Skyler lifted her eyes to the room at the end of the hall, where there was also light bleeding out from underneath the door. She listened for sounds of movement from the back room, but heard none. *Good girl,* she thought.

Skyler heard the toilet flush, and scurried out of the hallway so she wouldn't be standing there like an idiot when Peter came out of the bathroom. She headed over to the entryway to the kitchen and stood there awkwardly, her hands shoved into the back pockets of her jeans.

The bathroom door opened, and to Skyler's relief, Peter turned away from the hallway without so much as a glance. He walked up to her and smiled. "God, so much better! Thank you."

"Of course," Skyler said with a nod of her head.

They lingered in the foyer, the silence of the house filling the space between them. Skyler heard a soft thud come from down the hallway. "Hey!" she exclaimed, hoping to cover up the noise. "I have ice cream!"

Peter laughed. "Wow, that's a lot of enthusiasm." He made no indication of hearing the thud. "I thought you didn't want any dessert."

"I think my stomach might have made some extra room. Would you like some?" Skyler's fear of Peter hearing Athena quickly transitioned to fear that he might turn down her offer for dessert. Her stomach did a nauseating back flip as she waited for his response.

"What *kind* of ice cream?" he asked.

"Chocolate Fudge Brownie, I think."

"Oh, thank God! If it was Praline Pecan I was going to have to run out of here screaming."

Skyler laughed, relieved. "No, I'm definitely a chocolate girl." She walked into the kitchen, Peter trailing behind her. She grabbed a couple of bowls and spoons and placed them on the counter, willing her hands not to shake as she did so. She then went to the freezer to grab the ice cream. She opened the door only wide enough to retrieve the carton, not wanting Peter to see the pounds of frozen meat that filled the majority of the compartment.

"Ah, I was mistaken," Skyler said, closing the freezer door and looking down at the label. "It's actually Chocolate Fudge Brownie *Swirl*."

"And the swirl is the best part!" Peter clasped his hands together with exaggerated delight.

"One scoop or two?"

"Two, of course. Do you even have to ask?"

Skyler scooped ice cream into the two dishes and handed the bowl with two scoops over to Peter. He took it with a smile, shaking his head. "You really are something, you know that?"

"Why's that?" Skyler asked, alarmed.

"Ice cream. Not beer, or a nightcap. *Ice cream.* I love it."

Skyler blushed. "God, should I have offered you a beer? I have some! Do you want me to—"

"No no no! I'm saying I *like* that you offered me ice cream. It's very sweet."

"Ice cream is supposed to be sweet," Skyler said, her eyes lowered to the floor.

Peter reached out and gently tilted her chin back up with his finger. "I meant *you* are very sweet."

Skyer bit down on her lower lip, unable to look away from his piercing green eyes. She allowed him to lead her out of the kitchen and into the living room. They sat down on the couch, a foot of electrifying space hovering between them.

Skyler could feel lingering warmth on the cushion from where Athena had been sleeping. She glanced over at Peter to see if he had noticed, but he was already busy working on his ice cream. She smiled and took a tentative spoonful from her own bowl.

"This place is pretty impressive," Peter said between bites. "You live here all by yourself?"

"Yeah, it was my parents' place. Hence the superb decor."

"I like it," Peter said. He set his bowl down on the coffee table and licked chocolate from the corner of his mouth.

Skyler chewed on her lower lip as she watched him. *Shit, I'm staring again. At his mouth. At his perfect freaking mouth.* She looked up to Peter's eyes. He was watching her watch him. A small smile crept up his lips, where chocolate had been only seconds before. *Shit, he caught me,* Skyler thought, defeated.

Peter reached across the couch and took Skyler's bowl from her hands. He gently placed it on the coffee table next to his own, and then turned back to Skyler. She held her breath, both knowing what was about to happen and not believing it at the same time.

Peter leaned in, took Skyler's cheek in his hand, and pressed his mouth softly against hers. His lips felt cold from the ice cream, but his breath was warm and smelled of chocolate. Skyler leaned in to him, the kiss deepening as their mouths parted.

His hand drifted down from her cheek to her shoulder, and his other arm wrapped around her waist. Skyler let him shift her onto her back, her legs coming up from the floor and onto the couch. *God, he's a good kisser,* she thought. He brought his weight on top of her, his body feeling heavy and warm against hers. She placed her hand on the back of his head as he kissed her, feeling the softness of his hair between her fingers. *Oh my God, I can't believe this is happening.*

Peter's hand drifted from Skyler's shoulder down to her chest. She reached up and gently moved it to her waist. *Not ready for that one just yet. Let's save that for date number two.* Seconds later, his hand slid back up to her chest, and again, she moved it away. "I'm not ready for that yet," Skyler whispered, the words coming out between kisses.

When Peter's hand returned for the third time, rougher than before, the butterflies in Skyler's stomach gave way to something darker. *Bats. Not butterflies anymore, but bats.* She tried to move his hand away, but this time he would not allow her to move it.

Suddenly, Skyler became aware of just how strong the man on top of her was; trying to move his arm felt like trying to bend a lead pipe. All that time staring at his muscles, and yet she never even considered the strength behind them. And now, to her dismay, that strength was being used against her. Why had she been so naive? So trustworthy? What did she even know about this guy? He was only a volunteer, so no background check. She didn't even know his last name.

The kissing started to change—no longer tender, no longer affectionate. Peter grabbed at Skyler's breast painfully, causing her to yelp. "Peter," she gasped, "that hurts." She tried to shift out from underneath him, but was unable to move with his weight on top of her. "Peter," she struggled to say, but was barely able to get the name out with his lips pressed so hard against hers.

"Peter . . . *No.*" Skyler could feel her teeth digging into her inner lip as Peter's mouth bore down harder and harder. His lips didn't feel like lips anymore—they felt like wet, slimy worms, wriggling around on top of her mouth. His breath was no longer warm and sweet—it was now hot and suffocating, and forced into her mouth since she was unable to pull away from him. She tried to turn her face to the side, but that only caused him to force his lips down even harder. Skyler felt a sharp pain inside her upper lip as her teeth split the skin open, and then the taste of copper filled her mouth. "Peter," Skyler pleaded, "I'm bleeding. *Please . . .*"

Peter made no indication of hearing her. His breath came out in hot, heavy grunts, bathing her face and filling her mouth. The muscles in his chest and arms bulged and contracted, like snakes writhing beneath his skin. Skyler placed both of her hands against his chest and pushed up with all of her strength, but he didn't move as much as an inch. Instead, he pressed down harder against her. Skyler sunk deeper into the cushions, feeling like she was getting pulled down and not just pushed. *I'm going to suffocate.*

"Don't act like you didn't want this," Peter hissed, his voice muffled and his lips still smashed against hers. "You were practically begging for it all night." He reached up and pulled hard at the respectable V-neck of Skyler's painstakingly selected sweater, and she could hear the fabric ripping—the scream of a thousand carefully woven threads. The chain of her mother's necklace broke in the process, and Skyler felt the diamond slip off her chest on its way to the floor.

"Peter, get off of me!" she screamed. She beat at his back, but the effort was futile. His back felt like a piece of concrete. "Stop it! *Please!*"

"Keep begging. That shit gets me hard." Peter reached down between them and yanked violently at her jeans. The button popped off and tumbled to the floor, coming to rest next to her mother's necklace. *"I want you begging the whole time, you fucking slut."*

Skyler heard the sound of a belt buckle—*his belt buckle.* She beat at him furiously, trying to claw at his eyes and wriggle out from underneath him. In response, he grabbed her wrists and pinned them painfully over her head with his left hand. His other hand went back to the belt buckle. *"No!"* Skyler screamed. *"NO NO NO STOP IT NO PLEASE NO STOP!"*

"Yeah, just like that," he whispered into her ear. He squeezed down harder on her wrists, and Skyler cried out in pain. "I'm gonna make this last all night."

Skyler felt tears welling in her eyes and tried to will them away. She didn't want to give him the dignity of her tears—if anything, she wouldn't give him that. She heard the zipper of his pants as it made its descent, and then something else, barely audible over the sound of his ragged breathing and the blood pulsating in her ears. The sound came again—not from him, but from the hallway. And then a third time. It was a banging sound, followed by the sharp crack of breaking wood. It was the sound of a door breaking.

Peter pulled his face away and looked over the back of the couch, in the direction of the hallway. "I thought you lived alone," he snapped. Skyler's lips, suddenly free from his forced embrace, felt burning hot and numb all at the same time. Without the pressure of his mouth on hers, the cut inside her lip opened further, and blood began to drip into her throat.

Peter stared at the hallway, a bewildered expression on his face. A heavy silence filled the house, replacing the sounds of harsh breathing and breaking wood. Peter peered into the darkness, his eyes narrowing as he struggled to see what was hidden there. Tense seconds ticked by, and then Peter's eyes widened and his mouth fell open as he began to scream. His hand released Skyler's wrists and shot up to protect his face.

An instant later, the weight of Peter's body was pulled off hers. Skyler felt a wave of cold air fill the vacant space above her, and her skin prickled into feverish, almost painful, gooseflesh. She stared at the ceiling in horror and disbelief, her hands hovering over her face and her body still feeling like it was pinned to the couch.

Peter was screaming somewhere off to her left. His deep bellows of fear quickly transitioned into high-pitched, choked-off cries—the screams of pain. One cry followed the other, increasing in intensity instead of lessening.

Skyler jerked upright on the couch and turned to where the sounds were coming from. Peter was on his back, his pants open and pulled down to mid-thigh. His gray shirt was no longer gray—splatters of red now covered the fabric and the flesh beneath. Athena was on top of him, her paws firmly planted on his chest. Her claws were protracted, and were digging deeply into the muscles Skyler had once admired.

Athena bent down and bit at Peter's face. One of her saber-teeth scraped across his eye, and he let out a wail as it hooked into the soft tissue below the socket and split it open. Peter howled and flung his hands desperately through the air, trying to shove the cat off his chest. She was less than half his size, but the suddenness of the attack seemed to have rendered Peter defenseless. That and his pants were still pulled down around his thighs and restricting his mobility. Peter wriggled and screamed underneath her, but Athena barely budged. She took her paw off his chest just long enough to swipe at one of his flailing arms, and Peter let out another screech as her claws tore through the flesh of his forearm.

Skyler watched in horror, frozen in place and unable to comprehend what was happening. *Two minutes ago I was eating ice cream,* she thought. She tried to move, but her limbs felt like they were submerged in some sort of viscous sludge. *Submerged in tar.* Peter's wails continued, and he was now trying unsuccessfully to shove Athena away from his face and neck. His efforts reminded Skyler of her own pathetic attempts to push *him* away only seconds before.

Peter kicked his legs out and his sneakers squeaked across the wooden floor as he tried to gain traction and wiggle out from underneath Athena's firmly planted paws. Her head dipped down and she bit at his throat, causing Peter to curl into the fetal position. He threw his bloody, bitten hands over his head and neck, trying to block as much of his throat as he could. Athena instead swatted at his head, and bright streaks of red appeared and opened like flowers on his scalp. Peter whimpered and rolled onto his stomach. He began crawling across the living room floor, his open belt buckle dragging across the hardwood. Athena allowed him to crawl three or four feet before pouncing on his back, once again pinning him to the floor.

"ATTY NO!" Skyler shrieked, finally feeling her paralysis melt away. She jumped up from the couch and ran toward them, not swerving wide enough to miss the coffee table which had been knocked askew during the attack. Skyler's boot struck the table leg, and she was sent careening to the floor a good five feet away from Athena and Peter. She pushed herself up quickly, but not before she heard a gut-wrenching screech come out of Peter's mouth. The scream abruptly cut off, and a gurgling noise replaced it.

Skyler scrambled across the floor and grabbed at Athena, trying to pull her away from where Peter lay unmoving. Athena went willingly, looking from Skyler to Peter and then back at Skyler again. Her muzzle was red, and her saber-teeth dripping.

"Oh my God," Skyler mumbled. She pushed Athena further away from Peter and crawled over to him. As she drew near, her hand slipped in something warm and wet and she almost fell face first onto his back. He was lying on his stomach, his head turned to one side and his eyes fixed straight ahead. His throat was open, and blood gushed from the shredded flesh in steady intervals. The gurgling sounds were not coming from his mouth, but from the opening in his throat.

Skyler frantically looked around the room, searching for something to press against the wound. When she didn't see anything nearby, she tore off the remains of her sweater and pressed it down hard on his neck. "It's okay. You'll be okay," she said rapidly. "Just hold this here and I'll call 911. It's gonna be okay."

Peter's leg twitched once, twice, three times, and lay still. The muffled gurgling noises ceased. Skyler watched as the pool of red surrounding his throat spread, the blood seeping into the weave of her parents' area rug. She gaped at the spreading puddle, unable to look away. A trickle of blood worked its way down her chin, coming from the laceration inside her lip. A drop fell and landed in Peter's blood, creating a small, sickening ripple.

Skyler fell back onto the floor, releasing her grip on the torn sweater. More of Peter's blood spilled out from underneath. She sat on the living room floor in her bra, the front of her jeans ripped open and her knees stained red, staring at Peter's body.

Athena came over and lay down beside her, resting her head on Skyler's lap. Skyler looked down at her, her wide, hazel eyes locking on Athena's calm, golden ones. The entire front of Athena's face was smeared with blood, droplets even clinging to her whiskers. She licked at her lips and yawned.

"Oh, Atty," Skyler whispered. She looked from Athena back to Peter, and began to cry.

CHAPTER 25

March 6, 2018
10:41 p.m.

The top of the grave loomed overhead. The rain was coming down hard, and black dirt was crumbling from the walls and tumbling into the viscous substance that filled the bottom. *Tar. It's tar,* Skyler thought. *Has it always been tar?* It was up to her waist now, and she had to hold her arms overhead to keep her hands from sinking into the thick, stinking fluid.

Skyler searched the grave with growing panic, blinking hard to rid the rainwater from her eyes. She was alone. The small animal was gone, unless it had been sucked down by the tar and was now hidden somewhere below. Her mind raced, trying to decide if she should reach into the tar and search for it, although she doubted anything could be alive under its black, inky surface.

Up above, the growling had also ceased. Instead, she heard the sounds of crunching and grinding—teeth grinding together, bones cracking. *Eating. It's eating something up there.* The relentless chewing went on and on, somehow audible over the pouring rain. "Help me!" Skyler screamed into the gray, swirling sky. *"Stop eating and help me!"* The sounds of splintering bones and scraping teeth continued, unphased.

Skyler dug her hands into the soft earth and tried to pull herself up from the tar. The soil came out in sodden clumps, and she stumbled backward, falling deeper into the black sludge. Her hand dipped below the surface, and black slime sucked at her fingers in a desperate attempt to pull her down and into itself. She cried out in disgust, yanking her hand from the sticky goo. She rubbed her fingers together, feeling the tacky ooze lubricating her fingertips. *"Help me!"* she screamed again. *"Help—"*

Skyler jerked awake, violently slammed back into a reality she wasn't quite sure was real. She was lying on her side on the living room floor, the room dark except for the table lamp next to the couch. *"All a dream, all a dream, all a dream,"* she whispered to herself, trying to will the sense of dread from her body. She felt cold, and her shoulder ached from her position on the floor. "It was just the grave dream again. A tar grave. That's all. Nothing but a tar-filled grave . . ."

Skyler pressed her hand against the floor and tried to push herself up, but it slid across the wood and she fell back onto her aching shoulder. The floor was covered with something wet that wasn't quite yet cold. Her hand slipped around in the substance, and she felt it sluggishly running over the tops of her fingers. She lifted her hand and curled it into a fist, the slime oozing out from between her clenched fingers and dripping lazily down her forearms. *Is it tar?*

Skyler's vision was blurred and hazy, and she struggled to regain focus on the room. Her eyes were burning and felt puffy, like she had been crying. And her upper lip was throbbing and swollen. She looked down to her tar-covered hand, confused as to why she could still feel the tar there even though she had woken up.

Only it wasn't tar—it was something else. Something red. And thick. And sticky. Skyler splayed her fingers and looked at her hand with dawning horror. The grave might have been a dream, but the attack in her living room was not. Her parents' hardwood floor—smears of red everywhere. The mustard-colored area rug—saturated with blood. And her body, bare on top except for a light purple bra—also covered in blood. And, somehow, the chewing noises were still happening. The crunching and grinding of teeth on bone that she heard coming from above the tar grave—those sounds hadn't faded along with her dream.

Skyler groaned. She felt like she was in a drunken stupor she was unable to pull herself out of, just like her predicament inside the tar grave. Trapped and unable to free herself. She squeezed her eyes shut, willing the red smears and sounds of chewing to disappear. When she opened them, nothing had changed—the red smears were still there, and the relentless chewing continued.

Skyler sucked in a deep breath and forced herself to look over to where the grinding noises were coming from. Athena was there, hunched over Peter's body. She had his leg pinned down with one paw, and her head was turned to the side as she chewed on a whitish-gray cord that was coming out of an opening in his exposed thigh. A mash of bright red gore had been gouged from his upper leg—or what remained of it—and Athena was eating it. She pulled her head further to the side and the grayish cord broke free. Peter's body jerked lifelessly and was still again. Athena chewed on the piece of muscle and tendon she had severed, and then swallowed it.

Skyler retched. A chocolaty bile rose up into her throat, threatening to bring more stomach contents with it. She tried to force the vomit back down, and ended up hiccuping stomach acid that seared her throat and stung the inside of her lip.

Athena repositioned, crouched down, and used her saber-teeth to slice off another piece of Peter's flesh. The chewing sounds resumed, along with a guttural vibration emanating from deep inside her throat.

Skyler rolled over onto her side, away from the gore, and willed herself to faint again. *I rather be in the tar grave. I rather have the tar swallow me. Take me down into the darkness. Take me away from this moment. Away from the chewing sounds. Away from all the red. Just take me back there. Anywhere but here. Black, not red . . . black, not red . . .*

She closed her eyes and pressed her fingers against her ears, blocking out the sounds of Athena eating Peter's body. *God, please just take me back to the tar grave. I won't struggle this time, I promise. Let the tar swallow me forever. Just like we thought it did to the last of the saber-toothed tigers.*

Dear Reader

(II)

Remember when I said that love can be the death of you? That if you aren't careful, love can kill the person that you were? And suddenly, before you know it, you are a completely different person. A person who is capable of doing completely different things. Things you never thought you would be capable of doing. Good things, bad things—I suppose it doesn't matter. For some, love drives them to better themselves—to become doctors, artists, scientists. For others, love drives them to do crazy things, dangerous things, *insane* things. I guess the point I'm trying to make is that you change, and you do it without even being consciously aware that you are changing. You are completely oblivious to the metamorphosis. You just wake up one day, the fog finally clearing in your mind, and you think, *Now how the hell did I wind up here?*

That was me, lying on the living room floor in my blood-splattered purple bra, listening to the sounds of my foster kitten chewing on a chunk of my would-be rapist's hamstring. *Now how in the name of God did I wind up here?* I saved what I thought was an abandoned, sickly kitten . . . got a little too attached to said "kitten" and justified my way into keeping her . . . and now I'm lying on the floor with a dead body in my parents' living room. WHAT. THE. HELL. And before you hop up on your high horse and start lecturing me . . . *YES*, I am fully aware that anyone who keeps a big cat as a pet is bound to have this happen eventually . . . *BUT*, I guess that is the point I'm trying to make. I *knew* it was wrong. I *knew* it was dangerous. Hell, I have even participated in protests about big cats belonging in the wild and not in peoples' homes, yet I threw that all out the window without a second thought. And my question is: When? When did I change? When did I become this cavalier, reckless, morals-abandoning person? Because I sure as hell don't remember it happening.

The *old me* would have been appalled that I kept a wild animal in my home, and even more so, that I lied to Trish about it. The *old me* would have brought that not-a-kitten-after-all cub to a sanctuary the second I realized she was what she was. The *old me* would have done the *right thing.* But where did she go? Where did she run off to? No clue— not even an inkling. All I know for sure is that the *old me* was gone when I suddenly found myself lying on the living room floor next to the oh-so-charming and oh-so-dead Peter—who *apparently* was never a good guy in the first place. Joke's on me, I guess. Hardy-har-har.

What you have to understand is this: I didn't think she was dangerous yet. Yes, she was growing pretty dang fast, but she still hadn't reached her full size. Not even close. On that fateful night, Athena was just over eighty pounds. But, then again, so is a Rottweiler. And *tons* of people have Rottweilers in their homes. If Peter attacked me and Fluffy the Rottweiler came out and saved me from that horrible situation, would anyone even bat an eye? Would anyone care that that jerk got attacked, or would they just say he got what he deserved and give Fluffy a pat on the head for being a good dog? It was self-defense, after all. To be honest, I'm kind of surprised Peter *wasn't* able to fight Athena off; I know from experience that he is a pretty strong guy. I guess catching him with his pants down—literally and figuratively—worked to Atty's advantage. Not to mention, she's built to hold down prey much larger than herself. Duh.

Anyway, I'm getting off-track. Hell, this is my confession letter and I'm talking about the fictitious Fluffy instead of what I really need to be talking about. So back to it then. I previously mentioned that love changes people, for better or for worse. Now, love changed me—that we can already agree on. I kept an animal I shouldn't have, and I lied about it. But I *loved* her by then, you see? More than anything. My Athena, who sleeps next to me every night. Athena, who greets me at the door when I come home every day. Athena, that saved me from being raped by a very handsome and ultimately very disturbed individual. I loved her *so damn much.* And for someone who didn't receive a lot of love early on in life, that feeling can be pretty damn intoxicating.

You hear about those people—crazy people, jealous people—who hack into their exes' social media accounts and dig through their messages. Or how about the ones that break into their ex-lovers' houses when they aren't home? Or follow their soon-to-be ex-spouses from place to place while they run their weekly errands? And then there are those people who are *really* off their rockers and stroll into a restaurant or supermarket and shoot their ex-wife or cheating husband in the face. Do you think when they first met that person they thought, *I'm gonna blast this person's head off one day while they're in the meat department picking out a pot roast?* I doubt it. Maybe the Ted Bundys and Jeffrey Dahmers of the world thought that, but I think most of those lovestruck people had no freaking idea. Love changed them, alright, and *not* for the better.

So where do you draw the line then? At what point do you realize enough is enough? *Stop acting like a crazy person or you're actually going to become a crazy person.* Is it when you hack into your lover's Instagram account? Is it when you stand outside their window and watch them getting ready for bed? Is it when you grab the 'ol handgun and make a hasty trip to the Applebee's—because if you can't have them, nobody else can? *Is* there even a line when love is involved? When you wake up one day to find out you are a completely different person, what are you supposed to do? You don't even know this new person that you've become; how the hell do you know what they are capable of?

Apparently, the *new me* was capable of doing quite a few unexpected, and unsavory, things on that fateful spring night. When I finally dragged my blood-caked self off the living room floor, I had two options: call the cops, tell them what happened, and then watch them take away my date in a body bag and my Athena in a cage . . . OR . . . don't call the cops. *Old me* is screaming to grab my phone and dial 911, but *new me* has no intention of listening to those pleas of sanity. *New me* loves Athena, and *new me* isn't going to do anything that would cause her to be taken from me; to be poked, prodded, and to spend her life being studied in a cage. Not to mention, they put down man-killers, don't they?

Ya know, you really *can* justify any action you take, as long as you put your mind to it, huh? And I had A LOT of justifying to do on that particular night. So here's the part where I get up from the murder scene that was my late parents' living room, pull Athena off of the charming Peter's partially consumed body, and begin the cleanup process that ended with me outside of an Outback Steakhouse at 2:30 in the morning. The floor was easy enough to clean—not by black light standards, mind you, but I was hoping there would be no need for a forensics team anytime soon. The area rug, on the other hand, was a goner—no point in even *trying* to get the blood out of that thing. I used my dad's box cutter to cut the rug into pieces, and then used those pieces of rug to wrap up the pieces of Peter. Oh yeah, that's another thing the *new me* apparently decided was an okay thing to do—dismember a body. Carrying the dead weight of a muscular male is not something I am physically capable of doing, no matter how many pounds of him Athena managed to devour while I was still in shock. So, you know how I used my dad's box cutter for the rug? Well, I used another one of my dad's tools for Peter. An electric one. I won't go into details. Let's just say I'm happy my parents opted to get a home that had some ample distance between it and the neighboring houses. In the end, I wound up with five garbage bags filled with parts of Peter and parts of rug.

And I wasn't done there. Not even close. I still had to clean up the rest of the floor, the tub, Athena, me . . . what a goddamn mess. You might think of me as cold and heartless—and maybe I am those things now—but then . . . then I was horrified. I cried the entire time, and threw up twice. Goodbye steak dinner from Minstrel's—not nearly as pretty on the way back up as it was on the way down. And it wasn't just nausea that I was feeling, but guilt. Overwhelming, all-consuming guilt. Mixed with a pretty hefty amount of shame. Shame for not seeing through Peter's facade. Shame for letting him attack me. Why is it that victims of sexual assault always end up blaming themselves? Pretty fucked up if you ask me, yet it happens damn near every time. Anyway, there was shame for keeping a wild animal in the house, especially when I knew damn well just how dangerous it could be. Shame for not calling the police after Atty did what she did. And, mostly, shame for what I did with the tools and the garbage bags and the trip to the Outback dumpster. Lots of shame. Inordinate amounts of shame. Gut-wrenching, maybe-I-should-kill-myself, amounts of shame. But if I did that, what would happen to Atty? What would become of her? A rat in a cage having countless experiments done to her? Trying to breed her with other big cats? Yeah, sick shit like that. And what should I be more ashamed of? Disposing of a rapist (and c'mon, we both know I wasn't Peter's first trip to the land of sexual assault) or letting a horrible fate befall an innocent animal? And she was innocent—I'll go to my grave believing that. She was doing what she was born to do: kill prey. And beyond that: protect me. She's innocent, and Peter's not. And me? Well, who the hell knows the answer to that anymore?

The guilt and shame were going to have to go on the back burner, though, because I had more important matters to attend to. As I'm sure you may have already guessed, cleaning up the house wasn't my only problem that night. Peter's damn car was parked right outside, for starters. That was easy enough—into the garage it goes. If the cops are investigating anything to the point of looking inside my garage, I'm already toast, so his FJ Cruiser being in there didn't seem to be too big of an issue.

Then it was time to figure out the rest of the details, and if *Forensic Files* has taught me anything, it's attention to detail. Gotta dot all the I's and cross all the T's. So that meant I needed an easily believable story for what happened that night—something I wouldn't mix up the specifics about when telling one person or another what happened. Pretty damn simple when I finally figured it out. *He never showed up.* The end. There's poor Skyler, all dressed up and no date to go on. He stood me up, simple as that. No details that could change or stories that could differ. I got dressed up, waited for the alluring Peter to show, and ended up sitting on the couch watching horror movies by myself. I figured it should be horror movies since the whole night was pretty much a horror show as it was.

I was a little concerned about the restaurant, since we were seen there together. But there wasn't a whole lot I could do about that. He paid in cash, so nothing there to bring the cops running. And he was also new in town, so I'm pretty sure none of the employees or patrons had recognized him—or so I hoped. And that was it. That was all I could do.

When it comes to covering up a crime, there (of course) is a lot of intellect involved. But I think it also has a lot to do with luck. Luck to get away with it, or luck for the police to get their handcuffs around your wrists. Ted Bundy was captured because of a routine traffic stop. It didn't happen because of DNA samples and hair comparisons, it happened because that officer was lucky. One of Jeffrey Dahmer's victims escaped, only to have the police give him right back to his killer. In that case, unfortunately, Dahmer was the lucky one. It's all just a game of luck, isn't it? That's all life really is, an endless game of luck and love and blood and loss. And in this particular situation, I was banking on the luck being on my side, not the cops. So I did what I could, and then all that was left to do was sit back and let the chips fall where they may. With Atty by my side.

There's one other thing about luck, though: it runs out. Ask anyone who ever lost it all in Vegas—luck runs out. Mine didn't run out in regards to Peter. That came later. Much later. Luck, as it turns out, can only get you so far.

It looks like I'm going to have to leave you for now, dear reader. I promise to write more later, though. I know I still have a lot to fess up to. But for now, I will leave you with this: Love can be the death of you. *But*, if you're lucky, I also think it can be the birth of a *new you*. And it's up to you to decide if the *new you* or the *old you* is the person you want to be. For better or worse, I chose the *new me*. And there's no going back now.

Skyler Seabrooke

CHAPTER 26

March 8, 2018
10:16 a.m.

"*So . . .* tell me what happened!" an eager voice exclaimed. Skyler jumped and dropped the litter scooper she was holding. It fell to the bottom of the kennel with a clang. Gordito, the large, black-and-white tuxedo cat in the neighboring kennel, glared at her with annoyance.

Skyler whirled around and saw Trish standing behind her, watching her with barely contained excitement. "I wanted to call you yesterday," Trish gushed, "but I thought I should be a good work mom and wait until you came in today." Trish wrapped her arms tightly across her waist, as if she was trying to physically restrain her enthusiasm.

Skyler sighed and turned back to the kennel, making a show of grabbing the litter scooper and bag of droppings, when really she was trying to muster up the courage to recite the lie she had spent all of yesterday rehearsing. She closed the kennel door and looked back at Trish.

"Well? Tell me!" Trish released her waist and clasped her hands together instead.

Skyler shrugged. "He never showed," she said simply. She left the words hanging in the air. Better to undertell than overtell—overtelling makes it look rehearsed, and the lie all the more obvious.

"Never showed?" Trish asked incredulously, her brow furrowing into confusion as she mulled over Skyler's response. Her mouth slowly opened into an "O" of disbelief, then quickly converted into one of disgust. "He didn't even call to explain?"

Skyler shook her head and looked down at the floor, feeling the guilt parasite as it wound sinuously through her intestines. "Nope, nothing," she said. "I ended up just watching movies and then going to bed."

"That little piece of *shit*." Trish closed the distance between them and took hold of Skyler's shoulders. "Sky, I'm so sorry. I—I really thought he liked you. The way he looked at you . . . he seemed absolutely smitten."

Skyler forced a weak smile. "Guess not," she said, and gave her aching shoulders another shrug. They were still sore from her recent late-night activities. "Has he been in yet? Yesterday or today?"

Trish shook her head. "Not that I've noticed. He's scheduled for this afternoon, but I haven't seen the little asshole yet. There's going to be *a lot* of kennel scrubbing in his future." Trish released Skyler's shoulders and crossed her arms over her chest, studying Skyler's face.

Skyler looked away, feeling an unpleasant heat growing in her cheeks. Even with all the rehearsing, she still wasn't sure if she was lying well enough. What if Trish could read right through her? What if the police had already been in, asking about Peter, and they told Trish to approach her first? Maybe Skyler would open up to Trish, but not to the cops . . .

Trish surprised Skyler by wrapping her arms around her and hugging her with a fierceness that was almost startling. Skyler brought her hands tentatively up to Trish's back and rested them against her narrow shoulders. "Trish?"

"I am so, so sorry, Skyler. I encouraged you to go out with that little jerk. And after what happened with you and that foster kitten . . . Christ!" She released Skyler and studied her face again, her gray eyes searching Skyler's hazel ones. "Are you sure you're okay?"

Skyler laughed, hoping it sounded more carefree than she felt. "Trish, it was just a date. People get stood up all the time. It's no big deal."

"Well, someone standing up my work kid is a big deal to me. He just lost a shit ton of points. Like I said, kennel duty until the cows come home."

"Thanks," Skyler said. "I've got a lot more litter boxes to scoop. I better get to it."

"Okay, Sky," Trish said, and walked over to the exit. She looked over her shoulder before she left, her hand resting on the door. "You want me to keep him in the Dog House today? Give you two some space?"

"Yes, please," Skyler said. "The Dog House, both figuratively and literally."

"You got it," Trish said, and left the room.

Skyler turned to Gordito's kennel, where he was lying on the top shelf and watching her with half-closed, accusing eyes. "How do you think I did?" she asked, and opened the kennel door. She reached inside and scratched behind Gordito's ear. He glared at her a moment longer, then began to purr. "So you think I nailed it then?" Gordito continued to purr, stretching out his neck so Skyler could ruffle the white fur underneath his chin. "I'd like to thank the Academy," she said, and continued to pet Gordito until he fell asleep.

CHAPTER 27

March 14, 2018
9:14 a.m.

"Did you hear about Peter?" Samantha asked Skyler as soon as she arrived for her shift the following week. They stood at The Center's service desk, Samantha's green eyes sparkling with the excitement of untold gossip.

Eight days had passed since the night outside the Outback Steakhouse, and not a word had been said about Peter on the news or around town. Skyler's back stiffened at the mention of his name, and her heart rate doubled in a matter of seconds. "What about him?" she asked, trying to sound casual.

"They took him off the schedule." Samantha brushed a long strand of blonde hair behind her shoulder. She bent forward and placed her slender forearms on the counter, leaning in and assuming the standard gossip position. "I guess Trish was waiting a few days to see if he'd turn up," Samantha said in a low voice. "But after three no-shows, he's off the schedule for good."

"Wow." Skyler raised her eyebrows to show her surprise. "So they don't think he's coming back then?"

"Guess not." Samantha shook her head. "I thought he was gonna stick around, too. He kept talking about wanting to work here full time."

"Yeah, I heard him mention that, too. Pretty weird." Skyler waited for Samantha to divulge more gossip goodies, inside hoping there wasn't anything left to tell.

Samantha shrugged. "Yeah, weird," she said. "Sucks, too."

"Why's that?"

"He was so yummy to look at." She giggled.

Skyler's tongue ran along the partially healed cut inside her lip, still warm and slightly swollen a week later. An image flashed through her head, one of Peter's unmoving body sprawled across the hardwood as his blood poured out on the floorboards. "Yeah, super yummy," she mumbled.

"I thought you two might hit it off."

"Me, too," Skyler said with a sigh. "Alas, it is still just me and the animals."

Samantha patted Skyler's shoulder and pushed herself up from the counter. "Your prince charming is just around the corner. I'm sure of it." She gave Skyler a warm smile—the smile of a hopeful youth that hasn't yet realized just how harsh and unjust the world could be.

"I'm sure he is," Skyler said, trying to return the same heartfelt, if not naive, smile. Inside, her upper lip throbbed dully.

An eager-looking couple approached the desk and asked Samantha if the dog in kennel 92 was still available. They watched her with hopeful eyes as she clicked away on the computer.

Skyler took the opportunity to slip away from Samantha and the optimistic love chitchat. She walked across the lobby, taking a moment to replace a feathered cat toy that had fallen from its display hook. She wasn't able to make out what Samantha's response to the inquiring couple was, but when she glanced back and saw the excitement on their faces, she already knew the answer.

CHAPTER 28

Summer 2018

The summer drifted by, pleasantly warm and blissfully uneventful. Skyler never heard another word about Peter, either on the news or at the shelter. It wasn't uncommon for volunteers to up and leave, especially after finding out how much work the job entailed, and nobody seemed to notice Peter's sudden absence other than Trish and Samantha. And as for the police, if there ever was any question as to Peter's whereabouts, they were never pressing enough to make it onto the local news. Skyler at first thought it was being kept from the press while the police pursued various leads, but as the months passed by, Skyler's worry began to fade along with the summer heat. By September's arrival, the only ones in Diamondback that remembered Peter were Athena and Skyler.

Athena continued to grow, and before the summer was up, she had surpassed Skyler in both weight and size. Skyler worked hard to train her following the March mishap, knowing that the bigger Athena got, the harder she would be to control. Luckily, what Skyler thought would be a daunting task turned out to be much easier than she anticipated. Athena took to the training so well that on more than one occasion Skyler wondered if the saber-tooth she was raising could in fact read her own thoughts. A crazy notion, except for the obvious insanity of a saber-toothed cat existing in the first place.

By the time the first leaves of fall started their transition from green to gold, Athena had mastered all of the traditional verbal commands—*sit, stand, up, down, roll over, heel*—as well as a few non-verbal ones. She would now wait patiently to begin eating a meal until Skyler snapped her fingers to signal that it was okay to begin (very important if you don't want to lose a finger when setting down dinner), and she would always stop what she was doing, regardless of the activity, whenever Skyler held her hand to her side with her fingers splayed—a necessary command when it came to managing a rambunctious saber-tooth.

Late in the evenings, once Athena was well trained, Skyler would let her go out in the backyard for some outdoor time, the house seeming to become smaller and smaller as Athena became bigger and bigger. None of the neighboring houses overlooked the backyard, only the surrounding trees having a vantage point over her parents' high, well-constructed fence. Athena would bound around the enclosed space, roll in the grass, and tear up clumps of earth as she explored, but she never once tried to jump the fence, and she never made a sound while she was out there, as if she knew the importance of remaining concealed.

Athena's intelligence often baffled Skyler, and she spent many hours of the summer attempting to google the intellectual capacity of a saber-toothed cat. However, all her searches turned up empty, probably because the animal in question had been extinct for over ten thousand years.

On the first day of fall, Athena was two and a half feet tall at the shoulder, with a coat very similar to that of a lion's, albeit somewhat thicker and with a splattering of brown spots. Her bobbed tail never grew more than a foot from her body, and her forelimbs became much more pronounced as she aged. Skyler researched that a saber-tooth's forelimbs were more powerful than those of modern-day big cats; they were needed to hold down the giant mammals of the ice age while administering a lethal bite with their canines. That was probably why Athena had been so successful when attacking Peter—she was built for it.

Athena's canines, which never stopped growing, were now five inches long, and there was now no mistaking her for anything but what she truly was. There were also two more canines that recently erupted alongside the baby saber-teeth. From what Skyler read online, those were the adult teeth. For a time, Athena would have two sets of canines, the baby teeth acting as an anchor for the adult teeth as they grew in and became more durable. Eventually, the baby canines would fall away, and the adult saber-teeth would continue to grow until they reached seven inches in length. That would take time, though, and Athena still had a lot of growing to do.

Life at the shelter continued on as it normally did, with the staff grateful for every day more animals were adopted out than were brought in. Samantha went off to college in August, and Skyler felt particularly sad watching her go. As always, more volunteers eventually came in to replace the ones that moved on, and to Skyler's relief, none of them were exceptionally handsome.

As the months ticked by, life took on a normalcy that Skyler was grateful for. At times it even felt like the incident (which was what Skyler decided to refer to it as) that took place in her parents' living room that past spring hadn't even happened—like it occurred in a different life she was no longer a part of. The only time she remembered that horrible night was when she had the dreams, the tar now reminding her of the blood she discovered upon waking from one nightmare and finding herself in another.

The dreams always started with her inside the grave, submerged in tar and rain pouring down from above. The tar grew steadily deeper, and no matter how much she tried to crawl out, she was never able to pull herself up to safety. The sodden sides of the grave always crumbled when she tried to grab hold of something, raining down earth as well as water.

And something was up above her, a growling animal that she was never quite able to see. Skyler originally thought the animal was enraged, but the more she heard it, the more she realized it was frightened. But of what? What could possibly frighten something that could make such a monstrous roar?

What could possibly be scarier than the creature that was above her?

Skyler always woke in a sweat, the answers to the dream riddles still a mystery. She would wrap her arms around Athena and bury her face in her fur, willing her heart rate to slow and her breathing to regulate. Athena would lick Skyler's face with her rough tongue, as if to calm her down or ask if everything was alright. Skyler would sometimes weep when she woke from the nightmare, terrified not only for herself, but also for the frightened animal up above. How could she save it if she could never find a way out of the grave? How could she stop what was about to happen up there? Was it even something that she could stop?

Sleep would eventually come again, always empty and black following one of the nightmares. And in the morning, with the sun filtering in through the window and Athena peacefully sleeping beside her, the memory of the nightmare would simply fade away. Skyler would go about her day, not giving the dream a second thought, and leaving the dream's riddles unanswered.

CHAPTER 29

October 31, 2018
5:08 p.m.

Skyler walked down the grocery store aisle in a slow, meandering fashion, one wheel of her cart wiggling spasmodically as she went. Piece after piece of raw, crimson-colored meat lay before her, Saran wrap covering their cold surfaces and keeping the blood from seeping out. Chuck roast, rump roast, sirloin, pork shoulder, turkey breast. She had already selected enough poultry and beef to get Athena through the next couple of weeks, but she still had one more item to pick out—something special for Athena's first birthday. Her eyes scanned the New York strips in their plastic sheathing, then moved on to the rib eyes, before finally settling on the beef tenderloin. She sorted through the packages, found the largest cut of filet, and placed it in her shopping cart. *A filet for my feline,* she thought, satisfied.

Athena's appetite was steadily increasing, along with her size, and Skyler was now having to stock up on meat on a seemingly endless basis. She alternated her shopping expeditions between various grocery stores and butcher shops, not wanting to be the weird girl with a meat fetish at one particular store. That would only arouse suspicion, and Skyler didn't want anything to derail getting Athena her meals on time. She needed to make sure that Athena was always well-fed, and that she did not have any desire to leave the house in search of something else to eat—a roaming squirrel, a neighborhood pet, the Amazon delivery guy.

Having picked out Athena's birthday meal, Skyler redirected her cart and started heading down the seasonal aisle of the store, toward the registers. She was passing the Halloween candy when she saw someone familiar turn down the same aisle, walking in her direction.

"Skyler!" Trish exclaimed, and hurried over to meet her. "I wanted to pick up a few more bags of Halloween candy, just in case. I don't want those little costumed buggers egging my house 'cause I ran out of the good stuff and had to give them Smarties."

Skyler laughed. "I always liked Smarties, actually. The Dubble Bubble—not so much."

"You picking up some Halloween candy as well?" Trish asked. "You never were one for handing out candy, from what I recall." Trish glanced down at Skyler's shopping cart. "Jesus girl. What's with all the meat? You handing out Kobe for the trick-or-treaters this year?"

Skyler blushed. "I—uh . . ." she stammered, her mind working on overdrive to find a suitable explanation. "I'm trying out the keto diet," she said finally.

Trish raised an eyebrow and took another look inside Skyler's shopping cart. "Goodness girl. You're a woman, not a puma. I think you could probably start off a little smaller than that."

"Well, I was researching about the importance of meal prep. If I have the fridge stocked and ready to go, I will feel less like snacking on something carby." She shrugged sheepishly. "It made sense in the YouTube video."

Trish's eyes lingered on the cart of meat. "I *guess* so. Why keto, though? You are in no need of a diet, my dear."

"I just thought I'd try something new," Skyler said, feeling the stirrings of the guilt parasite deep within her abdomen. She tried to swallow, but her mouth had gone dry. "We can take bets on how long I last," she joked, hoping to clear the awkwardness from the air.

Trish's incredulous expression softened and she smiled. "Well, with the amount of meat you're buying, I hope you last over a month. It's going to take you at least that long to make it through all that protein. Where's the vegetables? Isn't that part of the diet?"

"You bet. The produce department is my next stop."

"Can I give you a bit of advice, Skyler?"

"Always."

"Don't start until after Halloween," Trish said.

"Why's that?"

"Take advantage of all this Halloween candy." Trish gestured to the shelves of lumpy orange bags that were beside her. "Fatten up a little. You're already too thin as it is. Then you can start your crazy meat diet in November."

"You know, that's a pretty good idea," Skyler said, and felt a wave of relief wash over her. The guilt parasite drowned in it, silenced again until the next time she would have to lie to Trish.

"Okay, Sky. You take care. See you tomorrow?"

"You bet," Skyler said. "Have a good night, Trish."

Skyler left the aisle and changed course, going toward the vegetables instead of the registers. If Trish ended up behind her in line, she didn't want to get caught in yet another lie. Not so soon after the last lie anyway. "Guess I'm eating salad for dinner," she said to herself, and entered the produce department.

CHAPTER 30

October 31, 2018
6:10 p.m.

The porch was dim and shrouded in shadows when Skyler pulled into her driveway. She had broken the golden Edison bulb that served as the single porch light almost a month ago while trying to sweep a sizable spiderweb off the porch's roof, along with the web's inhabitant. After a momentary, spastic freak-out when she thought the spider had fallen into her hair, she swept up the shards of glass, but never got around to bringing out a step stool and actually removing the shattered remains of the bulb. With the curtains always drawn nowadays, the porch light always seemed to slip her mind as soon as she got inside the house. Skyler made a mental note—again—to change out the bulb tomorrow, a chore that would most likely fade from her mind the second Athena bounded over to say hello.

Skyler hit the garage door opener and waited for the door to rumble up on its track. Inside, the garage was orderly and well kept, thanks to her father's organizational skills and personal pride in his tool collection. Storage boxes and tools were arranged on various shelves, roughly in the same spots they had been in when her parents were still alive. Skyler had rummaged through some of the boxes following her parents' passing, but the pain of seeing their Christmas decorations—a holiday she'd never get to celebrate with them again—and her mother's various craft projects—never to be finished—hurt too much. Skyler put each box back exactly where she found it, crying as she did so, and then never touched them again. A heavy layer of dust now covered the boxes and the majority of her father's tools—all except for the box cutter and electric hand saw, which were used much more recently than the rest.

There were two bikes leaning against one of the walls, one pink and the other yellow. They were also covered in dust, their tires long since deflated and their chains heavy with rust. The pink bike was Skyler's, and the larger, yellow one had been her mother's. Another relic from the past that Skyler refused to part with.

Next to the bikes was a new chrome freezer, standing out in stark contrast to the dusty remains of her parents' lives. Skyler had purchased it a couple months ago, when Athena's appetite surpassed the freezer compartment of the kitchen's refrigerator. The chest freezer looked like an alien craft in the dusty garage, a piece of Skyler's new life surrounded by the ghosts of her past.

Skyler pulled up next to the covered FJ Cruiser that took up the other side of the garage. She had purchased the car cover with cash at a store in Phoenix. She still wasn't sure what to do with Peter's vehicle, but she hoped keeping it under wraps—literally—would make her neighbors less suspicious if they were passing by the house when she happened to be pulling in or out of the garage. A shiny, black FJ Cruiser—much nicer than her actual car—sitting there unused would look all too conspicuous. Now she could just say it was a hunk of junk she inherited from a distant relative, or some other believable but unmemorable shit like that.

The garage door rumbled down, and Skyler waited until it completed its descent before she got out of her Sentra. Once alone in the garage, she unpacked her trunk of meat and transferred it to the freezer. The filet she left on the roof of the car, wanting to take that one inside as a birthday treat for Atty.

Athena was already in the kitchen when Skyler entered the house, a low rumble of pleasure reverberating in her throat as she rubbed her head against Skyler's hip. "Hi, sweet girl," Skyler said, only having to lean slightly over to kiss Athena's forehead. Athena rumbled again, more urgently this time, having smelled the tenderloin in Skyler's hand. She lurched forward, trying to get within reach of the beef, but Skyler raised it over her head before she could grab it.

"Manners, Atty," Skyler said. "You don't get your birthday present just yet. Sit your butt down and wait." Skyler pointed to the floor with one finger, and Athena obediently sat down, the muscles in her haunches rippling as she did so.

Skyler went about taking the filet out of its wrapping and placing it in one of Athena's stainless steel food bowls. The bowls were from the kitchen department at Target, the largest of PetSmart's dog bowls no longer being large enough. Skyler placed the entire tenderloin into the bowl. She rinsed her hands at the sink and then stooped down to face Athena straight on. Skyler ruffled the fur along her neck, being careful not to snag her skin on Athena's canines.

"Alright, my dear," she said. "I have a little song I have to sing before you get your present. It's traditional before a birthday, you see. Not that you'd know, since this is your first one." Athena watched Skyler with unwavering interest. "Okay, here we go . . ."

Skyler sang the birthday song, surprised by the burning sting of tears in her eyes that emerged during the third line. She couldn't remember the last time she sang that particular song to anyone, including herself. Athena rubbed against her as she finished singing, not understanding the words, but sensing Skyler's change in emotions.

"I'm fine, I'm fine. Just being silly." Skyler wiped at her eyes, her hand feeling wet when she pulled it away from her face. "You're just growing up so quick, Atty." She kissed Athena's head once more, then grabbed the food bowl. She set it down on the floor, Athena flinching forward but not moving from where she was sitting. She looked up at Skyler expectantly.

Skyler brought her hand down to her side, paused for a moment, then snapped her fingers. Athena lurched at the bowl, causing it to skitter across the floor. She wrapped a heavy paw around it to stop it from moving, then sunk her teeth into the chunk of meat.

Skyler sat down beside her and watched her eat her birthday meal. Her heart swelled with love for the animal before her, even when the wet, ripping sounds of Athena's chewing reminded her of the time she awoke on the floor to the sounds of her chewing . . . something else. That wasn't going to happen again, though. What happened that horrible March night was a one-time thing—a horrible incident for everyone involved. And Skyler wasn't going to let anything like that happen again. She was sure of it.

CHAPTER 31

November 16, 2018
4:40 p.m.

It was a week before Thanksgiving, and Skyler had just returned to the shelter after rescuing a litter of abandoned puppies from behind a Circle K. The puppies were dehydrated and covered with fleas, but Skyler was certain with some meds and a little loving care they would mend up and be ready for adoption within a few weeks. A couple years back, she would have welcomed the infant Labrador mixes into her home without a second thought, but now fostering any rescues was out of the question. She told Trish she just wasn't capable of withstanding the heartache of losing another foster pet, but really, the thing she was incapable of withstanding was losing the two-hundred-pound saber-toothed cat who now had free rein of her home.

Skyler was in the locker room, having just finished showering off the dirt and fleas she acquired in the course of collecting the abandoned puppies and bringing them to the shelter. They were now in the process of getting cleaned up and evaluated by the veterinary staff, and tonight they would be warm, free of fleas, and no longer hungry.

Another successful day, she thought as she grabbed her keys and phone from her locker. She had just thrown on a spare set of clothes and was thinking about stopping in for a beer at Sawyer's, when she felt her phone buzzing in her back pocket.

Skyler felt the familiar jolt in her stomach that always accompanied an incoming call. She used to think it was someone calling to ask her about strange noises coming from inside her house, but more often than not, it was just a recorded message telling her that her car's extended warranty was about to expire. Funny thing, since her Sentra was over fifteen years old. *That is some extended warranty,* she thought, and glanced down at the screen.

It was a number she was unfamiliar with, but with a Diamondback area code. *Still probably a solicitor,* she thought. She was about to let the call go to voicemail, then decided against it and answered.

"Hello?" Skyler pressed the flat screen against her ear. Phones could sure do a lot these days, but talking on them was not nearly as comfortable as it used to be. They used to be shaped to easily fit on the side of a person's face, but now it felt like pressing a brick onto your ear.

"Hello," an elderly sounding man said. "Is this Skyler Seabrooke?"

"Um, yes." Skyler closed her locker, shifting uncomfortably from one foot to the other. She felt a knot growing in the pit of her stomach. "Who's this?"

The man chuckled. "I'm sorry to disturb you, dear," he said. "My name is Walter Brindle. I was a friend of your parents. I live in Alpine Ridge, just around the block from you actually, on Cedar Ridge Drive."

The knot in Skyler's stomach deepened, tying itself tighter and pulling at her organs. She knew who Walter Brindle was, remembering him vaguely from her childhood. He would come over sometimes to fix things around the house—broken screen doors, leaky faucets, that kind of thing. He always brought along Dum Dums lollipops, and gave Skyler one on his way out. That was probably why she remembered him at all.

"—not sure if you remember me." Brindle's voice faded back into focus. Skyler struggled to register the words he was saying over the heavy thudding of her heart against her rib cage. *Is this about Athena? Did he hear something? See something?*

"Yes, of course I remember you," she said. "You would always give me a lollipop when you came over. How are you doing, Mr. Brindle?" *Talking too fast. Need to slow down, act normal.*

"Walt! Please call me Walt. And I must say, you have quite the memory on you, Skyler."

"It's hard for a kid to forget free candy," Skyler said, trying to sound the exact opposite of how she felt. *Did Athena get out somehow? Is she running down the street, waving her saber-teeth at the neighbors? Oh God.* "What can I do for you, Walt?"

"Well, I got your number from that nice fella at your work. Justin, I think he said his name was. See, I know you work over at the animal shelter. I guess everyone knows that, since you go all over town saving those animals. Admirable work you're doing."

"Well, I do my best," Skyler said, trying to will pleasantness into her voice. "Is there an animal in the neighborhood that is requiring some help? I'd be happy to—"

"No, dear. Nothing like that," Walt said jovially. "I'm actually calling because I wanted to help *you* out."

"Really?" Skyler asked, feeling a flutter of relief. Maybe there was nothing wrong with Athena, after all. "How so?"

"Well, I've noticed your porch light has been smashed to smithereens for some time now. I go on a late afternoon stroll around the neighborhood every day, and now with the nights coming on so quick, I couldn't help but notice your porch light was broken."

Freaking porch light. "Oh, yeah." Skyler forced a small laugh. "I broke it trying to get rid of a spiderweb. I guess I keep forgetting to change it out. I'll make sure to do that tonight, though."

Walt laughed. "Oh, no dear, I'm not asking you to do that. I just know how busy you are helping all those animals, and *I* wanted to help *you*. I was a maintenance man once upon a time, and even though I'm retired now, I still enjoy doing odds and ends jobs for people around the neighborhood. I thought I could fix up that porch light for you, make sure you don't end up getting cut on the glass while you're trying to remove it. It looks like it might require some tools to get it out of there safely."

"Really? Wow. Well, thank you for letting me know, Mr— Walt," Skyler said. The phone's screen was starting to feel hot against her skin. "I'm pretty sure I can take care of it myself, though. I'll be sure to be careful and wear gloves when I remove it. Thank—"

"Oh dear," Walt said, sounding a little flustered. "I don't want you to have to do a thing. After all you've been through with your parents and then your cousin—"

"Aunt, actually. Anyway, I appreciate your offer, but I can take care of it myself."

"Nonsense," Walt said. "I would be more than happy to help. I already brought a spare bulb over and have the key in hand. I'll just run on in and make sure the power is off, then I'll change it out for you. It will be up and running by the time you get home."

"What key?" Skyler asked, unable to keep the alarm from her voice. Her hand felt slick with sweat, her phone threatening to slip free from her clenched fingers.

"Under the turtle," Walt said, seeming not to notice the agitation in Skyler's voice. "Your parents always kept a spare key under the turtle planter on the porch. Said I could just use that and head on in if there was ever something we had discussed fixin' and they weren't home when I got around to it."

Skyler sucked in a gulp of air, unaware she had been holding her breath. She felt dizzy. *"There's been a key under that turtle pot all this time?"*

"Yes, dear," Walt said, and chuckled. "Nothing to worry about, though. We live in an awfully safe neighborhood, and a safe town as well. Anyway, I'll be in and out in a jiffy—"

"Mr. Brindle," Skyler said, any trace of forced sincerity leaving her voice, "I do not need your help to change that light. Please put the key back where you found it and—"

"I'm already inside, dear. I'm sorry if I upset you, I just wanted to help. I'll flip that switch off and be out in no time."

"Mr. Brindle! Please get out of my house *right now*." Skyler waited for a response but didn't receive one. "Walt! I do not like people being inside—"

"Do you live with someone, dear?"

Skyler felt her stomach drop hard, and the sharp, sickening taste of bile and stomach acid rising into her throat. She tried to swallow it back down. "No, I don't. Walt, please get out of my—"

"I think somebody might have broken into your home," Walt whispered.

No shit, Skyler thought. *I'm talking to him.* "Get out of the house right now," she demanded.

"I can hear thumping noises upstairs," Walt continued. His voice sounded farther away, like he no longer had the phone up to his ear.

Skyler felt all the muscles in her body tense. Her jaws clamped together, and she felt dangerously close to losing consciousness. *"Mr. Brindle! Get out of the hou—"*

"Skyler, dear," his voice near the phone again, "somebody is upstairs. I'm going to call the police."

"No! Just get out of the house. *Right now!*"

Seconds ticked by with excruciating slowness. Skyler was about to speak again when she heard Walt gasp. "Jesus, Mary, and Joseph," he whispered into the phone.

"Mr. Brindle? Walt? *Walt!*" Skyler pressed the phone hard against her ear, straining to hear anything on the other end of the line. When Walter Brindle screamed, the noise was as piercing as it was painful. She instinctively jerked the phone away, then quickly returned it to her ear. *"Walt! WALT!"*

Nothing. She had lost the call.

Skyler ran. Out of the locker room. Through the building. Toward the exit. Her footsteps echoed down the length of the hallway as she went, but all she could hear was the pounding of her own heart and the blood pulsating in her ears.

CHAPTER 32

November 16, 2018
4:40 p.m.

Walter Brindle was a Diamondback resident, born and raised. He went to the local high school when the graduating class was still under thirty students, and he learned to drive on dirt roads that were still two decades away from getting paved. Diamondback had grown substantially since Walt Brindle was a kid, but it was still a small, welcoming city, with a comforting familiarity that only a hometown could bring.

Walt had little desire to leave the area when the time came to make decisions about college and the future, and inevitably decided to stay in Diamondback for the long haul. He had always had a knack for gadgets and appliances, and found himself plenty of work as a maintenance man around town. He was the go-to call for the high school and grade school (both his alma mater), the small but efficient hospital on

Diamondback's northeast side, and a number of the local businesses around town. The Wash-O-Rama Laundromat often said they didn't know what they would do without Walt's expertise in washing machine antics, and Walt suspected they were right. He made a modest yet comfortable living, and that was all he could ever really ask for.

The only time Walt felt any real hardship was when his beloved wife, Alma, took ill a few years back. Alma had been a smoker most of her life. Back when they were kids and took up the habit, four out of five doctors were still recommending one brand of cigarettes over the other. Walt had managed to quit the darn things cold turkey when his prostate got a bit of cancer, but Alma was addicted through and through. She moved her pack-a-day habit to the backyard, at least, but was never able to bid the cigarettes farewell. When the COPD took hold of her three years ago, it was a startlingly quick decline. By the following New Year's Eve, Alma was in that small but efficient hospital, watching Walt light sparklers outside her window to celebrate the New Year. She only made it one month into that new year, and passed away one cold February night with the oxygen tube still in her nose, although her lungs weren't able to take enough of it in to keep her body going.

Walt had long since been retired by that awful February night, and now at seventy-eight, he was only able to do a few maintenance jobs a week, just for friends and acquaintances around town. He still enjoyed being the neighborhood handyman, and took on any odd job that his aging body could handle. It got him out of the house and allowed him an hour or two of precious socialization with the neighbors before he had to return to his empty house to eat his TV dinner and watch the latest episode of who-gives-a-shit on the tube.

Walt met the Seabrookes shortly after they moved into the blue house at the end of the cul-de-sac—the one that would eventually prove to be their last. He was one of the first in the newly developed neighborhood of Alpine Ridge to stop by and welcome them when they arrived. He offered to help with anything that needed fixing around the house, and was pleasantly surprised when Sean Seabrooke called him not five days later to help him figure out how to hook up his new dishwasher. Teresa was also wonderfully pleasant to be around, and always offered Walt a glass of sweet tea and some cookies when he was finished with whatever project he was working on. When that lovely couple had their little girl, Skyler, Walt started carrying candies when he came over, wanting to give the sweet little girl playing on the lawn something just as sweet as her. When Sean and Teresa died so suddenly in that car accident, Walt was beside himself. He wondered what would happen to the little girl who always played on the lawn with her stuffed animals, her auburn pigtails shimmering in the summer sunshine.

A rather severe-looking woman moved in shortly after the Seabrookes' passing, and that little girl was rarely seen playing on the lawn anymore. When Walt did see Skyler around town, the pigtails were gone and so was the happy, carefree smile that had always been on her lightly freckled face. The smile had been replaced by a look of sadness, acceptance, and—most of all—loneliness. Walt didn't see a carefree smile on that girl's face again until she started up at the local animal shelter. Walt could still remember the day he saw her, fully grown and just as beautiful as her mother had been, corralling an injured German shepherd that had been running up and down Cedar Ridge Drive for the better part of a day. When that frightened pup finally approached her and licked her hand, Walt saw that smile on her face again, revealing a ghost of the pigtailed girl he remembered on the lawn so many years ago.

Walt first noticed the broken porch light three weeks back, when the afternoons started giving way to night much too eagerly. He always went for an afternoon stroll around the neighborhood; it kept his heart in check and helped ease the achings of arthritis that had taken up residence in his hips and lower back. With the sun dipping below the horizon before it even reached six o'clock, the broken porch light at the Seabrooke house started standing out more and more as he made his daily trek down Oak Ridge Drive. The girl had started keeping her curtains drawn a year or so back—he wasn't sure why—but Walt wondered if maybe she hadn't even noticed it was broken.

Walt, always being the type to want to help someone in a pinch, thought it would be the least he could do for her. Maybe it would even bring on one of those carefree smiles, and he would be able to get a glimpse of the sweet, freckled girl he remembered, before life had played her such a cruel hand. Skyler had spent half her life helping animals in need, and he could certainly spend ten minutes helping her, even if it was only a silly porch light. At least it would be something to let her know she's not alone—that people in the neighborhood still care about her. All those years in that big, empty house must wear on you over time. It had only been a couple years since his Alma passed away, and already their house seemed way too big and way too empty. How Skyler had gone over a decade alone in that house of hers, Walt didn't know.

Walt ascended the porch steps at the Seabrooke residence and peered up at the broken light. Shards of glass stuck out from the socket, and it didn't look like it was going to be an easy twist of the wrist job to extract the bulb. He ambled home and came back with a few tools—a wrench, pliers, a screwdriver. He found the step stool Sean always kept on the side of the house, although it took a moment to locate it since a few overgrown bushes had all but concealed the rusty, old thing. Walt was about to get to work when he realized he didn't know if the power was still switched on for the bulb. Stupid, old man—forgetting something as obvious as that. If he jammed his pliers into that socket, he'd be electrocuted in no time. *Dumb dumb dumb,* he thought, just like the lollipops he used to bring for Skyler. Now he was the Dum Dum.

Walt considered coming back another time, when Skyler was home, but he had already brought the tools over and gotten the ladder out—might as well get this done now. He'd only have to step into her place for a second, flip the switch off, and right back out he'd go. Walt saw the ceramic turtle on the porch, sitting next to the rocking chair that Teresa used to sit in while she was pregnant, reading and enjoying the breeze. Walt stooped over, feeling his hips grumble in protest as he did so, and moved the turtle planter to the side. Underneath, the house key was still there, although it was now rusted and covered in a layer of filth and cobwebs. Walt dusted off the key and went back to the front door. He was about to let himself inside, when he thought maybe it would be best if he at least let the lady of the house know what he was up to. If she did happen to be home, he just might give her a heart attack.

Walt didn't know Skyler's phone number, so he called the next best thing: the Agave Animal Care Center. A friendly young man answered the phone at the service counter. He let Walt know that Skyler was in fact working that day, but he wasn't sure if she had returned from a call yet or not. Walt thanked Justin, and was about to hang up, when Justin offered him Skyler's cell phone number. He said she didn't mind getting called on her home phone, especially if it concerned the welfare of an animal. Walt wasn't calling about an animal, but he felt he could let that one slide. He jotted down Skyler's number on the pad of paper he always kept in the breast pocket of his shirt, thanked Justin, and ended the call.

Skyler answered on the fourth ring, and Walt hoped he wasn't interrupting her if she was in the middle of corralling another German shepherd. He introduced himself, and was pleasantly surprised to find Skyler remembered him from her days playing on the front lawn. Unfortunately, she didn't sound as carefree as she did in those days, but that didn't particularly surprise him.

Walt let Skyler know what he was up to, and let himself in through the front door. She sounded a bit agitated on the other end of the line, but his hearing wasn't what it used to be, and he was only partially listening to her once he began searching for the light switch. He thought he remembered exactly where it was, but once inside, he realized his mind also wasn't what it used to be. The switch was not right next to the door like he thought it was. Skyler was saying something on the phone, but Walt barely heard her. *Where could the switch be? Probably in the kitchen.*

Walt glanced into the living room as he walked by, taken aback by how everything in the house looked exactly the same as it did back then. Same couch, same coffee table, same decorations. It was like the girl hadn't updated one thing since her parents' death, which both pained him and made him feel nostalgic at the same time. The TV was at least new, thank goodness. And she had gotten rid of that god-awful yellow rug he never quite cared for—at least one thing a young woman and an aging, forgetful old man could agree on.

Walt entered the kitchen, but still couldn't find the dang light switch to the porch. How could he remember the area rug that was no longer there, but not the location of the light switch? Was Alzheimer's something he was going to have to start worrying about? Forgetting where he put the keys, if the stove was on, or—even worse—forgetting his beautiful Alma and the way her hair always fell across her forehead when she looked at him cross.

Skyler was saying something on the phone. Walt was about to ask her where the light switch was, when he heard a heavy thump come from upstairs. "Do you live with someone, dear?" he asked, his eyes focused on the ceiling where the thump originated from. More thumps followed, heading across the ceiling and toward the staircase. And then some sort of scratching noise.

"I think somebody might have broken into your home," Walt whispered into the phone. "I can hear thumping noises upstairs." Floorboards creaked under the weight of whoever was up there. From where the sounds were located, Walt assumed the intruder was standing at the head of the stairs, deciding whether or not he should come down and investigate. *A burglar?* he thought. He just happened to be a good Samaritan the same day a burglar decided to break into the Seabrooke house?

He needed to call the police. And he needed to let Skyler know not to come home right now—it wasn't safe. "Skyler, dear," he said, "somebody is upstairs. I'm going to call the police."

Skyler was yelling into the phone, telling him to get out of the house. She was right—he shouldn't be in here with a burglar, who knows how reckless the man might be. Walt crept through the kitchen and into the foyer. The stairs loomed to his right, the nostalgia of the house now replaced by an ominous presence. Walt took a step toward the front door, and a floorboard creaked below his foot. He stepped back, not wanting to alert the intruder to his whereabouts. Too late, though—he could hear heavy footsteps on the staircase now. The burglar knew he was there. And by the sounds of it, the man was *huge*. Body builder, maybe. Don't convicts work out a lot while in prison?

Walt hurried toward the front door, throwing a hasty glance over his shoulder. What he saw caused him to stop dead in his tracks. It wasn't a burglar. It wasn't a man. It wasn't even *human*. It was some sort of animal. A lion, maybe. But no, it wasn't. Its teeth were all wrong. And its upper body was too big. Walt sometimes flipped over to that Animal Planet channel when nothing else was on to watch, and that thing on the stairs was no lion. Or a tiger. *What in the name of God?* "Jesus, Mary, and Joseph," he whispered into the phone.

The animal growled, a low, rumbling sound he could feel reverberating in his chest. It stood on the platform midway up the stairs, watching him. Its upper lip withdrew into a snarl, revealing more of those unnaturally long teeth. It hunched down, the muscles in its forelimbs rippling and flexing. Walt felt his bladder let go.

He took a step backward, and then another. The front door was only a few more paces away. He could perhaps get there in time, but he refused to turn his back on that lion thing. If he turned away, it would almost certainly lunge at him. He took another step. He thought about those Animal Planet shows, and how they always said to move slow and look big. *Look big?* There was no way he was going to make himself look bigger than that thing. It had to be close to the *size* of a damn lion, even if that wasn't what it was. Walt took another step back, reaching behind him for the door handle. Still too far away.

The creature lunged without warning. Walt screamed—the hoarse, sad-sounding wail of an old man who knew his time was up. Its powerful-looking forelimbs collided with his chest, and he stumbled backward and into the foyer wall. Something cracked inside of him. The flip phone flew from his hand and hit the floor, the battery popping out on impact and sliding across the hardwood.

The growling continued, loud and hot against his face. The animal swiped at him, and he felt the front of his chest burning and wet. He fell to the floor, his head coming to rest near the front door—the door he never should have gone through in the first place. The creature pounced on top of him, and he felt more of his ribs snapping like kindling. The air whooshed out of his lungs, and the pressure of the thing on top of him was too much to take another breath. Its face came down to his, and he felt a searing, tearing sensation in his neck as it cut into him with those strangely long teeth.

Walt gurgled, his throat now open. Things were fading quickly, all the light from the room drifting away. He also felt his fear leaking out of him, along with the blood. The oncoming darkness felt warm—inviting even. Almost like an embrace from a loved one you had been waiting for years to see again. Almost like his Alma was wrapping her arms around him and welcoming him home. Walt went to her, and the Seabrooke house—and whatever was inside of it—faded away completely.

Dear Reader

(III)

Remember that ever-present, all-important line I was talking about? Well, I'm about to cross it. Because Walter Brindle was not a bad person. He wasn't a rapist. He wasn't a killer. He was just a kind, elderly, widowed handyman who liked to help out the neighbors. For free, no less. I'm not saying that justifying Peter's death was easy—because it wasn't—but it was a hell of a lot easier than justifying Mr. Brindle's death. Rapist = bad. Neighborhood handyman with lollipops = good. Even if he was a little presumptuous to let himself into my house without permission, he was still a good person. And the punishment he received was by far worse than the crime.

By the time I got home, it was all over. I suspected it would be, but I still had hope back then. Hope hadn't been completely stripped from my mental psyche, not at that point anyway. So after receiving that call, I hauled ass back home, driving much faster than the roads of Diamondback were intended for, and practically careened into my driveway. I'm surprised I didn't go straight through the garage door and right into Peter's damn FJ Cruiser. Wouldn't that look just great? A smashed-in garage door, a missing person's vehicle, and a body in the house? *Awesome.* You can stay tuned for my upcoming episode on *Forensic Files.*

I didn't even bother opening the garage—just threw the car into park, flung myself out of the driver's seat, and ran for the front door. There were some tools lying on the porch, ones I didn't recognize, and a rusty old step ladder that I might have recognized. No time to think about that, though.

I was about to pull out my key to unlock the door, then realized Mr. Brindle had already accomplished that task. So I just grabbed the doorknob and opened the door—well, *tried* to open the door. It only opened a few inches, then got stopped by something. So I tried to open it again, and again, but every time it bumped up against something and wouldn't budge. So I tried to push it in. It did move a few more inches, but then stopped again. It was just enough for me to see the red on the foyer floor, though. So bright, so thick, and so *familiar.* I stood there, looking down at it and contemplating just how many times blood can get on a hardwood floor before the wood starts to warp. That's how out of it I was.

So I gave up on the front door and ended up having to go back to my car and open the garage. In goes the Sentra, down goes the garage door. I wanted to take my time now, you see? I had already seen the red, and I had already felt the dead weight that was blocking the door. Did I really want to see the rest of it? Nope. No, thank you. I'd rather just take up residence in the garage from now on so I'd never have to see the source of all that red.

I walked into the house in a daze, reality having evaded me for the moment. I was back to that night in early March, using my dad's tools in a way they were not intended to be used. I was back in the tar grave, being swallowed by darkness and heavy, coagulating sludge.

Athena didn't greet me at the kitchen door when I came in, but I could hear her. I could hear the wet chewing noises, and the occasional cracking sound that I could now identify as bones breaking. Usually it was pig bones or cow bones, but this time it wasn't. This time it was handyman bones.

She was in the living room, gnawing on a piece of Mr. Brindle that was no longer identifiable. I couldn't figure out what it was exactly until I got a look at the body. His arm was no longer there, so I'm assuming that's what she had spent the last twenty minutes going to town on. There were also large gashes across his chest, and his plaid shirt was saturated in a thick molasses of congealing blood. The blood might have been from his throat, though, because that was split wide open. I could see white bone deep inside the gore; she had practically decapitated him.

I stood there for a long time—I don't know how long. Athena chewed, I stood, and Mr. Brindle lay there in a heap. I wish I could say I cried, or that I at least threw up in horror and revulsion. But in all honesty, I just stood there. Like a statue. Like a man who had stolen a glimpse of Medusa despite his better judgment. I don't know how long I was there, staring at poor old Walter Brindle. It must have been awhile. He wanted to help me, and because of my choices, he was dead. He died an awful death, and it was all because of me. How do you go on from that? How do you keep living? How do you rationalize the death of a *good* person? The fact of the matter is . . . you don't. You can't rationalize that, because it isn't rational.

The *old me*—the rational me—said that this is the end of the line. *Your actions have single-handedly led to the death of an innocent person. Turn yourself in and be done with it.* But then there was the *new me*, piping in and reminding myself that it wasn't *my* fault Mr. Brindle went into my house without permission. It wasn't *my* fault that I was unaware of the house key under the damn turtle. Athena was just defending her territory, right? Actually, don't answer that. The *old me* already knows the answer, and the *new me* doesn't want to hear it.

Remember when I talked about those heartbroken people—the Twitter hacker, the desperate stalker, the disgruntled ex with a handgun in the supermarket? They were normal people at first, at least to some degree, until love messed everything up. I'm not sure when the rational thoughts started giving way to the irrational for those folks— I'm sure they don't either—but I do know when it happened for me, and it was when I decided to not call the police about Walter Brindle.

Instead, I got my daddy's tools out of the garage and went to work. I left Athena with the arm. What was the point in trying to wrestle it away from her now? Walter sure as hell didn't need it anymore. I did what needed to be done in the bathtub, just like I did with Peter. I didn't throw up this time. And I didn't make a midnight trip to the dumpster either.

Anyway, back to that line. That *all-important* line. I don't think I crossed it when I decided not to call the police. What were they gonna do? Not help Mr. Brindle, that's for damn sure. I think the pivotal moment I stepped over that line was when I decided to keep the body and—God, this is hard to write down. I kept the pieces of the body for . . . well shit, I better just say it already. I put the pieces in the freezer in the garage so I could use them to feed Athena. There. I said it. But really, what would be better? Walter in a trash bag in some dumpster, or Walter helping to feed Athena? He did say he wanted to help, after all. So there it is. There's me crossing the line and laying the *old me* to rest, once and for all.

So into the freezer Walter goes. And then another floor-to-ceiling cleanathon to get rid of all the evidence that I could. Again, *CSI* would take me down in mere seconds, but I was still hoping it wouldn't come to that. Oh, hope—that little stirring of joy that flutters in your chest like a baby bird about to take flight for the first time. And then you have to wait and see if that baby bird is able to sail through the air with effortless ease, or crash down to the rocks below. Will your hopes fly, or will they plummet and splatter into bloody, broken carnage on those jagged rocks that we call despair? Only time will tell. Yippy.

I'd like to say I was overcome with guilt after what happened to Mr. Brindle, but it seemed like the guilt parasite was starting to lose its hold on my mind. It no longer had mountains of guilt to feed on now that the *old me* was dead, and without nourishment, it was withering away. It squirmed a bit for the following few weeks, slinking around my insides like a stubborn child not wanting to go to sleep just yet, but finally it retreated into the shadows and mercifully disappeared.

Well, I'm guessing by this point you're thinking I'm pretty much beyond saving. I've crossed the line, dug my own grave, I've made my bed and now I must lie in it. Basically, I'm a wicked monster on a one-way trip to the eternal hellfire of damnation. I can't blame you for thinking that, not after what I just told you. I don't *deserve* to be saved, I know that. Or, maybe, if you're optimistic, you might think there is still a small chance—a small chance I could be saved from this new reality I have found myself in. Like I said, my rational thinking seems to have deserted me, so I'm going to have to let you be the judge of that one. Again, I don't want to hear the answer.

Until next time,

Skyler Seabrooke

CHAPTER 33

December 24, 2018
10:08 p.m.

Skyler sat on the couch, flipping through TV stations and absentmindedly stroking the fur around Athena's neck. Athena chuffed in approval and nuzzled against Skyler's stomach. "Easy there, Atty," Skyler said, gently turning the big cat's saber-teeth away from her midsection. "Those things are getting sharp."

Skyler stopped on the local news station—something she had done every day for the last five weeks. She watched the pretty blonde news anchor rattle on about this and that as she ran her fingers through Athena's fur, waiting to see if there were any new developments regarding the disappearance of Walter Brindle.

Walt had made his first appearance on the evening news three days following his visit to the Seabrooke house. The report, once the lead story on all the local stations, had been downgraded week by week until it was nothing more than a prerecorded blurb at the end of the broadcast, following the weather forecast and sporting announcements.

"The police continue their search for a local retiree in Diamondback, Arizona. Walter Brindle, age seventy-eight, was last seen leaving the hardware store on Sagebrush Avenue on November sixteenth. People around town knew Brindle as a kind man, but that he was starting to get more forgetful as he aged. Many fear that he got confused while going on one of his evening walks, and that he might have wandered into the forest and gotten lost. If you have any information regarding the disappearance of Walter Brindle, please call . . ."

Skyler turned off the TV. She was relieved the news had moved on to other headlines, but also felt a profound sense of sadness over Mr. Brindle's death. She didn't mean for it to happen, and neither did Athena. It was just a horrible accident. Much like if Mr. Brindle had been hit by a car, or suffered a fatal stroke or heart attack. Things like that happen all the time, and although you might not feel guilty about those things happening, you can still feel very sad that they did happen.

Skyler grabbed her phone and checked for any missed calls or texts. She was on call for the shelter tonight, but so far no reports had come in. It was Christmas Eve, and she always volunteered to cover the on-call shift for the holiday so everyone else could be with their families. And as it turned out, she was getting to spend the evening with her family as well—all 240 pounds of her.

Trish had insisted that Skyler come over for an early holiday dinner, which Skyler agreed to do on the premise that Trish would not go overboard with the cooking just because of her. Of course, Trish did anyway, and Skyler offered to stay after dinner to help with the cleanup, barring any incoming calls from the shelter.

Trish's husband and two visiting children—both no longer children—were in the living room watching *A Christmas Carol* while Trish washed and Skyler dried the dishes.

"You sure you don't want to stay and watch the movie?" Trish asked as she handed Skyler a serving platter that matched the color of the freshly fallen snow outside.

Skyler grabbed it and started drying. "Naw, I'm more of a *Die Hard* kinda girl myself. Anyway, I should be getting back soon."

"And why's that?" Trish asked. "I don't want you alone in that house on Christmas Eve. Just stay here. Sam and the kids won't mind. I even think Brian might be taken with you."

Skyler laughed. "Brian is seven years younger than me. And aren't we somehow related? You being my work mom and all. That would be downright incestuous."

Trish chuckled, but followed it up with a stern look to let Skyler know she was not okay with her going home alone.

"I'll be *fine*, Trish. Scout's honor." Skyler held up two damp fingers.

"Boy Scouts is three fingers."

"My bad," Skyler said, and added another finger.

"Raising two boys has filled my head with all kinds of useful information." Trish handed Skyler a crystal salad bowl, still dripping with sudsy water. "Well, you have to stay for at least a bit longer, because I got you a little something."

"Triiiiish," Skyler whined. "I told you not to get me anything."

"It's just a little something. Everyone has to get a present on Christmas, even badass, independent women such as yourself."

"Alright, fine. Just know that all I got you was a new Agave Animal Care Center mug."

"That's perfect. I needed more room for my pen collection anyway."

Skyler got up from the couch, Athena watching her from beneath heavy eyelids. "C'mon, Atty. Bed time. You can't be sitting down here when Santa shows up." Skyler snapped her fingers, and Athena perked up and jumped off the couch. She followed at Skyler's heels, sniffing at her new, fuzzy paw print slippers (courtesy of Trish) as she went. They ascended the stairs, Skyler in the lead and Athena obediently following behind her.

Skyler crawled into bed, shivering between the cold sheets. "Up, Atty. I'm freezing!" Athena jumped onto the bed and lay down beside Skyler. "Nope, inside the covers tonight. It's gonna be a cold one." Skyler pulled down the blankets and Athena crawled inside. Skyler threw the covers over them both, then wrapped her arms around Athena's body and snuggled up close. The cub's warmth felt good against her skin, and before long her goose bumps began to fade.

"Now go to bed, my dear. You don't want to be awake when Santa gets here. And for Santa's sake, he doesn't want you to be awake either." They drifted off to sleep, Skyler's arms wrapped around Athena, as snow fell lazily down from an inky Christmas sky.

CHAPTER 34

June 24, 2019
3:32 p.m.

Justin was waiting outside the AACC locker room when Skyler stepped into the hallway, a timid, nervous expression on his face. "Hey, Skyler. I know you were just about to leave, but I wanted to let you know Cinder is back again. She's with Dr. Fischer right now."

Skyler's hands curled into fists, her fingernails digging into her palms. "Is she okay?"

"Well, not exactly." Justin shrugged helplessly. "He brought her in half an hour ago. She was, um, she wasn't moving."

"That asshole," Skyler hissed. She strode down the hallway toward the vet center, Justin scurrying after her. Anger surged through her body in steady waves, prickling the surface of her skin. "Where is he?"

"He left already," Justin called, having fallen behind. "He said he'd be back to get her in a few days."

"Like hell he will," Skyler snapped over her shoulder. She reached the entrance to the vet center and yanked the door open with such force that it whipped around on its hinges and banged against the wall of the hallway.

Kelsey jumped, startled by the loud clack of the door against cement. "Sky—"

"Where is she?"

"She's in exam room two," Kelsey stammered. "Skyler, remember what Trish said—"

"Uh huh." Skyler walked swiftly past the nurses' station and into the hall of exam rooms. She pressed her hands onto the opaque glass of exam room two, took in a deep breath, and entered without knocking. Fischer looked up from the exam table, where Cinder was lying in a crumpled heap. "That fucking bastard. I'm gonna—"

"Skyler, please," Fischer said. "Calm down."

"How the hell am I supposed to do that?" Skyler clamped her jaw down so hard it made her muscles ache. She took a step closer to the exam table, the menace draining from her voice as she looked down at Cinder. "How bad is it?"

Fischer shook his head. "Not good. Looks like a broken leg, most likely infected, a few broken ribs, and two lacerations on her head that are going to require sutures."

Skyler stopped at the edge of the table, where Cinder was looking up at her with sad, blue eyes. Her gray fur was matted and dirty, and there was blood caked to the top of her head and around her muzzle. One of her front paws was swollen and bent at an awkward angle.

"Oh, my poor Cinderella," Skyler whispered. She gently stroked the pit bull's head, being careful not to touch the open wounds. Despite her condition, Cinder whimpered eagerly and tried to wag her tail. "What did he do to you?" Cinder licked at Skyler's hand, her whole body shivering.

"Call the police," Skyler said to Fischer. "Right now. This is freaking ridiculous. It has to stop."

Fischer sighed and shook his head. "Skyler—"

"This is the *third time* he's brought her in like this. Animal cruelty is a crime. Why the hell are the cops not involved in this yet."

"He said she got hit by a car," Fischer said. "We have no way of proving otherwise."

"How about the fact that she's had horrible *accidents*"— Skyler brought her hands up to make air quotes—"three times in less than two years? He did this on purpose, Alan. Just like he did the other times."

"I know that. You know that. Everyone here *knows* that. But we can't *prove* it. If he takes us to court over custody of Cinder, he's going to win."

Skyler snorted. She looked down at Cinder and placed a comforting hand on her shoulder. Cinder's breathing was heavy and labored, probably from the broken ribs Fischer mentioned. "He can't keep doing this. If a kid gets beat to shit over and over, social services takes the kid to a safe place. This is the same thing—"

"Only it's not the same thing, Skyler. This is an animal. Not a human being. The rules are not nearly as stringent as they are for a child. Hell, at the federal level, animal cruelty is barely even considered a crime."

"That's going to change soon. But by then it will be too late for Cinder. She needs a new home. *Now.* We can't keep returning her to that monster."

"And if he gets a lawyer? How are you going to prove this wasn't caused by an automobile accident?"

"God, Alan! Look at her. You don't even want to try to stop this?" Skyler felt the rage boiling inside of her again. Her chest was burning, and if she screamed, she wouldn't be surprised if fire spewed from her mouth instead of air.

"We've tried in the past, and failed."

"Well, might as well just give up then," she snapped. Cinder tried to sit up, whimpered, then lay back down on the table. Skyler could see her anger was starting to upset the injured dog. She took in a deep breath and let it out slowly, willing herself to calm down.

"Skyler, I'm sorry. I wish to God we could be more proactive about this, but you know how it goes. Unless we have proof he's beating her, he's going to maintain custody. Hell, even if we did have proof, that is still what's probably going to happen."

"That's bullshit. I'm calling the police anyway. Somebody has to fight for her."

"I'll talk to them, too, if you want. See if we can convince them this is a cruelty case."

"Yeah, okay." Skyler leaned over and lightly kissed Cinder on the crown of her head. "You be strong, my Cinderella. This doctor guy may look scary, but he's here to help you." Skyler looked up at Fischer. "Take good care of her, Doc."

"Now *that* I can do." Fischer paged for a vet tech to come in and assist him.

Skyler left the room, feeling the rage pulsing throughout her body. She walked down the hallway toward the exit, not turning around when she heard someone behind her calling her name. First she would call the police, and if that didn't work, she would take care of it herself.

CHAPTER 35

June 26, 2019
1:06 p.m.

"Skyler, I don't know what else I can do. I hate this as much as you do, but . . ." Trish threw her hands in the air. "God, people can be such horrible monsters sometimes." She removed her glasses and started massaging her temples.

"The police said if we can't prove it, then they can't do anything about it. But I think we *can* prove it. Doctor Fischer can tell them the lacerations and the broken bones aren't consistent with a car accident. We can give them the operative report and—"

"And what?" Trish groaned. "The police will take a look at the medical mumbo jumbo in that report and say, 'By God, this proves everything'? No, Skyler. You know that isn't going to happen."

"But Trish . . . *we can't.* We can't send her back to Rick the Dick." Skyler stood in the center of Trish's office, her arms crossed and a deep groove etched down the middle of her brow. Trish sat at her desk, still massaging her temples.

"Sky, if Rick *Hansen* ever catches you guys calling him that, he's going to bring down a hailstorm of shit on me—*your boss.*"

"But he *is* a dick. And an animal abuser. He doesn't deserve to have Cinder. She deserves a loving family that is going to treat her well." Skyler collapsed in one of the chairs across from Trish's desk. She hated how useless she felt—how completely incapable she was of saving an animal. Of saving *this* animal. Her little Cinderella.

Rick the Dick Hansen had brought Cinder to the vet center on three separate occasions, each time with a different excuse as to how she acquired her injuries. First, he said she got into a fight with a neighborhood dog that somehow got into his backyard. As a result, she suffered multiple cuts and abrasions on her head and torso. Skyler suspected there was a fight, but not one involving another dog, and not one that was an accident. She knew a thing or two about *accidents.* The second time he brought her in, he said she jumped out of the back of his pickup truck while he was driving on the highway. That time she had two fractures in her hind leg, an eye that was swollen shut, and multiple broken ribs. And now here she was again, brought in with another bullshit excuse as to why she was injured.

Everyone who worked at the shelter had nicknamed Cinder's crotchety, abusive owner Rick the Dick after the second time he brought her in, once it was clear to all involved (cops excluded) that he was the source of Cinder's abuse. Skyler fought tooth and nail to not give Cinder back to the guy after the second hospitalization, but in the end, there was no way to prove any wrongdoing. Two days later, when Rick the Dick strode into the shelter, an uncomely man of five foot ten with a sweat-stained T-shirt and a trucker hat covering his greasy hair, Cinder was handed right back over to him—all because the abuse couldn't be *proven*.

And now it was happening again. And again, nothing could be proven. The police said so much when Skyler called them the other day. She got the runaround, getting transferred from one desk to the other, before finally having them agree to file her complaint, which basically meant nothing—especially not to Cinder, who was going to have to go back into Rick the Dick's custody as soon as she was out of observation at the vet center.

"He's picking her up tomorrow," Trish said. "He already called."

Skyler groaned and covered her face with her hands. "Trish, you can't let this happen. Not again."

"I hate this as much as you do," Trish said, agitation creeping into her voice for the first time. "But I have to do what is in the best interest of the shelter. We need all of our resources to keep this place going, not to pay expensive legal fees because the man sues us."

"But—"

"I'm sorry, Skyler. My hands are tied."

"Rick is the one who should be tied up," Skyler huffed. "In jail. With Jeffrey Dahmer."

"Now there's a pretty picture." Trish put her glasses back on. She looked Skyler up and down, as if studying a newly discovered species. "Maybe you should take the day off tomorrow. Relax. Cool off. I don't know if I want you and Rick to have a go at it when he arrives."

"Why? Because you think he'll hit me, too?"

"No. Because I think *you'll* hit *him*."

"The thought has crossed my mind," Skyler muttered. And it was true—the thought of what to do with Rick the Dick Hansen had been running through her mind all day.

"Skyler, we have a problem," Kelsey said in a low voice.

"Why? What's going on?" Skyler had just walked into the vet center, her shift done for the day. She wanted to check on Cinder one last time before heading home.

"I just got off the phone with Trish," Kelsey said. "She's on her way over."

Skyler's stomach dropped. Did Cinder's infection worsen? Was she even more damaged than Fischer originally thought? Internal bleeding? Brain damage? "What happened?"

"He's in there," Kelsey said, and gestured toward the ICU with her chin. She leaned forward in her chair and lowered her voice to a barely audible whisper. *"Rick the Dick."*

"Oh shit," Skyler grumbled. "How'd he get in there?" She looked at the door to the ICU, but couldn't see anything through the opaque glass.

"He walked right past me. When I tried to tell him he couldn't go back there, he just ignored me." Kelsey considered for a moment. "I guess that's better than him telling me to go screw myself, I suppose. Anyway, I called Trish right after he went in."

"You did the right thing. I don't want that guy antagonizing you. Where's Trish?"

"Here," Trish said as she stepped through the doorway and into the vet center. She joined them at the nurses' station, her lower lip trapped between her teeth and a flustered expression on her face. She smoothed down her pencil skirt and straightened her jacket, momentarily looking like an anxious child who had been caught trying on mommy's work clothes. And then it was gone, her nervous demeanor swiftly replaced by a look of assertive professionalism. "Where is he?" she asked Kelsey.

Kelsey raised her hand and pointed at the ICU. Trish gave her a curt nod, then turned to Skyler. "Stay here."

"No way!" Skyler protested. "I'm not leaving you alone with that bastard."

"Shhh," Trish whispered. She glanced over her shoulder at the ICU door.

Skyler crossed her arms over her chest. "I'm not letting you go in there alone."

"Fine, you can come. But keep your mouth *shut.*" Trish raised her eyebrows and pointed a finger at Skyler, waiting for a response.

Skyler sighed. "Fine. Let's go."

Rick Hansen was standing in front of one of the ICU kennels, watching Cinder, who was asleep and still on an IV antibiotic drip. Her broken paw had become infected prior to Rick bringing her in, probably because he took his sweet time before finally seeking medical care.

"What the hell are you doing in here?" Skyler snapped.

"Skyler!" Trish exclaimed. She gave Skyler a deathly serious look, and Skyler begrudgingly shut her mouth. "Mr. Hansen—"

"I'm in here because there's no damn security in this place," Rick said. He had a lump of chewing tobacco tucked inside his lower lip, but nothing to spit it into. Instead, his Adam's apple bobbed up and down each time he swallowed some of it down.

"It's an animal shelter, not a prison," Skyler said, and got another look of warning from Trish.

"Walk up and down them kennels and tell me it ain't a prison," Rick said.

Skyler opened her mouth to respond, but Trish cut her off. "Mr. Hansen, how can we help you right now?"

"I want to know why I can't take her home today. Seems like bullshit to keep her locked up in here when she can go home with me right now." Another swallow.

"She can't go home today because she is still ill," Trish said. She sounded calm, but Skyler could see the muscles in her jaw working, and the cords in her neck were taut with strain. "She has an infection in her fractured forelimb. She needs continuous antibiotics. That's why she is still here."

"You people are just tryin' to charge up my bill. Extra days, extra dollars. You won't be happy 'til you've bled me dry."

"I know I won't," Skyler chimed in. Trish's hand shot out and clutched Skyler's arm, squeezing until it hurt. She didn't let go until Skyler clamped her mouth shut.

"I assure you, Mr. Hansen, we are not keeping her here unnecessarily."

Rick gave Trish a wary stare, then shot a much ruder look at Skyler before turning back to Cinder. "She's my dog. You can't keep her without my permission."

"We strongly encourage you to allow Cinder to stay here until she has received her course of antibiotics," Trish said. Skyler looked down at Trish's hands, which were clenched tightly into fists, her dainty knuckles gone white.

Rick cursed under his breath. "Fine. Sounds like bullshit to me, but fine. I will be back t'morrow to pick her up."

Skyler's eyes searched the room. A few IV poles, a tray of gauze and bandages, a fire extinguisher. Her eyes stopped on the fire extinguisher. *If I could just get one good swing in . . .*

"Yes, Mr. Hansen," Trish said. "Can we show you out now?"

"Not yet," he said. "I want another minute here with my dog." Swallow.

Trish bit down on her lower lip so hard Skyler thought it might draw blood. "Just a minute more then. These rooms are for rest." Trish grabbed Skyler and led her out of the room.

Once the door was closed, Trish leaned over the desk and whispered to Kelsey, "Call Justin. Or one of the other guys that are on today. Get him in here to escort Rick out once he's ready. I don't need any more shit from that guy today."

"Yes, ma'am," Kelsey said, and picked up the phone.

Trish turned to Skyler. "You—go home. You're done for the day. I don't want you standing here when he comes out. I have to get back to my meeting."

Skyler nodded, her eyes lingering on the door to the ICU. When she looked away, her gaze landed on a pair of scissors that were lying on the edge of Kelsey's desk.

"I mean it, Skyler. Out." Trish pointed her finger at Skyler, and then at the exit. She gave Kelsey a nod and left.

Skyler listened to Trish's heels clicking on the tile as she walked back down the hallway. Once the sound faded away, Skyler whirled around and bolted back into the ICU. Kelsey's startled cry of protest was muffled by the door as it swung closed behind her. Skyler stood just inside the doorway, staring at the back of Rick's grimy T-shirt, too enraged to speak. She could feel the scissors pressed against her thigh, snuggly tucked into the pocket of her cargo pants.

Rick slowly turned away from the kennel and looked Skyler up and down. A lewd smile crept across his face, emphasizing the grotesque bulge of tobacco that still resided beneath his lower lip. He sucked some stained saliva through his teeth and then swallowed it down. "She got hit by a car."

"You can't treat her like that," Skyler said through clenched teeth.

"I can treat her however I damn well please. She's my property."

"She's not property, you sick fuck—"

"Hey now," Rick cut in. "Language, language, little lady. You sure do got a mouth on ya, don'tcha?" He licked his lips, and Skyler felt her skin prickle and her stomach churn. The scissors felt heavy in her pocket.

Silence hung in the air, thick as syrup. Finally, Rick said, "I'll be back t'morrow for my dog." He walked past Skyler, purposely brushing up against her as he went.

Skyler's hand went to her pocket, and her fingers wrapped around the handle of the scissors. If she moved now she could get him in the back . . . the neck . . .

But she couldn't move. She stood where she was, frozen in place, the blade of the scissors trembling against her leg.

Rick yanked the door open. He was going to get away! From her. From punishment. But she couldn't let that happen—not again. "She won't be here tomorrow," Skyler called after him.

Rick looked back at her, letting the door fall closed. "Now why in the hell not?"

"You heard Trish," Skyler said. "Cinder needs around-the-clock care. IV bag changes every few hours to complete her course of antibiotics. The vet center is closed at night."

"Closed at night? Ain't this a hospital?"

Skyler shrugged. "Budget cuts," she said, barely recognizing her own voice. "Anyway, Cinder will have to be fostered for the night at a house that is equipped to handle her medical care."

Rick took a few steps closer to her. She could smell the chew on his breath, and the sickly sweet stench of what she thought might be bourbon. "And let me guess whose house that's gonna be."

"I have the appropriate equipment for Cinder's continuous antibiotic drip. I will foster her tonight, and tomorrow you can pick her up at my house."

"How do I know she's gonna be safe at your house?" Another swallow.

"Because I'm not the one that beats animals," Skyler said, taking a step closer to him. "You are."

Rick looked her up and down once more, his eyes lingering on her chest. He met Skyler's glare and nodded. "Fine. Whatever. I'll get her from your place. But something makes me think you are just tryin' to find a way to get me alone. You got lust in your eyes." He winked. "Honey, all you really need to do is ask."

Skyler kept her ground, refusing to break his stare. Rick was right about seeing something in her eyes, but unfortunately for him, what he saw there wasn't lust. "I'll call you when Cinder's ready. We have your number on file."

"I bet you do," Rick said, and grinned his lopsided, leering grin again. He walked back over to the door. "See ya t'morrow, pretty lady."

Skyler watched him go, letting out a tremulous breath once the door swung closed. Her arms broke out into a wave of gooseflesh, and her whole body began to shake. When her fingers started aching, she looked down at her hand. The scissors were there, out of her pocket and pointed at the door. She couldn't even remember pulling them out.

CHAPTER 36

June 27, 2019
11:14 a.m.

Rick Hansen received a call from the shelter bitch at a quarter past eleven the following morning. Why in the hell she had to call so damn early was beyond him, but at least she said that the IV whatever had finished running its course. Something like that. He shoved himself up from his recliner, where he had fallen asleep at some point during the early morning hours. The bottle of whiskey he finished off the night before was lying on its side next to the chair.

Rick stumbled over to the bathroom and turned on the shower, keeping the temperature on cold because he needed to wake himself up. Usually he liked to have the shower piping hot as he rubbed one out, but today he had places to be. Hell, if he was right about the shelter bitch, maybe she wouldn't mind rubbin' one out for him.

Rick stepped under the frigid stream, let out a startled cry, and then jumped back out. He almost slipped on the wet tile, and had to grab the towel bar to steady himself. "Christ," he muttered, and reached back into the shower to adjust the temperature. There was a cold shower, and then there was a freezing shower. Damn water shouldn't be so cold this time of year—it was the middle of the damn summer, after all.

When the water lost its icy chill, he stepped back in and did a half-assed job of washing the important parts—pits and balls—and then rinsed off. He was hoping he had time for a beer before he left—something to subdue the throbbing in his head. He pulled on a pair of dirty jeans and gave the T-shirt draped over the nightstand a sniff. Deciding it was tolerable, he threw it over his head.

Rick stopped by the fridge on his way out to the truck, and was irritated to find he didn't have any more beers left. He was gonna have to deal with the lecturing bitch stone-cold sober. Maybe he should have rubbed one out, after all. He muttered a few curses under his breath and headed out the door.

She had told him the address when she called, but hell if he could find a place to write it down. He headed toward Alpine Ridge—that he remembered—and spent the majority of the drive trying to figure out what the broad's address was. It was Oak Street or something like that. But what number?

Rick reached into his back pocket and grabbed the can of Skoal that lived there. He shoved a generous pinch between his gum and lower lip, working it down into its usual resting place. He then jammed the can back into his jeans with a grunt.

His mind turned to Cinder as his truck rumbled along, exhaust spewing out in its wake. He didn't know what he was gonna do with that damn dog. Always gettin' into shit. She had torn up one of his good work boots while he was at the bar last week, and with the liquor coursin' through his veins, he couldn't help himself. He gave Cinder the lesson she deserved and just wanted to be done with it. But then the damn bitch couldn't walk right, and kept hoppin' around with one of her paws in the air. He gave it a few days to heal on its own—she didn't deserve no special treatment—but then the damn leg started swellin' up. Fuckin' dogs. The last two were just as much a pain in the ass as this one was turning out to be.

She'd best have learned her lesson this time, Rick thought as he turned onto Oak Ridge Drive. *That was the name—not Oak Street, Oak Ridge.* His thoughts returned to Cinder, and what he was gonna do with her if she ended up gettin' into his shit again. She had three strikes against her now—she shoulda been out after this last offense, but he just didn't have the heart to do it just then. He was a kindhearted guy, after all.

Rick watched the houses going by, sucking some tobacco-stained saliva through his teeth before swallowing. He still couldn't remember the number, but she did say the house was blue and her shitty tan Sentra was gonna be in the driveway, so he could at least keep an eye out for that.

That's what I'm gonna do with her, Rick thought, again thinking of Cinder. *Next time she gets into any of my shit, I'm gonna put peanut butter on the end of my Remington, and then she'll get a lesson that she will never forget. And I won't have to deal with those shelter fucks anymore neither—just bury the bitch in the backyard next to the others.*

A tan sedan appeared in the distance, parked in front of a large house painted blue. Rick slowed the truck as he got closer. *Yup, Sentra. This is it.* He pulled in behind the Sentra and got out of the truck, stretching his back before shutting the door. If the shelter bitch did want to get lustful, he wanted to be limbered up. She looked like she could get into some pretty kinky shit. Probably would need more than one go at him, too.

He headed up the stairs, noticing but not caring that all the curtains were drawn. He rapped on the door and waited. Nothing. *Goddamnit, I ain't got all day.* He knocked again, harder this time.

"Come in," a woman's voice called from inside.

Can't even come and get the damn door for me? When the hell did these women stop knowin' their place? Rick yanked open the door and stepped inside. He slammed it shut behind him and slowly walked the length of the foyer, sizing the place up. It looked dated as hell; like he had stepped back into the 1990s or somethin'. Back when he was young and spry and could give the girl two or three goes at it without having to limber up first. But where the hell was she?

He heard footsteps coming down the stairs and glanced up. There was a landing halfway up the staircase, with the lower stairs facing the foyer and the upper stairs facing the living room. He couldn't see her at first as she went down the top steps, but then there she was, standing on the landing and looking down at him. She didn't make a move to go down the remaining stairs. *Christ, she really does want to do me dirty,* he thought. *She's just waitin' for me to go up to her bedroom with her.* He could feel himself stiffening in his jeans. He hadn't put on any underwear, and the jeans zipper was rubbing against him. Better get these pants off real quick. He swallowed.

The girl just stood there on the landing, watching him. *Scarlett? Skylynn? Somethin' like that.* He supposed it didn't matter. And she just kept standing there—playing coy, no doubt. She didn't want to be *too* forward, throwing herself at him like she was.

"Whatcha doin' up there, darlin'?" he asked. "I was just joshin' about that lustful look in your eyes yesterday, but hell, there it is again."

Scarlett/Skylynn didn't answer, nor did she move. This coy shit was getting annoying. Let's fuckin' get started already. "I told you ya coulda just asked if ya wanted to jump my bones. Didn't have to bring my dog into it. Where is she anyway? Still sleepin'?"

"She's at the shelter," Scarlett/Skylynn said softly. "Where she's been all night."

"Hot damn girl, you really are jonesing for some action, aren'tcha? Not that I take too kindly to you lying about the whereabouts of my dog. But if you wanna be a bad girl, I'm more than happy to teach ya a lesson. More than one, in fact." Rick took a few steps toward the stairs. The zipper on his pants was becoming painful, and he wanted them off already.

She smiled, a sly smile that made her lips look sexy as all hell. What a tease she was! "Actually," she said, "I thought I would teach you a lesson."

"Me? Honey, when it comes to S and M, I am much fonder of being the *'S'* than the *'M'*."

She shook her head. "That's not what I'm talking about, Mr. Hansen."

"Well, what in the hell are ya talkin' about then?" he asked, frustrated. He was sick of playin' games with this broad, sexy mouth or not. He sucked some more brown saliva through his teeth.

"I'm talking about teaching you a lesson for how you treat animals." Scarlett/Skylynn took a couple steps down the stairs, then stopped again. "You beat that dog. The one you are so desperate to get back. You beat her, more than once, and I'd bet good money she's not the first animal you've abused."

"So what of it?" Rick snapped. He didn't like where this conversation was going. What the hell was this bitch up to? This is a weird-ass way to start a sex game—that's for damn sure.

"Animals aren't meant to be mistreated like that, Mr. Hansen."

"Stop calling me tha—"

"And if the police aren't willing to punish you for the crimes you have committed," she took another step down the stairs, "then I will."

"You!" Rick scoffed. "You don't even weigh a hundred pounds soakin' wet. What in the name of God are *you* gonna do? Spank me?"

She shook her head and descended a couple more stairs. "Not me," she said. She was now only a few steps from the bottom—only a couple yards away from him. If he lunged at her, he could grab her. But then what? Rick had taught his fair share of canines a lesson or two or three, but never a woman. Not more than a backhand anyway, when it was deserved.

"Listen, bitch," he said, raising his voice. He spat the soggy tobacco onto the floor of the foyer. "I'm sick of playin' games, so if you could just give me my damn dog, I'll be on my way." He heard a muffled noise come from down the hall to his left, and then scratching against wood. Cinder was down there. Rick looked down the hallway and saw that the doors at the end of the hall were both ajar. If he called her name, Cinder would come runnin' if she knew what was good for her. "Cinder—"

"I told you, your dog is at the shelter getting the medical treatment she needs."

"Then what in the hell did I just hear down the hall?" Rick felt something building in his chest, and it wasn't the all-too-familiar rage that usually stirred there—it was something else. Something that fluttered more, and made his stomach cramp down. Fear. That's what it was. *Fear.* The hairs on his neck stood erect, just as another part of him that was erect dwindled away, the zipper no longer rubbing painfully against him. He swallowed, but the chew was no longer tucked inside his lip.

"Down the hall?" Scarlett/Skylynn asked. "Oh, that's your lesson. Are you ready for it?"

"No, I'm not. I don't want no fuckin' lesson."

"Do you think that Cinder wanted her lesson?"

Before Rick could respond, the girl snapped her fingers. Just one snap, her right hand hanging down by her side. Rick looked at the hand, confused. Before he could ask what the hell that was about, he heard a single, sharp bang come from down the hallway. It was the door to one of the bedrooms, thrown violently into the adjacent wall. The door started to swing back, its hinges creaking, but before it could shut, something hurtled through.

Rick let out a startled cry and stumbled backward. It was some sort of lion or jaguar or something. Only it was shaped different, and its teeth were too big. It stalked down the hallway, its head low to the ground and the muscles in its shoulders rippling. It growled, a deep, guttural sound that filled the confines of the hallway. It pulled its lips back into a snarl, stalking closer to him as he backed up one foot after the other.

Rick came to a stop with his back against the wall of the foyer. He looked helplessly at Scarlett/Skylynn on the stairs. "Jesus Christ! What the hell is that thing?" When she didn't respond, he asked, *"Are you just gonna stand there and let it attack me?"* Rick's face felt wet, he must have started crying at some point. "Please!" he sobbed. "I'm sorry. I'm sorry I hit her! I won't do it again. *I swear!*"

"I don't believe you," she said.

The lion thing crept toward him, sinking its body even lower to the ground. It was only five feet away now. Rick pressed his body against the wall, wishing the plaster and wood could swallow him whole and create a barrier between

him and whatever demon creature this was—some freakin'
jungle cat from hell.

Rick looked back at the stairs, his eyes wide and lower lip
trembling. The girl had returned to the landing, and her right
hand was still hanging by her side with the thumb and middle
finger pressed together. Rick opened his mouth to plead with
her some more, but then she snapped her fingers.

The lion thing lunged at him, springing up and colliding
with his chest. It held him there, pressed against the wall, its
front claws digging painfully into his skin. Rick cried out in
fear and surprise. He tried to wriggle out from beneath its
immense paws, but found he was unable to move even an
inch. Rick screamed, and the thing pulled away. He thought
maybe his yelling had frightened it off, but instead it swiped at
his midsection with its paw.

Rick stumbled and fell to the ground. His stomach felt
funny, like he had leaned against a lit grill. He didn't bother
looking down, just crawled across the floor toward anything
that looked like safety. A sliding glass door stood on the
opposite side of the living room. He already knew it was too
far away, but panic made his body move forward even though
his mind had already determined the effort was futile.

The lion thing jumped on top of his back, pinning him
down on his stomach. He flailed his arms and tried to scream,
but all the air had left his lungs. He couldn't make a sound, not
even a whimper. He tried to crane his neck to look at the girl
on the stairs—maybe she could still stop this—but she was no
longer there. The stairs were empty. And then he felt teeth on
his face, impossibly long and impossibly sharp, scraping

across his flesh. It tore something away—part of his cheek maybe, because now his mouth was filling up with blood. It wouldn't take long for him to start choking on it, although it would be hard to choke when he couldn't even inhale.

The thing's head came back down to his, and this time he felt the teeth on his throat. At the same moment, he started to feel snapping pops across his rib cage. One, then another, then another.

He wanted to tell the girl that he had learned his lesson. He wanted to tell her that he would never hurt another animal again. He wanted to tell her anything to make this stop—to just get it over with already.

It turned out he didn't need to say anything, though, because within a few more seconds it was over. Rick's vision faded away shortly before his hearing went out. The last thing he heard was a wet, ripping sound, followed by chewing.

CHAPTER 37

June 27, 2019
12:07 p.m.

Skyler sat in the upstairs hallway with her back to the living room. Her knees were drawn up to her chest, her eyes squeezed shut, and her fingers pressed firmly against her ears. She rocked back and forth, waiting for it to stop.

She thought she would be able to handle watching the attack, but as soon as it began, she realized she couldn't stand having the image of Rick's final moments seared into her memory. She fled up the remaining stairs and collapsed on the hallway floor, her eyes shut and ears plugged. She hummed a tuneless melody in an attempt to drown out the sounds of Rick dying, all the while thinking to herself, *I had to do it, I had to do it, I had to do it*, on an endless repeat. When she removed her fingers from her ears some five minutes later, all she heard was that wet chewing sound.

Skyler wasn't sure how long she sat there listening to the chewing and the silence that followed, but by the time she got up, Athena had already sprawled out on the floor and fallen asleep. Skyler took one shaky step down the stairs, then another, clinging to the banister to steady herself. When she finally made it down to the foyer, she took a slow, deep breath, then turned around to face the aftermath in the living room.

Rick lay there, his eyes open and forever staring at a beast he could no longer see. His throat was torn out, the cords of tendon shredded and the arteries severed. Athena had also managed to flip him onto his back and opened up his stomach. Rick's midsection looked like some sort of cioppino seafood stew—the one with the red broth and the pieces of fish and shellfish floating in it. Only it wasn't broth, and it wasn't seafood. Skyler turned away, disgusted. Her body retched, so violently that it hurt. *I did this. This happened because of me. He's dead because of me.*

Athena was snoozing peacefully a few yards away from Rick's body. The front of her face was smeared with blood, as was the floor and a portion of the coffee table. Something pink and gooey was stuck in her whiskers; Skyler didn't want to investigate any further into what it was. Instead, she started the cleaning process she had come to know all too well, compartmentalizing what she was doing as she worked. Just a chore, nothing more. It became a mantra as she made trip after trip from the bathtub to the reach-in freezer. *Just a chore, nothing more. Just a chore, nothing more.*

Later, as she lay in bed with Athena, who was freshly washed and free of gore, Skyler went over how tomorrow was going to go. She knew she had just entered the land of premeditated murder—no point trying to deny that one—but, even worse, this time there was a link between her and the deceased. Sure, there were links with all of them, but this link multiple people knew about—the entire shelter, to be exact. Every employee there knew she hated Rick the Dick Hansen. Every employee knew how short-tempered she could get when it came to animal abuse. Not to mention, she had no idea if Rick told anyone about the meeting at her house. He wasn't exactly a socialite, but it was possible he could have told someone. A coworker? A fellow bar patron? People mostly saw him at the mechanics shop where he worked, or in the corner of one of the local bars, downing whiskey and grumbling at the TV. Could he have told the bartender he had a meeting with the chick from the animal shelter?

Skyler rolled over onto her side. She had messed up this time. She let her temper get in the way, and when the temper came in, the reasoning went out. Her mind started running through the facts, or should she refer to it as evidence? There was the phone record—she had called him to tell him when to come over. There was his truck, which she wiped down and drove over to the local bar—but who knows if someone recognized her while she was driving it? It must have looked conspicuous whether she was recognized or not—somebody wearing a sweatshirt with the hood up in the middle of summer. It was almost ninety degrees out there. And then there was the fact that Rick was supposed to pick up Cinder at the shelter today—something he had never failed to do before, no matter how much he mistreated her.

Skyler fidgeted with the duvet, unable to keep her hands still. She had become something of an expert at lying in the past year and a half, but even with all her practice, she wasn't sure if she could pull this one off. This might be three strikes and you're out.

Athena sensed Skyler's unease and moved closer to her, leaning her heavy body against Skyler's back. Skyler rolled over and put her arms around the big cat. "Oh, Atty," she whispered, "I screwed up. I really screwed up this time." She pressed her face into the scruff of Athena's neck and began to weep. Athena nuzzled against her, chuffing softly.

Skyler sniffled, attempting to force away an onslaught of tears. This wasn't the time to cry. That wasn't going to get her anywhere. What she needed to do was figure out a plan—a contingency plan. If the shit hit the proverbial fan, she needed to be able to act fast and get out. She paused, thinking. *That's it,* she thought. *Get out.* That was the plan—really the only possible plan, if she wanted to be honest with herself. She messed up big this time, and leaving Diamondback might be the only way to fix it. If the police started looking in her direction, she would have to run. *They* would have to run. Before the police arrived on her doorstep, with their questions, with their handcuffs, and with their high-powered black lights.

Skyler's mind raced, her tears forgotten. She could put a few sleeping pills into Athena's meal, or at least something to make her drowsy, and then get her into the back of the FJ Cruiser. Then they could haul ass for somewhere else—

anywhere else. She had a decent amount of money in her savings account; money from her parents she refused to touch even when she was strapped for cash. This could be the time to use it. She could empty out the account and go. And if the bank asks why, she could just say she wanted to buy a used car in cash, or—who the hell cares? She'll be gone before it ever becomes an issue.

Mexico would be the best bet. There's plenty of secluded places down there. And if they could just get across the border, then they'd be safe. They would need to be ready to act quickly, though, when and if the police caught wind of her vigilante tactics. Otherwise she would just be a sitting duck— or a seal floating in shark-infested waters. Just one or two officers would come at first, like the shark nudging the seal with its snout to see if it was worthy prey. But then they'd be back, with guns and handcuffs and black lights—the shark shooting out of the water and clamping its jaws around the unsuspecting seal. Jaws . . . handcuffs . . . different objects, same results. Leaving Diamondback would be hard, but if she knew the sharks were getting ready for an ambush attack from below, Skyler thought she'd be able to leave. Like Chief Brody would say . . . get the hell out of the water.

Skyler sighed heavily, her hands clutching at the comforter even though she was sweating beneath it. Diamondback had been her home all her life. Outside was the yard she played in while her mom read her romance novels on the porch. That sidewalk was the one she walked down with her dad on Halloween, dressed like a pirate or whatever, and trick-or-treating with the rest of the kids. And it was that street she rode on when she first learned how to ride a bike; after she fell off, her mom used a bright pink Band-Aid to cover the scrape on her knee.

Leaving the AACC was going to be the hardest. She loved it there—the people as well as the animals. But she had another animal to think about, and that was the most important thing. Protecting Athena. *Saving* Athena. Before the police came, and before she got taken away in handcuffs and Athena in a cage.

But when? And how would she know if the sharks were closing in? Should she wait until she gets nudged? Or jump out of the water at the first hint of a shadow down below? Would she even notice the shadow? The seals sure don't.

Skyler figured she still had at least a little bit of time to figure it out. And there was always the possibility that all this planning would be for nothing. Maybe Rick's disappearance would fade away just like the others. If so, they could stay right where they are, and Skyler would vow to never go all vigilante justice on someone ever again. Scout's honor. But if the police did start putting it together—if the sharks began circling in the depths below—then they would run. She just needed to make sure they had a plan, that they had *the* plan. Because their lives would depend on it.

Skyler drifted off into an uneasy sleep, one where she woke often but not completely. She was never sure if she was awake or dreaming, instead just fading in and out of consciousness in a dark, swirling haze. It wasn't until she opened her eyes and saw the sides of the grave that she realized she was actually dreaming.

She stood at the bottom, the tar surrounding her almost up to her shoulders. She held her arms overhead, trying to keep them out of the putrid goo. Black, viscous sludge clung to her breasts, and the tar had managed to work its way into the ends of her hair, which were now sticking together in slimy clumps.

She reached for the side of the grave, although she knew trying to escape was useless. The earth was too soft, too wet, and every time she grabbed for it, a clod broke free and tumbled into the tarry soup that was enveloping her. She needed help to get out of here, something to hold on to—a branch, a root, *something*.

Rain pelted down, and Skyler heard the familiar roar of fear and desperation up above. The roar startled her this time. Why was it still up there? She had saved the animal. She had done away with the abuser. *She had done it.* Why was the animal still there, and why was it still scared?

"I saved you!" she yelled up into the gray expanse of weeping clouds. "I already saved you!" Skyler grabbed at the sides again, and more black earth crumbled down into the tar. *"Why are you still afraid!?"* she screamed into the sky.

Skyler jerked awake. Morning had come, and she could already feel the summer heat bleeding through her bedroom window along with the sunshine. Athena was awake, sitting on the floor next to Skyler's side of the bed, her head level with Skyler's. Skyler looked into Athena's amber eyes and was surprised to see fear there. Had she been crying out in her sleep? That's why Athena is scared, right? It must be. "I don't understand," Skyler said aloud to the room.

Athena chuffed and licked at Skyler's hand, which was hanging over the side of the bed. Skyler placed the hand on top of Athena's head and ruffled her fur. She looked at Athena closely—her penetrating eyes, her honey-colored fur, her long, ivory saber-teeth. "Is it you?" she asked. "Is it you up there in the dream? You that I'm supposed to save? Has it been you all along?"

Athena nuzzled Skyler, then returned to where she was sitting, her eyes twinkling in the morning light. "But I already saved you, Atty. Back in the storm drain. *I already saved you.*"

Athena jumped over Skyler in one graceful motion, landing on the opposite side of the bed. Skyler felt like she might get launched off the bed completely, but managed to stay in place with the help of the covers Athena landed on.

"Atty!" she exclaimed. "No knocking me off the bed!"

Athena let out a low, rumbling noise from her throat—a sound that Skyler knew well. Athena was anxious about something. Skyler wrapped her arms around her. She listened to the big cat's heart thumping strong and steady in her chest.

"You're okay," Skyler whispered. "Everything is going to be okay. I'll figure it out, I promise." Athena grumbled again, although softer this time. Skyler kissed her head. "You're so big and tough, Atty. What could you possibly be afraid of?"

Skyler lay in bed with Athena until her alarm went off some thirty minutes later. She wanted to call in sick, but knew that would only make her look even more suspicious than she already did. Skyler switched off the alarm and sat up with a groan. Her muscles ached from the previous day's exertions. She stood up, stretched gingerly from side to side, and then headed toward the shower. It was going to be another long day.

CHAPTER 38

June 28, 2019
8:47 a.m.

Skyler arrived at the shelter at quarter to nine. There were no police cars, no sirens, no FBI agents. Just a peaceful parking lot on a lazy summer day. She could hear a dog barking in the outdoor exercise pen on the opposite side of the building, and a warm breeze tugged at her hair as she walked across the lot. The morning was pleasant and calm, in stark contrast to her insides, which were a chaotic, swirling mess of anxiety, apprehension, and downright fear.

Skyler reached the employee entrance and punched in the code. *Here we go,* she thought, and entered the building. She went a short distance down the hall and into the locker room, frustrated to see her hands were shaking when she opened her locker door. *Just breathe. Be calm. Just breathe. Be calm.* She took in a deep breath and slowly let it back out, repeating the process until her heart rate began to slow and her hands stopped shaking. She then went back into the hallway and headed toward the vet center, behaving as she would on any other day.

Kelsey was sitting at the nurses' station when she arrived, her thumb flicking at her phone and her face in a zombie-like trance. "Kelsey?" Skyler asked.

Kelsey's head popped up and the zoned-out look vanished from her face. She pressed a button on the side of her phone and tossed it onto the desk. "Hey, Sky. What's up?"

Skyler placed her hands on the counter to steady them, keeping her expression neutral. "Just checking to see how it went with Rick the Dick yesterday. How was Cinder?"

Kelsey's eyes widened at the mention of Rick's name. Skyler felt a pang of fear cut through her chest. *Shit shit shit. Did she mess up already? Say the wrong thing? Her face . . . God, it must be written all over my face . . .*

"He didn't show!" Kelsey exclaimed, and slapped her hands down on the desk. Skyler flinched at the sound. Kelsey went on, talking fast. "We were waiting for him *all day* but the jackass never came in. Trish even called, but no answer. Can you believe that?"

"Wow, that's . . . crazy." Skyler forced what she thought was a look of relief. "So now what?" she asked, leaning closer to Kelsey and assuming the gossip position. "What's Trish gonna do?"

Kelsey shrugged. "Dunno. If enough days go by and Rick the Dick doesn't come in to claim her, she goes up for adoption." Kelsey picked up her phone and flicked the screen back on. "God, wouldn't that be great?" she said, and began scrolling through her Instagram feed.

"So great. So Cinder's still in the ICU then?"

Kelsey glanced up from her phone. "You bet. She's awake and doing great. You should go say hello, she always gets excited to see you."

"Awesome, thanks." Skyler walked toward the ICU, stopping when Kelsey called after her. She felt a lump materialize in her throat, like a sudden and rapidly growing cancer. She tried to swallow it back down.

"You know what, Sky?" Kelsey asked.

Skyler turned around and looked at Kelsey with what she felt was a ridiculous smile plastered to her pale face.

"*You* should adopt her," Kelsey said. "Ya know, if the jackass doesn't come back."

Skyler's smile shifted to one of genuine relief. "Well, I guess we'll see," she said in a hopeful voice. Kelsey went back to Instagram, and Skyler entered the ICU.

"Skyler!" Trish called across the lobby. She hurried over to the service desk where Skyler was standing, her sensible heels clicking on the tile floor as she went.

Skyler had just finished going over the adoption paperwork with a middle-aged woman who adopted a bonded pair of senior cats. The woman had gone out to her car to retrieve her pet carrier, and Skyler was supposed to meet her in the Cat Cabana in a few minutes to help her load her new furry companions into said carrier.

"What's up, Trish?" Skyler asked. *Just breathe. Be calm. Just breathe. Be calm.*

Trish reached the desk and placed her manicured hands on the counter—clear polish, nothing more. "I'm assuming you heard about Cinder?"

"Yeah! That Rick the Di—sorry—that Rick Hansen didn't come back in to claim her?" *Just breathe. Be calm. Just breathe. Be calm.*

"Yeah," Trish said, sounding honestly bewildered. "I was pretty damn surprised, actually. I thought maybe he was sleeping off another bender yesterday and would show today, but so far . . . nothing." Trish shook her head in disbelief and stared out the window, lost in thought.

Skyler shrugged and turned her palms up. "Maybe he finally decided to be a decent human being."

Trish rolled her eyes. "Doubtful," she scoffed. She looked over at Skyler, her eyes narrowing. "So what did you say to him?"

Skyler cleared her throat, the malignant mass having returned to her windpipe, and looked down at the counter. *Shit.* "What do you mean?" she asked, trying to sound innocent.

"I know you went in and talked to him after I left. Kelsey told me. I'm just curious what you said to get him to finally back down."

Skyler met Trish's eyes. She didn't see any accusations or threats lurking there, only curiosity. "I—uh . . . I just told him he's not a good pet owner and Cinder deserves better," she mumbled.

Trish laughed. "Seriously? That's all it took?"

A nervous giggle escaped Skyler's lips. "Well, I might have used more colorful language than that."

Trish smiled and shook her head. "Well, whatever you said, I'm sure Cinder is grateful. We've got to wait a few more days to see if he comes in, but if not, she can go up for adoption."

Skyler noticed the middle-aged woman coming back into the building. She was holding a large pet carrier in one hand and struggling to open the door with the other. A man with an armful of dog treats rushed over and held the door for her. The woman said something to the man, smiled, then went in the direction of the Cat Cabana, glancing briefly at Skyler.

"Gotta go. That's my adopter." Skyler jerked a thumb at the woman just as she entered the Cat Cabana. "She just adopted Bonnie and Clyde."

"That's fantastic news! I love when a bonded pair gets adopted." Trish flicked her wrist a few times, shewing Skyler away. "Go, go. Get those kitties ready for their forever home."

Skyler grinned and said, "I'd be happy to." She went through the partition in the desk, expecting Trish to wander off to wherever she was needed next. Instead, Trish remained where she was standing, watching Skyler closely. Skyler gave her a quizzical look. "Anything else?"

Trish shrugged. "No, not really." Her eyes drifted back to the main entrance and to the sun-soaked parking lot beyond the glass. After a moment, she looked back at Skyler. "You go on. Your adopter might be getting impatient in there."

"Yeah, okay." Skyler took a few steps away from the service desk, and when Trish still didn't look away, she pivoted on her heels and started walking across the lobby. She allowed herself one quick glance over her shoulder, and to her dismay, Trish was still watching her.

Skyler turned back and hurried toward the Cat Cabana. *Oh God, does she know I'm lying?* She felt as if her heart and lungs had lost their ability to function—like at any moment she would keel over and collapse on the lobby floor. *Is this what a heart attack feels like?* She tried to swallow, but couldn't. *Why is she looking at me like that? Like she knows something.*

Skyler quickened her pace, but she could still feel Trish's eyes burning a hole in the back of her head.

CHAPTER 39

July 2, 2019
10:04 p.m.

Rick's haggard, prematurely wrinkled face appeared on the evening news on June thirtieth. His hair was unkempt in the photo, and his brown-going-on-gray five o'clock shadow hid his ruddy cheeks, forever flushed from drinking.

The blonde news anchor described Rick Hansen as a local mechanic, known by many in the town of Diamondback, where he has lived all his life. *"He was last seen on the evening of June twenty-sixth at a convenience store near the auto shop where he worked. When Hansen didn't arrive for his scheduled shift for the second day in a row, one of his coworkers went to check on him. His house was empty, and there were no signs of foul play. If anyone has any information as to Hansen's whereabouts, please call . . ."*

The next night, the pretty, blonde news anchor said the same spiel, but added that Hansen's truck had been found behind one of the local bars that he frequented. Police suspect he was too intoxicated to drive home and attempted to walk, and subsequently was injured.

The following night, the prim and proper blonde on Channel 8 News also threw in that an unidentified person was seen driving Hansen's truck the day following his disappearance. *"The identity of the person is still unknown, but the witness is fairly certain that he or she was much smaller than Hansen. Due to the person's small size, investigators believe it was a woman driving the vehicle. No one familiar with Hansen knew of him having a girlfriend . . ."*

Skyler stared at the TV screen, clutching an unopened beer with one hand and resting the other on Athena's shoulder. When they began to shake, Athena stirred and looked up at her, becoming immediately concerned. She chuffed softly and nuzzled Skyler's arm, but Skyler barely moved. She stared at the screen as if in a trance, her lip quivering and eyes unblinking.

The witness. The police. Skyler's heart was thudding so hard she thought it might crack her ribs—a sound with which she was now intimately familiar. The sharks were in the water now. *That's it. Game over. Next week on* Forensic Files . . .

It wouldn't take long now. They would find out Rick's dog was at the shelter. They would learn that one of the shelter employees had a problem with Rick the Dick Hansen. They'd talk to Trish, and from the odd way Trish was looking at her a few days ago, she might have something to say. Possibly *plenty* to say. Which meant the sharks—err, police—would be arriving at Skyler's house in the next few days. Which meant the *Forensic Files* people would come next, with their black lights and their luminol. Her living room would light up like a goddamn Christmas tree, not to mention her bathroom. And what about the FJ Cruiser in the garage? An FJ Cruiser that is registered to another missing person?

Skyler shuddered despite the warmth of the room. Athena rested her forehead against Skyler's side, her saber-teeth pressing into the couch cushion and threatening to puncture the fabric. Skyler let the beer bottle fall to the floor and wrapped both arms around the big cat. "I hoped it wouldn't happen, Atty, but it's time," she whispered. "We gotta get out of here." Athena draped a massive paw over Skyler's lap and looked up at her with golden eyes.

In the background, the weatherman was droning on about the weekend forecast. It sounded like nothing but a monotonous slew of words, Skyler barely hearing them, but when the man mentioned the Fourth of July, her ears perked up. She raised her head and looked at the TV.

"—with the holiday forecast," the weatherman said, "we are in for quite a treat this Independence Day. With a cold front headed this way, we can expect highs in the mid-seventies on the third, fourth, and fifth. And as you can see," the man gestured to the screen behind him, "plenty of sunshine all week long."

Skyler stared at the screen, transfixed. Athena, who was watching her closely, turned to look at the screen as well. She looked back at Skyler, confused. The extended forecast was up, showing day after day of smiling suns, and a bunch of numbers below that Skyler didn't bother to look at. *The holiday weekend*, she thought. *That's it. That's our way out.*

The blonde news anchor returned, thanking the bland, forgettable weatherman for yet another exciting weather report. Skyler didn't hear her. Her mind was elsewhere; her thoughts racing through her synapses and ideas shooting through her brain like sparks of lightning. *The Fourth of July. The holiday weekend. This is it. This is our chance.*

There would be a lot of people on the road traveling for the holiday—going to campsites in the mountains, to the beaches of California, or to visit relatives for backyard barbecues and fireworks. If they left at the same time, her and Atty, they were bound to fade into the sea of other cars on the interstate. No one would remember the FJ Cruiser as it went through checkpoints along the state borders, because there would be so many of them. So many people traveling, so many people congesting the highways and pouring over state lines. It would all be a monotonous blur to those Border Patrol agents. No one would take notice of the FJ Cruiser, or that it belonged to a missing person. What were they gonna do? Run the plates of every single car passing through? This was the chance she had been waiting for—the opportunity to disappear. *Safety in numbers, or better yet, anonymity in numbers.*

Skyler looked at her phone. It was half past ten on the night of July second. Leaving tomorrow was out of the question; there were quite a few things she would need to take care of first. *So the Fourth it is then.* They'd hopefully still be in the middle of the prime traveling rush—lots of cars on the road, less chance of being noticed. Especially since it was going to be quite the task to keep Athena concealed in the back seat. That's why she couldn't take her own car—Athena would stick out like a . . . well, like a saber-toothed tiger in the back of a small sedan. She'd have to leave her phone, too, otherwise they would be able to track her whereabouts.

Two days then, Skyler thought. They would have to be ready in two days—less, actually. All packed up and ready to hit the road at first light on July Fourth. Well, maybe more like nine or ten, so plenty of people have already started their own road trips. Road trips that led to hot dogs and fireworks, not running from the law and trying to slip past the border. If all goes according to plan, they would be well into Mexico before the police ever show up on her doorstep.

And what happens after they get into Mexico? Where would they go? Skyler shook her head. *One thing at a time,* she thought. She can worry about that when—and if—they make it across the border. Right now, all that mattered was getting out. Right now, the sharks were circling. Right now, the tar was threatening to pull her down into the darkness for good—to pull them both down—just like it did to the saber-toothed tigers all those centuries ago.

CHAPTER 40

July 3, 2019
8:12 a.m.

Skyler called out sick the following day, carefully reciting the script she had constructed, equipped with sniffles, a clogged-sounding voice, and *one* cough—she didn't want to overdo it. Justin sounded mildly irritated he would be solo for kennel duty that day, but still told her he hoped she'd feel better soon. Skyler wished she could tell Justin he turned out to be a really good coworker, and a pretty decent guy, but instead she just said thanks and ended the call.

She went to the bank next, to where her parents kept their savings account. She didn't plan to take all the money that was there—that would be too suspicious—but she would take enough to at least get started in Mexico. She thought fifteen grand would be feasible. She planned to tell the bank she needed it to buy a used car she saw in someone's driveway, if they even bothered to ask. She could say the guy would only accept cash. She doubted it would even come up, but hey, better to be overprepared than under. As it turned out, the teller that assisted her didn't bat an eye when she said she wanted to take out fifteen grand in cash. She mentioned the used car, but he barely even looked up from his computer. So far, the luck was falling on her side of the proverbial fence.

Half an hour later, Skyler was at the grocery store, picking up some canned goods, bottled water, and various boxes of food that didn't require refrigeration. Cereal, crackers, beef jerky, mixed nuts—not great, but at least something.

She was more concerned about how she was going to keep Athena fed. There was still plenty of Rick in the freezer, but she obviously wasn't going to be able to bring it along. This venture was going to be a big enough risk as it was, no need to throw some frozen body parts into the mix. She would let Athena eat her fill the night before they left, and then rely on grocery stores along the way. A turkey breast here, a ham steak there. When they got to where they were going— wherever that ended up being—she would try to figure out a more permanent solution. But again, that was something she would have to worry about later. One problem at a time.

Skyler spent the remainder of the day packing—clothes, hygiene products, blankets, food. By the time she was done, the FJ Cruiser was loaded with as much stuff as space would allow. She still had Athena to think about; she was going to take up the bulk of the back seat. And to get through Border Patrol, Skyler was going to have to put some blankets over her. But how was she going to explain *that* to the Border Patrol agents? A giant mound of blankets in the back seat?

She settled on telling them, if they asked, that it was for camping. Sleeping bags, extra blankets, pillows . . . maybe that would be enough. Hopefully that would be enough. If a ton of holiday travelers were heading across the border, maybe they wouldn't even notice. It's not like they really care about you going *into* Mexico; it's the coming back that matters. And she wasn't going to come back—this was a one-way trip, for better or for worse.

The last thing was the sleeping pills for Athena. Skyler wished she could have a moment alone in the pharmacy at the vet center, but she knew there was no way in hell that was going to happen, so instead she picked up some Benadryl at the store. She had no idea about the proper dosing, but hoped it was a mild enough drug that it wouldn't be too harmful if she gave Athena a little too much. She planned to stick some into a piece of Rick, and then give it to Athena in the morning an hour or so before they departed.

Skyler glanced out her kitchen window, pulling the curtain back just enough to see Oak Ridge Drive. It was sunset, and the sky was alight with splashes of orange and pink. It would be her last sunset in the only home she had ever known. Tomorrow she didn't know where she would wind up sleeping, but as long as she had Athena by her side, she didn't care.

CHAPTER 41

July 4, 2019
6:17 a.m.

The morning of July Fourth was bright with sunshine, just as the weatherman predicted. By the time the sun crested the horizon, Skyler had already been awake for some time, watching the shadows on the ceiling transform as night gave way to morning. A brilliant shaft of golden light was now cast across her bedroom walls, chasing away what remained of the darkness. If only she could banish the darkness in her own life so easily.

Athena lay beside her, also awake. Skyler suspected the big cat had picked up on some of her unease. Athena's body felt tense, and her breathing quicker and more labored than usual.

Skyler glanced at the clock on the bedside table. It was a quarter past six in the morning. She didn't want to get on the road until at least nine. By then, the highways would be thick with traffic, like plaque in one's arteries after consuming one too many of those Fourth of July cheeseburgers. She ran over the details of the day in her head again, listing the various things that could go wrong, and how she would attempt to handle them. The U.S.-Mexico border was less than three hundred miles from Diamondback, and if all went well, they would be safely across the border and hidden somewhere in the Mexican desert by four that afternoon.

As the clock neared 7:00 a.m., Skyler decided to get up and shower. It would possibly be her last shower in many days, so she took her time, letting the steam rise and the hot water pelt her skin until the heat began to fade. She threw on some jeans and a tank top, fastened her boots, and gave her bedroom one final, lingering stare. Her bed, her reading chair, the animal pictures on the walls. Thirty-four years of memories, reduced down to a single look as she stood in her doorway, her heart heavy and her stomach aching. Skyler left the room, rested her hand briefly on the door to her parents' bedroom as she walked past, and then descended the staircase for the last time.

At 8:00 a.m. it was time to call Agave and let them know she was still sick, but hopefully she would be able to come in for at least a little while tomorrow. It was one of the new volunteers that answered, and she had to ask for Skyler's name twice. That was good, though—the less memorable the conversation, the better.

After ending the call and turning off her cell phone for good, Skyler went into the kitchen and prepared Athena's go-to-sleep breakfast. She took out a piece of thawed Rick from the fridge, then went about sticking the pink Benadryl tablets into the thigh muscle. She had inserted four pills when she heard a knock at the door.

Skyler jumped at the sound, dropping the fifth pill onto the floor in the process. She looked down at the tiny pink tablet that resembled candy more than it resembled medication, temporarily paralyzed with fear. When the knock came again, louder this time, she squeezed her eyes shut as tightly as she could and held her breath. *Go away go away go away go away.*

After the third knock, Skyler knew whoever it was had no intention of leaving. She scurried out of the kitchen and into the foyer, debating whether she had time to shove Athena into the FJ Cruiser and peel out of the driveway before the police gunned her down. *Man, they work fast,* she thought, staring at the front door.

Skyler was about to snap her fingers for Athena to come over, when she heard a voice call from the other side of the door. Not a rough, takes-no-shit detective's voice, demanding for her to come out with her hands up, but a woman's voice, soft yet stern, and undoubtedly familiar.

"Skyler? Are you there?" the woman asked.

Athena came down the stairs to the first landing, her eyes locked on the front door. Skyler pointed to the top of the stairs. "Go up." Athena looked from her to the door, then reluctantly headed back up the stairs. They creaked and groaned under her weight. The noises stopped at the top of the stairs, which meant Athena had not gone down the hallway to Skyler's bedroom, but simply sat down at the top of the staircase.

Skyler hurried over to the door, then stopped. Her hand hovered over the doorknob as her mind ping-ponged over whether she should answer the door or just pretend she was asleep. *But then she'll just come back. And then she'll know I'm gone, and Athena and I will have less of a head start.* Skyler stared at the door until another knock jolted her back to reality. *Just answer it,* she thought, and grasped the doorknob with fingers that had gone white. She pulled the door open partway and peered outside.

Trish stood on the porch, her arms crossed and a concerned expression on her face. The worry lines that were etched into her brow only deepened when she saw Skyler. She looked her up and down, then noticed Skyler had not opened the door all the way. Her eyes narrowed. "Skyler?"

"Hi, Trish," Skyler said, holding the door open only enough for her body to show.

"Skyler, what on earth is going on? I need to talk to you."

Skyler shook her head slowly. "Now's not a good time, Trish. I'm still not feeling well—"

"Bullshit," Trish snapped, cutting her off. "And what are you doing with the door? Am I not allowed inside?" Trish tapped one of her sensible heels impatiently on the porch, waiting for Skyler to answer.

"I'm just—I might still be contagious. I don't want you to catch it." Skyler's grip tightened on the inside doorknob. She heard creaking behind her, on the staircase. With her free hand, behind her back, she jabbed her index finger at the staircase and then pointed up. She heard another creak, back on the upstairs landing.

"The hell with that," Trish said. "You aren't sick. I need to talk to you. Inside. Right now."

An anxious whine escaped Skyler's lips. *Shouldn't have answered. Stupid stupid stupid.* She looked tentatively over her shoulder at the staircase. It was empty. She reluctantly relinquished her grip on the doorknob and let the door fall open. Trish brushed past her and into the house. She stopped at the foot of the stairs, gave the living room a once-over, then turned back to Skyler. Skyler shut the front door and softly clicked the deadbolt into place.

Trish let out a frustrated, weary sigh. "Skyler, I know something has been going on with you lately," she said. "You've been acting strange for a while now, and don't even try to say that isn't true. Please tell me what's going on. *Please.*"

Skyler shifted from side to side, her arms wrapped tightly across her chest and her eyes darting to the stairs every few seconds. Trish caught her looking, glanced over her shoulder at the empty staircase, then looked back at Skyler. "Well?" she asked.

"I'm sorry, Trish. I don't know what to say. I've just been depressed lately."

"It's more than that, Skyler. You've *changed.*" Trish took a few steps away from the staircase. "I love you to death, and I've always considered you something of a daughter to me—not a work daughter, a *real* one—and I can tell that something is happening to you. Or has happened. What was it? What *is* it?"

Skyler felt her eyes burning, and tears lingering just below the surface. She tried to blink them away before they had a chance to spill. The guilt parasite—the one she thought was long since dead—stirred inside of her, this time in her chest instead of her gut. Her lip trembled. *"Trish,"* Skyler whispered, *"I fucked up real bad."*

Trish rushed forward and took Skyler's hands in her own. "Let me help you. Tell me what's going on."

Skyler shook her head vehemently. "I can't. You need to go. Right now."

Trish shook her head, just as vigorously. "Not a chance. The animal that died—that kitten—you've never been the same since then. You stopped fostering, for Christ's sake. By God, Skyler, that was your life."

"I couldn't handle any more loss," Skyler said softly. Inside, the guilt parasite savagely chewed on something in her chest—her heart maybe. "I just . . . couldn't."

"That I can understand," Trish said. "Hell, I can even accept that. But that's not everything."

A single tear rolled down Skyler's cheek. "It's not?"

Trish lowered her voice to almost a whisper. *"Rick Hansen, Skyler."*

Skyler tried to take a step back, away from Trish, but Trish tightened her grip on Skyler's hands. "Trish, you have to go now," she said, her voice shaking.

"It's all over the news," Trish went on. "The police think there was foul play involving his disappearance. And their only suspect is a petite woman that was seen driving his car." Skyler tried to pull away, but Trish held her hands so tightly that it hurt. "Skyler . . . *the police were at the shelter yesterday.* Asking questions."

Skyler looked at Trish with wide, frightened eyes, her struggle to get away momentarily forgotten.

"Please tell me you have nothing to do with this," Trish begged. "I know you, Skyler. I know you couldn't hurt anyone. Please tell me you had nothing to do with it. Please. Please tell me that. *Please.*"

The stairs issued a soft creak up above. Trish didn't seem to notice, but when the stairs creaked for a second time, further down and more pronounced, she glanced over her shoulder. The stairs were empty. She looked back at Skyler, bewildered.

Skyler took the opportunity to jerk both her hands down and out of Trish's grasp. "Trish," Skyler said, the shakiness in her voice giving way to something harder, something colder. "You need to go right now. I don't want you to disappear, too."

Trish's eyes widened. She took a step back, away from Skyler. "Oh dear God, Skyler," she stammered. "What did you do?" She continued to back up until she bumped into the banister of the staircase. She stopped there, staring at Skyler in disbelief.

The stairs groaned, and Athena appeared at the midway landing. Her eyes were locked on Trish, her lips pulled back from her teeth. A low growl emanated from deep inside her throat.

Trish whirled around, her mouth falling open when she saw Athena. She let out a startled cry, darted away from the stairs, stumbled on her sensible heels, and fell to the floor near Skyler's feet.

Skyler's hand went down to her side, her thumb and middle finger pressed together. Tears ran down her cheeks, Skyler no longer able to keep them at bay. "I'm so sorry, Trish," she said.

Trish's eyes were locked on Athena, who was slinking down the few remaining stairs. The big cat stopped at Trish's feet, crouched low to the ground and still making the same deep rumbling noise from inside her throat.

"Oh God," Trish whispered. *"Skyler, what did you do?"* She was crying; Skyler could hear it in her voice even though she couldn't see her face. Trish tried to scoot backward on the floor, but bumped into Skyler's legs and stopped. "She never died, did she?"

"No," Skyler said, choking on the word. "She didn't." She sucked in a mouthful of air, then let it out in a long, tremulous breath. Her hand remained at her side, her thumb and index finger pressed together and blanched of all color. Athena stayed where she was, crouched and waiting.

"You had Rick come here?" Trish asked.

"Yeah."

"And then you . . ."

"Yeah."

Trish was quiet for a moment. "And now me, Skyler?" she asked. She made no attempt to stand or flee. When Skyler didn't respond, she said, "I loved you like a daughter, Skyler. I still do, even after what you just told me."

Skyler let out a single, wretched sob. Her whole body was shaking, and she could feel the malignant mass in her throat threatening to close off her windpipe completely. She had already made her decision, and now it was time to go through with it. Skyler closed her eyes, took in a deep breath, then opened her hand—the sign for "stop". She turned her open palm to Athena, her fingers spread and her eyes still closed.

The growling faded away, and when Skyler opened her eyes, Athena was sitting on her haunches and looking up at her with a quizzical expression. The menace had drained from her face, and she now just looked confused by the entire situation. She looked at Trish, still on the floor, then back up at Skyler.

"Back up, Atty," Skyler said, defeated, and Athena obediently went back to the foot of the stairs. She sat down and started licking her paw, casually grooming herself.

Skyler offered a hand to Trish, who took it without hesitation and allowed Skyler to help her to her feet. Skyler looked at her, expecting to see fear, or at least anger, in her eyes, but all she saw there was awe. "What is she?" Trish asked.

"A *Smilodon*," Skyler said softly. Trish looked over at her, confused. "A saber-toothed tiger."

"My God . . ." Trish said. *"How?"*

"I have no idea. She was just . . . there, one day. In the storm drain."

Trish shook her head, speechless. Skyler waited for what came next—Trish saying she needed to notify the police, the inevitable sirens, the police cruisers on the lawn, the cage for

Athena, the handcuffs for herself. Instead, Trish said, "She's beautiful." She took a tentative step toward the big cat, then stopped and looked back at Skyler. "Can I . . ."

"Yes," Skyler said. "Of course." She looked at Athena. "Atty, come here."

Athena went to Skyler, then sat down beside her when Skyler pointed at the floor. Trish reached out, her hand trembling, and lightly touched the top of Athena's head. A small gasp escaped her lips. She stroked Athena's fur, a smile spreading across her face. Athena chuffed and started sniffing at Trish's skirt.

"I'm so sorry, Trish," Skyler said through fresh tears. "I just—I didn't want to give her up. They'll experiment on her. *They'll hurt her.*"

Silence filled the room, the only sound being Athena's breathing and the soft ticking of a clock coming from the living room. When Trish finally spoke, her voice was calm and determined. "No, they won't," she said. "Because they're not going to find her."

"But . . ." Skyler trailed off. "But aren't you going to call the police? Turn me in? Turn *us* in?" She gestured between herself and Athena, who was still seated beside Trish and rubbing her neck against Trish's leg.

"No, I'm not," Trish said.

"But after what just happened . . . I almost let her . . . I . . . I *deserve* to be locked up." Skyler sniffled and used her forearm to wipe away the tears on her face.

Trish gave Athena a final pat and turned to Skyler. She placed both her hands on Skyler's shoulders and leaned in. "I knew you wouldn't do it," she whispered. "I know you better than that."

"But I didn't even know if I was going to do it or not," Skyler mumbled. Another tear rolled down her cheek.

Trish smiled, a tired, weary smile that showed her age. She brushed the tear away with her thumb. "Then I guess I know you better than you know yourself." She glanced over at Athena. "At least sometimes anyway."

Trish grabbed her purse, which was lying on its side on the foyer floor. "Here," she said, digging through the bag until she found her wallet. "Take this."

"No, no, I have some. Please don't give me money when I almost had you killed. It's bad enough already."

"Yeah, you did. Which means you have to do what I say right now." Trish shoved a handful of bills into Skyler's hand, various presidents looking up from the worn green paper. "Take it. And go. That's what you're planning on doing, isn't it?"

Skyler nodded. "Yeah. Car's already packed."

"Where will you go?"

"Hoping for Mexico. Then I don't know. Somewhere . . . away."

Trish nodded. "I saw this movie where a man on the run went to Zihuatanejo. Looked like a pretty nice place. Maybe start there?"

Skyler smiled. "Worth a try."

"I can't stop the police forever," Trish said, "but I could at least give you a head start. I can try to delay talking to them for another day."

Skyler wrapped her arms around Trish, startling herself with the strength of her own embrace. If Athena didn't kill Trish, then this hug just might. However, Trish hugged her back just as fiercely.

"Oh, Skyler, I'm going to miss you so much. Please send a postcard every now and then, just so I know you're alright. You don't have to write anything on it. I'll know it's from you."

"I promise," Skyler said, not wanting to let go. "I love you like a real mom, too, you know."

Trish kissed Skyler's forehead. "I know you do. Now go, get out of here. While you still can."

"Goodbye, Trish."

"Goodbye, Skyler." Trish gave Athena one more wondrous stare, then hurried through the front door and disappeared.

CHAPTER 42

July 4, 2019
8:46 a.m.

Skyler watched Trish hurry back to her car, then locked the door and turned to Athena. "Okay, Atty. It's time for a snack." She snapped her fingers, and Athena followed her into the kitchen.

Skyler grabbed the fallen Benadryl off the floor and shoved it into the meat she had abandoned on the counter. She was about to set the plate down when a knock came at the door.

Skyler looked up, startled. *Did Trish forget something?* Skyler walked through the kitchen and back to the front door, opening it quickly without thinking. "Tri—" She stopped. It wasn't Trish.

A man stood on the porch, and Trish's car was gone. She had already left. The man was roughly six feet tall, with a lean frame and thick, brown hair that was just starting to gray. He wore a button-up plaid shirt, blue jeans, and heavy work boots, giving off the impression of a lumberjack, if it were not for his lean build and dazzling smile. Skyler had never seen him before—not at the shelter, and not around town. Her eyes fell to what was slung over his shoulder. It looked like some sort of gun, a rifle maybe, but something was off about it.

"You ready for the fireworks?" he asked cheerfully. Before Skyler could respond, he swung his fist and hit her in the face, putting his full weight into the punch. Skyler stumbled backward into the house, and everything went dark.

Dear Reader

(IV)

Well, well, well. Things have certainly gotten a bit sticky, haven't they? Like . . . oh, I don't know . . . tar, maybe? Black, viscous tar that pulls you down and never lets you go. Yeah, just like that.

So, before I can talk about that man coming out of left field—a shocker to me as much as it is to you—I gotta back up a little bit. If you are going to make a decision about me—about my supposed guilt or my possible (or impossible) salvation—you need to know the *whole* story. Then you can decide just how guilty I am. But story time isn't over just yet, kiddies—in fact, you haven't even made it to the best part yet. Let's try an analogy, shall we? If this was Alfred Hitchcock's *Psycho*, Detective Arbogast would be ascending the stairs right about now—to see who's hiding in Norman Bates's mommy's bedroom, of course. If you've ever watched that movie (and if you haven't, I do judge you just a bit—but hey, you're judging me, too, remember), then you know the most horrifying parts of the story are still yet to come. Same goes with this story, it just wasn't directed by Alfred Hitchcock.

So, we've already established that I crossed the line—that all-important line—with what I did to Walter Brindle. And I guess what I have learned since then is that once you have crossed that line, it's a hell of a lot easier to continue down the path of self-destruction. The guy who shoots his ex-wife in the head? Well, I would equate Walter Brindle to that man buying the gun. It's only a matter of time before he drives to the supermarket—the one his ex always shops at on Saturdays. Walter Brindle was me buying the gun. Rick Hansen—now that's me going to the supermarket to finish the job.

Let's talk about Rick Hansen for a little bit, shall we? I'm sure you already know he wasn't exactly a stand-up fellow. A sleazeball through and through. He certainly liked his booze—but hey, no judgment on that from me. What you do to your own body is your business. What's *my* business (or what I decided was my business) was his mistreatment of animals. Now *that* is just not okay. It never was, and it never will be. Harming an innocent animal is something only a disgusting, horrible, monstrous human being could do. A human being that, in my opinion, doesn't deserve to live. And if you saw poor Cinder, coming in bruised and broken—not once, not twice, but THREE times—at the hands of that cruel bastard, then you'd hop right over that line and onto my side, too. I'm certain of that one.

So I invited him over, knowing full well what would become of him. First-degree murder—I know, I know. Shame on me. But if I didn't *actually* kill him, does it still count? Eh, I suppose it does. *It was the bullet that killed him, Your Honor. I just pulled the trigger.* Anyway, we've already established that the line has been crossed—the *old me* has been laid to rest, and the *new me* thinks it's quite alright to be judge, jury, and executioner. To an animal abuser anyway.

So Rick comes over, and Athena does what she does. It was harder to watch than I thought it would be. In fact, I couldn't watch it. That's why I went upstairs and hid in the hallway until it was over. As it turns out, I was fine with issuing the sentence, but I didn't really want to stick around for the execution. I wouldn't say what I felt was guilt exactly, but just some sort of awed horror that I could be capable of such a thing. The *old me* probably wouldn't have even had the nerve to go into the ICU to yell at him. But she's dead, remember? I killed her, too. Just like poor, old, dog-beating Rick the Dick Hansen.

Once the shock of it wore off, I found I didn't even have much remorse for what I had done. Not even when I put the pieces that were left of him in the freezer. Athena had simply done to him what he had done to Cinder, albeit with a little more gusto. What I do regret is just how cavalier I was about what I was doing. I let my anger do the talking, and inevitably got the police looking in my direction. In all honesty, I'm surprised it didn't happen sooner. For those of you in law enforcement who are reading this—I don't blame you for not catching on sooner. It's not like murder was something Diamondback saw all that often. Hardly ever, in fact. Until now.

Anyway, back to the story. Back to Arbogast ascending the staircase to see what might be lurking up above. Great movie—you really should watch it sometime. So after that third news report, I realized I couldn't keep getting away with . . . well, murder . . . and that I needed to get the hell out of Dodge before it was too late. I took all the necessary steps, was pretty much all ready to go, then Trish showed up. You know Trish Morgan—she's the woman you police fellas have been grilling relentlessly in an attempt to get information about my current whereabouts, or to get her to confess to being involved in the murders. Well, I want to put the old kibosh on that *right now*, because Trish Morgan had absolutely NOTHING to do with the events that unfolded inside 9713 East Oak Ridge Drive. She was my employer, not my accomplice. Yes, she did show up at my house on July Fourth, but no, it was not to "aid and abet" me. She just wanted to see if I needed anything because I called out sick. That's it. I played the whole "I'm sick" charade when she arrived, and then I sent her packing. She had nothing to do with ANY of this, so STOP hounding her. Trish is a wonderful woman, and I miss her dearly. The. End.

Well, actually, I do have one last thing to say about Trish. And I'm sure you will be just *thrilled* to know this . . . *drum roll* . . . Trish ended up adopting Cinder! That's right, my little Cinderella has ended up with the best mom in the world, hands down. And before you get your panties in a bunch about how I gleaned this little tidbit of information, it was not because Trish has been in contact with me. *It was on the AACC website.* They have a photo gallery of adoption pictures on there. We call it the "Happily Ever After" page. Anyway, Trish and Cinder's picture was featured on there, front and center. You should check it out, super cute photo.

So, I guess we're back to my not-so-friendly morning visitor. Mr. Punch You in the Face Before You Can Say Hello. That hurt, by the way. See, when all this was going on—from the night I found Athena to the morning in question—I never even so much as considered the bigger picture. Why was she there? Where was her mother? How did a goddamn saber-toothed cat end up in Diamondback, or in the twenty-first century, for that matter? I just kinda took it as it was, and went from there. STUPID. Stupid, ignorant girl—that was me. Don't let them tell you that ignorance is bliss. Ignorance is actually a death sentence. Curiosity didn't kill the cat—ignorance did.

If I hadn't been so ignorant, I would have considered the possible reasons why Athena was in Diamondback. I would have considered who might be looking for her. I would have had a plan if that person ended up on my doorstep. I wouldn't have been completely taken by surprise. But hey, ignorance killed the cat. Not this cat, though—not if I could help it. When something threatens who you love, you can do some pretty amazing things you never thought you were capable of—lift cars, jump in front of bullets. All kinds of crazy, life-threatening shit like that.

The *old me* would have just wept and pleaded and let whatever was going to happen next happen. But she's gone, remember? I killed her. And the *new me* is *fucking pissed*. The *new me* is a murderer, after all—caution has already been thrown to the wind. I gotta say, thank God love changed me the way that it did, because the *old me* would not have survived what happens next. Actually, I think most people would not survive what happens next. Possibly not even you.

You know that cliché? Not the curiosity killed the cat one, I already used that. I mean the one in that movie, *The Jazz Singer*, where Al Jolson says, "You ain't heard nothin' yet." Well, this is the part where I use that tiresome, overused cliché myself, because . . . *You ain't heard nothin' yet*. Stay tuned, dear readers, whoever you are, because here is where things start to get really crazy.

Skyler Seabrooke

CHAPTER 43

Light started to filter in first—soft, hazy, and barely there. The colors came next, all browns and blacks and grays. And then the sounds, frightened growls competing with rumbling thunder. Skyler opened her eyes, not surprised to find herself inside the tar-filled grave. The tar was up to her neckline now, and her arms were almost completely submerged in thick, black sludge. Only her fingers managed to stay above the surface, so white and skeletal as they poked out of the tarry soup. Skyler tried to lift her arms, but found she could hardly move them. *Not long now,* she thought, elevating her chin to keep the tar from coating her face.

Up above, thunder continued to boom, and bright flashes of lightning illuminated the gray swirls of clouds in brief, violent bursts. Skyler raised her chin further, pointing her face directly toward the sky. She felt the tar greedily grabbing at her hair, attempting to pull her down by the scalp. The rain must have stopped, because she no longer needed to squint against the torrential downpour of her previous dreams. She peered up at the clouds as she waited for the tar to reach her mouth, her nose, her eyes . . . but something was odd about them. Skyler's eyes widened, the tar momentarily forgotten. The clouds didn't look right somehow. They were not storm clouds, with bulging curves and dark, bloated bellies, but just a single sheet of gray haze. Almost like . . .

Smoke, Skyler thought. *It's not clouds, it's smoke. The sky is full of smoke.* Another rumble of thunder blasted through the air, only that sounded wrong, too. It was too brief and pronounced, more like a gunshot than a rumble. A bright flash accompanied the boom, filling the smoke with twinkling blue splashes of light. Another boom, this time followed by red sparkles. The blue and red filled the smoky air, then disappeared just as quickly as they arrived. *Fireworks,* she thought, the realization slamming into her as if one of the fireworks had been aimed directly at her chest. *It's the fucking Fourth of July.*

Skyler struggled to pull her arms from the muck. Her fingers had disappeared somewhere below and her hair was now covered in tar up to the scalp. Only her pale, horrified face remained above its inky surface. In moments it would creep into her ears, and then what would she hear? Bubbles? Her own heartbeat? Or just all-consuming silence? Would she be able to hear the fireworks anymore? Probably not. Once she was pulled down, there would only be silence. And darkness. Forever.

Green filled the smoky sky, accompanied by crackling sounds that reminded Skyler of milk getting poured over Rice Krispies. When the crackling dwindled away, she could hear the growling again. *Athena.* She was up there, and she was terrified. Skyler tried to call to her, but no sound escaped her lips. Where had her voice gone? Had the tar sucked it out of her at the same time it was attempting to suck her down?

Skyler opened her mouth to try again, but instead she heard somebody else's voice. A man's voice. The same man that had been on her doorstep with the weird-looking gun. The same man that punched her in the face before she had a chance to speak. He was up there, above the grave, with Athena. The man was angry, shouting something Skyler couldn't quite make out.

Tar spilled into Skyler's ear canals, and the man's voice disappeared. She heard a few gurgles as the tar made its way to her eardrums, then silence. *No,* she thought. *No, please. I don't want to go down into the blackness. Please.*

Tar crept into the corners of her eyes. She struggled to keep them open, despite the biting sting as the tar seeped under her eyelids. The sky shimmered in brilliant white sparkles of confetti, although she could no longer hear the crackles that accompanied them.

But I have to save her! she thought. *There has to be a way that I can still save her. It can't end like this.* Skyler took a final breath, and felt the tar envelop her completely. Her eyes throbbed, her ears ached under the pressure, and her lungs began to burn. And it was dark. It was all so very, very dark . . .

CHAPTER 44

The Fucking Fourth of July

Skyler gasped, sucking in a great mouthful of air that made her chest heave and her throat clench. The tar was gone, taken away with the dream, but the darkness remained. She blinked her eyes, willing the comforting light of her bedroom to filter back in, but nothing came. Just blackness. Was she not out of the tar, after all? She was lying down, that much she knew, and below her the floor was moving. It was a monotonous feeling of movement, something that would fade away if she wasn't focusing on it.

Skyler tried to sit up, but her wrists pulled her back down. Startled, she fell onto her side and her shoulder thudded painfully against what felt like metal beneath her. She groaned. The sudden jolt to her shoulder reminded her that wasn't the only thing that was hurting—the side of her face felt like she had been struck by a baseball bat. Her cheek gave off a constant deep ache, and her eye felt swollen and hot. Paul Bunyan had punched her in the face. And hard.

Skyler reached up to assess the damage, and was bewildered when both hands came up instead of just one. Before she could touch her throbbing cheek, her arms came to a sudden stop. Something hard dug into her wrists, and she let out a frustrated grunt. She tried to raise her arms again, but again something prevented them from coming more than a foot off the floor. Skyler yanked up repeatedly, feeling the first stirrings of panic trickling through her veins. The sounds of metal clinking and clattering filled what sounded like a very small space.

Small like a coffin. Skyler stopped tugging, the trickle of panic opening into a steady stream. *I'm in a coffin. I'm dead. They buried me. They threw dirt on top of me.* She began to tremble. *But first they tied me down?*

The panic dulled as confusion took over. Skyler felt around the floor, searching for what was holding her down. Her hands came in contact with a metal hook that was embedded into the floor. Attached to the hook was a metal chain, and attached to the chain was a set of handcuffs—with her wrists inside.

I'm handcuffed to the freaking floor. What the hell what the hell what the hell? Tears stung at her eyes, and she could feel herself starting to hyperventilate. *Calm down calm down calm down. Panic is only going to make things worse.* Skyler concentrated on her breathing, doing her best to not let the panic take over her body and drive it around like a kid on a go-kart. *You're not dead. This isn't a coffin. It's too big to be a coffin. You're not buried alive. Breathe. Just breathe.*

As her breathing fell into a steady rhythm, Skyler noticed it had also fallen in sync with another sound in the small space. More breathing—slow, soft, and regular. Like when someone's asleep. *I'm not alone in here,* she thought. Something—or someone—was in the dark with her, although they seemed to be a lot less distressed about their current predicament than she was. Skyler listened to the calm, rhythmic inhales and exhales of her mystery cellmate, coming from somewhere off to her left. The only other sound was a persistent hum that accompanied the sense of movement she felt when she first woke up.

I'm in a car, she realized. *No, not a car—a van. I'm in the back of a van.* It all made sense—the metal floor, the monotonous hum, the constant but easily forgettable movement beneath her. She was in the back of a van that was going down . . . *What? A freeway? Yeah, definitely a freeway.* There was no stopping and starting, no turning or twisting— just a slow, continuous hum of tires moving along pavement.

Skyler returned her focus to the breathing of her cellmate—a sound that was somehow soothing and familiar. *Because it is.* She had slept next to that sound for the better part of two years. It was Athena. Skyler reached across the darkness in front of her, eager to feel Athena's comforting warmth and soft fur, but the handcuffs bit into her wrists and stopped her before she could make contact. Skyler extended her fingers as far as she could, but still, Athena was just out of reach.

"Athena?" Skyler whispered, not wanting whoever was driving the van to know she was awake. No response. "Atty?

It's me. Atty, wake up." Skyler reached forward again, and again the metal handcuffs stopped her. "Shit," she muttered.

What's wrong with her? Is she dying? "Atty," Skyler whined, "please wake up. Atty, I'm scared." Athena breathed peacefully in and out, undisturbed by Skyler's desperate pleas. *It was that guy,* she thought. He had that weird gun around his shoulder. It wasn't a regular gun—a bullet gun—it was the kind that has the little fluffy dart things that go into it. It was a tranquilizer gun. *He planned this.*

Skyler began to cry, no longer able to control her fear. The silent sobs racked her body as she lay on her side in the dark van, shivering despite the stuffy heat that hung heavy in the air. She hadn't allowed herself to cry with such unabashed intensity since her parents died, and the loss of control that came with it was alarming. The space suddenly felt like it was getting smaller. The walls coming closer. She couldn't see them—maybe the walls were inching closer and closer together and she just didn't know it yet. They were creeping toward her, and soon she'd feel them pressing against her from all sides. Against her back, her feet, her head. Coming from above and below. They'd press harder and harder, crushing her, until her ribs started to snap . . .

Skyler screamed. Forget panic, this was downright terror. *"Help! Somebody! Help me! Please! HELP ME!!!"* She continued to scream until her voice went hoarse and her throat burned. It felt like a firecracker had gone off inside her mouth and live, angry sparks had tumbled down into her lungs.

The van shifted beneath her, then veered to the right. She heard a faint clicking sound somewhere up front. *The signal,* she thought. Whoever was driving just took an exit off the freeway.

Skyler lay still, her body quivering in the dark. *"Breathe. Just breathe. Breathe. Just breathe,"* she said in a soft, shaky whisper. After all the screaming, she could barely hear the sound of her own voice. She recited the mantra again and again as the van turned, slowed, and finally came to a stop.

Whatever happened, at least she wouldn't be in the dark anymore. At least she'd be able to see that the walls weren't closing in on her. At least she wouldn't feel like she was in a coffin—even if that's exactly what this space ended up becoming. For her, and Athena.

CHAPTER 45

July 4, 2019
Midday

Harsh sunlight cut into Skyler's corneas like a scalpel, and everything became a blinding, ethereal white. One of the van's back doors had just been yanked open, and there was a blurry silhouette in its place, surrounded by a brilliant halo of midday sunshine. Skyler squinted against the brightness, her eyes locked on the hazy ghoul standing in its center. She opened her mouth to cry for help, but the ghoul hopped into the van with lithe grace and slammed the door shut.

Darkness returned, if only briefly. Skyler heard the ghoul fiddling with something on the floor near the door, and then the cool light of an LED lantern filled the van, making it look almost sterile—like an operating room. "Scream all ya want, sweetheart," the ghoul said. "There's nobody out there to hear ya."

Skyler took in her surroundings in dazed bewilderment. The interior of the van was a lifeless, dreary gray. There were two windows, one on each of the rear doors, that were heavily coated with some sort of black paint. Nothing else was in the van—no shelves, no tools, nothing. Athena was sprawled out on the floor beside her, taking up the majority of the space. If the chain that bound Skyler's wrists to the floor was only a few inches longer, she would have been able to feel Athena beside her.

The ghoul was crouched in front of the back doors, watching her. She recognized the heavy work boots, the jeans, the plaid shirt—it was the same Paul Bunyan outfit he had been wearing when he hit her. The tranquilizer gun was slung over his shoulder, the metal barrel glinting in the cold light emitted from the lantern. His eyes went from Athena to Skyler.

"Please don't hurt me," Skyler stammered.

The ghoul laughed, a hearty chuckle that sounded like it belonged at a Thanksgiving dinner table more than in the back of an abductor's van. "Well, hello to you, too, chickadee." His voice was cheerful, with a Texas accent that reminded Skyler of those old western movies her dad used to watch. It was the same voice she heard above the grave in her dream. This was the monster she had been dreaming of all along. He finally found her.

"Please let me go."

Another holiday party laugh. "Now why in the name of God would I do that after I just went through so much trouble gettin' ya in here?" The ghoul's face was tan and somewhat wrinkled from too much sun, and he had a scruffy five o'clock shadow that was just starting to show the first hints of gray. His facial features bordered on charming, if not for his eyes, which were sharp, alert, and the color of melting icebergs. Skyler guessed he was probably in his late forties or early fifties.

"You, my dear, weren't all that difficult," he went on. "Went out like a light with one punch, actually. Best if ya never take up boxin', if ya don't mind me sayin'. This bitch, though . . ." He shoved Athena's hind leg with his boot. "Now *she* was a challenge."

Skyler looked at Athena to see if the kick had woken her, but the big cat hadn't so much as stirred.

The ghoul took a few steps closer to Skyler, so he was squatting over one of her legs. She tried to pull away, but the chain only gave her a few inches of movement. "What do you want?" she asked.

"How 'bout I introduce myself first? Then we can get to what I want."

Skyler stared at him with wide eyes. *Money? Rape? Murder? Need to escape. Escape. Escape. Escape.* She looked at the rear doors of the van, then back at the ghoul.

"Carter Grayson," the ghoul said. "Pleased to meet your acquaintance." Carter held out his hand to shake hers, looked down at her shackles as if he was seeing them for the first time, then raised his hands up and shrugged. A smile spread across his tan face, revealing dazzling white teeth.

"No need to introduce yourself, though," Carter said. "I already know who you are. Skyler Seabrooke of

Diamondback, Arizona. Works at the local animal shelter. Lives alone on Oak Ridge Drive, in the blue house at the end of the street—the one with the biggest yard and the most *seclusion*." He winked. "I betcha needed all that extra space for what you've been up to." Carter looked down at Athena, who was sleeping deeply. His eyes went back up to Skyler. "You've been a busy girl, haven't ya?"

Skyler pulled feebly at the chain and said nothing.

"I saw what ya had in that freezer, sweetheart. *Woo-ee!* You've been doing some crazy shit, girl. Glad I'm not on the menu." Carter considered Athena for a moment, then shifted the tranquilizer gun to his other shoulder. "By the way . . . *Benadryl?* That wasn't goin' to do shit with an animal of this size." He jerked a thumb at the tranquilizer gun. "One shot from this baby and she went out like a light. Kinda like you, actually." He flashed her another smile, making his face look almost handsome.

"Gave me a chance to look around, anyhow," Carter continued in his Texas twang. "Nice place. Needs a redecorator, but hey, to each his own. From the looks of that Cruiser, you were about to turn tail and run, though." Carter's eyes locked on Skyler's. "Now why on earth would ya wanna do a thing like that for? Leave your lovely home in such a rush. Did ya do somethin' naughty, perhaps?"

Skyler scanned the van again, looking for a way to escape. *Nothing. There's nothing.* She kept looking anyway, partially because she didn't want to give up, but mostly because she didn't want to look at the ghoul's creepy blue eyes anymore.

When she didn't respond, Carter said, "Peter Holloway. Walter Brindle. Rick Hansen. Those names ring any bells?"

Skyler's mouth fell open and her eyes involuntarily went back to Carter. "H-how?"

"Oh, honey, ya really think you were that good at coverin' up your tracks?" Carter tilted his head and looked at Skyler with mock sympathy. "God, the last guy ya got—now that was just plain *sloppy*. You're lucky I came along before the cops did." Carter fell silent, contemplating his own thoughts. "Ya know, most serial killers get better over time—not worse."

"I am not a serial killer."

"Oh, yes you are," he said. "You just don't use a knife." Carter raised his eyebrows and slowly moved his eyes from Skyler, to Athena, and then back to Skyler again.

Skyler looked away, again trying to avoid those icy blue eyes. They felt like they were penetrating her mind somehow—some sort of mental rape. Instead, she watched Athena, who went on sleeping the sound sleep of sedation.

"My employers aren't too keen with what you've been doin' in that death chamber house of yours," Carter went on. "You're certainly bringing a lot of attention onto somethin' they don't want no attention on."

"Employers?"

"Yeah! Great bunch. Definitely not too stingy on the 'ol purse strings, if ya know what I mean." He gave her an exaggerated wink.

"They paid you to kidnap me?"

"They paid me to do a hell of a lot more than that."

Skyler felt stomach acid working its way up her throat. She tried to swallow it back down, but the sour taste of bile remained. *I'm going to die. He's going to kill me, but first he's going to finish what Peter started.* Skyler could almost feel the pressure of Peter's hand clutching at her wrists, and her eyes drifted down to the shackles that had taken its place.

Carter glanced at his watch. Skyler strained to see the time, but he lowered his wrist out of view before she could make it out. "Ya know," Carter said, "I've got a little time to kill, since ya started all that hollerin' a bit ahead of my schedule." Carter's mouth smiled, but his eyes did not. "So I guess I can tell ya a little story while we wait. And since I only got a few minutes, I'd appreciate you savin' all your questions 'til the end." He raised his eyebrows and tilted his head. "Ya got it, honey bun?"

Skyler nodded once, saying nothing.

Carter settled himself onto the floor, kicking one leg up to rest on Athena's body. His other leg he stretched out between her and Skyler. Skyler pulled her leg away, not wanting it to come in contact with him. The mere thought of his touch made her stomach churn. Carter smirked as she pulled away, but he said nothing.

Once comfortable, Carter made a dramatic show of clearing his throat. "So," he began, "once upon a time, these . . . let's call them *financially endowed gentlemen* . . . got it in their noggins that makin' some extinct species un-extinct sounded like a damn good idea. I mean, they got the *money*. They got the *resources*. So why the hell not, right? Ya see, people with that kinda money aren't the same as us regular folks. Sometimes I think they do this crazy shit just to see if they can. *And boy can they*." Carter gave Athena another shove with his boot.

"Anyway, they figured out a way to get their hands on some old fossil bones or whatever they're called—for the DNA shit they needed to get started. Then they set up some sort of genetics lab and got themselves some scientists—ones that can keep their mouths shut, of course. Ya know, people will do damn near anything if the price is right. And with my employers, the price is *always* right.

"So they start havin' some success with this whole cloning thing or whatever, but then they realize they need some live animals to make this shit happen. So they buy themselves a ranch in north Texas, where all they need is a permit to have as many big cats as they want. Make themselves a little *sanctuary*," Carter said, using his fingers to make air quotes, "and they are ready to go. Buy themselves some kitty cats—lions, tigers, no bears, though—and bingo. They have just what they need to make their little science project a reality. Shove whatever they cooked up in their lab into one of them lady cats in Texas and then see what comes out. Somethin' about embryos and surrogates—I don't really pay much attention to that part.

"Now here's where I come in. 'Cause whenever a knocked up tiger or lion is ready to give birth to whatever they put inside her, I'm the one that picks her up and brings her to them so they can cut it out. They can't risk a live birth, ya see? Just in case their special project gets damaged in the process.

"Only here's the important part." Carter held up his index finger, his eyes gleaming. "They ain't got it right yet. Not even once." He twirled his finger in Athena's direction. "'Til her."

Skyler looked down at Athena, asleep and blissfully unaware of her current predicament. Skyler almost envied her.

"And here's where *you* come in, sweetheart." Carter twirled his finger toward Skyler. "'Cause everythin' was goin' fine and dandy 'til I made me a little pit stop in Diamondback. I find a secluded spot, open the back *right* on schedule, and a fucking Siberian tiger comes shooting out of the goddamn door." Carter's expression shifted, his lips pulling back from his near-perfect teeth. "It's not my fault they didn't give me the correct dosage and it woke up," he said, his voice hard and accent gone. "That's *their* job. Not *mine*."

Skyler shrank back. *Where did his accent go?*

The rage on Carter's face disappeared just as quickly as it arrived. His brow relaxed, and his charming smile returned. He gave Skyler another wink.

What the hell is wrong with this guy? she thought.

"So I track down the damn tiger," Carter said in his Texas twang. "Tranq her, get her back in the van, and then get her to my employers just like nothin' ever happened. Except something *did* happen, 'cause when they go to get their Frankenstein baby out of her, the damn bitch had *already given birth*." Carter slapped his hand on the van floor. The sound made Skyler flinch.

"We assumed the thing rotted away or an animal got hold of it. What we did not assume was that someone found the damn thing while it was still alive and took it in as a fuckin' pet!"

Skyler swallowed and looked away. When her eyes went back to Carter, he was checking his watch again.

"All the same," he said, lowering his wrist, "they started watchin' Diamondback. Hired some PI's or God knows who else to watch the area. Ya know, to keep an eye out for any strange occurrences, sightings, disappearances—you name it. They *weren't* disappointed." Carter smirked. "And that's all she wrote, sweet chickadee."

"What are they going to do with me and Athena?" Skyler asked.

"Athena," Carter said with a laugh and a shake of his head. "Cute. Very cute. Anyway, I don't know what they're gonna do with it, but I can tell ya, when they were done with the last one, there wasn't much left of it."

"That's sick," Skyler muttered under her breath.

"What's that now?"

Skyler looked up at Carter, her anger overshadowing her fear. "She's a living creature, not a science experiment."

"That's how science works, sweetheart. Think about all those bunnies with makeup in their eyes, just to make sure your mascara doesn't make you go blind. Or monkeys gettin' shot into space just to see what happens. This ain't no different than that."

Carter's watch beeped. He raised it, looked at the time, then hit a button on the side to silence it. "Story time's over, chickadee." He pushed himself up from the floor and made his way to the back of the compartment, crawling between Skyler and Athena.

Skyler heard metal scraping on metal, and a latch popping open. Her skin broke out into a wave of gooseflesh. What was up there? Was he going to kill her right now? *I should've kept my damn mouth shut,* she thought, instinctively drawing her knees up toward her chest.

Carter reemerged, but instead of approaching her, he went over to Athena. Skyler tried to see around him, but with his back to her, she couldn't make out what he was doing. She pulled against the handcuffs. "What are you—"

"Relax," Carter snapped. He returned to the area overhead, and Skyler heard the latch sound again, and more scraping on metal. "I have to give her meds every few hours to keep her under." Carter crawled back to the rear doors. He clicked the lantern off and shoved one of the doors open.

Glaring sunlight blasted into the dark space, and Skyler squinted against it. It was hot outside, and she could hear freeway traffic somewhere off in the distance. An expanse of desert surrounded them, with no people in sight. They really were in the middle of nowhere.

Carter stood just outside the van, stretching his legs and back. His shirt sleeves were rolled up, his sinewy forearms just as tan as his face.

"And what happens to me when we get to where we're going?" Skyler asked. "What are they going to do to me?"

Carter regarded her with his frigid blue eyes. He watched her for what felt like an eternity, not speaking, then shrugged.

"They don't want anythin' to do with ya, sweetheart. You're a *liability*."

Skyler felt a small, dull ache of dread, somewhere deep inside. "If you were going to kill me, why didn't you just do it back at the house?"

Another holiday laugh. "Because that, my dear, would have been *sloppy*. We already talked about this—*sloppy is bad*. If you're in there with your brains all bashed in, they're gonna know somebody else is involved. Now you're just a missin' murder suspect. And no one will be lookin' for ya in the grand state of California anyway."

"California?"

"Yessir. Have ya ever seen the Fourth of July fireworks in LA before? Simply stunnin'." Carter smiled and let the door close halfway, then jerked it open so suddenly it caused Skyler to jump. He lunged into the van, pulling something out of his pocket that glinted in the midday sunshine. Skyler barely had a chance to register that it was a knife before she felt it sliding into the flesh of her upper arm. It sliced across the width of her arm, splitting open her bare skin with ease. A wave of blood poured from the wound.

Skyler screamed, in shock as well as pain, but it was cut off by Carter's hand as he clamped it down over her mouth. The calluses on his palm were rough against her lips. A muffled whimper escaped from behind his harsh grip.

"That's for all the screaming earlier," he said without an accent, his voice as cold as his eyes. "That shit gave me a fucking headache." He shoved Skyler's face away. Her head jerked backward and banged painfully against the van floor.

"Every time you start screaming, I will come back here and do it again. Do you understand me?"

Skyler forced herself to open her eyes. She looked up at Carter and nodded her head.

Carter left the van without another word, then turned back to stare at her. He wiped the blade of the knife against his pants, then closed it and clipped it into his pocket. The hate on his face transformed into a cheerful smile as soon as the knife was tucked away, as if he had just slid on a mask.

"Alright, honey bun," he said, his accent having returned. "You hang tight. I'll be back in a few hours." He winked, then shut the back door, almost delicately. Darkness reclaimed the small space, and once again, Skyler began to cry.

CHAPTER 46

July 4, 2019
Afternoon

The monotonous drone of the van's tires resumed. Skyler lay in the darkness of her cell for an unknown amount of time, quietly weeping. *Oh God. This can't be happening. I'm going to die in here. I'm going to die in the back of a van. Nothing. I'm going to become nothing. Oh God oh God oh God.*

Her arm throbbed in steady, unrelenting waves. The sharpness of the cut had faded away, but the deep ache that followed was almost worse. Skyler had tried to stop the bleeding, but found there was nothing much she could do. Not with her hands bound, and not without a towel or cloth to press to the wound. Mercifully, the bleeding seemed to have stopped on its own.

Skyler listened to Athena's steady breathing beside her. "What should I do, Atty?" she whispered. "I want to be strong for you, but I don't know how." Skyler reached for the big cat, but the handcuffs stopped her. If only she could rest a hand on Athena, then she wouldn't feel so alone.

Skyler's mind drifted to the lantern sitting near the door. Carter turned it off when he left, but he didn't remove it. He probably figured she wouldn't be able to reach it, and even if she could, who cares? Skyler began scooting her body across the floor, further down, toward the rear doors. She bent her knees, shifted her hips downward, and then wiggled her shoulders along. *Scoot, then wiggle. Scoot, then wiggle.* Her arms started to raise up, held taut by the handcuffs. The gash in her arm screamed at her, but she fought hard to ignore it. A few more scoots and her arms were stretched over her head.

Skyler tentatively felt along the floor with her foot. Her boot touched the rear door, and she then moved it along the door's edge to where she thought the lantern might be. Her foot bumped up against something, and she heard the scrape of the lantern as it shifted on the metal floor. *Got it. Now how do I get it up to my hands?*

Skyler placed one foot on either side of the lantern, being careful not to make any noise. Her shoulders were beginning to burn, stretched tight over her head, and she felt a fresh, warm trickle of blood oozing down her upper arm. *If nothing else, at least this is getting my mind off the ghoul in the front seat,* she thought.

Ignoring the pain, Skyler flattened her back against the floor, then wrapped her hands around the chain of the handcuffs, using it for leverage. "Wish I had done more crunches when I had the chance," she whispered to Athena.

Skyler squeezed the lantern between her boots, then took a deep breath and lifted her feet into the air, bringing the lantern up with them. She kept her legs elevated as she pulled herself back to where her hands were tethered, praying silently for the lantern to not slip and fall to the floor.

The pressure in her shoulders began to ease off as she got closer to where the chain was attached. Her abdominals were burning with the effort to keep her feet hovering in the air, and to her dismay, her legs were beginning to tremble. Once she wiggled far enough to have her hands near face level, Skyler used all the strength she had left to lift her hips and bring her knees to her chest. The lantern was now directly over her face and hands.

Skyler released the lantern from between her feet. It dropped heavily into her hands and almost slipped out of her grasp. She strained to keep a hold of it, sucking air between her teeth as a fresh wave of pain shot through her upper arm. Finally, her fingers wrapped firmly around the base. She lowered her legs to the floor with a grunt of relief, then rolled onto her left side and set the lantern down. She felt around for the power button, found it, and clicked it on.

Cold light flooded the dark space. Skyler squeezed her eyes shut and waited for them to adjust to the brightness looming just behind her eyelids. Carefully, she opened one eye, and then the other. Athena's chest was directly across from her, slowly rising and falling. Skyler smiled; just the sight of the big cat was enough to dampen her fear. She reluctantly pulled her eyes away from Athena and looked down at the wound on her left arm. The cut was around three inches in length, the skin hanging open and the flesh inside a shiny, unpleasant pink. It was definitely worthy of stitches, but nothing fatal. All the same, she didn't want another one.

Skyler started looking around the van. She stretched her neck to see above her, saw nothing but the top of the van's partition wall, then pivoted herself so she could get a better view. *What was he messing around with up there? And is it still there?*

She recognized her purse, lying on its side in the upper right corner. *Why'd he bring that?* Maybe his employers wanted it. Or perhaps he just wanted all the cash from the bank that she put in there when she thought they were making a break for Mexico. Regardless, there wasn't anything in that purse that was going to help her now. Even if her phone was in there, it's not like she could call the police—they'd just arrest her and charge her with murder. And she didn't even have a pocket knife or a nail file in there that she could brandish as a weapon. *Worst serial killer ever,* she thought.

Skyler craned her neck over her shoulder, trying to see the metal thing she heard Carter moving around up there. Her eyes landed on a metal case, army green and with a silver clasp. The case looked like a toolbox of some kind, and if it *was* a toolbox, maybe there was something in there she could use to get the handcuffs off. How in the hell was she going to reach it, though? If she could just . . . twist around maybe? Crawl over Athena and end up in the front of the compartment instead of the back? Maybe that would work. *Nothing like a little bit of van acrobatics to get the blood pumping,* she thought.

Skyler began scooting herself counterclockwise, like her body was the dial hand of a clock. Her legs came in contact with Athena, and for a moment she wanted to just stay there, feeling Athena's breathing and pretending they were lying in bed at home. Skyler forced the urge away and continued her upward rotation. She crawled the rest of the way over Athena's body, grimacing when her foot sunk into her abdomen. "I'm sorry, Atty," she whispered.

Once she made it to the front of the compartment, Skyler flipped over onto her stomach and let out a sigh of relief. The metal toolbox was now resting against her leg. She got onto her knees and elbows, her hands held taut by the handcuffs overhead. She straddled the toolbox and, inch by inch, worked the box and herself toward the handcuff chain until the box was beneath her chest and she had some slack on the chain so she could use her hands.

Skyler looked down and inspected the box. It didn't appear to be anything special. Not new, but not old. She flipped up the latch and opened the lid. Her eyes widened. There were no tools inside, nor was there anything she could use to try to pick the lock of the handcuffs. Instead, there were needles. Hypodermic needles. She counted eight in all, arranged neatly in a row with packaging foam to keep them in place. Each vial was filled with cloudy white fluid, except for two, which had apparently already been used.

Skyler reached inside and carefully removed one of the syringes. She held the vial up to the light and turned it over in her hand. There were small dashes along the side, designating milliliters of liquid. The vial was a little less than half full of the opaque fluid, which came up to . . . she counted the lines as best she could in the available light . . . fourteen. Fourteen lines of fluid. Whatever that meant.

Skyler inspected each syringe, and in every filled vial the liquid came up to the fourteenth dash. *Tranquilizer,* she thought. *Already filled to the right amount.* What did Carter say earlier? That he had to give Athena meds every few hours to keep her under? And how much time had gone by since he was last in here? In the darkness, she couldn't be sure.

Skyler looked down at the syringes, not sure how to proceed. *How can this help you? Focus focus focus.* She thought about pocketing one of the needles, but the risk of sticking herself with it seemed too great. That, and she wouldn't be able to stab him with it anyway, not while she was tied down. *So what else can you do? Think think think.*

Before she realized what she was doing, she squirted half the liquid from one of the syringes onto the floor. She looked at the small hazy puddle, then back at the needle. The contents was now seven dashes lower—half the potency it was before. Skyler debated squirting a little more out, then decided against it. There was already a chance it would be noticeable that some was missing—any more and he would know for sure.

Skyler grabbed the next syringe and ejected the same amount onto the floor. Then the next syringe. Then the next. When she was done, there was a small puddle of poisoned goo beneath her. She looked down at it, her mind racing. Now what?

Screw it, she thought, and pressed her knee onto the puddle. The liquid seeped into her jeans, turning their light denim color to a darker shade of blue. She mopped up as much as she could with her pant leg, then turned her attention to the toolbox. She grasped the lid with her fingertips, carefully brought it around, and then lowered it softly into place. She flipped the latch closed, then started the arduous task of moving the toolbox back to where she found it. Skyler then crawled around the van—clockwise this time—to get back into her original position. Once she made it over Athena, she dropped back onto the floor with an exhausted huff.

Just the lantern now, she thought. She held her thumb reluctantly over the power button, not wanting to be plunged into a sea of blackness again, then switched it off with a defeated sigh.

Skyler grabbed the lantern with both hands, lifted it over her face, then brought up her feet to grab it. She lowered it carefully to the floor below her, then tried to scoot it to where she thought it had been, although the dark made it impossible to know if she had pushed it into the correct spot or not. She nudged it over a bit further, then decided that was as good as it was going to get.

Skyler readjusted herself so the handcuff chain had some slack on it and her hands were close to her chest. She lay on her side, savoring the coolness of the metal against her throbbing arm. Her wrists felt like they were on fire, and her face ached where she had been struck so many hours ago. *God, you certainly are a mess, girl.*

Skyler closed her eyes, searching out and finally finding the sound of Athena's breathing. She let the sound soothe her as best it could, trying to match her rapid inhales and exhales to Athena's slow and steady breaths. There was nothing else that could be done now. All there was left to do was wait.

CHAPTER 47

July 4, 2019
Night

The van glided up and over a bump in the road. Skyler could feel the front wheels go over, and a second later, the back wheels. *A speed bump.* She had felt the van leave the freeway at least half an hour ago, although it was hard to tell just how long in the dark. What followed was a lot of stopping and starting, which she suspected was moderate to heavy traffic along surface streets. And now a speed bump.

The van went over another bump, and then another. They had to be in some sort of parking lot or on a residential road or something. Which meant they had arrived at their destination—wherever that was.

A few hours earlier, Carter had returned to the back of the van to administer another injection for Athena. Skyler didn't dare speak, and Carter didn't bother. He wove his way between his captives, and Skyler held her breath as she heard him open the toolbox to retrieve a syringe. She waited for the accusation to come, his voice cold and flat—*You've been busy back here, haven't you, chickadee?*—followed by the knife, but neither made an appearance.

Carter injected Athena with the sedative, then returned the empty syringe to the toolbox before shoving it back up to the front of the van. Once he was finished, he stood just outside the back doors, stretching his arms overhead and giving the compartment a once-over.

"You've got blood all over ya, girl," he said. Something was different about his accent as he spoke; it now sounded more southern than Texan. *Does he even know it changed?* Skyler said nothing.

"It's just that yellin'," he went on. "It gives me such a goshdarn headache. You understand, right sugar pie?"

Again, Skyler said nothing. Her eyes went from the tranq gun on Carter's shoulder, down to the knife clipped into his pocket, and then back to the tranq gun. The sun's glow was warmer than it had been before, and the shadows longer. She guessed it was mid to late afternoon.

"Well, the cat certainly got your tongue, huh?" Carter said, and then burst out laughing. He continued to laugh until tears were streaming down his sun-worn cheeks. "Get it?" he asked through bouts of laughter. "'Cause it's a cat." He pointed at Athena and continued to laugh.

Skyler's body tensed. Was this the happy charade before the stabbing began? She watched Carter, listening to the hysterical, unnerving laughter and willing for him to not lunge back into the van. Had he noticed the syringe was different, after all? Was he just trying to trick her into thinking she had gotten away with it? Skyler watched, waiting.

"Anyhoo," he said, rubbing at his cheeks with the back of his hand, "not much longer now. See ya soon, chickadee." Carter shut the door, and Skyler could still hear him laughing outside.

The van slowed to a stop, the engine vibrating as the vehicle idled, and then silence filled the back compartment. Silence except for Athena's breathing, which had quickened in the past half hour and lost some of its steady rhythm. And Skyler was certain she heard a soft snort come from Athena's direction not too long ago. Was the sedative wearing off? Was she waking up? *God, please let her wake up. Now. Please. Right now. RIGHT NOW.*

The front door opened, then closed. Skyler felt the van rock gently on its wheels as Carter slammed the door. Footsteps crunched along the ground outside as he went around the side of the van.

"Atty," Skyler whispered. *"Wake up—"*

The rear door jerked open, Carter bounded inside, and then the door swung shut again. For a moment they were all in darkness, the sounds of breathing filling the small space— Athena's steady (but not *that* steady), Skyler's light and quick, and Carter's loud and labored. He sounded anxious about something. Skyler heard him fumble around for the lantern, find it, then click it on.

Without a word, he crouch walked between Athena and Skyler until he was hovering somewhere overhead. Skyler heard metal scraping on metal as he pulled the toolbox over to where he was crouched. She grimaced, again expecting his monotone voice to drift down from up above, but once again, the voice never came. Instead, she heard the click of the metal latch, and then a clang as he flung the lid open. From what it sounded like, Carter was in a hurry.

He shuffled over to Athena, holding one of the syringes in his hand. He lowered it toward the big cat, his hand shaking as the syringe hovered above her body. Carter let out a frustrated grunt, steadied his hand, then plunged the needle down into Athena's fur. Once the contents was injected, he sighed with relief. When he returned from the toolbox a moment later, his hands were no longer shaking.

"Goodness gracious, was that a close one!" he exclaimed in a southern drawl. He hopped out of the van and turned back to look at his captives, making a dramatic display of wiping the sweat from his brow. "There's too much damn traffic nowadays, if ya don't mind me sayin'."

Behind Carter, night had fallen—the day having died while Skyler was tied up inside the van. She searched for someone nearby to help, but with the bright light of the lantern obscuring her view, everything behind Carter was a dark haze.

"Where are we?" she asked.

Carter looked over his shoulder, then back at Skyler. "At our final destination, darlin'. But don't bother screamin' for help, 'cause no one will hear ya. Except for me, of course. And ya know how I feel about screamin'." Carter raised his eyebrows and gave her a knowing look. In the cold light of the lantern, his eyes almost seemed to glow in the dark, like a hyena's.

Skyler looked away. *Just try screaming anyway. He could be lying. There could be someone out there, somewhere. After he stabs you, maybe they'll be able to get you to a doctor in time. Just open your mouth and scream—*

Skyler scrunched her nose against a foul odor that was spilling into the van. She snorted against the stench. "What . . . *is that?*"

Carter sniffed at the air as if he was smelling a bouquet of flowers. He twirled his hand toward his face, trying to waft more of the aroma into his nostrils. He let out a satisfied sigh and looked at Skyler, grinning. "That, my sweet honey bun, is tar."

Skyler's body went rigid. *Tar? I'm dreaming. I must be dreaming.* She jerked on the handcuff chain, and the pain in her wrists assured her that she was very much awake. *He heard me dreaming then. Earlier. He must have heard me talking in my sleep. He's just messing with me.* She opened her mouth to say something, but no words came out.

Carter glanced at his watch. "Hang tight, chickadee," he said. He slammed the back door before she could reply, and Skyler heard his footsteps crunching on the ground outside. She listened to them as they faded away.

She looked over at Athena, dismayed to find her sleeping peacefully again. She should have squirted more out of the syringes. It was still too much sedative. Athena was still asleep. *Shit shit shit. I'm going to die. Oh my God, I'm going to die.* Skyler felt tears pricking her eyes. She tried to sniffle them away, but the smell of tar made her gag.

"Athena," she whispered, "you have to wake up now. We're running out of time." The big cat didn't stir, but Skyler saw movement beneath her heavy eyelids. Athena was dreaming. Feeling the embers of hope rekindling in her chest, Skyler leaned closer. Dreaming was good. Dreaming meant brain activity. Dreaming meant not comatose. *"Atty,"* she whispered louder.

The sound of footsteps returned, approaching the rear door of the van. Skyler scooted backward, as far away from the door as she could go. *Please not be Carter. Please not be Carter. Please not be—*

Carter yanked the back door open. His expression was blank, and his eyes dark and emotionless. In his hand, he held the knife. It glinted in the cold light of the lantern, looking more like an icicle than a blade. He stepped into the van, grabbed the rear door, and slammed it shut.

CHAPTER 48

April 19, 2016
7:32 p.m.

Carter Grayson stood in the back of his maintenance truck, sorting through one of the truck's side-mounted storage compartments with growing frustration. Not finding the hammer he was looking for, he shut the lid with a grunt, then turned around to search the compartment on the opposite side. This one he kept locked, and he cursed under his breath when it took him more than a few seconds to pull out the keys from the pocket of his cargo pants. Once he got the damn thing open, he sighed with relief, having found the long-handled framing hammer he was looking for. It was resting on top of a medium-sized toolbox that was shoved into the far back corner of the storage compartment. The toolbox was dinged up and not much to look at, but the lock that hung from its clasp was heavy, high quality, and most likely expensive. Carter didn't know how expensive; he hadn't been the one to purchase it.

Carter inspected the various pockets of his cargo pants, starting with the back and working his way down to the zippered pouches on either side of his legs. All were empty. He was fairly certain he had already placed all the items into the run-down toolbox, but checking twice wasn't going to hurt anyone. In fact, his employers often insisted on it. Satisfied, he shut the lid of the truck's side compartment and locked it.

Carter hopped out of the truck bed, hammer in hand, and landed gracefully on the road below. *Near perfect landing,* he thought. *Should have been a gymnast.* Except there was no way in hell he was putting on any of that stretchy fabric all the gymnasts wore. He'd rather stick to his Levi's and his plaid, or if it was a workday out at the tar pits, a plain black T-shirt and some cargo pants. Can't forget the cargo pants—the pockets they provided was the most important part of his ensemble. The most important part of the entire job he was doing out here, actually.

Carter grabbed hold of the truck's tailgate and slammed it closed. He adjusted his grip on the long handle of the framing hammer, not wanting it to bite him in the shin while he was walking. It had been a long day, and the last thing he needed was a cracked kneecap.

The fatigue Carter felt wasn't new to him; having two jobs was bound to tire a man out. First there was his secret job— *the real job*—and then there was the one he was pretending to do out at the tar pits. What a shithole. Literally. They should just call the place the pits, because that's what it was. *The pits.*

The place always stunk to high heaven—it was a never-ending assault of pungent asphalt on the nostrils, although the winding paths throughout the park had not been paved in quite some time. It was the sludge oozing out of the earth's surface that was causing the stench; it just kept seeping out of the ground in the middle of fucking LA. Why the idiot city planners built high-rises around an active tar pit was beyond him. Each day when he arrived for work, he scanned the tops of the surrounding buildings, half-expecting them to be at a slant. The tar pulls everything down eventually. *Everything.*

Carter walked along the path in the direction of Pit 91. It was the only active dig site at the La Brea Tar Pits since he started working there eight months ago. He stepped to the side to allow a family of four to pass by, giving the parents a nod and their snot-covered children a goofy grin. The little girl giggled, then ran ahead to catch up with her brother.

Carter checked his watch. It was getting pretty late for visitors. Soon the paths would be dark and the park uninhabited. There were always some people relaxing in the grass near La Brea's visitor center, but as for the many footpaths that wove their way around the tar pits, there wasn't much to see once the sun went down. Which it already had.

"This place sucks," Carter muttered under his breath, then snickered at his own joke. What wasn't funny were the long hours he had to work as a maintenance man at the pits, with pay that was mediocre at best. You'd think they'd want to shell out a little more cash for the guy that keeps the tools running at the dig site, keeps the equipment in top shape, and keeps the pit's walls from caving in—but he hadn't seen so much as a raise in his eight months of service. Not that it mattered. It wasn't the paycheck from La Brea that kept him coming back, it was the *other* paycheck. The one from his *secret* job. To La Brea, he was just the maintenance guy, fairly new and moderately experienced. To his other employers, he was the *bone guy*, and at that he was an expert. Not at identifying the bones—he couldn't tell a sloth bone from a mammoth bone, except that mammoth bones were bigger— but at getting the bones out of La Brea and into the hands of his employers. Hence the cargo pants.

Carter wished he could get some mammoth bones to his employers; he thought that would be a lot more impressive than what they were actually working on, which was essentially just a damn cat. He read about scientists in Siberia recovering DNA from the bone marrow of a woolly mammoth they found frozen in the ice, and damn did that sound exciting. It didn't sound like those people had gotten very far when it came to cloning the damn thing, though. Not like his employers. His employers had bypassed all the obligatory laws and regulations that came along with genetic engineering, all by simply not telling anyone about it. And now their prototype was going to be one of the first animals brought back from extinction, even if it was only an overgrown house cat, albeit with bigger teeth.

With all the bone fragments Carter brought his employers since beginning his exciting career as a La Brea maintenance man, he had hoped some other prehistoric monstrosity would come out of it—something bigger, at least. But alas, out of all the bones he collected, the only ones that had any viable DNA were of the cat. Something about tooth pulp, from what he overheard them saying once while he was delivering his pilfered items. Carter supposed it didn't matter if it was a mastodon or a saber-tooth—all that really mattered was the paycheck. Let them clone all the kitty cats they want, as long as he keeps getting paid.

Carter went over the small bridge that led to the gated entrance to Pit 91. On the other side of the bridge was a small wooden building that housed the pit's observation deck. He went through one of the two open doorways and into a small room with a slanted glass wall. He walked up to the window and peered down into Pit 91. Twenty feet below, wooden platforms surrounded two tar pits, one big and one small. The larger pit was the main dig site—it was where he collected all his bone pieces anyway. Large pieces of scapula and vertebrae stuck out of the tar, as if reaching up desperately to be saved from the black death surrounding them. Each visible bone had a small label next to it, identifying the different species present in the stinking, black soup.

The smaller pit off to the side was really just a square-shaped hole with a ladder. The tar below was much further down, and not nearly as easy to sift through. Carter had once considered going down there to look for bone fragments, but once he mounted the ladder he changed his mind. How far down did the tar go? Feet? Miles? To hell itself? He wasn't going to risk falling into that shit. And he knew it would be waiting for him to do just that. To fall in. To be *consumed.* He knew the tar was waiting, and that it was hungry. All those scientists and paleontologists kept taking stuff out of it, but they never bothered to put anything back in. Nature had to have a certain balance, and they were disrupting that balance with their greedy hands.

Every now and then, to Carter's delight, the tar did manage to take something back. Not long ago, he noticed a squirrel that had gotten trapped in one of the other pits in the park. He made a show of fixing up a nearby perimeter fence, so he had a reason to stay and watch. The squirrel struggled feebly to free itself, but the tar had already claimed the majority of its hind leg and there was no way out. Carter watched it for some time, an hour maybe, his lips curled into a small smile. When the squirrel stopped struggling and collapsed into the tar, defeated, Carter decided the fence was fixed, and he called it quits for the night. He drove home whistling an indecipherable tune, thinking about the squirrel's fate. He wondered if the tar was satisfied, having claimed another victim. He suspected that it was.

Carter left the observation deck of Pit 91. He walked through the doorway and over to the perimeter fence, his framing hammer dangling by his side. He shuffled through the keys on his key ring and unlocked the gate. After stepping through, he pulled hard on the gate to make sure it was securely latched behind him.

He went along the exterior wall of the observation deck, which came to an abrupt stop at the edge of Pit 91. His eyes went up to the deck's window, but there were still no parkgoers around. No strolling couples, no giggling children. He wondered what it would look like if one of those kids got stuck in the tar. One limb getting sucked down at a time as the kid slowly lost the battle to free itself. *Not giggling anymore, are you little Jimmy? Now you're screaming.*

Carter walked along the pit's edge, working his way over to the single wooden ladder that led down to the platforms some twenty feet below. His eyes scanned the platforms for lingering scientists, but it appeared everyone had already left. Pit 91 was a giant, empty grave—just the way he liked it.

During the day, the site was often bustling with activity, both with employees working inside the perimeter fence and tourists walking around its edge, peering at the scientists as if they were exotic animals in a zoo. Now, as dusk began its inevitable transition into night, the area was quiet and its human presence absent. *Just like it was thousands of years ago,* Carter thought. No people, no high-rises, no traffic. Just the animals, and just the tar. The hungry, insatiable tar.

The wooden ladder didn't make a sound as he descended into the pit—proof of his upstanding maintenance abilities. He strolled across the platforms, holding the hammer with both hands as it rested across his shoulders. The hammer was a prop to make it look like he had a purpose for being down in the pit, if anyone happened to stroll by. It was pretty late to still be at work, but if it was something important like the integrity of the pit wall, he would be greeted with looks of gratitude and not suspicion. *If* anyone happened to show up. Carter had been playing this little game for months now, and not once did he have company down in the pit at this hour— except for the dead, of course.

After poking around one of the wooden planks that lined the pit wall, assessing it for possible "damage", Carter set the hammer down and meandered over to the large pool of tar. He knelt down and began feeling along the edge of the platform, to where he had nudged a small piece of a jawbone earlier that day. He grunted with the effort, frustrated it wasn't hidden where he thought he left it. Had one of the paleontologists found it before he had a chance to pocket it? *Damn, that looked like a good piece, too. It might even have had some of that tooth pulp shit they were excited about before . . .*

"What are you doing?" a voice called out. It was coming from directly behind him, not from above, which meant whoever it belonged to was inside the pit with him and not standing at the railing up top.

Carter stood and turned around, rubbing his tar-smeared fingertips on his cargo pants. He threw a guilty grin on his face, one that was equal parts sheepish and charming. "Hey there, Toby," he said, laying on his accent extra thick. "You startled me! I just accidentally dropped my goshdarn toothpick in the tar and didn't want nobody thinkin' that our prehistoric friends had dental problems." He chuckled and shoved his hands into his pockets.

"Uh huh," Toby said, his blond eyebrows raised. He was pretty young to be a paleontologist, and Carter suspected he was probably just a grad student volunteering at La Brea in hopes it would look good on his résumé. He'd seen him around the park, always smiling and eager to please. Too eager. Like a kid trying to make his absentee father happy, even though that father didn't give two shits if the kid lived or died. It made Carter sick seeing someone act that pathetic.

Toby made Carter sick. All that "yessir, nosir" business. Grow some fucking balls and act like a man for once.

Carter's grin widened, showing off his dazzling teeth. He found that straight teeth set people at ease, while crooked teeth were seen as something undesirable—sinister even. People were fucking stupid. "What can I help ya with, Toby?" Carter asked. "I thought you woulda called it quits hours ago. Gone downtown to chase some tail, or whateva it is ya college boys do nowadays."

"I'm studying to get my doctorate in paleontology. And I'm a little bit past going out to *chase tail*."

Carter shrugged, not caring what the little shit did with his time off. From the looks of him, he probably wasn't all that good at chasing tail anyway—not quick enough, that Toby. "Okie dokie, boss," Carter said. "Well, it's gettin' late and I still got me some work to do, so if ya wouldn't mind–"

"What work?" Toby asked, an edge to his voice. Not a sharp edge, though. A sharp edge was beyond Toby's skill set. A sharp edge required balls, of which Carter was quite sure Toby was lacking.

"One of the planks on the east-facin' wall is loose. I was just comin' down to fix 'er up. I don't want this place cavin' in anytime soon, or I'm outta a job."

"I haven't seen any loose planks."

"Well, there are." Carter chuckled. "That's why I'm the maintenance man, and you're the scientist man." He took a few steps closer to Toby, mildly impressed when Toby didn't take an instinctive step backward. Maybe this little shit had some balls, after all. Small ones, of course.

Carter leaned over and picked up the framing hammer that was lying near Toby's feet. He threw it over his shoulder and brushed past Toby on his way over to the east wall. When he arrived, he made an exaggerated show of wiggling a loosened plank that was at chest level. He had pried it up long ago, just in case this exact situation presented itself. He pulled a nail from one of his cargo pockets and clamped it between his teeth. When he threw a glance over his shoulder, Toby was still standing there in the growing gloom.

"Ya need somethin' else, my man?" Carter asked, the nail waggling up and down as he talked. When Toby didn't respond, he turned his attention back to the wall. He lifted the loosened plank into place, then took the nail from his mouth and positioned it on top of the plank. He swung the hammer back, but before he could drive the nail home, Toby found his voice.

"I know what you did," he said. Not loud, not soft, but certain. "What you *have* been doing."

Carter pivoted on his heels and dropped the nail. He lowered the hammer down to his side, feeling the heavy, unforgiving weight in his hand. He tightened his grip. "Whatcha talkin' about, Toby?" He took a step forward, then another.

Toby held his ground until Carter was only a few feet away, looking down at him. He then stumbled back a step. Toby was pushing six feet, but Carter still had a few inches on him. Not to mention a hefty amount of muscle mass. Apparently, being a grad student didn't allow for much time at the gym. If the kid had ever decided to work a real job and get his hands dirty, maybe he wouldn't be so pitifully weak now. And maybe he wouldn't have felt the need to take a step back as Carter drew near.

Carter watched him, his face blank and his eyes locked on Toby's. The kid shrunk back a few more steps, but still refused to drop the subject. Probably because he was so goddamn eager to please—not Carter, but the La Brea head honchos.

"You've been stealing," Toby said, holding his chin up and puffing up his pathetically small chest. "Bones from the tar pit. I've seen you do it."

"Have ya now?" Carter asked, his voice low as he took another step toward the hard-willed Toby.

Toby trembled, but instead of retreating to the ladder, he bunched his delicate hands into fists. "Those are important discoveries," he said. "And they are the property of La Brea. You have no right to sell them or put them up in your house, or whatever you're doing with them."

Carter smirked. This kid actually did have balls. "Is that whatcha think I'm doin'?"

Toby shrugged, flustered. He was losing some of his bravado. "I don't know why you would steal them. But I'm not going to let it happen anymore. I'm going to tell La Brea, and if you don't return everything you stole, then I bet you're going to be hearing from the police pretty soon."

Carter's voice fell flat. "You know, for being a graduate student, you really aren't that smart, are you, Toby?"

"Wh-why's that?" Toby stammered. He took a few generous steps backward, his main objective transitioning from confronting Carter to getting out of Pit 91.

"All that time studying, and yet you think it wise to come to a deserted location, unaccompanied and unarmed, to threaten somebody." Carter continued walking forward, matching the speed of Toby's retreat.

Toby's hands found the ladder, and he clung to it like a life preserver. "Wh-where did your accent go?" Instead of waiting for a reply, Toby turned and tried to scramble up the ladder. He missed the second rung, slipped, and almost fell off completely.

Carter reached out and placed a hand on Toby's shoulder, steadying him. "You're not welcome here," Carter said. Toby's body tensed under his hand, and he looked over his shoulder to meet Carter's eyes. "This is a cemetery, you idiot. We're all dead down here."

Carter swung the hammer down in one swift motion. It connected with Toby's temple, and the kid fell to the platform below like a bag of rocks. *Or a bag of bones,* Carter thought as he looked down at the grad student's body.

Blood gurgled out from where the hammer entered Toby's skull, and Carter had to press his boot down on the kid's back to dislodge the tool from the side of his head. It made a meaty crunch as it broke free, like the sound of a coconut opening.

An idea shot through Carter's head, and with it a sense of excitement he rarely felt. He knelt down over Toby's body and turned the kid's head so he could get a good look at his face. Toby's brown eyes were open and fixed straight ahead. Carter looked at the hole in Toby's skull, where a gray, jelly-like substance was spilling out along with the blood. The kid was dead. With only one hit from the hammer? *How pathetic,* Carter thought.

Carter's eyes darted up to the observation deck, but there was still no one watching beyond the glass. Satisfied, Carter leaned down and grabbed the kid's ankles. He dragged Toby toward the pool of tar, barely breaking a sweat as he moved Toby's dead weight. When he reached the edge of the larger tar pit, Carter changed course and instead went to the smaller, deeper pit beside it. The large pool was too risky, since it was the main source of all the fossil finds. He didn't want the young, valiant Toby being the next discovery.

Carter tossed Toby's body into the smaller pit, then peered over the side. Toby landed with a heavy plop at the bottom, and Carter watched, fascinated, as the body started its descent into whatever lay below. Carter sighed wistfully when the tar claimed an arm without even an ounce of struggle from its victim; he wished Toby had still been alive when he went in. Carter thought of the squirrel and realized he wanted to— *needed to*—give the tar something living. The struggle was important. He could see that now. Unfortunately, both Carter and the tar would have to settle for a dead body. This time.

It was full dark by the time Toby's body disappeared, and the depths of Pit 91 had become a treacherous maze of buckets, tools, and equipment boxes. Luckily, Carter already knew the way, since he had spent many evenings inside the pit's walls, pocketing bones and "maintaining things". He went back to the edge of the larger pool, reached beneath the platform, and within a minute found the piece of jawbone he had been searching for before he was so rudely interrupted. He wiped the majority of the tar off on his pants, studying the white piece of history in his hands. Part of a tooth was attached to the jaw fragment, and Carter felt a wave of satisfaction that made up for Toby's swift demise. Maybe this piece had that tooth pulp stuff his employers always seemed to be excited about. If so, there might be a little bit of a bonus coming his way. The attached piece of tooth had a sharpened edge. Carter ran his thumb over it, pleased. The edge was blunted after all the centuries it spent trapped beneath the tar, but Carter imagined that it was razor-sharp before the cat that it belonged to got trapped and met its fate. Way before humans took over the globe and constructed high-rises alongside a mass grave of black death.

Carter zipped the jawbone into one of the larger pockets of his cargo pants, grabbed his framing hammer, and looped it through his belt. Looks like his long day was about to get even longer, since he now had a bit of cleanup to take care of. If Toby was so eager to please, you'd think he could have bled a little less all over the damn dig site.

When Carter reached surface level, his cleanup complete, he took one final look down into Pit 91. He wondered if Toby's bones would surface anytime soon, or if it would be another ten-thousand years before the college kid made another appearance. Whatever. It didn't matter. What happened to Toby's remains wasn't his problem, Carter thought. After all, he was just the maintenance man.

CHAPTER 49

July 4, 2019
Sometime Before the Fireworks

"Why are you telling me this?" Skyler asked, her voice soft. She was sitting on the floor of the van, her knees pulled up to her chest and her wrists shackled between her feet. She was pretty sure she was going to die tonight, and she wanted some sort of barrier between her body and the man in front of her, even if the only thing she could use as a shield were her own legs. *He wouldn't tell me a story about murdering someone unless he was certain I wouldn't be around to tell anyone else.* She pulled her knees closer to her body, fighting the urge to cry.

Carter was leaning against the back door of the van, one leg kicked out and his arm casually draped over the opposite knee. The light from the lantern danced across his face as he moved, much like a fire does when people are telling ghost stories around a campfire—only this fire was made of dry ice and permafrost. He idly flipped his knife open and closed, and Skyler could still see traces of her blood on the blade.

"Just tryin' to pass the time," Carter said with a shrug. "I thought you'd like me to tell ya a little bedtime story, chickadee." He winked. "Sorry, but I don't know no *romantic comedies.*"

Skyler saw movement out of the corner of her eye. She stole a quick glance at Athena, whose eyelids fluttered briefly, then settled back into place. "Pass the time until what?" she asked, wanting to keep Carter's focus away from the big cat.

"The fireworks, silly! It's the Fourth 'o July, in case ya forgot." He rapped his knuckles on the side of his head. "One too many hits on the noggin, I reckon?"

Skyler swallowed, although her mouth was so dry there wasn't much to swallow. Outside, she could hear a few faint voices somewhere off in the distance. She wondered if they would hear her if she screamed, but the sight of her blood on Carter's knife was enough to stop her from trying.

"Why'd you bring me here? If you were always planning to—" she stopped. She didn't want to say the words. If he was by any small chance not planning to kill her, she certainly didn't want to put the idea in his head. "Why here?"

Carter looked up from beneath his brows, a smirk on his face and his eyes as emotionless as melting glaciers. "*That* I did for me," he said. "Almost everythin' I do is for my employers, but this little field trip was my idea."

Athena's eyelids fluttered again. *Come on, Atty. Please wake up. I've never needed you more than I do right now. I'll even take what Peter was going to do to me over getting stabbed to death. Please wake up, Atty. Please.* "I don't understand," she said to Carter.

"It probably woulda been less risky to toss ya in the desert somewhere along the way," Carter said. "But gosh, I just couldn't help but bring ya here. It seemed almost *poetic* that the thing that brought your precious kitty cat into existence is the same thing that takes you out of it. *Fuckin' Shakespeare!*" He slapped his hands down on the floor of the van. Skyler winced against the sound. Beside her, Athena's eyes opened, her pupils unfocused, then closed again.

"The same thing . . ."

"You remember the guy I tossed in the tar?"

"Hard to forget," Skyler muttered.

Carter laughed, one short, harsh bark of laughter. Athena's eyes opened, and her pupils focused on Skyler. Skyler extended her fingers and flattened her hand as best she could without being noticeable. *Oh God, Atty. Please wait until his back is turned. Wait until he goes to open the door. Please please please.* Athena's eyes drifted closed again.

"Pretty neat stuff," Carter went on, " but not very excitin'." He shook his head regretfully. "He was already dead, ya see? He just . . . disappeared. No strugglin'. No beggin'. Nothin'. Pretty *anticlimactic*. But *you* . . . you're goin' in alive. Now *that* is what I call excitin'."

Skyler gaped at him. "You're going to . . ." She started to hyperventilate. "You're going to . . . *throw me in the tar?*"

"Yessir," Carter said with a nod of his head.

Skyler felt on the verge of panic. *In the tar. Down into the tar. Pulled down by the tar. Pulled down . . .* "You don't have to," she blurted out. She shook her head rapidly from side to side. "You don't have to do this. I won't tell anyone, I swear. You don't have to. *I swear.*" She was rambling, but unable to stop herself. She had hoped it wouldn't come down to her begging the ghoul for her life, but here it was. She looked down at Athena, but her eyes were still closed. *"Please. Don't."*

Carter opened his mouth to speak, but before he could, a muffled *boom* rippled through the air outside. Carter closed his mouth and pressed a finger to his lips. He cocked his head to the side and listened. Another *boom*, and then a few seconds later, another. He laughed, a quiet, composed laugh that sounded almost polite. "Ah, it's time," he said, and smiled.

"Please . . . No . . ." Skyler begged. Another *boom* went off, somewhere overhead.

"The fireworks," Carter said, acting as if he hadn't heard her. "They've begun."

CHAPTER 50

July 4, 2019
9:00 p.m.

Carter lurched up from where he was sitting and moved quickly across the van. He squatted over Skyler, grabbed her by the shoulder, then struck her in the face. His fist collided with her cheekbone, just shy of her nose.

Skyler cried out, the sound piercing in the small space. Carter released her shoulder and she collapsed onto the floor, trying to cover her head before he swung his fist down again. Instead, he brought his knee in, hard and fast. It hit her squarely in the gut, and a firework of pain exploded inside of her. She tried to scream, but only a gurgling whimper came out.

Skyler lay on her left side, unmoving, as Carter hovered over her. *Oh God. I'm going to die. No no no. I'm not ready.*

Please no. She squeezed her eyes shut, bracing for the knife that would surely come next.

Carter pulled something out of his pocket, but it wasn't the knife. Skyler heard the delicate tinkle of metal jingling together. *The handcuff keys.* She opened her eyes and looked past Carter's boot, which was only inches away from her bleeding nose. Athena was looking directly at her. Her eyes were wide, and Skyler could see fear and confusion lurking below glints of swirling amber.

Carter wrapped his hand around Skyler's wrist and pulled her arms up as far as the chain would allow. She grimaced as the metal cuffs dug in. Even worse, the cut on her arm issued a sharp stab as the skin was stretched taut and the wound reopened.

Athena tried to lift her head, but was only able to raise it a couple inches before it dropped back down to the floor. Carter's back was to the big cat, and he didn't notice her movements as he messed with the chain of the handcuffs. Skyler felt a click on one of her wrists, and then, mercifully, the metal was pulled away. She kept her gaze locked on Athena, who lay still and watched her with frightened eyes.

The second handcuff fell away a moment later, and Skyler's arms collapsed onto the van floor along with the metal chain she was no longer attached to. More *booms* went off overhead. Skyler tried to lift her hands to ward off any additional blows that might be coming, but before she could defend herself, Carter's arm was beneath her shoulder and he was pulling her up from the floor. He dragged her toward the exit, moving her dead weight with not so much as a grunt.

Skyler stole one more glance at Athena as she was removed from the van. Athena's eyes followed her out, but she was unable to move her head.

The van door slammed closed, just inches from Skyler's face. Carter removed his arm from where it was supporting her, then used it to shove her against the back door. Skyler's shoulder collided with the van, and she felt a bolt of pain shoot up her neck. She tried to scream—maybe someone was close enough to help her now—but just more garbled whimpering came out. He must have hit her diaphragm when he kneed her in the stomach. She slouched against the van door, curled in at the waist, with her left arm pinned behind her. It was a struggle to remain standing, but she didn't want to fall to the ground, where he would almost certainly kick her. Or stab her—can't forget about that one.

Skyler looked up, searching for help. She expected to be standing in some sort of parking lot, but instead, the van was parked alongside a narrow, deserted road. A maintenance truck was parked a few yards behind the van, its lights off and cab empty. There was nobody nearby.

To the left, palm trees butted up against the road, their trunks disappearing into a scattering of bushes and shrubs. Skyler squeezed her eyes shut and reopened them, trying to allow her vision to adjust to the darkness around her, but all she could see were the blurry shapes of the surrounding foliage.

Boom. The sky exploded with pink light, revealing a black, welded wire fence just beyond the palm trees. And what was past the fence? Skyler squinted, straining to see what lurked on the other side. *Boom.* The fence lit up blue, and behind it . . . a pond? A lake? *Boom.* No . . . a tar pit.

Carter stood over Skyler, dwarfing her small body as she leaned against the back door of the van. He was close enough for her to smell his sweat, and she could hear his heavy breathing above her head. His left hand was jammed inside his pocket, searching for something—*the knife?*—and his right hand was holding the tranquilizer gun.

Skyler felt dizzy and disoriented. Something crackled overhead—*Rice Krispies,* she thought—and the wire fence was illuminated again. Beyond the fence, a dark lake that did not reflect the fireworks up above. Apparently, the tar could swallow anything—mammoths, saber-toothed cats, even the light.

Her head throbbed dully, her vision blurring with each throb. Her arm was still behind her back, pressed against the van's door, and she started feeling along its smooth surface. Her fingers stumbled upon grooved metal and stopped. *The license plate.*

Carter cursed above her. "Fucking keys. I just had them . . ." He kept the tranq gun aimed at her chest as he struggled to search his pockets with the opposite hand. He reached across his body and jammed his left hand into his right pocket, grunting from the effort.

The keys? Shit, he's gonna lock the door. Behind her back, Skyler's hand crept up past the license plate. She brought her arm as high as her shoulder would allow, and her hand wrapped around a long, cylindrical piece of plastic. *The door handle.* She curled her fingers around the handle, her left shoulder threatening to pop from its socket. She extended her legs an inch, then two, moving slowly to not bring attention to what she was doing. The pain in her shoulder eased off as she rose up. *Don't let him lock the door. C'mon. Hurry hurry hurry.*

Keys jingled in front of her, followed by a relieved sigh from Carter. *Boom.* The surrounding trees lit up a sickening shade of red. Skyler thought of all the red on her living room floor. All the red in her bathtub. All the red on her daddy's tools. Her thumb slid over a button on the side of the handle. *The door latch.* She pressed down hard. The keys rattled as Carter selected what must have been a key fob, because a second later there was a clunking sensation directly below Skyler's thumb as the lock engaged. She felt the rear door of the van push an inch into her back. It was open. *Bingo.*

Carter's rough hand began to feel around her chest, not to grope her, but to get a hold of her again. He was having trouble seeing in the dark as well. *That's the problem with murder,* she thought. *You need a dark spot so nobody can see you, but then you can't see either.*

Carter found Skyler's arm and jerked her forward. She stumbled over her own feet and would have fallen to the ground if he hadn't stopped her. He scooped his arm around her waist and used his other hand to press the tranquilizer gun into her rib cage. He spun them around, toward the trees, the fence, and the dark lake beyond.

Boom. Everything turned green, then faded to black again. Darkness crept into the corners of Skyler's vision, somehow darker than the blackness of her surroundings.

Unconsciousness threatened to take her away. *Don't pass out, don't pass out, don't pass out,* she thought. *If you pass out now, you'll never wake up.* Her head felt swimmy, and she was having difficulty wading through the muck in her mind. She still felt dazed from the beating in the van, almost like she had one too many beers at the bar. She stumbled over her feet again and again as they walked through the trees, Carter having to keep her from falling multiple times.

Carter came to a stop when they reached a gate in the fence. "Don't you fucking move," he hissed into her ear, "or I'll stab you right here."

Skyler grimaced woozily at the sound of his voice. *No accent. That can't be good,* she thought. *Time to focus. COME ON. This is literally life or death right now. Yours and Atty's.* The thought of Athena sobered her mind a little, and the dark haze at the corners of her vision began to clear.

Boom. The lock on the gate lit up a brilliant purple. Carter jammed one of the keys on his key ring into the lock, and the gate clicked open. "How . . ." she mumbled, unable to articulate the rest of the question.

"I work here, remember," he said into her ear, and dragged her through the fence.

CHAPTER 51

July 4, 2019
9:05 p.m.

Timmy Palmer sat atop his daddy's shoulders, watching the fireworks as they burst and sparkled above his head. His eyes twinkled, reflecting the rainbow of colors as they shimmered across the LA sky. He wasn't sure why his parents picked Hancock Park to watch the fireworks this year. He thought it was a funny sounding name—Hand Cock. His friends at the playground had giggled endlessly with him about it. But it wasn't that bad of a place, just another city park really—except for the stinky smell. It smelled like when they repaved the road outside their house earlier that year. His daddy had been mad about it, saying something about tacks and dollars, although Timmy wasn't sure how those two things were connected. Either way, this was how it smelled at their house when they were paving—it smelled just like Hand Cock Park.

There were other families in the grass, too, all pointed in the same direction. Some were sitting and others were standing, all craning their necks to look at the sky. Two grown-ups were kissing—gross—and it looked like their faces were painted different colors when the fireworks went off. Timmy looked around at the other people, little boys and girls, mommies and daddies, and even some old, wrinkly people. He glanced over his shoulder, enjoying his high vantage point from his daddy's shoulders. He couldn't wait until he was this tall for real. He'd be able to see all the way to Tim Buck Too—somewhere he always wanted to go since *his* name was in the title.

Behind him, in the direction of the stinkiness, was a black lake surrounded by a tall fence—a *tar pit* was what his daddy had called it. They walked past it on their way into Hand Cock Park. At the front of the lake there were some plastic, furry-looking elephants that were standing inside the tar. Timmy didn't like the way they looked—they were scared. His butt-faced sister said it was cool, but he didn't think so.

He was about to turn around and watch some more fireworks when motion on the opposite side of the lake caught his attention. There were people inside the fence! He didn't know they were allowed to go in there! Why didn't his daddy bring him inside earlier? Maybe the *tar pit* was cooler up close. Those people certainly seemed to think so. The lady was so excited that she was even on her hands and knees to get a closer look!

Timmy narrowed his eyes, studying the people inside the fence. On second thought, that lady looked kinda sick. The way his mommy looked after she found out his grandma and grandpa were coming to stay with them for a week. She was *drunked*—that's what his friend Kevin said it was called.

Timmy didn't want to watch them anymore. Not with how drunked that lady was. She needed to go to bed, not look at the *tar pit*. Timmy turned around and looked back up at the sky. More fireworks went off—three or four in a row this time! "Wow!" Timmy exclaimed, and his daddy patted his leg in agreement. Standing beside them, his mommy wrapped her arms around his butt-faced sister, and they all watched the show together.

CHAPTER 52

July 4, 2019
9:05 p.m.

Skyler looked down at the black, inky water. It wasn't the heavy, viscous slime from her dream—groundwater and rain had thinned it down. Swirls of rainbow-colored oil drifted across the top. Somewhere off in the middle of the lake, a large bubble floated to the surface and burst. The lake gurgled, then returned to stillness.

Carter shoved Skyler forward, and she stumbled and fell to her knees just inches from the lake's edge. Her hands hit the soil, which felt slick and sticky at the same time. She tried to crawl backward, away from the tar, but Carter pressed his boot into her hip and shoved her forward again. Her hands sunk into the cool, oily blackness of the lake, the raw skin on her wrists screaming as tar and oil seeped inside. "If you start yelling, I will stab you in the back," Carter whispered behind her, his voice cold and emotionless. "Now stand up and start walking."

Skyler felt paralyzed, stuck in the tar even though she hadn't entered it yet. Her fear felt like a tar of its own making, and it was pulling her down. She looked over her shoulder to where Carter was standing. He was just beyond her feet, with the tranquilizer gun aimed at her back. The knife was clipped into his pocket, the metal clasp glinting as a firework boomed overhead. In the distance, she could hear patriotic music playing.

Skyler's eyes panned the fence line that wrapped around the lake. To her left, beyond the fence, people were standing in a grassy area. That was where the music was coming from. She could see a little boy sitting on top of a man's shoulders and pointing up at the sky. All the people were far away and none of them were looking in her direction.

Skyler opened her mouth to cry for help, but thought of the knife and how easily it slid into her arm. It would go just as easily into her stomach, her back, her neck. She'd rather drown than be stabbed. Maybe the tar was a mercy; maybe that's what the dream was trying to tell her all along.

Carter shoved her again, harder this time. Skyler's arms, still weak and sore from being chained down for so long, gave out from underneath her. She fell onto her stomach, turning her head at the last second to keep tar and oil from coating her face. She felt the slimy water seep into her shirt and soak the front of her jeans.

"It's waiting," Carter snapped. "Now get up and go into the goddamn tar."

Skyler pushed herself back up to her hands and knees. Her arms quivered, and her hip ached from where he had kicked her. She felt like she was going to fall forward again, and widened her arms to keep her balance. Her right hand landed on something hard, just inches below the inky surface of the lake. Her fingers curled around it. A rock. At least the size of a softball.

Boom. Boom boom. Red, purple, and gold filled the sky. The lake gurgled, as if in protest of the fireworks, and more bubbles erupted from its center in what sounded like a wet belch. The chorus to "God Bless the U.S.A." drifted across the park.

"Let's go," Carter ordered. "It's hungry." He took a step forward, his boot sinking into the onyx-colored sand, and grabbed Skyler by the hair. He yanked her backward, pulling her up to her knees in one violent tug. The rock in Skyler's hand made a heavy *thup!* sound as it dislodged from the tarry sediment below. She dug her fingers into its jagged surface and pressed it to the front of her thigh, out of Carter's view. He gave her hair another agonizing tug, and she stumbled onto her feet.

Carter came up behind her, his body pressed against her and the barrel of the tranquilizer gun digging into the small of her back. "Last chance. Otherwise I will gut you where you stand," he spat into her ear. His breath felt hot and sticky against her neck.

Boom. Green sparkles. *Boom boom.* Pink and yellow flashes.

Skyler took one tentative step forward, and then another. Her feet sunk an inch into the tar, liquid creeping up the sides of her boots and coating their tops with oil. Skyler could feel the seat belt snakes coiling around her. She stood there, frozen in place, unable to step forward and unable to fight back. She could feel Peter's weight pressing down on top of her.

Boom. Blue splashes. *Crackle.* White sparkles.

When she didn't take another step, Carter jammed the gun between her shoulder blades, causing her to yelp. "Time's up—"

A grumbling sound, followed by a harsh snort. *Boom.* Orange starbursts. Followed by a low, drawn-out moan. *Crackle.* Gold glitter. Then a deep, guttural yowl coming from somewhere behind them. *Athena.*

Skyler's muscles tensed. This wasn't just her life Carter wanted to take away—it was also Athena's. And Skyler had promised Atty she would keep her safe. Today was not the day she would break that promise. She would *never* break that promise.

Another groan, somewhere beyond the fence. The pressure from the gun lessened between her shoulder blades. Carter's voice, no longer directed at her, but somewhere off to her left: "What the hell is tha—"

Skyler didn't hesitate. She pressed into the soil with her right leg and whirled her body around to the left. As she did so, she brought the rock up with her right hand in a forward sweeping motion, holding it out and letting her momentum carry it forward.

Time slowed down as she traveled through her arc of motion. The fireworks seemed to last longer, and their booms were a cacophony in her ears. Then Carter came into view. He had been looking over his shoulder, and was now turning his head back toward her, a startled expression contorting the features of his face. Their eyes locked briefly, both reflecting glints of silver from the light up above, and then the rock connected with Carter's temple. It made a wet, heavy crack as it collided with the side of his head, and then Carter's legs went out from under him. He crumpled down to the soil as if all the bones in his legs had shattered at once. The tranquilizer gun flew from his hand and landed in the lake some ten feet away. *Thumk!*

Skyler lurched for the gun, but it disappeared below the surface before she could reach it. Her feet slipped in the muck, and she almost fell forward into the lake. She jerked her body backward, managed to keep from falling, but ended up dropping the rock in the process. *"Shit!"* she exclaimed, and fell to her knees to retrieve it. Black oil soaked into her jeans. Her hands searched blindly below the surface, but she couldn't feel the rock anywhere. More fireworks boomed overhead, casting brilliant splashes of color across the park. Panicked, Skyler continued her search. She needed to hit him again, and again, and again. *But where the hell was the rock?*

Carter garbled something from the ground beside her, and she felt his fingers slide down her leg, searching for purchase. He was lying on his side, the knife hidden somewhere beneath him. Skyler launched herself out of the lake, avoiding his grasp, and half ran, half crawled away from the tar pit.

She broke into a full run as she neared the fence, throwing one terrified glance over her shoulder. Carter was stumbling up to his knees, his hand pressed against the side of his head. In a crackle of white light, Skyler saw the side of his face was now painted red. *Good.*

She bolted through the gate, screaming as she went. *"Help! Somebody please! HELP!"* Fireworks went off in rapid succession, followed by Rice Krispies crackles that spanned the LA sky. She looked over at the grassy clearing where the people were standing, hoping someone had heard her, but no one had so much as turned to look in her direction. Behind her, Carter was yelling something. She couldn't make out the words over "America the Beautiful", but was certain he wasn't using an accent.

Skyler ran to the van, forgetting about the people in the park. They wouldn't reach her in time, even if they did hear her. She collided with the side of the van, leaving two black handprints smeared on its white surface. She stumbled around to the back and grabbed the door handle. *Please be open. Please be open.* She yanked hard on the handle, and the door swung open and ripped free from her hand. It bounced on its hinges and whipped back around. Skyler threw her arm up to keep it from hitting her in the face.

"Atty!" she cried. *"We have to go RIGHT NOW!"* Skyler looked into the van, prepared to drag Athena out if she had to. Away from the dripping red ghoul that was creeping up behind them. Skyler reached inside with one blackened hand, then stopped. The van was empty.

CHAPTER 53

July 4, 2019
9:09 p.m.

Carter Grayson got to his feet, spitting out every curse word he could think of in a long, profane slur of rage. The rage coursed through him like fire, causing his hands to shake and his body to go rigid. He reached up to his aching temple and felt the slippery slime of fresh blood. *That bitch.* He glanced over his shoulder, and in a flash of blue light, saw her slip through the gate. *That BITCH.*

Carter looked down at his feet, searching for what she had hit him with. Nothing was there—just black, stinking water. And where the hell had his tranq gun gone? He dropped it when the bitch hit him, but where did it land? The lake was dark and oily, revealing nothing below its surface.

Carter let out another slew of curses, then steadied himself. His shoulders relaxed and his hands unclenched, the fire inside dwindling down to mere embers. Having regained his composure, he started making his way back to the fence. He threw one look toward Hancock Park to see if anyone was watching him, but all the idiots in the distance were still standing with their backs to the lake, watching the fireworks. A throbbing pain thudded in his temple, synchronized with his rapid pulse. And that damned music wasn't helping. He paused, waiting for the nausea and lightheadedness to subside. Once they did, he kicked the gate open and stepped through.

She couldn't have gotten far, and even though he'd lost the tranq gun, he still had his knife. He'd rather use the knife anyway. That murderous little bitch deserved to bleed out. She made him bleed, and oh boy was he going to make her bleed.

Carter walked toward the van, wiping the dripping blood from his face with his shirt sleeve. He needed to hurry. He wanted her tracked down and dying before the fireworks were over—dead would be even better. Once the fireworks were done, people would be much more apt to notice him. Especially after what the bitch did to his face.

Carter reached the van and saw there were black, smeared handprints on the side panel. She had definitely been here. A crackle of silver and gold illuminated the sky, and Carter stopped mid-breath. He held the knife at his side, his hand twitching nervously.

Why was the door ajar? Why in the name of God was the back door of *his* van ajar? He had locked it. *He had fucking locked it!* Carter shot out his hand and pulled the door the rest of the way open, ready to stab the bitch if she had somehow managed to get inside and was now trying to drag out her drugged cat. She wasn't there, though, and neither was the cat.

Carter said nothing. He stared into the empty compartment, tightening his grip on the knife. *That bitch.* He hurled himself inside the van, grabbed the box of syringes, and shoved himself back out. *I can't lose another one. First the tiger, and now this. They won't just fire me, they'll have me killed.* He slammed the door, his grip never loosening from the knife.

When the next firework went off, Carter scanned the ground for any sign of which way the bitch had gone. There were black footprints, faint but visible, heading further into the park. Maybe she was following the damn cat. If he could find them together that would be a hell of a lot easier than tracking them down individually. A knife for the bitch and a needle for her cat. And then everything would be right as rain.

A green explosion lit up the sky, and Carter used the fading, eerie green light to follow the tar-smeared footprints deeper into La Brea.

CHAPTER 54

July 4, 2019
9:09 p.m.

Skyler stood at the rear entrance to the van, looking into the dark, empty compartment. She knew Athena had woken up, but where the hell had she gone? She couldn't have gotten far, not until the effects of the sedative had completely worn off.

Skyler scanned the surrounding area. The lake was to her right, where she could hear Carter groaning. Far up ahead, she could see the grassy park and the people that were watching the fireworks display. *Not that way,* she thought. If Athena was hurt and frightened she would be looking for a place to hide. To her left, a small path broke off the narrow road and led down into the trees. *Boom.* Carter's groaning, closer this time. Skyler's eyes followed the path as it disappeared into the darkness. *That's gotta be . . .* The fence creaked as the gate swung open. *Boom.*

Skyler sprinted down the path, shadows engulfing her as she entered the heavy foliage. She followed the darkened trail as best she could as it cut through the trees and bushes. She swerved to avoid colliding with the branches of a tree, stumbled and nearly fell over a protruding rock, and then came to a clumsy stop when she emerged on a different, better lit footpath. *There are so many trails. How am I going to pick the right one?*

Another perimeter fence lay before her, wrapped around more tar pits. It gave La Brea the impression of a zoo, but with tar pits inside the enclosures instead of animals. Occasional lampposts casted circles of golden light onto the walkways, but otherwise the park was drowning in shadows.

Left or right? Left or right? The music was coming from the right, darkness and silence from the left. *She would have gone left,* Skyler thought. *Into the dark. To a hiding place.*

Skyler turned and bolted into the darkness. She ran blindly down the paths, picking the darker option each time she came to a fork in the road. She stumbled upon a short bridge which led to a small, wooden building. A sign was in the center, with open doorways on either side. *Dark doorways. A hiding place.* Skyler ran across the bridge and over to the building. The sign between the doorways identified the area as Pit 91.

"Atty," Skyler called in a harsh whisper. She was about to go inside the building, when she noticed another one of those perimeter fences. The gate was locked, but low to the ground some of the fence had been bent inward, leaving a two-by-three-foot opening. Tufts of tawny fur were caught in a few of the metal prongs on the fence.

Skyler scurried over to the fence and grabbed a tuft of fur. She rubbed it between her fingers, recognizing the downy fuzz of Athena's undercoat. *"Atty,"* Skyler whispered, louder this time. She dropped to her knees, not noticing the tarry smears she left on the ground, and crawled through the hole in the fence. Pavement gave way to dirt on the other side, and Skyler felt small rocks scraping at her palms as she wiggled the rest of the way through.

Once inside, she rose to her feet and followed the fence line, using it to guide her through the darkness to whatever was inside Pit 91.

CHAPTER 55

July 4, 2019
9:12 p.m.

Carter followed the winding path, sucking his breath in and out through his teeth. His head throbbed from where the bitch hit him, and blood kept dripping into his eye, causing it to sting and blur. He tilted his head to the side and used his shoulder to wipe the blood away. In his left hand, he carried the box of syringes. In his right, the knife—blade open and at the ready. This shit was ending tonight. How he was going to drag the goddamn cat back to his van was beyond him, but he had to solve each problem as it came. And right now, getting his knife into the bitch's throat was his top priority.

Carter arrived at another pit fence and stopped in the center of the path. Going right would lead him back to the people, and since she already had that chance and didn't take it, he decided to turn left and head deeper into the park. Just more tar pits going this way, including the one where he got the cat bones that started all this shit.

That's it—Pit 91. That's where it would have gone, and the same with her. It didn't get much more dark and secluded than Pit 91, not at this time of night. It's where he would have taken her in the first place, if only he could have gotten his van near it. This could work out in his favor; the pit was closed off to the public and he'd be able to take his time down there. And boy oh boy, did he want to take his time. All he had to do was drug the cat and then he could take all the time he wanted with the bitch. All the time he wanted. She was still going to end up in the tar, after all, he thought with a grin. Just more bones for the prehistoric ooze.

CHAPTER 56

July 4, 2019
9:12 p.m.

Skyler walked along the exterior of the small building, which came to an abrupt halt at the edge of an immense, square-shaped hole in the ground. A railing wrapped around the hole's edge, with the building—apparently an observation deck—on one side and a wooden ladder on the other. Down below the ladder: darkness.

Skyler hurried along the railing, heading toward the ladder. As she went, she scanned the bottom of the pit, which was some twenty feet below. There were wooden platforms down there, positioned around the tar, making it look like a grotesque swimming pool. Boxes and buckets were scattered about the platforms, making it difficult to search for Athena among the debris. And with so little light down there, Skyler had to wait for each new firework to erupt to see into the darkened corners and crevices.

A particularly bright—and loud—firework lit up overhead, and Skyler caught a brush of movement in the far corner of the pit. She wrapped her hands around the railing, leaning over the edge as far as the handrail would allow. "Athena!" she called down into the depths of Pit 91. Nothing.

"Atty!" Skyler yelled. *Where did she go?* Skyler called out again, nearly screaming this time, and saw two golden globes of light emerge, hovering in the far corner underneath the observation deck. Cat's eyes, reflecting what little light was available.

She watched the eyes, straining to make out Athena's shape in the darkness. A firework boomed overhead, and finally, Skyler saw her. Athena was crouched in the far corner, her shackles up and her head hanging low to the ground. She looked terrified, and drugged. The sedatives were still in effect, and it looked like she was having trouble with her motor control. She looked up at Skyler, recognized her, and let out a pitiful chuffing noise.

"Oh God," Skyler gasped, her heart racing. She grabbed hold of the ladder, whirled around, and began her descent into the pit. "Atty, I'm coming!" Skyler called over her shoulder. "Hold on, baby! I'm coming!" She went down the ladder, rung by rung, the light fading more and more as she went deeper into Pit 91.

CHAPTER 57

July 4, 2019
9:15 p.m.

Carter watched the bitch descend the ladder from the observation deck. He couldn't see the cat anywhere, but he was sure it was down there—he saw the bitch calling out to it before she mounted the ladder.

Carter raised his eyes to ground level and scanned the surrounding area. Equipment—containers of tools, boxes of supplies, storage crates—were positioned between the pit and the perimeter fence that blocked the public from entering the work zone. The only way to actually see *into* the pit was from the observation deck, which was deserted. He suspected it would remain deserted for the rest of the night.

Oh, this is going to be fun, he thought, and went over to the damaged fence, clutching his knife so tightly that the blood had drained completely from his fingers.

CHAPTER 58

July 4, 2019
9:15 p.m.

Skyler reached out tentatively with her foot, assessing the stability of the platform below. It felt solid enough, and she lowered herself down from the ladder. She turned slowly, keeping her hand on the ladder for support, until she was facing the interior of Pit 91.

There were two tar pits side by side. One was large, with the tar's stagnant surface lurking just below platform level, and the other was small and deep. *The swimming pool and the spa,* she thought, remembering the picture from the museum. Fossilized bones reached out from the larger pit—*the pool*— with small numbered tags positioned next to each bone. A metal ladder wrapped over the side of the smaller pit—*the spa*—and then disappeared.

Skyler worked her way across the platforms to where she saw Athena, being careful to watch her footing. She stretched her arms out in front of her as she neared the back corner, reaching for Athena. "Atty," she whispered, and took a few more steps forward. *"Atty . . ."*

Skyler's hands touched the far wall. Her fingers ran along the rough planks of wood, a splinter biting into the pad of one of her fingers. She drew her hand back, shaking it absentmindedly as if that would cause the splinter to fall out, then stuck it out again, feeling along the wall with growing panic. *Where was she? She was just here. She was JUST here!*

A bouquet of fireworks went off overhead, and the corner of Pit 91 lit up, revealing a stack of stained buckets and a few loose tools lying on the ground. Athena wasn't there. *"Shit!"* Skyler turned around and began searching for Athena in the opposite direction. All the corners of the pit were shrouded in shadows, and she would have to wait until another round of fireworks went off to see where she had gone. Where was the goddamn finale already? She needed the light!

Skyler heard a crunching noise up above, coming from the side of the observation deck. She pressed herself against the wall of wooden planks, willing herself to disappear into the shadows. She looked up. There was a little more light at ground level, and she saw the toe of a boot come into view. Skyler's eyes widened. She recognized the boot. *Carter.*

"Shiiiiit," Skyler said in a low, anxious voice. She looked around for a place to hide. If Athena could somehow hide down here, then so could she. Only, after a quick scan, she couldn't find anywhere nearby that would be an easy enough

place to conceal herself. She wasn't sure if Carter knew she was down here or not, but she sure as hell couldn't be standing in the middle of the platform when the next firework went off. If she hid well enough, and Athena stayed wherever she was, maybe Carter would leave and look elsewhere. Maybe . . .

Skyler looked down. The metal ladder that descended into the smaller pit was only a few feet away. She peered into the hole, which was square-shaped and around six feet wide. The surface of the tar was six or seven feet down below. *A hole within a hole,* she thought. It was almost pitch black inside—either from shadows, from the tar, or both. The putrid stench of asphalt drifted up from its depths.

Skyler looked back up to ground level, and saw Carter walking slowly along the railing. He was looking straight ahead, at all the crates that surrounded the dig site, and not down into the pit itself. Maybe he thought Athena was hiding behind one of those crates. And maybe, by some miracle, he hadn't noticed them yet.

She crouched down and crawled over to the edge of the deep hole. Her shoulder nudged a shovel that was leaning against the wall, and she shot out a hand and grabbed it before it had a chance to fall. *God, that was a close one.* She gently set the shovel down on the platform.

Skyler grabbed onto the metal ladder, swept her feet over the side, and without hesitation, lowered herself down into the smaller pit. One rung, then two, then three. Her hips disappeared from view, then her shoulders, then her head. A firework went off, and cold, white light filled the interior of

Pit 91. The hole she was in, however, remained engulfed in a thick layer of shadows.

Skyler hovered on the ladder, scared to go further down or back up. Her blood throbbed in her ears, hard and fast like her heartbeat. Her face felt wet; she wasn't sure if it was from sweat, tears, or blood. Inches below her feet, the tar waited, silently.

Up above, the sounds of Carter whistling filled the confines of Pit 91, drawing closer as he went down the main ladder. *He's coming down here!* Skyler's stomach lurched, and she almost lost her grip and fell. *He's going to look in here.* And when he did, he would see her cowering on the ladder. There was only one thing left that she could do. She had to go deeper. She had to go . . . *in.*

Skyler lowered herself down another rung of the ladder, and then another. Her boot touched the tar's surface, and she had to forcibly push it deeper into the viscous sludge. This was the tar from her dream—no water to dilute it, no rain to soften it. She went down another rung, and the tar began to fill her boots. It was cold. *Cold like a grave. Cold like death. Because that's exactly what it is.* She reached down, struggling to keep hold of the ladder with one hand while she used the other to remove her boots. They were going to be like dumbbells strapped to her feet otherwise.

Shoes off, Skyler submerged her feet into the tar, then continued to go down, rung by rung. The tar reached her calves, her knees, her thighs. She wasn't sure if the subtle yet persistent downward pull she felt was real or imagined. *Please let it be imagined.*

Skyler shivered as the tar crept up to her stomach. It was colder than she thought it would be, and thick like syrup—or congealing blood. She imagined a gigantic tub of blood, which had thickened on the top, like the film that develops on the surface of a bowl of soup that has been left out on the counter for too long.

She continued her descent, feeling the tar coating her breasts and sliding, thick and heavy, over her shoulders. She kept expecting to feel the bottom below her bare feet—in the dream she had always been standing on the bottom of the grave—but there was no bottom here.

Skyler stopped when the tar reached her neck. She hovered there, clinging to the ladder as a drowning man clings to a life preserver, not sure if she was either floating or sinking. Up above, something heavy landed on the platform. Carter had reached the bottom.

She craned her neck and looked up, feeling the tar grabbing at her hair like hands of the dead reaching up to claim her. She slowed her breathing, willing herself not to panic. *If I just stay real still, he'll go away. If I just stay real still, he'll go away. If I just . . .*

A series of fireworks boomed up above—way up above now—sounding like hollow gunshots inside the dark hole. The tar sucked the sound into itself, just like it sucked down all those animals—gone forever until the people at La Brea pulled them from their graves thousands of years later. She wondered how long it would be until they pulled her remains from this grave. Would they be bones? Would any flesh remain?

Carter's voice filled Pit 91, sounding like a kid on a playground more than a man hunting down his victim. "Oh, my little chickadee, you can't fucking hide from me," he sang, his voice empty and out of tune.

Skyler looked up from her hiding place. The walls of the pit stretched up above her, giving the impression that she had fallen down a well. A firework went off, somewhere out of view, and the sky flashed with blue, then red, then green. Smoke swirled through the air in various shades of aqua and purple, then drifted lazily across the starless sky.

CHAPTER 59

July 4, 2019
9:19 p.m.

Carter hopped playfully from platform to platform, humming an unidentifiable tune and relishing the moment. The bitch was down here, and before long she'd be dead. Another victim for the tar. Then he just had to snag the cat and this mess would be corrected.

"Oh, my little chickadee, you can't fucking hide from me," he sang as he made his way across the pit. He had his knife in one hand and a needle in the other, depending on which escapee he found first. The box of syringes he left by the ladder, where he could easily grab another one in case the cat needed a double dose.

Carter walked along the platforms, scanning the larger pool of tar as he went. He recognized some of the bones that were inside, partially obscured from the sludge that contained them. No meddling bitch bones in there, though—not just yet.

Carter neared the back corner where he saw the bitch hiding, carefully stepping around the smaller, deeper pit as he went. He glanced down briefly as he passed by, saw nothing but black death inside, and proceeded onward until he reached the corner beneath the observation deck. Gold and silver crackles lit the sky, and with a cry of outrage, he saw the corner was empty. *Empty!*

"Goddamnit!" he exclaimed. *"Where in the goddamn hell did she go?!"* Carter whirled around, his cold, blue eyes narrowed with rage, and scanned Pit 91. He didn't see her anywhere nearby. There's no way she could have gotten past him, though, so where the hell did she go?

Carter stalked back across the platform. He peered down into the deep pit as he went, his eyes following the metal ladder rung by rung into the darkness. "Chickadee?"

Behind him came the slight scrape of metal on wood. *That bitch is fucking with my toolbox.* He gritted his teeth against a new wave of rage, willing his hands to be steady. He wasn't going to give her a chance to hit him again, not this time.

Carter spun on his heels, his knife at the ready. However, when his eyes caught sight of the toolbox, the bitch was nowhere to be seen. Instead, the cat was there, standing over the toolbox with its eyes locked on Carter. Its lips were pulled back into a snarl, revealing its long teeth, which were plenty visible even in the deep shadows of Pit 91.

Carter instinctively took a step back. He waited for the cat to lunge, but instead it slumped to the side and just managed to steady itself before falling over. *Still drugged,* he thought. He flipped his knife closed and shoved it into his pocket, then transferred the syringe to his right hand. He put his left hand out into a calming gesture, much like one would do when offering a hand to a frightened dog to try and gain its affection. He took a step forward, then another, creeping closer and closer to where the cat stood, snarling.

As he closed the distance between them, the cat took a step backward and stumbled. This was going to be easier than he thought it would be. He was prepared to take a few swipes and bites if necessary, but now he might be able to get this done practically unscathed.

"Here, kitty kitty," he said as he crept forward.

The cat issued a low, grumbling growl that resonated in his chest. It sounded angry, but it also sounded scared.

"Not so big and tough when you're stoned, huh?" he said in a comforting tone. The cat must not have thought so, though, because it let out another grating cry.

"Now you need to keep your goddamn voice down," Carter snapped, the soothing tone leaving his voice. "I don't like yelling. It gives me a damn headache."

The cat took another step backward. Its hind legs gave out from underneath it, and it fell into a sitting position. It let out a long, frightened yowl. Carter thought he could even feel the sound reverberating in the fillings in his teeth, if that was possible. "Shut the fuck up," he hissed, and crept closer. Only a few more feet now, and he'd be within striking range.

The cat tried to get up, its legs quivering as it struggled to stand, and then it fell again. Carter took another step forward, closing in. The cat tried to shove itself backward with its front paws, but came in contact with the wall of the pit. "Say goodnight, kitty cat," Carter cooed, and reached forward with the needle.

Skyler's hands ached from her grip on the ladder, but she refused to let go, even for a second. She kept envisioning herself getting sucked down by the tar, her hands stretched up to the sky, with patriotic colors splashing across her skin as she was pulled below its black surface. From bright rainbows of light to eternal blackness, all in the course of a few seconds.

Instead, she gripped the ladder with a fierce tightness, willing Carter to go away. He was just above the tar pit grave now, heading toward the far corner where she had been only moments ago. At least she wasn't hiding there anymore, and as far as she knew, neither was Athena.

"Goddamnit!" Carter yelled from up above. "Where in the goddamn hell did she go!?" Skyler listened to him clomp across the wooden platform just beyond the tar pit grave, pausing near its edge. The top of his head appeared, hovering over the side. He was going to look inside! Skyler pulled herself against the ladder, pressing her body as close to the wall as it could go. His voice drifted down into the grave. "Chickadee?" She waited, not breathing. After a moment, his head disappeared from view. He then started walking toward the main ladder.

Skyler let out a silent sigh of relief. *He's leaving. It worked.* But now Carter was saying something, and it wasn't to her. Skyler strained to make out the words, but they were too soft and too far away. The angry yowl that came a few seconds later she heard, though. She was pulling up on the ladder even before her brain caught up with her body. *Athena was up there. Jesus Christ. He found her.*

Skyler's neck came out of the thick tar, and she could feel its black, dead fingers caressing her throat and threatening to pull it back down. To pull *her* down, like the seat belt snakes. To hold her down like Peter. To beat her down like Carter. She gritted her teeth, pressed her foot onto one of the submerged rungs of the ladder, and pushed herself up. She moved her hands up the ladder, struggling to maintain her grip with the slimy tar coating her palms. She reached out one hand and wiped it on the wooden side of the grave, then the other.

She lifted her leg through the goo, found the next rung, and pushed up. At the same time, she pulled with her arms. Skyler felt every muscle and tendon in her body straining against the dark embrace of the tar, but she wasn't going to let it pull her down this time—those days were gone. That *person* was gone. Her arms broke free, then her chest. Athena growled up above, and she could hear Carter's voice, angry and full of hate. *I'm coming, Atty. I'm not staying in the grave this time. I'm fucking coming.*

Her waist emerged from the tar, followed by her hips. She felt like a fly trying to loosen itself from spilled honey. Her knees came through, and finally, her feet. Her toes curled around the rungs of the ladder as she lifted her slick, tar-covered body out of the grave. One hand reached the top, and then the other. She hauled herself up and crawled onto the platform, dripping black death from every inch of her body.

Skyler looked across Pit 91 and saw Carter, holding a syringe and moving in on Athena. Athena was on her side and struggling to stand, but her legs wouldn't hold up her weight. There were only a few yards between them.

Skyler brought her feet underneath her. They slid across the wood, tar oozing out from between her toes. Her feet were bare; her socks must have been pulled from her feet as she tried to free herself from the tar. She looked to her side and saw the shovel she bumped into earlier. She reached out, grabbed the handle, and used the tool like a crutch to push herself up to standing.

She slipped, stabilized herself with the shovel, and then smeared her feet across the platform to wipe as much tar from the soles as she could. She then crept forward, now a ghoul of her own making, holding the shovel with both hands. When she was within striking distance of Carter, she lifted the shovel up and over her shoulder, like a baseball bat.

"Say goodnight, kitty cat," Carter said to Athena, and reached forward with the needle.

"HEY ASSHOLE!" Skyler shouted, and brought the shovel down with all her strength onto the top of Carter's head.

CHAPTER 60

July 4, 2019
9:24 p.m.

Carter's skull issued a sickening crack as the metal spade of the shovel made contact. The syringe flew from his hand and landed on the platform with a clatter. He staggered to the side, before tripping over his feet and falling with a thud onto the platform below.

Skyler followed him, the shovel raised for another blow. She stopped at Carter's feet and looked down at his crumpled frame. There was a large laceration on the top of his scalp, blood seeping out in a steady flow. It coated his face and spilled onto the platform beneath him. He looked up at her, the whites of his eyes standing out in stark contrast to the red mask he was wearing. Fireworks boomed, turning his coated face to a shimmering purple, and then back to red again.

"What are you going to do now?" he croaked. He spat, and red droplets flew from his mouth and landed on his shirt. "You tell the police, they'll arrest you. You run, I'll find you." He spat again, and more droplets flew. "I promise you that."

"What the hell makes you think I'd let you live?" Skyler asked, the shovel heavy in her aching arms. She saw movement in her periphery, and glanced over to see Athena standing beside her. The cat's body swayed, but she didn't fall.

Carter laughed, and more blood flew. "You can't kill me," he said simply. "Not without her help." He looked over at Athena, then back at Skyler. "And she can barely hold herself up right now."

"You think I need her to kill you?"

"It's one thing to hire a hit man, it's quite another to end someone's life with your own hands." Carter licked the blood from his lips and grinned. "You don't have it in you, sweet cheeks."

Skyler reluctantly lowered the shovel, and Carter's grin widened, revealing perfect teeth now stained red. She let out a low, weary sigh. Athena moved toward Carter, and his body tensed as he watched her approach.

Skyler dropped her hand to her side and stiffened her fingers. Athena looked at Skyler, and then down at her flattened hand. She turned to Carter, teeth bared, then took a step back and sat down heavily on the platform.

Carter laughed; it sounded clogged and wet. "See!" he said with glee. "She's got no fight left in her. And you—you never did."

Skyler smiled, one black ghoul to one red one. "Hey, Carter," she said, and raised the shovel over her shoulder. "*That* was the old me. *This* is the new me." Skyler brought down the shovel with everything she had.

Carter barely got out a scream before the spade collided with his forehead. The blade hit skull, then sliced down his face, cutting through his left eye and opening his cheek. Skyler pulled up the shovel and brought it down again. Carter turned his head away from the blow, and the shovel connected with his temple. The impact jerked his neck back at a grotesque angle, and Skyler heard a cracking sound from deep inside. Two teeth came free from his mouth and tumbled across the platform. Carter slumped down, his leg twitching. After a moment, he was still.

Skyler watched him, her mouth hanging open. *Boom. Boom boom.* His body lit up white, then yellow, then blue. The fireworks were building in frequency, and she suspected the finale would begin any second. They needed to hurry.

Skyler knelt over Carter's body, fished the keys from his pocket, and hastily shoved them into her own. She then dragged him over to the platform's edge. She took the shovel, widened her stance, and pressed the spade into Carter's side. His shoulder slumped over the edge, followed by his arms. For an agonizing moment, his upper body hung over the tar and his legs stayed put on the platform, looking like some sort of hideous pendulum. With one more shove, his legs went over the side, and Carter's body landed in the tar with a heavy *plop!*

Athena and Skyler stood at the edge and looked down. The body was already partially submerged, the desperate hands of the tar finally claiming their victim. Skyler lowered the shovel, made contact with Carter's back, and pressed down. The tar sluggishly moved inward from both sides of his torso, and finally met in the center. She watched as his body disappeared from view, the tar swallowing it completely.

When Skyler looked away, Athena was on top of a crate and struggling to crawl out of the pit. Her claws dug into the wooden planks, and after a few tries, she clumsily pulled herself up and out. Following suit, Skyler scrambled up the wooden ladder and reached the top of Pit 91 a few seconds later, where Athena was already waiting for her.

Brilliant rainbows of light reflected on Skyler's tar-covered skin as the Fourth of July fireworks display reached its crescendo in an overwhelming finale of overhead explosions. "Come on, Atty," Skyler panted. "We gotta go."

Skyler took off running along the side of Pit 91, toward the opening in the fence that Athena had made only moments ago. Athena followed at her heels. The big cat stumbled from time to time, but luckily the sedative was finally starting to relinquish its hold on her body. They crawled beneath the bent fence, one by one, and then ran back the way they came. The sky flashed with every color imaginable, and sound waves rippled through the atmosphere, competing with the cannons of the *1812 Overture* that was playing back by the lake. *Too bad we aren't able to stop and watch it,* Skyler thought as they ran beneath the trees and beelined for the van. *It certainly sounds like one hell of a show.*

CHAPTER 61

July 4, 2019
9:32 p.m.

The sparkling flashes disappeared long before the rumbling booms faded away, and Timmy took the opportunity to look behind him from where he sat atop his daddy's shoulders. His daddy and mommy were talking about how beautiful the show was, and his pig-faced sister was whining about wanting ice cream.

Timmy wondered if the drunked lady got a chance to enjoy the fireworks. Maybe the man helped her up, and they got to watch the ending together. However, when he looked over at the *tar pit*, he didn't see them anymore. He scanned the edge of the lake and the surrounding fence, but the drunked lady and the man were nowhere to be seen.

Timmy was about to turn back to his mommy to tell her that he wanted ice cream, too, when he saw movement near the fence. A big white van was parked there—the kind that Mommy and Daddy told him to never get inside, regardless of how nice the driver might be.

Someone was running across the road toward the van. It looked like the drunked lady, all dressed in black, only she didn't look drunked anymore. And she had something with her—some kind of animal. Timmy squinted, straining to make out what was running beside her. His eyes widened in awe when he realized what it was: the biggest kitty he had ever seen! Even bigger than the lion he saw at the zoo last week!

The no-longer-drunked lady and the giant kitty went around the side of the van. Timmy bopped his dad on the head—once, twice, three times.

"Hey, Timmy!" Chuck Palmer said. "Stop that." He reached up and patted his son on the leg. He knew keeping the kids up this late was going to make them cranky.

"But Daddy!" Timmy exclaimed. "There's a kitty! There's a giant kitty over there!"

Chuck turned around, both him and his son now facing the tar pit. Attached to the fence was a large placard with a drawing of a saber-toothed cat on it. It looked out from the sign, its long teeth extending far past its chin, as if it was surveying everyone in Hancock Park. "Yeah, bud," Chuck said, "I see it. You're right, that's a very big kitty!"

"No," Timmy said, and gave his daddy another frustrated bop on the head. "Not the picture. By the van. *There's a big kitty by the van!*"

Chuck looked over to the adjacent road, but saw nothing parked there except for a maintenance truck. His son really must be tired. It was going on ten, after all—well past his bedtime. "I don't see a van, bud," Chuck said.

"But it was right there!" Timmy insisted. "By the trees. A big kitty and a drunked lady wearing black went into a van by the trees." He pointed one chubby finger in that direction so his daddy would know where to look; however, when he looked back to the road where the van had been parked, it was gone.

Dear Reader

(V)

When I was a kid, four or five maybe, my dad told me a little piece of advice. I was upset, you see, because the girls in my playgroup were making fun of me because I was smaller and skinnier than them. Funny to be upset about such a thing, since most girls, once they reach adulthood, spend the rest of their lives trying to be smaller and thinner than all of their friends. But at the time, their teasing words stung. I came home in tears, asking my dad when I would get to grow up already, so nobody would be able to pick on me anymore. Back then, I didn't realize you could get picked on when you were a grown-up—picked on in much worse ways than teasing words and hurtful giggles.

My dad sat me down on his lap and said I needed to pay real close attention, because he was about to give me one big old whopper of advice—one that I should remember for the rest of my life. Which was . . . *drum roll* . . . that no matter how small I felt, I could still make a *big difference*. Not the most profound or unique advice that one could give a kid, but hey, it did the trick—it got me to stop crying.

When they died, that big old whopper of advice stuck with me—possibly because I still felt so small and insignificant, or possibly because I wanted to help those that felt small and insignificant just like I did. I started noticing animals around town—trying to find food in garbage cans, cowering under porches when it was pouring rain, injured and afraid because their human decided to harm them instead of protect them—and I wanted to help. Those animals were smaller than I was (and I was still pretty dang small), and I thought I could be the *big difference* for them.

So I started carrying cans of pet food in my backpack, which I bought with the little bit of allowance my aunt gave me. When I saw a hungry stray picking through the garbage, I'd pull out a can of food and offer them a meal that wasn't rotting or full of maggots. Then I started keeping a couple towels in my backpack, too, so when I saw a cat or dog that was cold and wet, I could offer them a little bit of warmth and comfort. Before long, there were very few books in my backpack and I was more like a walking pet shop than a schoolgirl. Blankets, food, treats, toys—anything I could find to be the *big difference* to that small animal.

Unfortunately, there were some animals I wasn't capable of helping. The injured ones, the sick ones—I didn't have anything in my backpack that could fix them. So I found the number for the local animal shelter and memorized that bad boy. Every time I saw an animal that needed more help than my handy-dandy backpack could provide, I ran home and called that number. I told the person that answered that there was a—cat, dog, bird, bunny—that needed their help on so-and-so street. Then I'd go back and wait for them to arrive and save the day.

That's how I met Trish, by the way. She was younger than I am now, and she was wearing a staff T-shirt back in those days—no sensible heels or button-up blouses back then. She started to recognize me, and I quickly became known as the little girl who wanted to save the animals. When the shelter expanded and Trish moved into a managerial position, she told me that when I was old enough, I should come and work at the shelter. I could even start volunteering there once I was fifteen. Which was how I wound up there on my fifteenth birthday, with Trish giving me a cupcake with a candle in it and singing me "Happy Birthday". It was the first birthday candle I got to wish on since my parents died, and there was only one thing I could think of when I wished my very special wish—to make a *big difference* to every animal I had the opportunity to help. I may still be small, but I certainly wasn't going to act like it when it came to saving animals. Then . . . then I was going to be *big*.

So I scrubbed the kennels, cleaned the litter boxes, hauled the food, walked the dogs, scratched the cats, and *eventually* became a full-time Agave Animal Care Center employee. My job was now to help animals, and God, I like to think my dad was proud of me with that one. I found a way to make that big old whopper of advice he gave me a reality.

Later on, as you know, I wound up doing some things that might have made my dad not so proud. But I suppose it all depends on how you look at it. Sure, my actions led to the alluring Peter bleeding out on my parents' rug—not a proud moment—but don't you think my actions made a *big difference* to all the women who never had to suffer the unfathomable amount of pain that is involved in being a rape victim? Don't even try to tell me I was going to be Peter's last victim—there would have been more. But Athena put a stop to that, and I'm happy she did.

And what about Cinder? She was one beating away from dying at the hands of a cruel, abusive asshole. Yes, I am well aware I committed first-degree murder with that one . . . but would you have done any differently? Sure you can say you would never do such a horrible thing as murder . . . but are you sure? Are you *really* sure? If it was your pet that was abused, if it was your daughter that was raped—would you turn the other cheek, or would you do something about it? We all like to think we are good, virtuous people—incapable of any wrongdoing or intentionally hurting others—but let me ask you this . . . isn't doing nothing just as damaging? Isn't standing back and letting evil happen just as criminal as putting a stop to it yourself? Can you be a bad person by simply *not* acting?

That's a choice you are going to have to make, and I'm afraid to tell you, you don't get to submit your answer ahead of time. It's not until you're actually in it—in that pivotal moment of "to act or not to act"—that you will really know who you are. Before that, it's all just a guessing game.

If a man with a gun walks into the office, we all like to think we'll be the hero in that scenario—jumping in front of bullets, knocking the gun from the would-be killer's hand, carrying out our shaken-but-otherwise-unharmed crush as they shower us with thank yous—but what if, when push comes to shove, you're the dude hiding under his desk and pissing his pants? What if you're the woman who shoves your fellow coworker into harm's way just so you can have an extra second to escape? What if . . . what if you're the *villain* in this little scenario, and you just don't know it yet?

I ended up being a little bit more of a villain than I ever thought I would be—but hey, like I said, you don't get to submit your answer ahead of time. To Rick, I'm the villain. To Cinder, I'm the hero. To you—well, that's a decision you are going to have to make for yourself. There's one thing you can't deny, though, and that's that I certainly managed to make a *big difference* for both of them.

Anyway, I'm starting to ramble. It's my last letter and I guess I'm just trying to make some sense out of all this. To make some sense out of how I went from point "A" to point "I've been involved in the deaths of four people". And that last one—*woo-ee!* I sure as hell didn't see that one coming. Did you?

Carter Grayson was a little gift out of left field that put a rather unpleasant hitch in my plans. A complete monster, through and through. There's no way you could *possibly* think that guy was worthy of keeping around. Unless you're looking for someone to fill Hannibal Lecter's shoes.

Carter's body was found a hell of a lot quicker than any of the other bodies that met their end in Pit 91. Maybe the blood-splattered platform and box of mysterious syringes had something to do with that. All I know is that in only two days time Carter's face was all over the news—and not just local, we're talking national coverage. The La Brea employee that died in the very tar pit he helped to maintain? What a story! And with the bizarre evidence that was left behind? What a mystery as well!

Foul play was obvious, given the condition of Carter's face and broken neck. Not the work of an accidental slip and trip, that's for sure. From what I read, it was a real head-scratcher for you poor, flabbergasted detectives. A bloody shovel, a box of needles (further investigation revealed they were filled with a cocktail of heavy-duty tranquilizers), deep scratch marks on one of the pit walls, and a steel fence that was somehow bent out of shape. *Bizarre.* Rumors started flying almost immediately—an animal crawled out of the tar and ate Carter Grayson, stuff like that. More on point than anyone might have realized, except for the eating part, but that was simply because we ran out of time.

Anyway, it wasn't until my fingerprints were identified on the toolbox and on some of the syringes inside that things really started ramping up for the conspiracy theorists. You see, I was already making some pretty big waves back in Diamondback—the contents of my freezer making it to the front page—and adding Carter Grayson to my list of victims certainly threw things for a loop. Why would this crazy girl from a small town in Arizona travel to the La Brea Tar Pits to murder a man she had no connection with? He must have been involved in something, right? Maybe they were involved in something together! All I know is that the FBI got involved and the news coverage all but stopped. It's just as well. I rather not spend any more of my time thinking about

Carter Grayson anyway. That chapter is *closed.* Permanently. So let's get back to it, shall we?

I never really planned to write any confession letters. I mean, why bother? I've already been labeled a deranged killer, and that's a hard title to live down. But then I thought, why not? Maybe there's a small chance I could set the record straight, ya know, before Athena and I disappear for good. Not so much for me, but for my parents' memory. I wanted everyone that knew Sean and Teresa Seabrooke to know their little girl wasn't a complete monster. Or at least know I had my reasons for doing what I did.

I guess, when it comes down to it, all I really wanted to convey with these letters is that ordinary people are capable of doing not-so-ordinary things. Small people can make a *big difference.* I led a small life before, and in case you were wondering, it has become small again. I don't have body parts in my freezer anymore—not human ones anyway—and I don't actively seek out people to punish. I pretty much just stay off the grid, which is fine with me. And although my life may be small, it isn't empty. I have love in my life, and that, I have come to realize, is *the* most important thing. Not every person has to make a *big difference*, but every person—and animal—deserves to know what love is. I think there would be a lot less Carter Graysons and Rick Hansens in the world if everyone had love in their lives. Love from a spouse, love from a child, love from a pet . . . just . . . *love.* It's when the love goes away that people become monsters.

Remember, way back when, when I said that love can be the death of you? I'd like to amend that just a little. I've come to realize that it's not *love* that can be the death of you, but the *absence* of love. It's when that love is taken away that people do horrible things. Stalking their exes? Bringing a gun to the supermarket? Love changed them alright, but it was the absence of love (or the fear of the same) that destroyed them. So I beg you, all of you, to find the love in your lives and hold onto it tight. Not in a homicidal, "if I can't have you no one else can" kind of way, but in a way that enriches your lives. Go adopt a shelter pet—I promise they will love you forever. Fall in love with painting or reading. Hell, fall in love with the person you want to be and then try like hell to become that person. Just make sure to love *something*. If not, your world will become very dark, and there are monsters lurking in the dark. I've seen them.

I've been reflecting on my life quite a bit lately—a lot of time on the road can do that—and I'm beginning to think that maybe it's *all* a pit of tar. Love, life, blood—all of it. Deep down, at their very core, they are all the same thing, really. Without blood, there is no life. Without life, there is no love. And love . . . what is love if not but a pit of tar? So thick and heavy there is no chance you will ever escape from its grasp. The tar—the love—will pull you down, threatening to drown you before you even realize you were trapped. There is no escaping it, no matter how careful you are and no matter how many precautions you take. One day, you will get trapped in that tar pit of love, and it will start to pull you down.

So do you fight it? Will fighting it even help, or will you just get dragged down quicker? You can't fight the tar, and you can't fight the love. So it's better to just let yourself go down, because struggling will only make it worse. And, if you are really, *really* honest with yourself, do you even want to fight it? To fight not to love someone? In the end, most of us will end up living, bleeding, and dying for the chance to be with the person we love. And maybe that's okay. I think it is anyway.

And as for Athena and myself? I'm sure you're just dying to find out what our plans may be. I bet you police fellas have your handcuffs packed and your stun guns at the ready. Sorry to disappoint, but these are *confession* letters, not *"come and find me"* letters—even though I'm sure you will still try your damnedest to do just that. I sure as hell am not going to make it easy for you, though. Remember what I said about keeping love in your life? Well, I love Athena, and I sure as hell am not going to let you take her away from me, or me from her. So unless you are planning to let us live happily ever after like in one of those Disney fairy tales (hahaha), I guess our only other option is to get gone and stay gone.

You may think there's no way we will be able to do that— to disappear, I mean. Where would we go? And how would we get there? Ah, the age-old question: where would a slightly deranged woman and a four-hundred-pound (and still growing!) saber-toothed cat go while on the run? Sorry to say, but that is a riddle you are going to have to solve for yourself. It's a big world out there, and one girl and one saber-tooth fading into the background might be easier than you'd expect. Locating us will almost be like trying to find a needle in a haystack—last cliché, I promise!

So, unless you are lucky enough to find this very small needle in that very large haystack, I guess this is farewell. Maybe, instead of asking yourself where we might be, you should be asking if you really need to be searching for us at all. Am I really *that* bad of a person? I guess that's up for debate. I don't really know either, to tell you the truth. All I know for sure is that I haven't dreamt of the tar pit grave once since that night at La Brea. Since the night I saved Athena, and saved myself.

So, when you toss this letter aside (or, for you police folks, stick it back into an evidence bag), just remember this one thing: *Everyone* is capable of doing horrible things. You are, too. You just don't know it yet. Maybe the *old you* isn't capable of doing the things I've done . . . but the *new you*? Well, you haven't even met that person yet. But you will. Someday.

Love,

Skyler Seabrooke & Athena

EPILOGUE

Frost clung to the brittle winter branches of the forest trees. The morning sunlight danced across the frozen crystals, looking like someone spilled glitter onto the hushed landscape. Delicate icicles dangled precariously from the thicker branches, doomed to plummet to the powder below at the first whisper of an oncoming wind.

Overhead, the sky was the palest of blues, looking almost translucent over the unadulterated wilderness. Even with hundreds of miles of untouched arctic terrain, the land still looked small in comparison to the great expanse of powder-blue sky up above.

Below the trees, a plume of heavy, white vapor filled the air, an exhaled breath that hovered in space with not a trace of wind to carry it away. Before the cold could claim the ghost of breath, another filled its place. And then another.

The stag stood in a small clearing, its hooves sunk deep into a pristine blanket of freshly fallen snow. The forest was deathly quiet, not even the birds daring to break the silence with their songs. The stag took a step forward, its antler brushing against a single, low-hanging icicle that made the softest clink of broken glass before it fell to the snow below.

The stag's ear twitched, then rotated toward the slight noise of what it thought was the icicle's impact with the drift of white powder underfoot. It exhaled again, its frozen breath momentarily obscuring its vision.

The collision came so suddenly that the stag barely had a moment to register the sudden movement in its periphery. It fell helplessly to its side some five feet away, just short of where the trees came in to claim the small clearing. Its heavy body sunk into the snow, pressed down by the animal above. The creature was immense, overpowering the stag in both size and weight. The stag sunk deeper into the snow as the animal's head came down. The rest came quickly enough. The plumes of white vapor from the stag's breath slowed, then stopped.

The animal stepped away from its prey, licking the blood from its teeth. Harsh, vibrant red coated the surrounding snow—no longer pristine, no longer sparkling like shattered diamonds. The animal stood among the splatters of crimson, patiently waiting for what came next.

Skyler Seabrooke carefully made her way through the shimmering trees, heading in the direction of the clearing. Her boots sunk into the soft snow with each step, and white clouds spilled from her lungs with every breath. She had seen her fair share of snow in Diamondback, but never a winter wonderland such as this. This far north, the snow would cover the ground well into April, and very likely through May.

Skyler could make out the clearing up ahead—a brilliant, red rose in the center of all that white. As she drew near, she could see movement between the trees. Not from the crumpled animal that lay partially submerged in a snow drift, but from something much, much bigger. It circled the edge of the clearing, waiting.

When Skyler emerged from the trees, Athena bounded over to her. Her muzzle was red, and the stag's blood dripped from her seven-inch teeth. Her muscles were thick and pronounced, even below her heavy coat, which had thickened in the frigid temperatures. Her head was level with Skyler's shoulders, and when she looked up, their faces were only inches apart. Silver flecks of winter danced in Athena's amber eyes as she watched Skyler. She chuffed a greeting, then rubbed against Skyler's shoulder.

"What did you get this time, Atty?" Skyler asked, letting her hands sink deep into Athena's fur. It was well below zero outside, and the heat coming off Athena's body was warm and inviting. She released Athena and pulled the fur-lined hood of her parka tighter over her ears. "Okay, okay," she said. "One sec."

Skyler used her teeth to loosen her glove, then pulled it off with her other hand. The cold bit into her exposed skin instantly, and Skyler hissed through her teeth against the sharp ache in her fingers.

Athena saw Skyler's bare hand and hurried back over to the fallen stag. She stopped just short of the steaming red mass, her six-hundred pounds dwarfing the deer beneath her. She looked over at Skyler and waited.

Skyler smiled. "Good girl, Atty," she said, and snapped her fingers.

THANK YOU FOR READING!

♥

If you enjoyed *Foster*, please consider leaving a review. I read every single one of them, and they mean so much!

A NOTE FROM THE AUTHOR

While the La Brea Tar Pits is a real location in Los Angeles, everything writing in this book regarding the La Brea Tar Pits is purely a work of fiction and meant for entertainment purposes only. To learn the real story about La Brea and the amazing work they do there, you can visit **https://tarpits.org**, or simply stop by and have a look for yourself the next time you are visiting Los Angeles.

Animals need our help, each and every day, and I want to thank everyone who has ever helped an animal in need. Whether it's taking the time to stop and help an abandoned animal on the side of the road, or welcoming a rescue pet into your home, or simply donating to your favorite animal shelter, thank you so much for your kindness. I believe the world would be a better place if we all treated animals with the love and respect they deserve.

And a special thank you to those who have dedicated their lives to helping animals—those working in animal shelters, those running animal rescues, those who open their homes to foster pets in need of a safe place to sleep at night, those who work in the veterinary field, those who advocate for animal rights, and those who work as animal rescue officers, risking their own safety for the welfare of animals in need—thank you to all of you, from the bottom of my heart. This world is a better place because you are in it.

ACKNOWLEDGEMENT

First and foremost, I would like to thank my incredible husband, Ryan McCrory, who has been with me every step of the way—and there have been a lot of steps—as I transformed Foster from a fledgling idea into the novel before you. This story turned out to be quite the undertaking, and I couldn't have done it without his love, support, and patience. Through countless rewrites, weeks not leaving my desk as I pushed toward the finish line, and a bout of pneumonia along the way, he has been by my side and cheering me on. And my thanks extend far beyond just moral support. Ryan has proved to be a fantastic developmental editor, and an asset in the writing process that I am so thankful to have on my side. Foster would not be the story it is today without the myriad of helpful—and sometimes downright amazing—suggestions he had to bring everything together into one frightening, fluid tale of love, suspense, and revenge. Ryan also did the cover design for Foster, and I am so proud of the fabulous designer he has become. There is no one else I would rather go on this journey with—both the journey of becoming an author, and the journey of life. I would shout my thanks from the rooftops if I could, but I'm rather clumsy and he doesn't want me going up there, so I will have to settle for saying my thanks on these pages. So, thank you, my love. This story is for you.

I would also like to thank my family, whose unwavering support in my abilities has meant so much to me along the way. Thank you to my mother, Nancy Dufour, to my father-in-law and mother-in-law, Mike and Betty McCrory, and to my brothers-in-law, Michael McCrory and Randy Ballesteros. I truly appreciate the time you have devoted to reading my manuscript, and for your unyielding encouragement while I pursue my dreams.

Thank you to my father, Larry Dufour, for passing his love of reading on to me. It was that passion for reading that led me down the path of becoming an author, and this book wouldn't be here without it. He will forever be missed, and I hope, wherever he may be, that he gets a chance to read this story. I think he would have liked it.

And finally, I would like to thank you—yes, you—dear reader. Thank you for giving my humble book a try. This is only my second novel, but I don't think it will ever stop amazing me that you found this book and enjoyed it enough to make it this far. Writing is something I do because I have stories I want to tell, but to tell a story you need to have somcone to listen. You. You may not always be thinking of me, but believe me, I am thinking of you—in every character, in every word, in every comma. Someday, I would like to dedicate all of my time into writing stories for you to enjoy, and that can't be possible without your help. So, if you enjoyed this book, please don't keep it a secret. Leave a rating on Amazon or Goodreads. Let your friends and family know about the time we've shared. Only with your continued support will we get to share more time together. Time where I can tell you another story. I'm already working on it. So thank you, dear reader, for reading this book. I hope you enjoyed reading it as much as I enjoyed writing it!

Until next time,
Danielle McCrory

Also by Danielle McCrory

WASP CANYON
A NOVEL

WHEN THE DARKNESS COMES, THE TEETH AND THE CLAWS COME WITH IT.

Jessica Cleary took up running the Arizona hiking trails as a way to cope with the recent loss of her father. While out on a run in Wasp Canyon, Jessica stumbles upon a gruesome scene and finds herself injured and running for her life.

There is something lurking inside Wasp Canyon—something vicious, cunning, and with an insatiable appetite. When people in town start falling victim to a mysterious predator and the police are unable to offer any explanation, Jessica decides it's time to stop running—it's time to stop running and fight.

ABOUT THE AUTHOR

Danielle McCrory was born and raised in Tucson, Arizona. She has degrees in Graphic Design and Physical Therapy. Danielle started writing because she believes there are still so many scary stories left untold. Danielle loves horror movies, animals, rainy days, and Halloween. She lives in Tucson with her husband, Ryan McCrory, and their two cats, Brodi and Jaxson.

Made in the USA
Middletown, DE
02 February 2023